Praise for Peter May

'Peter May is a writer I'd follow to the ends of the earth'
New York Times

'A wonderfully complex book'   Peter James, on *Entry Island*

'One of the best regarded crime series of recent years'
Boyd Tonkin, *Independent*, on the Lewis Trilogy

'He is a terrific writer doing something different'
Mark Billingham

'From the first page I know I was in safe hands. I knew I could
trust this writer'   Sophie Hannah

'Tightly plotted, with no skimping on either the nuances of
character or the wonderfully evocative descriptions . . . a true
pleasure to read'   *Guardian*

'May's novels are strong on place and the wounds left by old
relationships'   *Sunday Times*

'Will have the reader relishing every tendency of description
and characterization'   Barry Forshaw, *Independent*

'The characters were wonderfully compelling'   Kate Mosse

'Lyrical, empathetic and moving'   Alex Gray

'Dark, exciting and atmospheric'   *Scotland on Sunday*

'Powerful and authentic'   *Glasgow Sunday Herald*

Also by Peter May

FICTION

The Lewis Trilogy

The Blackhouse
The Lewis Man
The Chessmen

The Enzo Files

Extraordinary People
The Critic
Blacklight Blue
Freeze Frame
Blowback
Cast Iron
The Night Gate

The China Thrillers

The Firemaker
The Fourth Sacrifice
The Killing Room
Snakehead
The Runner
Chinese Whispers

The Ghost Marriage: A China Novella

Stand-alone Novels

The Man With No Face
The Noble Path
Entry Island
Runaway
Coffin Road
I'll Keep You Safe
A Silent Death
Lockdown
A Winter Grave

NON-FICTION

Hebrides (with David Wilson)

Peter May was born and raised in Scotland. He was an award-winning journalist at the age of twenty-one and a published novelist at twenty-six. When his first book was adapted as a major drama series for the BBC, he quit journalism and, during the high-octane fifteen years that followed, became one of Scotland's most successful television dramatists.

He has won several literary awards in France, received the USA's Barry Award for *The Blackhouse* – the first in his internationally bestselling Lewis Trilogy; and in 2014 *Entry Island* was awarded the ITV Specsavers Crime Thriller Book Club Best Read of the Year, as well as the Deanston Scottish Crime Book of the Year. May now lives in South-West France with his wife, writer Janice Hally.

PETER MAY

FREEZE FRAME

riverrun

First published in the USA in 2010 by Poisoned Pen Press
This reissue edition published in Great Britain in 2024 by

riverrun

an imprint of
Quercus Editions Ltd
Carmelite House
50 Victoria Embankment
London EC4Y 0DZ

An Hachette UK company

A CIP catalogue record for this book is available
from the British Library

PB ISBN 978 1 52943 475 0
EBOOK ISBN 978 1 78206 888 4

10 9 8 7 6 5 4 3 2 1

Typeset by CC Book Production
Printed and bound in Great Britain by Clays Ltd, Elcograf S.p.A.

Papers used by riverrun are from well-managed forests and other responsible sources.

For Eric the Viking

O death, where is thy sting?
O grave, where is thy victory?

1 Corinthians, 55

PART ONE

CHAPTER ONE

Munich, Germany, December 20 1951

Erik Fleischer was a man who counted his blessings.

His wife was an attractive woman, hair cascading in golden waves over square shoulders, a smile that lit her inner soul, and spellbinding blue eyes. Still adoring after five turbulent years.

He had two wonderful children, blond, blue-eyed clones of their mother. Magda's genes had predominated over his own Mediterranean looks.

He had survived the war virtually unscathed, inheriting his parents' Bavarian villa in this leafy suburb, establishing a lucrative practice among the new, burgeoning middle class rising now out of the ashes of Hitler's madness.

The good life stretched ahead towards an unbroken horizon.

How could he have known that this night he would lose everything?

As he sat reading the evening newspaper, he absorbed, almost unconsciously, the peals of laughter emanating from the dining room. Mother and children playing a simple board game. He dipped his head to peer over his glasses and glanced through the door towards them. And with the seeds of arousal sown by the merest glance at Magda, rose ambition for a third, or even a fourth.

He glanced at his watch, folded his paper and laid it aside. 'I'll be back down in fifteen.'

Magda half-turned her head towards the living room. 'Dinner will be ready in twenty.'

His study was an elegant room, oak-panelled, one wall lined with bookshelves that groaned under the weight of his father's books. Tall windows looked out across the boulevard to the brooding darkness of the park beyond. Full-length velvet curtains hung open, and he could feel the cold pressing against the glass, like icy palms pushing flat against the panes. He drew the velvet against the night and sat at his leather-tooled desk, patient files neatly laid out under the soft light of his desk lamp. He checked his diary. First appointment was at eight-thirty tomorrow. And he felt the smallest grain of discontent at the thought of the endless stream of pregnant women that would punctuate his days into the foreseeable future. But he wasn't going to let it darken his mood. His blessings were still in the ascendancy. He pulled the first of the files towards him and flipped it open.

The sound of the phone crashed into the ring of light around him, and he reached into the darkness beyond it to lift the receiver. The voice was little more than a whisper. Hoarse and tight with tension.

'They're coming! Get out! Now!'

He was on his feet, even before the phone went dead. He heard his chair hit the floor behind him. The nearest window was two paces away. He separated the curtains the merest crack, and felt the soft velvet against his cheek as he peered beyond them into a night filled now with demons. It was hard to see past the haloes of light around the street lamps below, but he was certain that he could see a movement of shadows among the trees. No time to think. He had put the possibility of such a thing far from his conscious mind, but now that it was here he reacted with what seemed like well-rehearsed efficiency.

Shaking fingers retrieved keys from his pocket and unlocked his desk drawer. The metal of the army issue pistol felt cold in his warm hand. He crossed to the walk-in cloakroom at the far side of the room and threw open the door. Rows of coats and jackets hung on the rail, shoes neatly lined up beneath them. He lifted a heavy wool overcoat and slipped the gun into its pocket, pulling it on over broad shoulders before stooping to pick up the leather overnight bag he had prepared for just this moment.

He did not stop to think. There was no regret-filled backward glance as he closed his study door and hurried along the landing to the back stairs. No time for reflection or sorrow. To hesitate would be fatal. Only briefly, as he hurried down the stairway, did the image of Magda and the children in the dining room flit briefly through his mind. No time to say goodbye. No point. It was over.

The cellar smelled sour. Freezing air, fetid and damp. He

stumbled through the darkness to the door, and fumbled with gloved fingers to unlock it.

Icy night air hit him like a slap in the face, and he saw his breath billow in the moonlight as he pulled on his hat. But now he stopped to listen, before peering cautiously along the alley between cold granite houses, to the street beyond. There was only the occasional car on the boulevard. But the shadows among the trees had taken form. He saw the huddled shapes of half a dozen men. The glow of cigarettes in the dark.

And then suddenly the screech of tyres. Lights blazing in the boulevard as several vehicles mounted the pavement, doors flying open. A cigarette discarded in a shower of sparks as men came running from the park.

Erik pulled the door shut behind him and sprinted along the alley to the lane behind the house, half-fearing they had sent men round the back. But no – they had not anticipated his forewarning. As he heard the hammering on his front door and the voices calling in the night, he hurried off into the dark, towards an unknown future full of fear and uncertainty.

CHAPTER TWO

Agadir, Morocco, February 29 1960

The view from the ancient city walls down to the harbour below and the sweep of the bay away to the south were spectacular. Yves never ceased to marvel at it. He had been fortunate to get an apartment in the historic kasbah, a studio in the roof of a converted riad in the heart of the old town. It was small, but all that a single man might require. From his terrace, he looked out over a jumble of rooftops and down into the narrow, shaded streets below. He loved the life of the kasbah, its noise, its energy, and he was used to shopping almost daily for fresh produce in the souk. He enjoyed waking to the sound of the calls to prayer that rang out each morning from the minaret of the mosque. Plaintive calls, summoning men to confer with their maker. And although he was not a religious man himself, there was something about the spirituality of the ritual that he envied, that his lack of faith would prevent him ever from sharing.

Today, as he drove out through the old city gates, the view unfolded below him as it always did. But this morning he barely noticed it. The mist gathering along the coast caught the first light of dawn as the sun rose over the desert to the east. Glowing. Pink. The restless ocean washing it up all along the sandy shore. A haze hung over the city spread out below him, new buildings expanding east and south as the population of this West African port exploded with the success of the Atlantic sardine trade.

But Yves was focused on his rear-view mirror. Amid the chaos of motor vehicles and horse-drawn carts and merchants' barrows in his wake, he caught a glimpse of the black Citröen. He had been watching for it, hoping that in the end it might prove simply to be a figment of an overactive imagination. But there it was. He cursed softly under his breath and followed the road as it serpentined its way down the hill towards the harbour. Fleets of rusting trawlers lined up along the quay, like the sardines that they had brought in overnight.

He glanced out of his driver's window, up the arid rocky slope and its tangle of pale green desert scrub, to the curve of the road above him. Dust rose from the tyres of the following Citröen. He had first spotted it nearly a week ago. It was probable that no ordinary person would have noticed it. But Yves was no ordinary person. His life possessed only a veneer of normality. There was not a minute of any hour of any day that passed when he didn't have an urge to glance back over his shoulder. It had become instinctive, as much a part of him as breathing. Always watching, scanning faces, focusing on anything unusual, no matter how small. Always expecting them, knowing that they were out there. Somewhere. Looking for him.

As the Citröen came round the bend behind him, he saw the driver's face, caught in a brief flash of sunlight, like a photograph engraving itself on Yves's retinas. A familiar face. Round. Bald. But familiar from where? He had no idea. He only knew that he had seen it before. He could see the shadows of other men in the car, and suspicion burgeoned into certainty and then fear. They had found him. They were following him. And sooner or later they would come for him.

With a deep inward sigh, Yves knew that it was time to move on.

A window along one side of his office looked down on to the floor of the indoor fishmarket below. It was a huge shed where long wooden palettes laid out on concrete displayed the day's catch. Sardines, mackerel, dorade, mullet, plaice. Boxes and boxes of them neatly arranged in oblong enclosures all across the trading floor, where buyers clustered to barter with white-coated marketeers. Raised voices floated up through the stench of fish and salt to rattle the window frames. Yves paused for only a moment to consider that it was the last time that he would gaze upon this scene. He had grown to love the smells and sights and sounds of the market during the nearly ten years he had worked his way up from humble trader to market manager. Considering that he had known nothing of fish or fishermen when he arrived from Munich, his ascent had been little short of meteoric. But his intelligence and ability to think on his feet had quickly singled him out from the crowd, and his bosses had not been slow to spot it. Increased responsibility had followed. Promotion. First to the running of the trading floor, then to assistant manager. And when finally his mentor had retired last year, stepping up, and into, his shoes had seemed the most natural progression to everyone concerned.

He turned away from the window, heavy with disappointment and regret. Each time, it seemed, that his future looked set, fate stepped in with a change of plan.

Run, Erik, run. Start again. Rebuild your life. But don't ever think you are safe. Never think for a moment that I am not right behind you, ready to pounce.

He removed the picture from the wall above his desk, and spun the dial on the safe behind it left and right. He heard the tumblers falling into place as he stopped it at the final digit, and the heavy door swung open. Inside lay bundles of documents, official papers, a cash box containing several hundred Dirham. And right at the back, a padlocked metal case, which he removed and placed on his desk.

A small key on his car key ring unlocked the padlock and he threw back the lid. Inside were the passports they had given him. All the paperwork he would require when the time came. He took them out and slipped them into a compartment of his briefcase, and picked up an old black and white photograph. Magda and the children. He felt a stab of self-pity, almost remorse. In all these years he had hardly ever allowed himself to even think what might have become of them. And now wasn't the time. It followed the papers into his briefcase, and he picked up the Walther P38 that he had taken from his desk drawer that fateful December night in Munich all those years before. Occasionally oiled, but never fired, in anger or self-defence. He dropped that, too, into the briefcase.

He looked up startled as the door opened. His secretary was a plump lady in her late thirties, dowdy and unattractive, with olive skin and dark eyes. Her long hair was tied up inside a black scarf.

'What is it, Aqila?' The sharpness of his tone startled her.

'I'm sorry, Monsieur Vaurs.' Her apology was both defensive and hostile. They had never got on. 'I have Monsieur Cattiaux from the bank on the line. Do you want to take his call?'

'No, tell him to call this afternoon.' His French, after all this time, was almost without accent and would never stand out in a country where almost everyone spoke it as a second language. But that was something he might have to work on.

She nodded and closed the door behind her. He breathed out deeply, trying to release the accumulating tension. He wouldn't be here this afternoon, and he would never speak to Monsieur Cattiaux from the bank, ever again. He took some satisfaction from that, at least. A single crumb of comfort floating in his sea of troubles. If there was one thing he did not mind leaving behind him it was debt.

He put the empty container back in the safe and locked it again, carefully rehanging the picture. Then he turned to his desk and began going through the drawers. There wasn't much here that he would take with him. It was almost impossible to anticipate what he might need in an obscure and uncharted future.

*

The *azan* call to prayer rang out across the kasbah, the voice of the muezzin carrying across the night, rising above the racket of the street markets and restaurants below. It was a familiar and comforting sound to Yves, coming as it did with the soft air through the open windows of his studio. Even in February the night air was mild. He would miss the climate. The heat of the summer, the mild winters, the clear, dry air. And the smell and sound of the sea. When silence settled across the city in the dead of night, it was always there, a sound like breathing. The deep, sighing, ever-present breath of the sea. In a way, he thought, it was what he might miss most of all.

The small leather suitcase was open on the bed. Prepacked and always ready, he was adding last minute items. Insignificant things. The detritus of a life to which he had grown too attached and was reluctant now to abandon entirely. An engraved silver cigarette case, a clock with luminous hands that he had bought at the souk, a gold wrist chain given him by Salima. He paused and wondered about her photograph. It stood in a pewter frame on the bedside table. When he hadn't wakened to her on his pillow, she had always been there at the side of his bed. On an impulse, he tore the cardboard backing away from the frame and took out the black and white print. He looked into her dark, smiling eyes, and ran a fingertip over her lips. Lips he would never kiss again.

He slipped it into the lining of his suitcase and stood debating whether he should call her. But he knew he could never explain the reason he was leaving, or make her understand why she would never see him again. And he wondered why that thought caused him more pain than the leaving of Magda and the boys.

In the end, he found a more practical reason for not calling Salima. It was just possible that his phone was being tapped, and he did not want to alert his pursuers to the fact that he was about to flee.

He closed his suitcase and sat on the edge of the bed looking around his studio. A glance at his watch told him it was not long after 11.30, and he suddenly felt very alone. And frightened. He had never planned for a life like this. Living in the shadows, watching for those who might be watching him. Forced to flit from one life to the next, always leaving behind the people and the things he loved. There was almost, he thought, no point in building a new life. Because somewhere, sometime in the future, they would find him, and it would all begin again.

Wearily he got to his feet and lifted his case. The bastards were relentless. And if they ever caught him, his life would be over.

At 11.38 he pulled the door of his apartment softly shut behind him. The old stone staircase was in darkness, the bulb on the landing burned-out or stolen. He would leave by the side exit in the corridor next to the caretaker's apartment on the ground floor, just in case they were watching the street. Once out into the maze of alleyways that riddled the kasbah, he could melt undetected into the night.

But the dark in the stairwell was profound, wrapping itself

around him like a cloak, very nearly tangible. His outstretched free hand followed the line of the wall downwards as he searched ahead with each foot for the next step. His own breath resonated loudly in the silence that resided behind the thick, stone walls of the old riad.

It was when he reached the landing below his that he first heard the voices. Whispers in the dark. Foreign tongues that he could barely discern and could not understand. But there was an urgency in the voices that conveyed itself without barrier of language. A tension in them. And he became aware that the men who owned them were on the next landing down, and on their way up.

Panic rose like bile to choke him. It was them! They were coming for him. Now. And there was nowhere he could go. He stopped, standing stock-still, mid-flight. The only course open to him was to retreat to his studio, and attempt an escape across the rooftops. But the very thought paralysed him with fear. He had felt safe to always leave his windows open, because no thief in his right mind would clamber over these roofs at night. And, besides, he had absolutely no head for heights.

They were getting closer. He heard his name, and blood turned to ice in his veins. No doubt about it. It *was* him they had come for. And still he stood rooted to the stairs, held there by a debilitating inertia. His only other course would be to charge down through them, taking them by surprise. But what if they had flashlights, and guns? There were several of them, he could tell. He would be totally exposed.

There was no advance warning. So he was taken wholly by surprise when the world came apart around him. Suddenly, and completely. What had seemed like solid matter supporting him turned to dust, and masonry, and timber, the air filled with the screeching and rending of metal and stone. A roar that rose up out of the very bowels of the earth, the hot, rancid breath of the devil himself exploding into the night. Yves was falling, flying, turning. Interminably. Fifteen seconds that felt like fifteen hours, before something struck him on the head, and the world turned black.

He had no idea how long he had been unconscious. But the first thing that struck him, as awareness returned, was the silence. An extraordinary, deafening silence, all the more striking for its contrast with the roar of destruction still echoing in his memory. Dust was settling all around him like the finest snow, and he choked on it, before looking up to see stars where once had been his apartment. He could make no sense of the confusion of masonry and brick all around him and had no conception at all of where he was. But to his surprise he found he was still clutching his suitcase, battered and scored, but intact.

He was lying at a peculiar angle over a chunk of what appeared to be the staircase, and he manoeuvred himself with difficulty into a sitting position. Miraculously, nothing seemed broken, but he could feel blood trickling down the side of his head.

Now he could hear distant voices calling in the night. And someone screaming. Closer to hand, something that sounded like moaning. But in his confusion he was unable to identify which direction it came from. He had no idea what had just happened. An explosion?

He tried to get to his feet and, as he turned, saw an arm protruding from a jagged chunk of masonry, frozen fingers clutching at nothing. He scrambled over the rubble, and with an enormous effort managed to pull the stonework to one side, exposing the hopelessly crushed body of a bald-headed man with with a round face, white now with plaster dust, and streaked crimson with blood. The Citröen driver. There were others here, too. He saw a foot. A hand. A leg. No sound. No movement. His pursuers were dead. All of them. Just three of the sixteen thousand who died that night during fifteen seconds of hell, in what he would soon discover had been the worst earthquake in Moroccan history.

Yet Yves had survived it, and who would know? How many bodies would never be recovered? His included.

This was the moment he realised that, with his own death, he was being given a second chance at life. No one would be looking for him ever again.

CHAPTER THREE

Paris, France, October 28 2009

It was nearly a year since the bullet had punched through Raffin's chest and almost ended his life. As far as Enzo could see he had never been the same man since.

He climbed the circular stairs to Raffin's apartment and heard clumsy fingers practising scales on a distant piano. The same fingers, he thought, which had been playing eleven months earlier when the shots were fired. They seemed to have made little progress since.

He hesitated by the door, remembering how the journalist had lain bleeding here in the hall as Enzo tried desperately to staunch the blood. There was no trace of it left on the tiles.

Raffin looked tired when he opened the door. His usual pallor was tinged with grey, and his pale green eyes, usually so sharp and perceptive, seemed dull. He smiled wanly and shook Enzo's hand. 'Come in.' Enzo followed him through to the sitting room, noticing how he no longer moved with the fluidity of youth. Still only in his mid-thirties, he had the demeanour of a man ten years older. His brown, collar-length hair seemed thinner, lank and lacking lustre.

He ushered Enzo to a seat at the table. It was strewn with documents and photographs and scribbled notes. A well-thumbed copy of his book, *Assassins Cachés*, lay open at the chapter about Killian. A half-full bottle of 1998 Pouilly Loché, Les Franières, stood beside an empty glass at Raffin's place, condensation trickling down the misted bottle. 'I'll get you a glass.'

'No, thanks.' Enzo could not resist a glance at his watch. It was not yet ten in the morning. Too early, even for him. And he watched with some concern as Raffin refilled his glass. He had never considered this fashionable young Parisian a suitable match for his daughter. Less so now. 'How's Kirsty?' She had not been in touch for several weeks.

'Fine, last time I saw her. She's still in Strasbourg.' But he wasn't going to be drawn on the subject. He sat down and sipped at his wine. 'I've been going through my research notes. I'd almost forgotten how much more there was about the Killian case than ever went into the book.'

'Why was that?'

'His son's widow, Jane Killian . . . she's still haunted by the call he made to her the night of his murder. He made her promise that nothing in his study would be touched, moved or removed, until such time as his son, Peter, could get to see it. He told her he'd left Peter a message there, something only his son would understand. Sadly, the son was killed in a road accident in Addis Ababa and never got to see it.'

'So what never made it into the book?'

'Any detailed description of what was in the room. She's had psychics, and journalists, and private investigators go over it with a fine-toothed comb but has always refused to allow publication of the details.'

'Why?'

'She's afraid that whoever the message was about might read and interpret those details.'

Enzo shook his head. 'But it's nearly twenty years since Killian was murdered, Roger. Can it still matter?'

'It might, if it gives a clue as to who killed him.'

'She still owns the house?'

Raffin took another sip of his wine. 'Yes. By law it went from father to son, but since the son was dead within a week of the father, it passed to his widow. No children involved, you see.'

'And she's still keeping her promise to the old man?'

'Scrupulously. His study remains untouched, just as it was the day of his murder.'

Enzo felt the first rush of adrenaline. It was like a crime scene preserved in a time capsule. 'Tell me a little more about Killian himself.'

'There's not much more to tell than appeared in my book. He was sixty-eight years old. English. He'd owned the house on the Île de Groix for almost twenty years, using it mainly for family holidays until he retired there in '87, one year after the death of his wife.'

Enzo consulted his own notes. 'A professor of tropical medical genetics at University of London.'

'Yes, he worked for the university's tropical medicine department. But insects were what really turned him on. According to his daughter-in-law, it was an obsession. He'd been a member of the Amateur Entomologists' Society in the UK for years, and couldn't wait to retire to devote himself to it full time.'

'Time wasn't on his side, though, was it? I mean, even if he hadn't been murdered, he didn't have long to live.'

Raffin shook his head. 'No. The lung cancer was diagnosed in the spring of 1990, and he wasn't expected to see out the year.'

Not for the first time, Enzo turned this information over in his mind and found it puzzling. 'Okay. And what about Kerjean? Is he still around?'

'He was when I was there. A thoroughly unpleasant character, from all accounts. Of course, he wouldn't talk to me. Hasn't given a single interview since the trial.'

'You don't give much of an account of the trial in the book.'

'It didn't merit it, Enzo. Sure, the guy had motive and opportunity, but the evidence against him was entirely circumstantial. It should never have gone to court.' He drained his glass and refilled it. 'Anyway, I had a long talk with Jane Killian on the phone last night. You can cancel your hotel booking. She's agreed to let you stay at the house, in the little attic room above the study.' He chuckled, but there was no humour in it. 'I think she sees you as the last hope of ever solving this case. I got the very firm impression that if you can't figure it out, she's going to give up and sell up.'

Enzo nodded slowly. 'So, no pressure, then.'

Raffin grinned. 'I'd have thought it was right up your street, Enzo, given that your specialty was crime scene analysis.'

Enzo canted his head in acknowledgement. 'I have to confess, it's an intriguing challenge. But I'd hate to be anyone's last hope.' He looked up to see Raffin pursing pale lips in faint amusement.

'Tell me . . .What was it you saw in that room that Jane Killian wouldn't let you write about?'

'Oh, I think I should leave you to see that for yourself.' Raffin looked at his watch, and Enzo noticed how his hands trembled. 'Shall we lunch at *midi*? I can call and book a table at the Marco Polo.'

Enzo felt the colour rising slightly on his cheeks. 'I can't today. I'm meeting someone.'

Raffin looked at him speculatively and nodded without comment. He took another sip of his wine, then after a moment, 'Have you seen Charlotte, lately?'

'No. Not lately.' Which was the truth. But he wondered why he was reluctant to confirm Raffin's obvious suspicion that it was the journalist's former lover that Enzo was meeting at *midi*. He wanted to leave right there and then, but it would have been churlish to do so. And he wasn't due to meet Charlotte for over an hour. 'Maybe I'll take that glass of wine now,' he said. As Raffin crossed to fetch a glass from the cabinet, Enzo glanced from the window into the courtyard below. Drifts of leaves from the big old chestnut blew across the cobbles on a chill autumn breeze, and he wondered why anyone would want to kill a dying man.

CHAPTER FOUR

Île de Groix, Brittany, France, August 12 1990

At the far side of the garden, beneath the shade of a gnarled oak, stood the shed that Killian used as a workshop. He had spent many hours here, pursuing his passion. Collecting and breeding, killing and preserving. He had constructed a rough workbench and lined the walls with shelves that were crowded with specimen jars and light traps, an insect tray, and a Tullgren funnel for trapping apterygotes.

In the corner stood a rack where he kept his nets. Several large ones for capturing flying creatures. A strong sweep net for sampling insects on vegetation. A pond dipping net for catching those that lived and bred on water.

He had just constructed a new pooter, two lengths of 3mm clear plastic tubing protruding from either end of a transparent plastic film canister. A small square of fine-meshed cotton was taped over the end of the mouthpiece which was inside the canister. Thus he would avoid the danger of sucking one of the insects into his mouth. Carefully, he inserted the other length of tube into the glass breeding jar where gossamer-winged creatures, trapped, demented, and hungry, whined and darted through the light that slanted from the window. He put the mouthpiece between his lips. A short, sharp intake of breath drew a single insect through the tube and into the canister.

Killian took a large magnifying glass from the drawer and lifted the canister to the light, peering at it through the lens with some satisfaction. This was what he had wanted. A female of the *culex pipiens* species, the world's most common mosquito. Unlike its malaria-carrying cousin, the *culex* fed mainly on birds, although was not averse to feeding on man to spread such delights as Saint Louis encephalitis and West Nile virus. It could be found on every continent on earth, except Antarctica, and was a common irritant here on this tiny, rocky island in the unpredictable Bay of Biscay.

Killian withdrew the collecting tube and sealed the hole in the lid with a square of tape. Fastidiously, he replaced the breeding jar in its heated container and cleared away his workbench. Everything had a place and had to be in it.

Satisfied, finally, with his work, he stepped out into the garden and locked the door of the shed. The shadows of trees fell darkly across the lawn towards the whitewashed cottage, in sharp contrast to the sunlight that slanted between their branches. Beyond, the same light shimmered on the sparkling waters of the strait that separated the island from the mainland port of Lorient, just visible in the far distance. The white triangles of sailing boats flashed in the clear summer air, tacking back and forth in the breeze that breathed through the channel.

The hum of myriad insects filled the hot air, music to Killian's ears as he turned away from the house and headed across the grass to the little annex where he had his study. A separate building with a tiny guest bedroom in the attic, Killian spent more time in the annex than he did in the house. Sometimes, when he worked late into the night, he would sleep upstairs. He had passed many more nights there than any houseguest. Visitors were rare these days, and when Peter and Jane came they always took a room in the main house.

The outside door of the annex opened into a tiny square of hall, from which narrow stairs led up to the bedroom. Straight ahead, a door opened into a small bathroom, while the door to the right led into his study. He knew he would have to take care not to leave it open for more than the few seconds it would take his visitor to enter. He closed it behind him now and crossed to his desk. He placed the film canister in his in tray and went to the window. He opened it to lean out and pull the shutters closed, adjusting the slats to let in some light, before closing the window once more and turning the key in its lock. Only the fan turning lazily in the ceiling stirred the hot air of the room.

Killian returned to his desk and eased himself into his captain's chair. He took out a handkerchief to mop away the perspiration that formed like dewdrops on his forehead, and ran a hand back through his head of thick, white hair. He looked at the book lying on his desk. A thin, well-thumbed paperback. He opened it at random, somewhere around the halfway point, and ran the heel of his hand up between the pages, breaking the spine so that it would remain open, an act that caused him some distress. But necessary, he knew, to accomplish his goal.

In the top right-hand drawer, he found a small jar of clear liquid and a clean wad of cotton wool. He smeared the cotton with a little of the liquid, and dabbed it lightly across the pages of the open book, then leaned forward to blow it dry. The combination of lactic acid and carbon dioxide would, he knew, prove an irresistible attractant to the winged messenger in the film canister.

Now he retrieved an aerosol of the repellent, *N,N-diethyl-3-methylbenzamide,* from the bottom drawer and closed his eyes as he sprayed it around his face and hands. He held his breath for as long as it took the fine liquid particles to disperse in the downdraft from the fan, then took a deep gulp of air.

He sat back in his seat and looked at the rays of light that zigzagged across the chair opposite and had a fleeting moment of doubt. But he forced it quickly from his mind and checked the time. His visitor would arrive any minute now. He reached for the film canister in his in tray and hesitated only briefly before flipping the cap off with his thumb and releasing the *culex pipiens* into the room.

The lines of sunlight that fell across the room from the shutters now followed the contours of Killian's visitor, striping arms and legs, as he sat in the chair which had been empty just a few minutes earlier. He was comfortable and relaxed, legs crossed, hands folded in his lap, smiling a slightly patronising smile across the desk at the Englishman. 'My goodness, it's hot,' he said, and he took out a fresh white handkerchief to wipe away the sweat gathering in the folds of his neck. 'Any chance we could open a window?' He was wearing a white, open-necked shirt, the sleeves carefully folded up to the elbows.

Killian shrugged. 'The air's warmer outside than in.' He glanced up at the ceiling fan, and wondered with a stab of concern whether the downdraught might discourage the mosquito. He felt a trickle of perspiration run down the side of his face. 'I'm sweating, too. But it's not the heat that's doing it.'

'No, of course not.' His visitor paused, raising one eyebrow and tipping his head as a sign of concern. 'How are you feeling?'

'Not good.' Some days were better than others. But lately there were more days when he felt worse. He supposed it was only to be expected. He tried to listen for the high-pitched whine of the *culex*, but his tinnitus was so bad now it was impossible to detect.

The other man leaned forward suddenly, half-turning his head to squint across the desk. He was looking at the open book that lay upon it, and for a moment Killian thought he had seen right through him. 'What are you reading these days?' he asked. But didn't wait for an answer, reading instead from the page heading. *The Life of the Mosquito, Part 4*. He looked up at Killian, and his incomprehension was patent, etched in the lines that wrinkled his nose and radiated from around his eyes. 'Of course. You're interested in insects, aren't you?'

'It's been a passion of mine for years.'

'Can't say I have anything other than a healthy dislike for them myself. Noisy, stinging, biting little bastards!' And he chuckled as if he had said something amusing.

Killian smiled indulgently.

'Well, I suppose we'd better get on with it.' The visitor leaned over to lift his bag from the floor and suddenly slapped at his forearm with his free hand. When he lifted his palm away, there was the tiniest smear of blood there, and for one dreadful moment Killian thought he had actually killed the *culex*. 'Damn! Missed him.'

Killian lowered his eyes and saw it just as it landed on the pages of the open book. Such a fragile, delicate creature, with its dark-scaled proboscis and golden head, abdomen swollen now from its last meal. 'There she is.'

His visitor frowned. 'She?'

'It's only the female of the species that bites.'

'Hah! Like most women, not to be trusted.' The visitor peered with annoyance at the tiny creature that had just fed on him.

'She needs the blood to feed her babies. Or, to be more accurate, to develop fertile eggs. Mosquitoes of both sexes actually feed on sugar. Plant nectar. Blood meals are reserved for egg production only.'

The other man raised his eyebrow again, this time in concert with a curl of his lip to demonstrate his distaste. 'As far as I'm concerned, the only good mosquito's a dead one.'

'Yes,' Killian agreed. And very carefully he slipped two

fingers beneath one half of the book, and quickly, deftly, flipped it shut. His visitor watched, with something like fascination, as Killian opened it again to reveal the creature perfectly squashed, its final meal now staining the paper of the facing pages. A small, crimson stain in *The Life of the Mosquito, Part 4*.

Killian smiled with satisfaction and looked up to meet the eye of his visitor. 'Gotcha!' he said.

Six weeks later

Killian closed the door of his study and climbed the narrow staircase in the dark. When he reached the little attic bedroom, he turned on the light and saw a stooped and putty-faced old man staring back at him from the mirror of the dressing table opposite. It was with something of a shock that he realised that the old man was himself. Most of the thick, silver hair that had so characterised his later years, was gone. There were deep, penumbrous shadows beneath his eyes, skin hanging grey and loose around his neck and jowls. He walked with the stooped gait of the elderly, and he wondered what had happened to the young man who had arrived with so much hope in his heart all those years before on the shores of England's green and pleasant land.

All that filled his heart now was fear. Not fear of death, for that was inevitable. But fear of not finishing what he had begun. That, in the end, his tormentor would get away with it. He had misplaced his trust in another and realised too late the mistake. He glanced from the window towards the house, across a lawn mired in shadow. There were no lights beyond the pale, colourless, illumination of the moon. And for a moment, he wondered if he saw movement among the trees. A figure flitting from shadow to shadow. He stood straining to see for nearly a minute before deciding it was just his imagination.

Turning away from the window he hobbled across the room, supported by his walking stick, a stout piece of hazel with an owl's head carved as a handle, the curve of it fitting neatly now in the palm of his hand. The bed gave beneath him as he sat on its edge, and he laid the stick beside him before picking up the phone. If only Peter had been at home, he would have told him everything. He cursed himself for not doing so sooner.

The phone, ringing shrill and metallic in a distant land, sounded in his ear, until he heard the familiar cadences of a young woman's voice. 'Hello?' And he wished he could lay his head on her breast and weep, curling up like a fetus, returning to the safety of the womb.

Instead he said, 'Jane, it's Papa. Don't speak, just listen.'

The alarm in her voice was clear. 'Papa, what's wrong?'

'You're not listening to me, Jane.' He was trying to stay calm. 'I need you to do something for me, and I don't want there to be any misunderstanding.' He paused and was greeted by silence from the other end. Almost. He could hear her short, shallow breathing. 'Good.' He had her attention. 'I know that Peter won't be back from Africa until next month. If I'm still around, I'll speak to him myself. But if I'm not – if something has happened to me – then I want you to tell him to come straight here.'

'For God's sake, Papa, what could happen to you? Have you taken a turn for the worse?'

'Jane!' His admonition was almost brutal, and he heard her stop midbreath. 'If for any reason I am not around any longer, he's to come to the house. I've left a message for him. He'll find it in my study. But, Jane . . . if he's still not back, I need you to make sure that no one moves or removes anything in the room. I need you to promise me that.'

'But, Papa – '

'Promise me, Jane!'

He heard the frustration now in her voice. 'I promise. But, Papa, what kind of message?'

'Nothing that anyone else will make sense of, Jane. But Peter will know straight away.' He had absolute confidence that his son would understand. And with understanding would come illumination. 'It's just ironic that it's the son who will finish the job.'

'Why can't you tell me?'

How could he tell her that it was too great a responsibility for a mere daughter-in-law? That he couldn't trust her with something so important. He tried to soften it. 'It's too much to place on the shoulders of a young woman, Jane. Peter will know what to do.'

'Papa . . .'

But he wasn't listening any more. A dull thud from somewhere deep in the building reverberated faintly through the bed. He felt it more than heard it. And as he got to his feet, he let the receiver fall back in its cradle. He lifted his walking stick, this time to use as a weapon rather than as an aid to walking, and shuffled towards the door.

The light from the bedroom spilled down the stairs to the tiny hall below, casting his shadow before him as he made his way slowly, step by step, down to the door of his study. It stood slightly ajar, but he remembered that he had closed it. Fear tightened around his heart like a clenched fist. Using his stick, he pushed it wide and saw the light that pooled on the green leather below his desk lamp, throwing his desk diary into sharp, clear focus. Beyond its ring of light, the rest of the room lay shadowed in semi-darkness. The door to the little kitchen stood fully open. He knew, too, that he had left it closed. He tried to listen, but the ringing in his ears obliterated all else.

He stepped into the room, and almost immediately was aware of a movement in his peripheral vision. He swivelled around as the intruder stepped into the light, the pistol in his hand raised and pointed at Killian's chest. His face was set and grim, and Killian thought he saw fear in his eyes. 'I figured it would be you,' Killian said. 'I knew it was a mistake to tell you. I could see it in your eyes.'

'Could you?'

'I saw all this, probably before you did.'

'Then you'll know how it ends.'

'Yes.' He was resigned to it now.

'I couldn't let you tell anyone.' It was almost as if he were pleading for understanding.

'No. You couldn't.'

The three shots from the pistol reverberated with deafening intensity in the stillness of the night. Propelled by the first of them back against the wall, Killian was dead before the other bullets left the gun.

The distant echo of gunshot was followed by the sound of a phone ringing in the bedroom upstairs. Frozen momentarily by the act of murder, the killer seemed startled by it and then moved to sudden action. He had no idea how much time he might have. But it was imperative that he find and destroy the evidence.

CHAPTER FIVE

Paris, France, October 28 2009

Enzo pulled up the collar of his baggy linen jacket and buttoned it against the bite of the wind. Beneath it, his light cotton shirt billowed around the hips of his cargo pants, and he wished he had dressed more appropriately for the weather. It had been sultry when he left his home in the south-west the day before. Cahors had been enjoying something of an Indian summer, and the cold winds blowing along the streets of Paris had come as a shock. Only the smokers sat out on the pavements along the Boulevard Saint-Germain. A hardy, if dying, breed.

His leather overnight bag bulged with the clothes he had crammed in to last him a week. He had told himself that a week really ought to be enough. In fact, he seriously wondered how he was going to occupy himself for that long. A look at the map had revealed that the tiny Île de Groix was only eight kilometres long and three wide. With a population of just over two thousand, there were only a handful of villages, in addition to the small town above the main harbour at Port

Tudy. It did not offer the prospect of very sophisticated living. And being out of season, his guide book had warned him, many of the restaurants would be shut.

He found a seat at a table in the Café Boneparte and glanced anxiously at his watch. His train left Montparnasse at one, connecting with the ferry from Lorient late afternoon. There would be no time for lunch. He would have to grab a sandwich at the station to eat on the train. The waiter brought him a glass of the house red, and he sat sipping it impatiently, watching the faces drift by in the square. He should have known that Charlotte would be late. She was always late.

It was nearly three months since he had last seen her. An encounter consummated by a bout of frenetic lovemaking at her eccentric home in an area of the thirteenth *arrondissement*, where once tanneries and tapestry-makers had lined the river. In the weeks that followed she had failed to return a single one of his calls, and he had finally determined to put his relationship with her behind him. A decision he had taken with some regret, for she was an attractive women, intellectually challenging, sexually stimulating. But she had made it clear, on more than one occasion, that while she enjoyed his company, they would never be more than friends, and occasional lovers.

She was more than fifteen years his junior, and he could see her point. He would be past retirement age when she was still in her forties. But after more than twenty years of widowhood, and with both daughters reaching their twenties, Enzo was looking for more now as he drifted towards the *troisième âge*.

'Still the old hippie, I see.'

He looked up to see her standing over him, dark curls tumbling luxuriantly over fine, angular shoulders, even darker eyes fixing him with their slightly quizzical smile. She wore a long black coat over black jeans and high-heeled boots. A colourful knitted scarf was thrown carelessly around her neck. He immediately felt his heart leap and butterflies stir. She had always had that effect on him, and all his resolve to put an end to it immediately dispersed like a dawn mist as the morning breeze stirs up.

'Hippie?'

'Last time we spoke you were talking of cutting off the ponytail. I'm glad you didn't.' She sat down and waved to the waiter. 'A Perrier,' she said when he arrived at the table, then turned to Enzo. 'Another of those?'

'No, I won't. I don't have much time.'

'Oh.'

He saw her disappointment immediately. The meeting had been at her suggestion. Roger, she said, had told her he would be in town. Enzo couldn't understand why she maintained contact with the journalist. They had been lovers for eighteen months, then broken up in acrimony. She had subsequently made it clear that she disliked him intensely. Yet for some reason they still exchanged calls, and met for the occasional drink.

'What's so pressing?'

'I have a train to catch in just under an hour.'

'Where are you going?'

'An island off the coast of Brittany. One of Roger's cold cases. Didn't he tell you?'

'No, he didn't.' She seemed put out that he hadn't. 'So how long will you be?'

'I don't know. A week. Maybe longer.'

'Will you come back to Paris afterwards?'

'I hadn't been planning to.' He noticed for the first time the dark smudges staining ivory skin beneath saucer eyes. And he wondered if she had lost weight. 'Are you all right?'

Her Perrier arrived and she took a long, slow sip, bubbles effervescing around her lips. 'I haven't been very well.' But she added quickly, 'Nothing serious.'

He reached out a hand to brush tumbling curls from her eyes, and held his fingertips to her cheek. He looked at her fondly, filled with concern. 'You need to take better care of yourself.'

'How would you know if I did or not? You're never around.'

Her rebuke stung him. It was so unfair. He took his hand away quickly, as if he had received an electric shock. 'Your choice, not mine.' He paused. 'Why did you want to meet me today?'

'I need to talk to you, Enzo. There's stuff we have to discuss.' There was a coldness now, in her tone.

Even as he moved imperceptibly away, he knew that she would pick up his body language, the psychologist's eye detecting all his *micro signes*. It annoyed him that he should be so easily read. 'I'm listening.'

But she shook her head. 'Not now. Not like this. What I have to say is far too important to squeeze in between a glass of wine and a dash for a train.' She abandoned her Perrier and stood up. 'Let me know when you're in town again, and I'll apply for an audience.'

And with a swirl of her coat she was gone, leaving Enzo to sigh in exasperation and pay the bill.

CHAPTER SIX

Île de Groix, Brittany, France, October 28 2009

Enzo gazed from the window of the *gare maritime* across a grey expanse of water towards a dock where container ships were lined up in serried rows, tall cranes breaking low cloud. The rain was so fine it was almost a mist. In Scotland Enzo would have called it a *smirr*. The wet, the cold, the brooding and bruised skies, all were reminiscent of his native country. He should have felt at home. Instead, he felt miserable. And a little guilty. If only by association.

Lorient was a dull town, characterised by the unimaginative post-war architecture of the 1950s. It had once been a thriving port on the Breton coast, a destination for the fleet of the French East India Company bringing goods from the Orient. But the Germans had commandeered it as a base for U-boats employed to attack allied convoys in the Atlantic. Over four hellish weeks in the winter of 1943, allied bombers had completely destroyed the town. Enzo had read somewhere that thousands of French civilians had been killed during the raids.

The irony was that the heavily fortified submarine base had survived intact. It was now a tourist attraction.

As he walked with the other passengers down the ramp to the jetty and the ferry beyond, the wind tugged at his jacket, blowing stinging rain into his face, and he hurried up studded metal stairs to the warmth of the passenger deck to find a seat. Rain smeared the view across to the distant Larmor-Plage, where the German commander, Karl Dönitz, had installed his headquarters. From there he had no doubt watched in awe as sixty thousand incendiary bombs fell on the city, his own private fireworks display.

The water in the bay was choppy, the colour of pewter, topped by occasional flashes of white. Demented seagulls wheeled and screeched overhead, like scraps of paper blowing in the wind. As the ferry sounded its horn and chugged slowly towards the defensive outer walls of the harbour, Enzo could see the formidable concrete construction at Keroman that had housed the U-boats, dark and sinister still on this most inhospitable of days.

He glanced around him, at the faces of his fellow passengers. Pale Celtic faces, buried in books, or glowering under skipped hats and anorak hoods. Island faces, shaped by race and climate, indistinguishable from the inhabitants of the Scottish west coast, sharing a common heritage, and a kinship that transcended language and national borders.

The ferry was about halfway across the strait when he realised that each time he turned his head, other heads dipped into magazines, and faces swivelled to look from windows.

And he was struck by the strange and uncomfortable sensation that people were looking at him. He was not unused to the curious stares of the French. A tall man, big built, with his dark hair and silver streak pulled back in a ponytail, he cut an unusual figure among the slighter-built, Mediterranean people of the south. But here, among fellow Celts, he had not expected to feel so conspicuous. And yet, no doubt about it, surreptitious eyes were upon him.

When the first dark smudge that was the Île de Groix emerged from the gathering gloom, Enzo stood up and moved forward to the arc of large windows that looked out across the bow of the boat. Driving rain distorted his view of Port Tudy between the twin lighthouses that marked the opening to the harbour. Beyond a forest of masts, he could just make out the white, pink, and blue-painted cottages built along the low cliffs that ran up the hill towards Le Bourg.

He turned around to find almost every face on the passenger deck looking at him. Almost expectantly. As if they anticipated that he might say something, utter some words of wisdom. They looked almost ready to applaud. He wanted to shout: *what are you looking at*! But an announcement over the loudspeakers welcoming them to the Île de Groix, saved him from the humiliation, and the moment passed. Passengers suddenly forgot about him in their haste to disembark, rising from their seats, gathering belongings, and hurrying for the stairs.

But the feeling of being watched returned once more as he stepped up on to the jetty. Fishermen on the rusted green fishing boat, the *Banco*, turned curious eyes upon him as they docked at the wharf, and he was aware of yet more heads turning in his direction as he hurried along the pier. He could see the lifeboat station away to his right, a white building with blue shutters. The *Societé Nationale de Sauvetage en Mer*. Ahead, beyond a small circle at the end of the jetty, stood a couple of hotels, bars with covered terraces looking out across the harbour. He was tempted by the prospect of a chance to escape the cold and rain, and a couple of whiskies to warm him. But he spotted the garish yellow frontage of Coconut's car rental and supposed he really ought to pick up his rental car and drive out to the house before it got dark.

He was about to cross the street, when he felt a firm tugging on his arm. He turned to find himself looking into the face of a man almost as tall as himself, but perhaps ten years younger. A broad-built man with dark hair rain-smeared across his forehead and straggling over his upturned collar. His jacket was soaked through, and his blue eyes fixed Enzo with a disconcertingly unblinking gaze. Enzo smelled the rancid stink of stale alcohol on his breath.

'You think you're so smart, monsieur.'

'What?'

'You think you'll come after me and prove what no one else could. Well, you're wrong.'

And it dawned on Enzo who he was. 'You're Thibaud Kerjean.'

'They still think I did it.'

'Who?'

'Everyone. Twenty years on. Even after the court acquitted me. Well, fuck them, monsieur. And fuck you. I wasn't guilty then, and I'm not guilty now. So if you're as smart as you think you are, you'll stay well away from me. And if you don't, you'll regret it.'

Enzo was aware for the first time that Kerjean was still holding his arm. He pulled it free, and stared back directly into the islander's hostility. 'How the hell do you know who I am?'

Kerjean's lip curled into something halfway between a sneer and a smile, and he turned away, walking briskly towards the bar at the Café de la Jetée. Enzo stood watching him go, angry, confused, before becoming aware once more of faces turned in his direction: passengers from the ferry, customers in the bars standing in doorways and at windows. A car, newly disembarked from the ferry, turned through a puddle, and Enzo felt the splash of it soak the legs of his trousers with muddy rainwater. He cursed and stooped to wipe at his trousers legs with the back of his hand, then turned to glare after the driver, which is when he saw the newspaper billboard wired to an Île de Groix welcome sign. It displayed the headline of that day's edition of *Ouest-France*. SCOTS EXPERT TO SOLVE GROIX MURDER. Beneath was a black and white photograph of Enzo. Taken a few years previously, but unmistakable, with the dark ponytail and white stripe that had earned him his nickname of Magpie.

'Your reputation goes before you, Monsieur Macleod.'

Enzo looked up to see a tall, solemn-faced gendarme regarding him with speculative interest. He wore a peaked *kepi* and a waterproof cape over his uniform, which looked a great deal dryer than Enzo felt. His arms were folded across his chest.

'And I see you have already met Monsieur Kerjean. I think he's afraid that someone is finally going to prove that he did it.'

Enzo cocked an eyebrow. 'And did he?' There seemed no point now in hurrying for cover.

'That's for him to know, and you to find out.' The gendarme extended a warm, dry hand to shake Enzo's cold, wet one. 'I'm Adjudant Richard Guéguen. Top cop around here. Big fish in a very small pool. And I'd like a word, if you can spare me a few minutes.' But it sounded more like an order than a request.

Enzo glanced anxiously towards Coconut's. He had no idea what time they closed. 'I've got to pick up my rental car.'

'Oh, I wouldn't worry about that. It won't be going anywhere without you. Besides, they've been told to expect you'll be a little late.' The hint of a smile crept across full lips.

The gendarmerie stood in a commanding position on the hill above the customs offices overlooking the port, a yellow-painted three-storey villa with a steeply pitched slate roof. Guéguen took Enzo in through a side entrance. He called into a small general office, where three *gendarmes* sat idling behind desks. He didn't want to be disturbed, he said, and led Enzo through to his own office at the rear of the house. Enzo felt eyes on his back as he followed the adjudant down the hall.

Guéguen indicated a chair facing his desk. 'Coffee?'

'I'd love one.'

'Two coffees in here please.' The adjudant called his order back down the hall and pointedly left the door open, apparently so that they could be overheard. He hung up his cape and cap and sat down behind his desk, then leaned forward, his forearms flat in front of him, interlocking his fingers as if in prayer. 'You're an interesting character, Monsieur Macleod.'

'So I've been told.'

'But I have to confess I'd never heard of you before I was instructed by brigade headquarters to lend you absolutely no assistance whatsoever.'

'And why would they instruct you to do that?'

'You mean apart from the fact that cops never like outsiders showing them how to do their job?'

Enzo grinned. 'Yes, apart from that.'

'Well, Monsieur Macleod, you have to realise that the economy of this little island of ours is almost entirely dependent upon tourism these days. The era of the tuna fleets and the fish processing are long gone. And to be perfectly frank, murder is not a great tourist attraction.'

'Even one that's twenty years old?'

'It's the only one in living memory, Monsieur Macleod. However, the fact that it was never solved makes it a little like a wound that has never healed. And we really don't want folk coming picking at the scabs.'

'Even if a resolution of the case would finally heal the scar?'

Guéguen sat back in his chair and chuckled, turning a

pencil over and over again between his fingers. 'And what makes you think you can succeed where no one else has?'

'I've got a pretty good track record.'

'That you have, Monsieur Macleod. I was amazed at just how much there was about you on the Internet when I looked. This would be the . . . fourth in Raffin's catalogue of cold cases, yes?' He opened a folder in front of him. 'And I see that before you came to France you specialised in crime scene analysis. No doubt Madame Killian will have high expectations.'

'I never make any promises.'

'Very wise. You know, a succession of people have come to study this case over the years, and none of them has exactly enhanced his reputation.'

'And I'm not here to enhance mine, Adjudant Guéguen. The publicity these cases attracts helps us raise funds for the Forensic Science Department at my university. So it's only the French *police scientifique* that'll be enhanced.'

Guéguen inclined his head and smiled in acquiescence. 'True, but nonetheless, I have to tell you that should you feel inclined to bend the law in any way during the course of your investigation, you can expect no quarter from me or any of my officers. And you will have no access to official records, or evidence.'

Enzo nodded. 'I take it you don't keep any of that kind of stuff here in any case.'

'No. All documentation and evidence is held at Vannes, a few kilometres along the coast from Lorient.'

'Which is where the trial was held, right?'

'Right.'

A young gendarme coughed and entered, a polystyrene cup of coffee in each hand. He placed them on the desk, along with sachets of sugar and plastic stirrers, and left. Enzo stirred in his sugar and cradled the cup in his hands to warm them, sipping on the strong, hot, black liquid. 'Thank you,' he said. 'I needed this.' He looked up and saw what looked like amusement in the younger man's eyes. Guéguen, he reckoned could only be in his early forties. Dark hair cut short, with some grey, like brushed steel showing now around the temples. He had dark eyebrows and friendly liquid brown eyes. A good-looking man who seemed not at all to fit the stereotype of the humourless, intimidating gendarme. 'And thank you, too, for warning me off so gently.'

The adjudant grinned. 'All part of the service, Monsieur Macleod.' He lifted the phone. 'I'll give Coconut's a call and ask them to drop your car off here. Save you walking back down the hill in the rain.'

When he finished the call Enzo said, 'Thank you. Again.' He glanced back along the hall. 'How many of you are there here?'

'Six. Myself, a *chef*, two *gendarmes*, and two trainees. During the summer months when the population of the island literally explodes, the brigade sends us another six.'

'And I guess any serious crimes, like murder, would be handled by investigators from the mainland?'

Guéguen laughed heartily. 'Monsieur Macleod, if you want to know how the investigation into Killian's murder was conducted, you only have to ask.'

'I thought you'd been instructed not to cooperate.'

'Not to give you access to official police records or evidence,' Guéguen corrected him. 'No one said we couldn't discuss things that were a matter of public record.' And there was a hint of wickedness in the smile that creased his eyes.

'So what happened?'

'Well, in theory, we were supposed to secure the crime scene until senior investigators arrived from Lorient. In fact, we made a complete mess of it. No one had the least idea what securing a crime scene entailed, so I'm afraid we trampled all over it, touched things we shouldn't, and failed to protect things we should.'

'You were here then?' Enzo was incredulous. 'Twenty years ago?

Guéguen grinned. 'I was one of the trainees at that time. I have spent most of my career since serving with other brigades in various parts of Brittany. I returned just last year for the first time in nearly seventeen years.'

'As the boss?'

'Yes. As the boss.' Guéguen's eyes crinkled again in amusement. 'A lot older and much wiser. If there were any serious crime committed on the island today, Monsieur Macleod, every one of my officers is trained in the treatment of a crime scene. There is a rota of island doctors who would be called out to determine whether or not a death was suspicious, although of course any autopsy would be carried out by the pathologist at the hospital in Lorient. We've had a few suicides and serious accidents to practise on.'

'So it was a local doctor who determined that Killian's death was suspicious?'

This time Guéguen roared with laughter. 'I would hardly describe three bullet holes in the chest as suspicious, Mr Macleod. But, yes. It was.'

Voices in the corridor interrupted their conversation. A young man from the car rental company knocked on the door and brought in paperwork for Enzo to sign. He seemed self-conscious, almost deferential in the presence of the senior gendarme, and was anxious to be away again as soon as possible.

'The car's round the back,' he said. 'The Suzuki jeep.' He handed Enzo the keys and was gone.

Guéguen rose from his desk and reached for his cape and hat. 'I'll walk you round.'

Enzo gulped down the last of his coffee and lifted his over-night bag, and the two men left by the same side entrance and walked around to the back of the gendarmerie. On the far side of a muddy parking area stood a concrete block with two heavy steel doors. Guéguen followed Enzo's eyes.

'The cells.' He walked towards the nearest door and pushed it open. 'Take a look. This is where we brought Kerjean when it was decided to charge him.'

Enzo walked into a dark cubicle. A hole in the floor at the back of the cell served as a toilet. High up in the wall above it was a window, allowing minimal light to penetrate thick cubes of unbreakable glass. A stone plinth was covered with a thin, unsanitary looking mattress. It was cold and damp, the walls scarred with the graffiti of drunks and petty crooks. Not a place you would want to spend any time.

'Myself and one of the more senior *gendarmes* were dispatched to bring him in.' Guéguen seemed lost for a moment in his memory of the event. 'We were pretty nervous about it. Kerjean was . . . still is . . . a big man. And he had something of a reputation for violence. He wasn't any stranger to these cells. He'd spent a few nights here after getting into drunken brawls in town. And he never came quietly.'

'You thought he might resist arrest?'

'Who knows what a desperate man accused of murder might do? As it turned out, he came like a lamb.'

'Do you think he did it?' Enzo watched carefully for his reaction, but the big gendarme just smiled.

'Of course he didn't. He was acquitted, wasn't he?' He reached into an inside pocket and produced a dog-eared business card. He found a pen and scribbled some figures on the back of it, before handing it to Enzo. 'Here.'

Enzo turned it over. It was a telephone number.

'That's my personal mobile. Officially, I can do nothing for you, Monsieur Macleod. Unofficially . . .' he glanced across the sodden car park towards the house, ' . . . I'll help you in any way I can. And I don't just *think* Kerjean did it, I'm *sure* he did. Even if he can't be tried again, I'd love to see him nailed.'

CHAPTER SEVEN

The brief rush of traffic following the arrival of the ferry had long since subsided. The sky had darkened, the last of its light squeezed out by the rainclouds. Le Bourg, the small town at the top of the hill above Port Tudy, was deserted. Lights shone in a few shop windows: *Le Relais des Mousquetaires*, the *Bleu Thé*, the *Île et Elles* hairdresser on the square opposite the war monument and the church.

Enzo lost his way several times in the narrow streets, terraces of gabled houses with steeply pitched roofs and dormer windows, painted pink and white, and brick-red, and blue. Finally he saw a roadsign for Port Mélite.

After he left the town, and the Ecomarché supermarket on its outskirts, place names and arrows painted on crumbling road surfaces replaced conventional roadsigns. His jeep, with its canvas roof and brutal suspension, proved draughty and damp and noisy as he steered it east through the gathering gloom along the island's north coast. This was flat, dull countryside, punctuated by the odd stand of trees and occasional clusters of isolated cottages. Finally the road turned into a long descent to the tiny village of Port Mélite, a small group of houses huddled around a short sweep of sandy beach. Through the rain and the gloom, Enzo could just see the lights of the mainland in the far distance across the strait.

He parked next to a white car beside two concrete benches overlooking the beach. The name of the village was painted on a stone set into the grass. An arrow pointed east. *Les Grands Sables 400m*. He found the house about twenty metres along the dirt track leading to the big sands. It stood behind a wall and blue-painted fence, half obscured by tall, over-grown shrubs and bushes. It was a square, white bungalow with blue shutters, a light burned in one of the windows at the front, warm and welcoming in the cold and wet of the approaching night.

He'd had no real sense of what to expect of Jane Killian, and yet Enzo found himself taken by surprise. She was petite, five-two or three, and slim built. Curling brown hair with blond highlights was cut short, tight into the nape of her neck, giving her an almost boyish appearance, an illusion aided by the way she dressed. Loose-fitting jeans, a pale blue, open-necked shirt out over narrow hips, well-worn high tops. But there was nothing masculine about her. She had full, almost sensuous lips, and below dark eyebrows large, bright eyes, brown flecked with orange, almost amber. She was, he knew from Raffin's book, forty-five years old, but looked ten years younger and had an air of fragility about her. As if she might easily be broken. She held out a small, elegant hand to shake Enzo's. 'Come in. You must be frozen dressed like that.'

Enzo followed her into the living room, where split logs

glowed on a grate in an open fire, throwing out their warmth, and filling the room with the smoky sweet smell of burning oak.

'Here, let me take that jacket. It's soaking.' She took his coat and draped it over the back of a chair in front of the fire. 'You could probably do with a drink. Whisky?'

'Perfect.' Enzo knew already that he liked her. Any woman who hung up his coat and offered him whisky went right to the head of the queue for his affections. He noticed the open book on the coffee table next to the armchair where the impression her body had left in the soft cushions still showed. *Chocolat.* So although she had never remarried, she hadn't lost her sense of romance. Or perhaps her dreams of it.

She handed him a whisky and refilled her own glass. 'Sit down.' She curled herself up in the armchair she had occupied before his arrival. 'It's nice to be talking English. My French isn't that great, I'm afraid.' Enzo had fallen back into his native language without even thinking about it, but realised now that there was a comfort in it. 'I suppose your French must be pretty good.'

Enzo shrugged modestly. 'It's okay. Although I think my Scottish accent sometimes bamboozles the French.'

'How long have you lived here?'

'About twenty-three years now.'

'Almost a native, then.'

'Well, my daughter is. One hundred per cent French. Although she speaks English with my Scottish accent.'

Jane smiled and tipped her head slightly, sipping her

whisky, and looking at him over her glass with an appraising eye. 'She has a French mother then, I guess.'

'Yes.' Enzo wasn't about to volunteer any more just yet. He looked around the small living room, made smaller by the clutter of soft furnishings. Pushed up against one wall stood a scarred French buffet, no doubt acquired at a local *brocante*. A gateleg table was folded against the back wall. Mounted above it a dozen framed cases displayed preserved insects pinned to white backboards. Ageing brown and cream floral-patterned paper covered the walls and the door, and a scatter of rugs protected polished oak floorboards. 'So . . . this is where it all happened?'

'Not exactly,' she said. 'Papa's study is out in the annex across the lawn. I'm sorry . . . I should say Adam. I always called him Papa, because Peter did.'

'That doesn't sound very English.'

She raised her eyebrows in surprise. 'Well, that's because he wasn't.'

And now it was Enzo's turn to be surprised. 'I thought your father-in-law was British.'

'He was. Well, at least, he took British nationality. But he was born in Poland, and didn't come to Britain until 1951. In the end, he was more English than the English. Not even the hint of an accent. I think he worked very hard at not being Polish anymore.'

This was news to Enzo. There had been no mention of it in Raffin's book. 'Tell me.'

'Not much to tell, really. He began his university education in Warsaw before the German invasion. Finished it after the war, and came to do a postgrad at University of London in '51.'

'In tropical medical genetics.'

'Yes. Over the years he spent a lot of time in the tropics, as well as other parts of the world. I think that's where he got the entomology bug.' She smiled. 'So to speak.'

Enzo ran his eyes over the lines of insect display cases hanging on the wall. Jane followed his glance.

'Not an interest he passed on to his son, I'm happy to say.'

'What was it Peter did?'

'He worked for a charity. Spent a lot of time overseas, just like his father.'

Enzo looked at her carefully. 'It's almost twenty years since he died.'

'Yes.' If there were still emotional scars, she kept them well hidden.

'But you never remarried.'

'No.'

He waited for more, but there was nothing forthcoming. Instead she changed the subject.

'I've prepared the bedroom directly above Papa's study. You can stay as long as you like, or for as long as it takes. I'll be here, in the main house, for about two weeks, so if there's anything you need to know . . .'

Enzo took a large swallow of whisky. 'You can tell me how the local newspaper knew I was coming.'

'Oh, God, did they?' She flushed with embarrassment. 'I haven't seen the paper, but I'm afraid it was probably my fault.

There's a woman in the village who looks after the house for me when I'm not here and gets it ready for my return.' She sighed. 'When I asked her to prepare the guest bedroom, I stupidly told her why.' She shrugged her apology. 'Impossible to keep a secret here. I'm sorry, I should have known better.' She drained her glass. 'Would you like to see the study?'

At the back door she took an umbrella from the rack. The door led straight from a large kitchen into the garden. Oddly the kitchen seemed cold and empty. Jane said, 'I'd have had a meal prepared for you, but I only arrived today myself. Haven't had a chance to go shopping yet. I thought we might eat out in town, if that's okay with you.'

'Sure.' Enzo groaned inwardly at the prospect of having to go out again into the night. It was fully dark now, and by the light of an outside halogen lamp illuminating the back garden, he could see the rain driving almost horizontally across the lawn.

They huddled together under the shelter of the umbrella and hurried over the grass to where the annex sat brooding darkly among the trees. He was aware of her slight, soft body pressed into his side as he crooked his arm around her shoulders to support the umbrella against the wind.

She unlocked the door, and they scrambled out of the wet into the small square of entrance hall, shaking the umbrella behind them. The flick of a switch caused a single, naked bulb to cast light down into the hall from the narrow stairwell. She pushed open the door in front of them.

'Bathroom in there. Bedroom up the stairs. And this . . .' she turned to her right and opened a door, ' . . . was Papa's study.' She leaned in and turned on a light, and Enzo found himself gazing back twenty years into the past.

He felt a strange thrill of anticipation, all his instincts on suddenly heightened alert. Here was the room where Killian had died. The room in which he had somehow created a message for his son. A message that the young man had never seen and which had never been deciphered by anyone since. He laid his overnight bag down in the hall and took three steps back in time to an early autumn night in September 1990.

The large, square room had a high ceiling. To the right, a tall, shuttered window opened on to what Enzo imagined would be a view across the garden to the house. Floor-to-ceiling bookshelves lined the facing wall and the wall to the left. A thousand volumes or more stood side by side, silent witnesses to the murder of the man who had placed them there. Their multi-coloured façade lent a warmth to this otherwise cold room.

Killian's desk faced the door, an austere, uncomfortable-looking guest chair set at an angle on the nearside. Against the door wall stood a wooden filing cabinet, and next to it a work table where, Jane said, Killian spent hours preserving and mounting species of insects gathered from the surrounding countryside. Each one was photographed and annotated in leather-bound volumes. Beyond that, another door led to a small kitchen with little more than a sink and draining board, an old refrigerator, a small electric oven, and a shelf with an electric kettle, teapot and tea caddy.

Enzo's first impression was of an almost obsessive sense of order. The desk was set at right angles to the window, carefully aligned with the run of the floorboards. The books on the shelves behind it were perfectly perpendicular, each spine meticulously lined up with the edge of the shelf it stood on. Enzo crossed the room and ran the tips of his fingers lightly along one of the rows, following the regularity of its contours. He noticed that the books were all arranged in alphabetical order, first by author, then by title.

On the desk itself two wire trays were placed one at each side. An in tray, an out tray. Each was empty. The brass desk lamp was set at a ninety-degree angle on the far left-hand corner of the desk. The only incongruity was a curled and faded yellow Post-it stuck to its glass shade with Scotch tape. On a pristine, unmarked blotter, a desk diary lay open at the week beginning September 23 1990. A pen nestled where the pages curled into the line of its spine.

'It didn't look quite this way when I got here,' Jane said. 'Whoever shot him had been searching for something. Whether it was anything specific, or just valuables, we'll maybe never know.' She sighed. 'Anyway, I straightened it up as best I could, trying to remember the way he kept things. Nothing has been moved or removed. And nothing introduced. Everything is exactly as it was then.'

She couldn't resist a glance towards the floorboards beneath the window, and Enzo was quick to spot it. Although it had faded with time, the blood that had seeped from Killian's fatal wounds had left an indelible, dark stain in the wood.

'I washed the bloodstains from the wall once the police were finished. There were two exit wounds, and you can see where the bullets pitted the plaster. The third lodged in his spine.'

Enzo wondered whether it was simply time and the no doubt oft-repeated phrases that lent the mechanical, emotionless quality to her voice. He nodded and lowered himself into Killian's captain's chair. Its leather seat had become dry and brittle after all this time, and the chair groaned beneath his weight. Perhaps by placing himself in the man's seat he could find someway into his mind.

There were four drawers in the desk. The deep one on the left contained a box of A4 printing paper. The drawer above it revealed an arrangement of open cardboard boxes filled with various items of stationery. Paperclips, drawing pins, staples, a Post-it pad, pens, pencils, erasers. The deep drawer on the right held a box of clear plastic sleeves for filing documents in clip folders. Lying on top of it was an aerosol can with a handwritten label. *N,N-diethyl-3-methylbenzamide*. Enzo lifted it out and examined it. He held it in the air, expelled a tiny blast and sniffed, wrinkling his nose. 'Mosquito repellent.'

'Yes.' Jane nodded. This was clearly not news to her.

'Are you troubled by mosquitoes here?'

'Not much. There's usually an onshore breeze that keeps us relatively insect-free.'

Enzo laid the aerosol back in the drawer and slid open the one above it. Here was a strange arrangement of clear plastic tubing exiting from either end of a transparent plastic film container of the kind that used to hold rolls of film in the pre-digital age. Enzo frowned.

'It's called a pooter, apparently,' Jane said. 'For catching single insects. You use one end as a mouthpiece, and suck the creatures in through the other end to trap them in the container.'

Enzo pulled off the lid and saw that the mouthpiece tube had a tiny square of gauze stuck over one end. Its purpose was obvious. He put it back in the drawer, and picked up the only other item. A small bottle of clear liquid. He held it up. 'Do you know what's in this is?'

'I had it analysed. It's lactic acid. No one seems to know what he might have used it for.'

Enzo thought about it for a long time. 'Lactic acid,' he said at length, 'particularly in combination with carbon dioxide, is a well-known mosquito attractant.'

'Oh.' Jane seemed surprised. 'No one's come up with that before.'

'Strange though.' Enzo turned it over in his mind. 'Repellent in one drawer, attractant in another.'

'Well, he worked with insects all the time, so who knows what he might have used them for.'

Enzo closed the drawer and looked at the desk diary open in front of him. 'The diary was open at this page?'

'Yes.'

Enzo flipped back several pages, screwing up his eyes to read the entries. 'Doctor's appointments,' he said. 'Twice a week by the looks.'

'He was getting some kind of palliative treatment for the cancer. It didn't seem to be doing him much good, though.'

Enzo returned to the entry for Monday, September 24, the day Killian was murdered, and reached into his canvas shoulder satchel to retrieve his half-moon reading glasses. He smiled ruefully over them at Jane. 'Vanity has to take a back seat to clarity these days, I'm afraid.' And he returned his attention to Killian's final entry. He read it out loud. 'P, I was lighting a fire, but now there's no more time, and all I'm left with is a half-warmed fish in the pouring rain.' He looked up, puzzled. 'What did he mean? Is this the message?'

His dead son's wife shrugged, and looked vaguely disappointed. 'Well, that's what I hoped you would tell me, Mr Macleod.' She approached the desk. 'If it is the message, it's only a part of it.' He left notes all over the place.' She touched the Post-it scotched to the desk lamp. 'This one was attached to the lamp, but kept falling off. So I stuck it on with sticky tape so it didn't get lost.'

Enzo leaned forward to read it, peering myopically through his half-moons at the faded scrawl. Again, he read aloud. 'P, one day you will have to oil my bicycles. Don't forget!' He looked up at Jane. 'I'm assuming that P is Peter.'

'That is the assumption everyone else has made.'

'So your father-in-law had more than one bicycle?'

'No, that's the strange thing. He didn't have one at all. And neither did Peter.'

Enzo looked again at the note on the lamp, then the scribbled entry in the desk diary, before flipping back for a second look at the previous entries. 'All the other entries in his diary,' he said, 'are written in a very tight, neat hand. Except this last one. And the note on the lamp.' He compared dots and t's and loops. 'But demonstrably the same handwriting. Just scribbled, as if done in a great hurry.'

'Yes. It was very uncharacteristic of him. He was a scrupulous and careful man.'

Enzo looked around the study again. 'Very tidy, very ordered.'

Jane nodded her agreement. 'Almost manically so.'

He stood up. 'What other notes were there?'

She led him through to the tiny kitchen, which was filled with the hum and rattle of the old refrigerator. Its door was covered with fridge magnets collected over the years. Cartoon insects arranged in ordered patterns, badges, and flags. A scribbled pencil note was fading now on a notepad for jotting down larder items to be restocked. The telephone numbers of the medical clinic in Le Bourg had dimmed too, and several washed-out family photographs were held in place by short magnetic strips carefully angled at each corner. A yellow Post-it was browning and curled at the corners. Stuck on at an odd angle, it was held in position by what appeared to be two randomly placed magnetic strips.

'What did he keep in the fridge?'

'Cold drinks, mostly. And cheese. Stuff like that, for snacking when he felt hungry.' He opened the door and its fluorescent light flickered to illuminate yellowing empty shelves within. 'It was empty when he was found.' She pulled down a flap at the top of the fridge to expose the build-up of ice and frost that choked the tiny icebox. 'And this was pretty much iced up then, too. I keep meaning to defrost it, but never have.'

'I'm amazed it still works,' Enzo said.

Jane just smiled. 'Actually I think it's more than thirty years old. They must have built things to last longer then. Unlike now. What's the catchphrase these days? Built-in obsolescence?'

Enzo grinned. 'Yes. So you have to replace them more often. Keeps manufacturers in business and people in jobs.'

She shut the door and Enzo peered at the photographs, their glaze cracked in places and starting to peel. He recognised Adam Killian from the photographs in Raffin's book. A healthy, tanned-looking man with a thick head of pure white hair grinning at the camera. And Jane Killian, looking much younger. Dark hair cascading over her shoulders. A shy smile.

'I guess the young man must be Peter.'

'Yes.'

Peter was taller than his father. Thin. With an open smile and warm eyes. Fair hair tumbled over his forehead, and he seemed very young.

Almost as if she could read his thoughts, Jane said, 'These were taken just before he graduated. His father was so proud of him.'

Now he turned his attention to the shopping list, and recognised the same hurried hand. 'The cooks have the blues,' he read out, and glanced up at Jane. 'Was he much of a cook?'

'Oh, not at all. His wife fed him all his life. I think he was terribly lost after she died. He seemed to live on convenience foods. Anything out of packets and tins.'

Enzo turned his eyes back to the fridge door and the scribbled Post-it. This time it was Jane who read it out, as she must have done countless times before. Perhaps she hoped that one day it would bring an unexpected revelation and suddenly make sense. 'A bit of the flood will boil the feast.'

Enzo repeated it, almost under his breath. 'A bit of the flood will boil the feast.' He straightened himself up and felt the tension in the muscles of his back. He placed his palms in the small of his back and stretched backward to loosen them. The cold and the damp were taking their toll. 'Is there anything else I should see.' He quite deliberately wanted to avoid focusing too much on any one of these things. He would let his subconscious do the hard work while he concentrated on more mundane matters, like eating and drinking and sleeping.

'The only other thing that seemed particularly significant,' she said, 'was over here, above his work bench.' He followed her over to the desk beside the filing cabinet. The scarred wooden desktop itself was empty, apart from a tray at one side laid out with entomology pins, setting needles, and forceps. Set alongside it were four grades of pencil, two six-inch rulers, a hand-held lens, and a binocular microscope. Two rows of wooden-framed glass cases hung on the wall above it displaying Killian's butterfly collection, each specimen carefully pinned to its backboard. A neat, handwritten paper data label beneath each detailed when and where it had been obtained.

Enzo noted that with Killian's usual attention to detail, they were arranged in taxonomic order.

'What's in the filing cabinet?'

'All his entomological records. Photographs in plastic sleeves arranged in date order in clip folders, and all his leather-bound notebooks. He noted every insect he ever caught. All described and identified. Or not. Apparently around one million insects have already been officially identified, but they think there may be as many as five million that have not. That seems to be the appeal for the amateur, that you could actually discover a previously unidentified species of insect.' He caught her eye and she smiled. 'Which would leave me quivering with apathy, I'm afraid.'

Enzo laughed. 'Is it worth my while going through them?'

She shrugged. 'I don't know. Only you can judge that. But no one else has ever found anything of interest among them.'

'Did the police look at all this stuff at the time?'

Jane sighed and folded her arms. 'Well, they did. But not very carefully. I'm afraid they didn't take my account of Papa's phone call very seriously. I think they just thought I was some hysterical woman, distraught by the murder of her father-in-law and the death of her husband, and that I was exercising an overactive imagination.' She blew air out through pursed lips, exasperated still after all these years. 'They were so keen to pin it on Kerjean, they simply took Papa's calls as an affirmation that he knew the man was coming for him.'

Enzo regarded her with interest. 'And what do *you* think, Mrs. Killian?'

'Oh, God, don't call me that. It makes me sound like some old dear. It's Jane.'

Enzo grinned. 'Okay, Jane.' He paused. 'So do you believe that it was Kerjean who did it?'

She shook her head. 'I really don't know. Everyone on the island seems to think so. I went to his trial. I sat in court day after day and listened to the evidence, and watched him in the dock. And I have to say, if I'd been on the jury I wouldn't have convicted him either.' She looked down and scuffed at the floor with the toe of her high top. 'But, you know, even if the evidence had been compelling, something about it wouldn't have felt right. I don't know how to explain that.' She looked up and met his eye very directly. 'It just didn't fit, somehow, with the call I got from Papa that night.'

Enzo nodded thoughtfully, then turned back to the work desk. 'So what was it here that I should see?'

'Oh, yes.' She snapped out of a reverie that had sent her back in time through nearly half her lifetime. 'The poem.' She nodded towards the wall above the rows of display cases.

A piece of poetry, handwritten in a careful script, was pressed behind glass in a fine, black frame. Enzo canted his head to one side and looked at it in confusion. 'It's hanging upside down.'

'That's exactly how it was when I got here. The poem's been there for years. I never paid it much attention. But it was always hung the right way up before.'

Enzo reached for it. 'May I?'

'Of course.'

He lifted the frame from the wall and saw that it had simply been turned the other way round and rehung, as if Killian had wanted to draw attention to it.

'It was a favourite of his. I have no idea why. He wrote it out himself to frame and hang on the wall.'

Enzo adjusted his reading glasses and scanned the lines.

> *This day relenting God*
> *Hath placed within my hand*
> *A wondrous thing; and God*
> *Be praised. At his command,*
> *Seeking his secret deeds*
> *With tears and toiling breath,*
> *I find thy cunning seeds,*
> *O million-murdering Death.*
> *I know this little thing*
> *A myriad men will save,*
> *O Death, where is thy sting?*
> *Thy victory, O Grave?*

The credited author was Ronald Ross. Not a name with which Enzo was familiar.

'What is it about, do you know?'

She shrugged. 'No idea. I do know that the last two lines are based on a quote from the bible.'

'Yes.' Enzo nodded. He could pinpoint the quote almost without thinking. 'First Corinthians. O death, where is thy sting? O grave, where is thy victory?'

Jane looked at him with naked curiosity. 'I wouldn't have taken you for a religious man.'

'Then don't. I'm not. But being the product of an Italian Catholic and a Presbyterian Scot, religion was never far from the dinner table in our house. I was force-fed the stuff along with my mince and tatties.'

She laughed and looked at her watch. 'I don't know about you, but it's a long time since lunch and my stomach is starting to complain.'

'Oh, that's *your* stomach making the noise? I thought it was mine.'

She grinned. 'I'll take you up to your room.'

It felt cold as they trudged up the narrow staircase to the tiny bedroom in the roof. Even the bulb in the ceiling cast a cold light around the room when Jane switched it on. The ceiling sloped down almost to the floor at either side. A small dormer window cut deep into the north side looked out across the lawn towards the house. On the other, a Velux window was set into the angle of the roof to capture the sunlight on the southern elevation.

A brass bed was pushed against the gable end and flanked by two, small, marble-topped bedside tables with matching lamps. On the left-hand table stood a telephone next to an old-fashioned answering machine. A smoked plastic lid protected the cassette inside. A pinpoint of green light glowed next to the rewind button. Jane crossed the room and switched cassettes. 'You'll probably want to hear this.' She rewound the cassette and hit the play button.

Enzo dropped his overnight bag on to the bed and perched on the edge of it, reaching for a stout walking stick that leaned against the wall, and listened in surprise as he heard what was unmistakably Jane's voice.

Papa? Papa, are you there? For God's sake, Papa, call me back. You've got to tell me what's going on. You must.

There was a long silence, during which it was possible to hear her rapid breathing. Then,

Oh, God, Papa, please!

Another silence, then the line went dead, and Jane leaned over to switch off the machine. He noticed how pale she had become.

She said, 'You can't know how it feels to listen to that. And I must have done it a hundred times. Like listening to a ghost. The me I was in a former life, when I still had a husband and a life ahead of me.' She turned towards Enzo. 'That was about two minutes after his call to me. For some reason I couldn't get through again straight away. And then it rang and rang, before the answering machine cut in.' He heard the tremor in her voice as she drew her breath. 'You can hear my distress. I've always thought I must have been uttering those words at the very time he was being murdered. That perhaps the killer himself heard them, and maybe even wondered what it was that Papa had told me.'

'What exactly did he say in that call, your father-in-law?'

'Just that he couldn't tell me what was wrong. But that if anything happened to him, Peter was to come here as soon as he returned from Africa. He'd left a message in the study that only Peter would understand. And he said it was ironic that it was Peter who would finish the job. Then he made me promise that if something happened to him before Peter got back, I was to make sure that nothing in the study got disturbed.'

'What did you think he meant by something happening to him?'

'That he was going to die.'

'He was terminally ill, of course.'

'Lung cancer, yes. I thought his condition must have deteriorated. But then, as things turned out, it wasn't that at all. He believed that someone was going to kill him. He must have.' Enzo heard the same distress in her voice that he had heard on the phone. 'Why didn't he just tell me? Oh, God, he was so old-fashioned! Some things you could only confide in another man. A woman had her place, and that was in the home. God forbid you should trust her with anything more than a shopping list!'

For the first time, she noticed the walking stick in Enzo's hands. He was running his palm over the smoothly carved head of the owl that was the handle.

'That was his,' she said. 'He must have been carrying it when he was shot. It was found lying beside the body.'

And Enzo felt a sudden, strange connection with the man. In a way, it was as if he had just met him downstairs in his study. Already he had formed an impression of an ordered and obsessive mind. And now, holding his walking stick, it was almost as if he was making physical contact, reaching back through almost two decades to the night his life had been taken, and the curved head of the owl in his hand had been the last thing he touched on this earth.

He laid the walking stick carefully on the bed and stood up. 'You know, Jane, even if he had told you that night, there was nothing you could have done about it. You were hundreds of miles away in another country.'

'I might have had some idea of who killed him, Mr Macleod. I might have been able to put this behind me and move on. As it is, there's not a day goes by that I don't think about it. Or a night when I don't wake up in the small hours and wish to God I was free of it. It's like he put a curse on me that night, and I can never escape it until the whole damned thing is resolved and his killer caught.' She looked at him, distraught, tears brimming in her eyes. 'I can't go on like this. I just can't.'

Almost without thinking, Enzo extended an arm and drew her towards him. She offered no resistance, and pressed her face into his chest as he held her, trying to quell the sobs he felt rising from deep inside her. 'If it was a message that only Peter could understand,' he said, 'then we have to understand why, so that we know how to look at what he's left us. We're looking with eyes that aren't Peter's. That has to be the key.' And he remembered his words to Raffin in Paris. *I'd hate to be anyone's last hope.* But for Jane, he realised, that is exactly what he was.

CHAPTER EIGHT

The Auberge du Pêcheur occupied a three-storey whitewashed building above the Eco-Museum, on the curve of the hill as it rose steeply up from Port Tudy towards Le Bourg. A hand-written menu chalked on a blackboard leaned against maroon doors in the yellow light of a coach lamp over the entrance. Heads turned curious eyes in the direction of the door as Enzo ushered Jane in ahead of him. A waitress in jeans and a knitted top led them to their table past tables and shelves crowded with island bric-à-brac: ceramic seagulls; pewter pots; an enormous, traditional, Groisillon cafetiére called a *grek*. Painted boats and seascapes hung on cream walls crowded with brass and glass and uplit by dozens of small table lamps.

Diners occupied several tables in the restaurant, and Enzo doubted if there was a single one of them who didn't know who they were. With the possible exception of a young couple in hiking boots and heavy sweaters, anoraks over the backs of their chairs, who looked as if they could be late-season tourists on a walking holiday. There was an audible lull in conversation as Enzo and Jane took their seats, and interested ears strained to hear what they might say. Enzo took some satisfaction from the realisation that whatever discernible conversation might ensue between Jane and himself, it would be in English and unlikely to be understood.

'They do wonderful seafood here,' Jane said. 'If you're into that.'

Enzo smiled. 'I am.'

The waitress brought a chalkboard menu to their table and sat it up on a chair for them to read. Her eyes lingered for a moment on Enzo, then she smiled. 'Nice to see you again, Madame Killian,' she said in French. Jane just smiled and said nothing, and the waitress left them to make their choice.

'The prawns are always good. And the dorade.'

'Then I'll have prawns for an entrée, and dorade for my main course.'

Jane grinned. 'Now I'll feel bad if you don't like them.'

'Don't worry, I'll pretend I do, even if I don't.'

She laughed, and some of the tension seemed to leave her. 'Such a gentleman.'

'Shall I choose a wine?'

'Please.'

Enzo cast his eyes over the wine list and picked out a 2005 *Mémoire Blanc* from Château Clément Termes. When they had ordered, he rested his chin on interlocked hands and looked appraisingly at Jane Killian. 'How come an attractive woman like you never remarried, Jane?'

She seemed to think about it for a long time. Perhaps deciding whether or not to speak the truth, or whether to brush his question aside, some superficial response to satisfy his curiosity. In the end her reply, Enzo was sure, came from the heart. 'They say that for every one of us, somewhere in the world, there is the perfect partner. They also say that most people never get to find theirs. I was lucky. When Peter came along, I knew I had met mine.'

'How did you meet?'

'Oh, it wasn't anything very exciting. We were both at Edinburgh University. Peter was from London. I came from Bristol. Edinburgh wasn't either of our first choices, but that's where we both ended up. As if fate had decided it for us.'

'You believe in fate, then?'

She smiled. 'No. But sometimes it's nice to think that something so right has been planned. That we actually do mean something in the great scheme of things.'

The wine arrived, and the waitress filled each of their glasses.

'Peter had always been interested in charity work. He was a great believer in the individual making a difference in the world. I never understood, after all that he saw and experienced, how he ever managed to hold on to that belief. He came back sometimes from his trips, usually to Africa, with stories that reduced him to tears in the telling. He saw awful things, Mr Macleod. Hunger, disease, war. Terrible suffering on an unimaginable scale. And still he thought he could make a difference. For a few, maybe he did.'

'You were never tempted to join him?'

'I didn't have his strength. In the face of such suffering, I think you have to remain resolutely dispassionate in order to be able to help. I would have been far too emotional, completely useless. Somehow Peter never let it affect him. Until afterwards. In the field he was only ever totally practical. He saved his tears for me. And in a strange sort of way, that made me feel very special. Admitted to a place in the very heart of him that no one else ever reached.' She looked very directly at Enzo. 'So you see, Mr Macleod, there was no way I could ever replace him.'

'It's Enzo,' Enzo said. 'Not even my students call me Monsieur Macleod.' He sipped his wine and let the smoky vanilla flavour slip back over his tongue. 'So how did you fill your life during his long absences?'

'I had my career. In publishing. Very prosaic, I'm afraid. I got to live my life vicariously through the authors we published. And through Peter, of course. How I wish we'd had the Internet in those days. It would have been so much easier to keep in touch. And I might have had a more enduring record of our conversations. These days I keep every email I send and receive. As if keeping a record of my life might give it some meaning.' She laughed, but too late to hide the bitterness.

From the moment he had met her, Enzo had sensed an emotional charge within her, almost like a controlled explosion, a part of herself on which she kept the lid firmly shut. Now, for the first time, he felt the force of that charge escaping, involuntary words betraying her disappointment with life and a feeling of self-pity.

'Are you still in publishing?'

'I work for a small house in east London. One of the few independent publishers left. But I'm not sure how much longer we can survive. Most of the small houses have been gobbled up by the conglomerates. Sales and profit are the only criteria that apply these days. Quality and diversity are dirty words in publishing.'

It was the same bitterness that had seeped out of her just moments earlier. This was a woman, Enzo realised, who had simply never been able to put her life back on the rails after the death of her husband and the telephone call that presaged the murder of his father. If fate had indeed brought her and her perfect partner together, then it had also torn her life asunder. And perhaps the only comfort she could take from the thought was that, after all, she really did mean something in the great scheme of things.

Almost as if she sensed his perception of her, she smiled, a wry smile dissipating the bitterness and self-pity. 'But I really do try not to think too much about such things, Enzo. I don't want to end up a bitter and twisted old widow.' Almost as if she feared that's exactly what she'd become.

The prawns arrived and for a few minutes became the focus of Enzo's attention, soft flesh dissolving in a creamy garlic sauce to be washed over by more *Mémoire*. When he looked up again, he found Jane watching him. 'Interesting eyes. One brown, one blue.'

'Waardenburg Syndrome. Which also gives me the silver stripe in my hair.'

She nodded. 'So what was it that brought you to France,

Enzo?' But before he could answer she added, 'Curious name for a Scotsman.'

'Italian mother. It's short for Lorenzo.'

'Ah.'

'The ferry.'

She frowned her confusion. 'What?'

'You asked me what brought me to France. Sealink ferry from Dover to Calais, then a ten-hour drive down to Cahors.' He saw dimples materialise in her cheeks as she pursed her lips, and he grinned. 'I'm sorry. It was a woman, of course. A French woman. That perfect partner that fate reserves for the lucky few, then takes away again – just so you don't get the idea that you're something special.'

'Oh.' Her smile faded instantly. 'What happened?'

'She died in childbirth.'

'How long ago was that?'

'My daughter has not long turned twenty-two.'

'I'm so sorry.'

He shrugged. 'I was, too. But it's a long time ago now. I always think I've put it behind me. But every time my daughter has a birthday, I'm reminded that it's the anniversary of her mother's death. I'd love to just let it pass, but you can hardly ignore your baby's birthday, can you?'

'You never remarried?'

He sipped his wine and glanced at her over his glass. 'No.' He was aware of the similarities between them.

'Why not?'

'Do I really need to answer that, Jane? You did it yourself.'

She nodded, and he realised that perhaps the only reason he had divined the bitterness and self-pity in Jane was because they were things he recognised in himself. They shared a moment of silent empathy before she abruptly changed the subject.

'How did you get involved in solving the cold cases in Raffin's book?'

He shook his head and grinned. 'Because I was an idiot. I worked as a forensic scientist in Scotland, Jane, but had to give it up when I came to France. I ended up teaching. Solving Raffin's cold cases started out as a bet. I'd kept myself up to date with the latest developments in forensics, and figured that new science applied to old cases could bring new results.'

'With a hundred per cent success rate to date, I'm told.'

Enzo inclined his head. 'It's never quite that simple. And there are some cases in which science plays little or no part.' He hesitated for a moment. 'Don't raise your hopes too high. I'm not sure I can live up to them.'

She nodded. 'In a way I have no expectations at all. After all this time, and the number of people who've come and looked and left none the wiser, it seems to me that whatever it was Papa wanted Peter to know, only Peter could divine.' She sat back as the waitress came and took their plates, and waited until they were alone again. 'They were terribly close, Peter and his father. Much closer than I ever was to either of my parents. In a way they were hard to separate. Peter was like a clone of his father, which I suppose is why I felt such an affinity with his Papa. And why I took his death almost as badly. One came so hard on the heels of the other it was almost too much to bear. The only thing that kept me focused during those dark days was the promise he forced me to make during that phone call. It was the reason I had to carry on.'

And it occurred to Enzo that if keeping her promise is what had motivated her to get through that time, the fulfilment of it might leave a hole in her life that could be very hard to fill. And that while desperate to be free, finally, of what she had earlier described as a curse, that freedom might also steal away her only *raison d'être*. She was an intelligent woman. And it was a dichotomy, he was sure, of which she was only too aware.

Enzo's fish arrived. Pan-fried whole dorade. Soft, moist flesh, butter, garlic, crumbling floury potatoes. And it took all his attention, separating white flakes from fine bones, as they ate in silence until looking up to exchange smiles of shared pleasure.

'That was great,' Enzo said. And after the cold and the rain, he felt almost restored. But he waited until their coffees arrived before asking the question that had been on his mind for some days. 'The thing,' he said, 'that has bothered me most since I first read about this case, was why anyone would bother to murder a terminally ill man.'

But Jane just shrugged. 'I'm not sure that many people knew he was dying. Relatives and close friends, really. It's not exactly the sort of thing you advertise.'

'No.' Enzo knew only too well from his brief experience

of being diagnosed with a terminal illness that it was not something you wanted to share. It was almost as if by acknowledging it, you were accepting it. 'Who did know, then?'

'I don't know exactly. His doctor, obviously. Peter and I. And I don't know who else he might have told. Certainly not Kerjean. Papa didn't really have what you would call close friends on the island. People knew him. He was regarded as something of an eccentric, I think. But he wasn't a man with an active social life and, after the diagnosis, he went out less and less.'

To Enzo's surprise, when they stepped out into the street, the rain had stopped. It had seemed as if it were set to last for days. But unexpectedly the sky had cleared, and stars crusted its inky firmament like frost on black ice. Jane had loaned him one of Killian's scarves, and he tightened it around his neck as they walked down the hill towards the harbour, breath billowing around their heads. The soft feel of it brought him in contact once again with the man whose death he had come to resolve. There was a smell from the scarf that he had noticed when she first gave it to him. A slightly stale, slightly perfumed smell. But masculine. Something that spoke of body sweat and aftershave. A long, lingering reminder of a man whose life had been so brutally taken all those years before. A presence that he had left on this earth, long after his passing. And, in an odd way, it connected him to Enzo. Made it personal somehow. As if the old man had bequeathed a message to him, too.

As they passed the Eco-Museum on their right, the harbour opened up below them, bathed in a wash of moonlight that shone on every wet surface, as if all had been newly painted and the paint had not yet dried.

Rows of sailing boats tethered along the quay clunked and bumped and rocked on the gentle swell of the inner harbour, the air filled with the sound of metal cables clattering against steel masts. Lights from the hotels and cafés that lined the harbour row reflected on the black waters of the bay, broken by its ruffled surface into myriad splinters that flashed and vanished, moments in eternity only fractionally less brief than the lives of men.

But although the rain had gone, the air was cold. A sharp, biting cold, laden with the portent of overnight frost and icy roads. Enzo was surprised to feel Jane slide her arm through his, and thought how natural it felt. Two people sharing warmth on a cold night, tragic lives that had led them to this place and time, and a mystery that had already begun to wrap its icy fingers around him after haunting her for half a lifetime.

He felt a sense of destiny in this, that he had not experienced in previous cases. And he wondered if, perhaps, it was his destiny this time to fail.

'You must have been over thirty, then, when you met your French lady,' Jane said suddenly.

'Yes. Just past my thirtieth birthday. We met at an international convention on forensic science in Nice.'

'And you'd been single up until then?'

'No. I was married when I met Pascale.'

'Oh. So you left your wife for her.'

'Yes.' Enzo half turned to catch her expression out of the corner of his eye, wondering if she disapproved. But if she did, there was nothing in her face, or her voice, to betray it.

'A good thing there were no children, then.'

Enzo hesitated almost imperceptibly. 'I had a seven-year-old daughter. Kirsty.' Without taking his eyes from the street ahead, he was aware of her head turning to look at him.

'And?'

'She spent most of the next twenty years of her life hating me for it.'

'Still?'

'No. In the end we managed to put it behind us.' And he deftly changed the focus of their conversation. 'How about you? Did you and Peter not have any children?'

'We were too busy.' And he heard that bitterness creeping once again into her voice. 'He with his charity work. Me with my career. We were still young. Had our whole lives ahead of us, after all. Plenty of time for children.' He turned his head to meet her gaze directly as they reached her car. 'It's the biggest regret of my life, Enzo. I could have had children with someone else, of course. But I didn't want to. I wanted Peter's children.' She pressed the remote on her key ring and unlocked the car. 'You're a lucky man.' And she opened the driver's door and slipped behind the wheel.

The annex felt even colder than when Jane had shown him around earlier. The light thrown out by the naked bulb in the stairwell seemed more depressing than he remembered it, devoid of any warmth. He lifted one weary leg after the other to climb the stairs. They had sat talking for nearly an hour in the house when they got back, and two large whiskies later Enzo could barely keep his eyes open. And so he had said goodnight and walked across the sodden lawn, feeling the ground squelch beneath his weight, wetting his shoes and chilling his feet.

Moonlight fell at an angle through the dormer, lying in a bright slab across the floor and the bed, and he resisted the temptation to put on the electric light. The room glowed in the light of the moon. He took a moment to set up his laptop computer on the dressing table, plugging in the 3G USB stick that would connect him to the Internet and allow him to check his email. Then he undressed himself hurriedly in the cold, anxious to slip beneath the blankets, even though he knew that the sheets would be frigid, possibly damp, and that sleep could be a long time coming, in spite of his fatigue.

As he tossed the last of his clothes onto a chair and prepared himself for the icy plunge, he saw a light come on in an upstairs window of the house opposite. He could see a washed-out patterned paper on the far wall of the room it exposed, then after a moment, Jane moved through his field of vision, disappearing momentarily, before returning to stand within the frame of the window, pulling her shirt up and over her head to reveal pale skin and a black bra. She bent over to slide her jeans down over slender thighs, stepping out of them, and straightening up to expose the skimpy black thong she wore beneath them.

She half turned, and he saw the curve of her buttocks, and felt guilty suddenly, like a voyeur, or a peeping Tom. He turned away from the window to throw back the covers on his bed, trying to keep his eyes averted. But he couldn't resist a final glance, only to see her silhouette filling the frame as she advanced to swing the internal shutters closed, to keep in the light and shut out the night. And Enzo. Almost as if she knew he was watching. Almost as if she hoped he might be.

CHAPTER NINE

Enzo woke on full alert, heart pounding, blood pulsing through his head. He sat upright in the dark listening to the silence of the night. The moonlight which had washed his room silver when he climbed into bed was long gone. The dark seemed profound.

Something had woken him. Something from the real world that had penetrated his dream world and triggered instinctive alarms. But he had no idea what, unable to recall or replay any sound in his head. He listened for a long time, trying to control breathing that seemed inordinately loud, before slipping from between the now warm covers of his bed to push his feet into cold slippers. He wore only boxers, and reached for the dressing gown he had draped over the chair. Black silk, embroidered with red and gold dragons. And he wondered why he had brought something so impractical for the late autumn Breton climate. Shivering, he wrapped it around himself, and tightened the belt. His hair, loosened from its band, tumbled over his shoulders in ropes and curls.

He looked around for something he might use as a weapon, and spotted Killian's walking stick with the owl's head, which he had left leaning against the wall. It felt stout and comforting in his hand, lending him a degree of reassurance with the sense of protection it provided. His sense of vulnerability, wearing only a dressing gown and slippers, was acute.

He opened the door of the bedroom and peered down through the inky blackness of the stairwell, reluctant to turn on the light, knowing that it would make him only too visible to any intruder. With one hand against the wall, he inched his way down the wooden stairs, wincing with each creak that tore holes in the silence of the night, feeling for the next step with an outstretched foot, until finally he was standing in the small, pocket handkerchief square of entrance hall. Listening. Hearing nothing.

He reached out a hand and gently pushed open the door of the tiny bathroom, then reached in to find the light switch.

The sudden glare of unforgiving, harsh, electric light blinded and startled him. He stood blinking, listening to the rush of blood in his ears. The bathroom was empty. Nowhere to hide. He turned towards the study. The door stood slightly ajar, and light spilled across the floor from the hall towards the far wall and the rows of books that lined it. He took two cautious steps forward, placing outstretched fingertips on the door to push it inwards, raising the walking stick in his left hand.

He heard, more than saw, the dark shape that fell from above, and released an involuntary yell of fear and pain as something like needles sunk into his forehead and his scalp, the weight of something warm and soft pressing down on his head.

His own voice was joined by the screech of another. A high-pitched, wailing scream that filled the room, and he stumbled forward, flailing at his head, until he felt the needles withdraw and the weight suddenly lift. He turned, gasping for breath, in time to see a dark shape darting up the stairs to the bedroom, and he fumbled for the light switch in the hall.

A pure black cat stood on the top step glaring down at him, back arched, hackles raised, a quivering tail pointing straight up behind it.

'Damn cat!' Enzo shouted at the night, both relieved and annoyed. Where in hell had it come from? He could only imagine it had slipped in unnoticed when Jane opened up earlier in the evening. An escape from the rain. But from its demeanour, it seemed to regard Enzo as the intruder. He waved his stick at it and hissed and called, but it stood staring implacably back at him as if he were mad. If he could have seen himself in his black silk dressing gown and tangle of hair waving a walking stick around in the stairwell, shouting names at a dumb animal in the middle of the night, he might have been forced to agree.

It was, perhaps, some fleeting, out-of-body image of himself that made him stop to consider his tactics. And it took him only a moment to decide on a course of action. He shut both the study and bathroom doors and opened the entrance door wide, feeling the rush of cold air from the outside. Then he began up the stairs, holding the stick in front of him.

The cat watched his approach, first wary, then alarmed, but waited until almost the last moment, before turning and sprinting into the bedroom. Enzo followed it in, chasing it around the room until finally it escaped back down the stairwell, and he arrived at the top step in time to see it vanishing out into the night. He hurried down the stairs and slammed the door shut.

He stood, breathing hard, leaning with his back against the door, glad that there had been no one around to witness the debacle. But there was no point, he knew, in going back to bed now. He was wide awake, with a slight headache from too much whisky and wine, and his exertions of the last few minutes. He opened the study door and turned on the light, and was struck again by the room's almost suffocating atmosphere. It seemed filled by the personality of the man who had lived and died there. Even all these years later. And he allowed himself a fleeting, fanciful moment to wonder whether the black cat had come like the spirit of the deceased man to draw him down into this room in the reflective small hours of the morning. Or maybe it had been some demon sent to scare him off, Death's messenger bearing a warning, a harbinger of inevitable failure.

Enzo went through to the kitchen and poured himself a glass of cold water, and as he drank it in small sips, wandered back through the study. The account of the murder in Raffin's book suggested that there had been no break-in. The intruder had simply entered through an unlocked door and lain in wait for his victim.

Killian had ended his call to Jane abruptly. Had he heard something? Enzo still held the dead man's walking stick in his hand, the stick that had been found on the floor beside the body. Had he hung up on Jane and taken his walking stick to come downstairs and investigate? If so, his assailant hadn't hidden himself for long. Killian's body was found against the window wall, just to the right of the door as you came into the room. The position of the body, and the trajectory of the bullets, suggested that his killer had fired on him from the direction of the kitchen. Is that where he had been hiding?

The bloodstained floorboards were evocative. Enzo could visualise the body lying there, twisted and broken, blood seeping from the exit wounds in his back, drained from his body by the force of gravity. The heart would no longer have been pumping. He looked around the study. If you were searching for something, where would you look? The desk drawers, the filing cabinet, the kitchen cupboard. You would barely notice a scribbled shopping list, or a Post-it, or a hurried diary entry that made no sense. Did Killian's murderer even speak English?

The best place to hide something, Enzo knew, was in plain sight. How often people failed to see what was right in front of them.

What else might his killer have failed to see? Enzo ran his eyes around the room again. Over the rows of books on their shelves, Killian's workbench, his desk, and through the open door to the fridge in the kitchen. Of course, it would depend on what he was looking for. Something, Enzo was sure, that Killian had hidden, leaving clues that would lead his son to its hiding place.

What could possibly have so spooked Killian that he feared for his life? For it was fear and a sense of desperation that had been conveyed by Jane's account of his phone call. Killian must have believed that something was going to happen to him, that he was in danger, and was afraid that some course of action upon which he had embarked would remain unfinished. What was it he had said to Jane? *It's ironic that it is Peter who will finish the job.* What job?

And what it is that a dying man fears?

Enzo wandered back through to the kitchen and rinsed his glass in the sink, then turned to the fridge door. *The cooks have the blues*, Killian had written on his shopping list. And on the Post-it, *A bit of the flood will boil the feast.* A Post-it that jumped out at Enzo for the simple reason that it did not line up with anything else that Killian had placed on the door.

Killian must have had no doubts that Peter would instantly understand. Some code, perhaps, that they had contrived or shared during Peter's childhood, the significance of which only they would understand. Father and son. Jane had spoken of how close they were.

Enzo shivered and went back through to the study. The cold was creeping into his bones now. He crossed the room and sat once more in Killian's chair, surveying the desk in front of him. His eye fell upon the Post-it stuck to the desk lamp. *P, One day you will have to oil my bicycles. Don't forget!* Addressing himself directly to his son. And again in the diary. *P, I was lighting a fire, but now there's no more time, and all I'm left with is a half warmed fish in the pouring rain.* Enzo closed his eyes and turned the phrases over and over again in his mind, as if the simple act of repetition might bring revelation, or clarity. Neither came, and he opened his eyes again to flip back a page of the diary to the previous week. Dr. S, 2.30 pm, Tuesday. And again at the same time on Thursday. He flipped back several more pages. Twice a week from the early summer.

Enzo knew he had to start somewhere, and this seemed as good a place as any. Tomorrow he would seek a consultation with Killian's physician. Dead men don't talk. But sometimes their doctors know more than they could ever tell while their patients were still alive.

CHAPTER TEN

The Maison Médicale stood at the end of a long, straight road heading east out of Le Bourg, surrounded by modern suburban houses and lush, tree-filled gardens. It was an angular building of cream-painted concrete and steeply sloping slate roofs, a relic of the utilitarian architecture of the 1970s. As Enzo pulled into the gravel parking area in front of it, he saw from the *panneau* that there were three general practitioners, a dentist, and two nurses based in the centre.

A middle-aged receptionist looked up at him from behind her desk, and indifference immediately gave way to smiles. *'Ah. C'est Monsieur Macleod, n'est-ce pas? Vous êtes malade?'*

Enzo produced a patient smile. He was not yet sure if it would be a help or a hindrance that everyone on the island seemed to know who he was. 'No, madame. I'm not ill. I wondered if I might make an appointment to see whichever of the doctors at the clinic was treating Adam Killian before his death.'

The receptionist could barely conceal her excitement. 'Well, of course, I don't have to ask why it is you want to see him.' She got her smile under control. 'But I'm afraid Doctor Servat senior retired a good many years ago now.'

'Oh.' Enzo wondered why he should be surprised. Many things would have changed in the passing of twenty years. 'Doctor Servat senior ... Does that mean there is a Doctor Servat junior?'

'Yes, of course. His son, Alain.'

'And he consults here?'

'He does.'

'Then do you think I might be able to talk to him?'

She raised an index finger, pointing it towards the ceiling. 'One moment please.' And she picked up the phone to punch in two digits. 'Doctor Servat, there's a Monsieur Macleod here to see you in relation to the murder of Adam Killian.' She raised an eyebrow in Enzo's direction as if to seek confirmation. Enzo released a long breath and nodded, resigned to the fact that everyone on this island would either know or want to know his business. She hung up. 'You can go in as soon as he's finished with his patient.' She pointed towards a row of plastic chairs in the waiting area, and he took a seat to wait.

Although he avoided her eye, he was aware that she was looking at him. He could feel her impatience, and with a sinking heart heard the deep intake of breath that preceded the question she could contain no longer. 'Did you enjoy your meal?'

He looked up, surprised. 'My meal?'

'At the Auberge du Pêcheur. I heard that you dined there last night with Madame Killian.'

'Did you?'

'They do the most wonderful seafood.'

'They do.'

'During the season you always have to reserve.'

'I'm sure you do.' After a moment, Enzo decided to exploit her eagerness to talk. 'When did Doctor Servat senior retire?'

'Oh, I'm not sure, exactly. It was before my time. Seventeen, eighteen years ago, perhaps.'

'And his son took over then?'

'Oh, no, Doctor Servat junior was already established in the practice by then. A lovely man. Never heard him utter an angry word in my life. His wife was a nurse here at one time. They have such beautiful girls, too. The son's a little older. I don't really know him. He's away at university, you know. But they're one of the nicest families on the island.'

Enzo was beginning to wish he hadn't asked, but was rescued from rudeness by the opening of the door to Doctor Servat's surgery. An elderly lady with a hat, a long coat, and a stout stick, was shown out into the hall by a man in his mid-forties who held her elbow as she steadied herself to leave. He shook her hand.

'Thank you so much, doctor.'

'Just take it easy, Madame Pouard. No horse riding or mountain climbing for the next few weeks.'

Madame Pouard laughed. 'Chance would be a fine thing, doctor.'

Doctor Servat looked towards Enzo as the big Scot got to his feet, and he came forward. His handshake was warm and dry and firm. 'Monsieur Macleod. Please come in.'

He ushered Enzo into his surgery. 'Take a seat, take a seat.'

Enzo sat on the business side of the doctor's desk and looked at the rows of medical books on the shelves behind it. The room was L-shaped, and the longer leg of the L contained an examination table, a sink and draining board, and a tall glass-doored cabinet full of bottles and boxes. Servat sat down opposite Enzo and folded his hands on the desk in front of him. He regarded the Scotsman with warm, brown eyes that crinkled slightly in a look of mild amusement. He was a man of medium height, inclining now to portliness, with a thatch of thick, sandy hair, greying just very slightly at the temples. 'So . . . you're here to find out who killed Adam Killian.' It wasn't a question.

Enzo said, 'I think if you were to conduct a straw poll in the street, nine out of ten people would probably tell you I was.'

The doctor laughed. 'Oh, I think you're wrong, Monsieur Macleod. I doubt if there's anyone on the island who wouldn't tell me that.'

It was Enzo's turn to laugh. 'Not an easy place to keep a secret.'

'Almost impossible.'

'All the more extraordinary, then, that a man's murder should go unsolved all these years.'

The doctor inhaled deeply. 'Well, if you were to conduct that same straw poll of yours, Monsieur Macleod, I think that nine out of ten people would tell you that Thibaud Kerjean did it.'

'And did he?'

'I have absolutely no idea. But according to the courts he

didn't. So who am I to argue with the considered opinion of the French justice system?'

'Of course, sometimes guilty men go free simply because the prosecution can't prove it.'

'That's true, monsieur.'

'In Scotland we have a third verdict. Guilty, not guilty, and not proven.'

The doctor sat back in his seat and nodded thoughtful approval. 'Ah. Interesting idea. Perhaps that would have been the verdict in this case, had it been tried in a Scottish court.'

'Perhaps it would.' Enzo smiled. 'I believe your father was Adam Killian's physician at the time of his death.'

'Yes, he was. And he retired not long afterwards. He was a good age, even then. He and a couple of other island practitioners were involved in setting up the Maison Médicale in the seventies. Prior to that he had his own *cabinet* in the family home in Le Bourg, where I live now with my own family.'

'And I don't suppose you could cast any light on his medical dealings with Killian?'

'I'm afraid not. I had only been in the practice a short time then, and I never had any contact with Killian myself. My father's really the only one who could have told you. But there wouldn't be much point in asking him now. He's over ninety.'

'He's still alive?' Enzo couldn't conceal his surprise.

'Oh, yes. Very much so. And still lives with us at home.'

'Do you think I might be able to talk to him anyway?'

'Well, yes, of course you could.' A momentary sadness seemed to flit across his face, so fleeting that Enzo almost missed it. 'But I'm afraid it won't do you any good.' He glanced at his watch. 'Look, it's almost *midi*. I won't have any more patients now before lunch. Why don't you come back with me to the house?' He lifted his mobile and hit the speed dial. 'I'll just call my wife and let her know to set another place at the table.'

The Servat family lived in a big rambling house on the corner of the Place du Leurhé opposite Le Triskell, a pub that offered coffee and rooms. This was a small square behind the church, at the centre of a maze of tiny streets that fanned out from it like the spokes of a buckled bicycle wheel. The tiny *terrasse* in front of Le Triskell was deserted, parasols tied up for the winter, the sun melting frost on plastic tables and chairs.

Opposite a peach-painted cottage with green shutters that housed the Crédit Agricole bank stood the building that characterised and dominated the square. It was a crumbling, white two-storey house with a square tower punctuated on three sides by rows of holes the size of cantaloupes. At first, Enzo thought it might be some elaborate sort of *pigeonnier*, but Alain Servat caught his curious glance in its direction and laughed. 'A hard one to guess, isn't it? It used to be the town's fire station. They hung the hoses up in the tower after use. The holes were to ventilate it so they would dry quickly.'

He led Enzo through a gate into a narrow path between extravagantly towering shrubs that almost completely obscured the pale lemon and blue of the house: giant hydrangeas with pink and blue flowers fading now in the late autumn; tall, corn-coloured fronds, sprouting through a profusion of yellowing leaves; spiky green grasses that grew taller than a man.

The front door opened into a long, narrow hallway that stretched all the way to the back of the house, where a glass door spilled dazzling sunlight on to polished wooden floors.

'We're home, *chérie*,' the doctor called, and steered Enzo off to their left, into a large, square dining room with a door leading through to a farmhouse-style kitchen. A slim woman with long chestnut curls appeared in the kitchen doorway. She wore a maroon apron over jeans and a white blouse, sleeves rolled up to her elbows.

'Hi, darling,' she said. 'Lunch won't be long.'

'Elisabeth, this is Monsieur Enzo Macleod. He's a private *police scientifique*, come to reopen the investigation into the Killian murder.'

'Oh.' Elisabeth Servat wiped her hands on her apron and stepped into the room to shake Enzo's hand. 'I'm pleased to meet you, Monsieur.' She smiled. 'I'm never very sure whether it would be better to solve the Killian case or to bury it. It's a little like Killian himself. Dead, but keeps coming back to haunt us.'

Enzo became aware that she was still holding his hand. Longer than he might have expected. But she was in no way self-conscious about it, and so he did not feel ill at ease. 'Well, I hope I won't be stirring up too many ghosts.'

She laughed and released his hand, a handsome woman with wide, cupid-bow lips and lively dark eyes. 'You never know, Monsieur Macleod, with Halloween just around the corner.' She glanced at her husband. 'Why don't you two sit in at the table. The girls will be back any minute.'

The table looked as if it might have been in the family for generations, its dense wooden surface scarred and burned and stained by countless meals. Who knew how many souls had sat around it, eating and drinking across the years, how many dramas and conversations it had witnessed. Enzo remembered his father telling him how he had been laid out on his kitchen table as a boy to have his tonsils removed by the family doctor. But it was not a thought conducive to sharpening the appetite, and he quickly banished it.

Mats and crockery now littered the Servat table, two sets of condiments, a large *grek*, and cloth napkins laid at each place. The smells coming from the kitchen were delicious.

Dressers were pushed up against blue walls beneath paintings and family photographs, and a large brass lamp hung low over the table from the ceiling. But its light was not required. Sunlight tumbled through the open kitchen door, and the room seemed to glow in its reflection.

'I suppose you must feel right at home here on the island,' Alain Servat said. 'A Celt among Celts.'

Enzo was no longer surprised by how much people seemed to know about him. 'I do. Groix feels like any west-coast Scottish island to me. Particularly yesterday, when I arrived in the rain.'

'Ah, yes. The famous Scottish rain. Is that why you went to live in the south of France, monsieur? To escape it?'

Enzo laughed. 'Yes. I'd spent so many years in the rain I was starting to go rusty.' He took his napkin from its holder and unrolled it. 'And what about you, doctor. A fellow Celt?'

'Near enough. My family came from the Paris area originally. But I'm island-born and bred. The only time I spent away from the place was at medical school, and earning my stripes as an intern at various hospitals.' He nodded towards the kitchen. 'Elisabeth, on the other hand, can trace her island roots right back to the fifteenth century.'

Elisabeth emerged from the kitchen with steaming bowls of leek and potato soup which she placed in front of the two men as the door burst open and two teenage girls bustled into the room, dragging cold air behind them.

'All right, girls, calm down. Behave yourselves now. We have a guest for lunch. Monsieur Macleod, meet Oanez and Seve. Twelve and fourteen, monsieur, and both with far too much energy.'

An energy immediately subdued by teenage awkwardness, as the girls self-consciously presented themselves to Enzo to be kissed on either cheek. 'Unusual names,' he said.

'Breton.' Alain waved the girls to their seats, putting a finger to his lips to quell their urge to chatter and giggle. 'Our son's called Primel. We wanted traditional Breton names for all of the children. He's now studying at the Sorbonne. Philosophy rather than medicine, I'm afraid.'

'Which means he probably won't be back,' Elisabeth said, bringing another two bowls to the table. There was the hint of regret in her voice. 'The young ones can't wait to get away from the island these days.' She returned to the kitchen to fetch a bowl for herself and then joined them at the table. Enzo noticed that there was no place set for Doctor Servat senior. He had expected the old man to join them for lunch, but decided not to ask about him just yet.

The soup was thick, and hearty, and delicious, great lumps of waxy potato breaking up in it as he ate. He looked up at Elisabeth. 'So did you not feel inclined to leave the island yourself?'

'Oh, I did. I trained as a nurse on the mainland, Monsieur Macleod. But in the end, something drew me back.'

Alain Servat chuckled. 'Yes. Me.'

Elisabeth grinned. 'Yes, you, Alain. Damn you!' She turned a fading smile towards Enzo. 'And an unfortunately ailing father.'

Alain said, 'He was one of the last of generations of tuna fishermen. You know, that's what Groix used to be famous for. Its tuna fleet.'

'When I was a girl,' Elisabeth said, 'we could see the boats from our house, as they sailed back into the harbour at Port Lay. Of course, they were motorised by then. But in the old days they used to come in under full sail. I have some pictures somewhere. A marvellous sight. All the more amazing when you see the harbour today. It seems so small. But in my memory it was huge, filled with boats, and the raised voices of men landing their catch, and the wagons that took them up the hill to the fish processing factory.' Her smile was tinged by sadness. 'All gone now. Just like my papa.'

Enzo swung his head towards her husband. 'And where is your father? I thought he lived here with you.'

But it was Elisabeth who answered for him. 'Oh, he does. But I'm afraid old Émile doesn't eat with us any more.'

'Elisabeth's been wonderful with him. If it wasn't for her, we'd have had to put him into care long ago.' Alain looked adoringly at his wife. 'And it's not been easy.'

Elisabeth laughed it off. 'It seems I have built a career out of looking after old people.'

Alain raised a hand, like a schoolboy in class. 'Me next,' he said. He turned to Enzo. 'A man couldn't be in better hands.'

'Oh, by the time you reach that stage, darling, I'll be needing someone to look after me, too. Then it'll be up to the children.' Elisabeth turned towards her daughters. 'Isn't that right, girls?'

They both pulled faces, embarrassed by suddenly being drawn into the conversation and clearly unattracted by the idea of caring for elderly parents.

Alain laughed aloud. 'God help us!' He turned to Enzo. 'My father has his own room at the back of the house. I'll take you to see him after we've eaten.'

Émile Servat's room was off to the right at the end of the long hallway that transected the house from north to south. Alain stopped to peer through its glass-panelled door before entering. It was a large, airy room, with high ceilings and tall windows that gave out on to the street that ran along the side of the house. The walls had been freshly painted a rich cream colour, in contrast to the dark wood of the floor and the furniture. Bookcases lined the walls and were cluttered with all manner of maritime memorabilia. A ship's brass bell. An enormous compass mounted on a mahogany pedestal. Paintings of sailboats and framed marine maps and charts lining the walls. Model boats on side tables fought for space with miniature lifebelts and globes of the world. 'This used to be his surgery,' Alain said. 'He was crazy about boats. We went out sailing almost every weekend when I was a boy.'

Enzo was struck almost immediately by the smell of stale urine, the perfume of old age and incontinence. The room was warm and was filled by the stink of it, a suffocating and depressing odour that signalled decay and loss of control.

A television against the near wall was switched on. The applause and laughter of a quiz show on FR3 rang around the room. Sitting in a wheelchair, with his head tipped in the direction of the set, was the shadow of what had once been a man. A wizened creature, shiny skin stretched tight over a skeletal frame, clothes hanging loosely on his shrunken body. Vacant eyes were directed towards the TV but were completely unresponsive. Thin wisps of pure white hair were scraped back over an otherwise bald skull. Old Émile Servat's jaw hung slack, purple lips shiny and wet, globs of drool hanging from his jowls and crusting down the front of his cardigan as it dried.

Alain immediately stepped forward, producing a handkerchief from his pocket and wiping the saliva from his father's face. 'Oh, Papa.' He whispered it, almost like a quiet admonishment, and he turned apologetically towards Enzo. 'It's no life, really. But we make him as comfortable as we can. Who knows how much he feels or understands. If I were to pinch his arm he would feel the pain. Sometimes he looks at me, but I have no idea what he sees. He's barely spoken in the last three years.' He drew a deep breath. 'So you see why there would be no point in asking him about Killian.'

Enzo nodded. 'I am sorry, I had no idea.'

'Of course not. He was already over seventy when Killian died. He should really have retired before then, but he wanted to carry on. Unfortunately, the dementia had already begun to set in, even then. We had to force his retirement. It was a difficult and heartbreaking time.'

'It must have been.' Enzo remembered his own father's descent into senility. A gradual process of forgetfulness and frustration. Forgetting how to spell, forgetting the songs he had played on the piano all his life, forgetting his friends, his family. And the day, burned forever into Enzo's memory, when he had arrived to take the old man out for lunch only to be met by a blank stare and the plaintive query, 'Who are you?'

'At least now he seems to have found some kind of inner peace. Some place inside his head that he inhabits, untouched by the world around him. We will look after his physical needs until such time as his body decides to give up. Which could be a week, a month, a year. Who knows?' Alain Servat shook his head sadly. 'It is a dreadful thing to see an intelligent and vigourous man reduced to this. All the more affecting since we know that it is what awaits us, too. If we survive.'

A knock at the door on the far side of the room interrupted morbid thoughts. It opened to admit a big man, only a little shrunken by age, a thick shock of wiry white hair above a deeply lined but fleshy face full of character and humour.

'*Salut, salut*,' he said. And shut the door behind him to approach them across the room, supported by a gnarled old walking stick with a brass tip, his walk stiff-gaited but steady. He wore a dark suit, tightly buttoned across a patterned pullover, and an open-necked shirt that was grubby and frayed around the collar. If Enzo had been asked to guess, he would have said that the old man was around eighty. His dark eyes twinkled with mischief and humour. 'How is the old boy today?'

Alain smiled patiently, and explained to Enzo. 'Jacques has a couple of years on my father, and always likes to refer to him as *the old boy*.' It was a joke that had clearly worn thin.

But Enzo was astonished and looked at the old man anew.

'Ninety-four,' Jacques said, answering the unasked question, fiercely proud of his achievement. He held out a hand to shake Enzo's. 'Jacques Gassman at your service, monsieur.' And Enzo detected the faintest hint of an accent that he couldn't quite place.

There was still power in the grip of the big, bony old hand.

Alain said, 'Jacques and my father each had their own practice on the island until they set up the medical centre together.'

'Oh,' Enzo said. 'So it's *Doctor* Gassman?'

'It is,' the old man said proudly. 'I come to see the old boy every other day, just to keep an eye on him. And he always asked me to keep an eye on that son of his, too.' He winked at Alain. 'So I do that as well.'

'You do,' Alain said. 'This is Monsieur Enzo Macleod, Jacques.'

'Yes, I know. I do still read the papers, young man.' He turned towards Enzo. 'Even if it takes a little longer than it used to.' He paused. 'You've come to solve our little island mystery.'

Enzo shrugged acknowledgment. 'If I can. I had been hoping to discuss Monsieur Killian's medical condition with his physician.' He glanced at old Émile. 'But clearly that's not going to be possible.'

'Well, you can still look at his medical records.' He looked at the younger doctor. 'Can't he Alain? I thought you had all Émile's old paper records brought here to the house when the centre was computerised.'

'Yes, we did. They're all in boxes up in the attic. I never thought of that. I suppose Adam Killian's records could be up there among them.' He looked at Enzo. 'Would you like me to check?'

Enzo nodded. 'That would be very helpful.'

The dust of decades covered every surface in this large, draughty attic. Cobwebs hung in theatrical drifts from skylight windows, and daylight leaked in all around the edges of the slates. Enzo followed Alain carefully over loose floorboards laid across open beams to where stacks of cardboard boxes were lined up against the far gable. The tape that had been used to seal them had long since lost its hold, and the flaps that closed them off were easily prised apart, raising clouds of choking dust into the cold air.

The files had been arranged in alphabetical order, so Enzo and Alain had to move A to J back into the centre of the attic to gain access to K. Alain then tore open the lid and started riffling through the files inside bulging folders of handwritten notes.

'Here it is.' He drew out a file in a faded purple folder that was thinner than the rest.

For a moment Enzo wondered why, but then reflected that Killian had only been an occasional visitor to the island until his retirement. Alain flicked through charts and yellowing pages of handwritten notes, ink fading now on brittle paper. Enzo squinted at them, trying to read. But the handwriting was almost indecipherable. 'Doctors!' he muttered. 'Do they take classes in bad handwriting?'

Alain laughed. 'Yes. I think my father got an A-plus.' He tilted his head a little to one side. 'But then I'm used to reading it.' He turned over several more sheets. 'Ah, here we are. Yes . . . Killian came to him in March 1990, complaining of night sweats and chronic fatigue, and a cough that had lingered long after the spring cold that kicked it off. In the end Papa sent him for an x-ray at the radiography centre in Lorient.' He went to the back of the file and pulled out a large green envelope. Inside was Killian's chest x-ray that the radiographer had forwarded to his doctor. Alain held it up towards the sunshine streaming in through the small rectangle of skylight, and Enzo saw a slow-moving cloud of dust drifting through the light beyond it. 'There.' He ran his finger along the bottom edge. 'The date it was taken. April 15 1990.' He slipped the transparency back into its envelope and consulted his father's notes once more. 'Inoperable tumour. Terminal. Three to six months, the radiographer thought.'

'But in fact he was still alive after five and must have been pretty close to the end by then.' Enzo was staring at the file in Alain's hands. But not seeing it. Gazing through it, beyond it. Lost in thought. 'If his killer had waited a week or two longer, maybe less, the cancer would have done the job for him.'

PART TWO

CHAPTER ELEVEN

The bar adjoined the Auberge du Pêcheur along the north gable, with windows looking out over the harbour. It was dark when Enzo climbed the steps to its door in search of a *digestif* after his bowl of pasta in the Thon Bleu, just a couple of hundred metres up the road.

He had no real desire to return to his cold bedroom above Killian's study, to sit on his own, haunted by the man and the mystery he had left behind him. He felt the need of something to warm him from the inside on this frosty night at the end of a frustrating day.

The search for Killian's physician had brought no real enlightenment, and he had spent the rest of the day acquainting himself with the island, driving out to its north-west tip and the lighthouse at Pen Men. There, an inhospitable sea devoured the coastline, eating into its hard, black gneiss, creating sheer cliffs and treacherous inlets where it vented its frustration in wave after wave of foaming spume. Then he had driven south-west, through the small coastal town of Locmaria, to the rocky outcrop of the Pointe des Chats, where he had stood warming himself in the late autumn sunshine, gazing out over calmer seas.

There were perhaps a dozen customers in the bar when he entered. Heads turned out of habit to register the newcomer, and a spontaneous silence fell across the tables. A strange, self-conscious silence that no one seemed to know how to break.

Enzo was almost amused by it. He smiled and nodded. '*Bonsoir*' he said, and walked the length of the room to the bar, aware of all the eyes upon him. He heard murmurs of *bonsoir* in return, and someone cleared his throat noisily. But not a single conversation resumed. The barman was a man in his thirties, with shoulder-length hair and steel-rimmed glasses, tall and thin. He wore a polo-neck sweater, and jeans that hung loose from skinny hips. He seemed quite unfazed.

He nodded. 'Monsieur Macleod,' he said, as if Enzo was a regular. 'What can I get you tonight?' Enzo looked beyond him to the crowded shelves above the counter, and saw to his surprise that they were well-stocked with good Scotch and Irish whisky.

'I'll have a Glenlivet.'

'Would that be the twelve or the fifteen-year-old, monsieur?'

'Let's live dangerously and go for the fifteen.'

As the barman lifted down the bottle, Enzo glanced around the bar. Dark varnished beams supported its sloping ceiling, and framed pictures, mostly of boats or the sea, crowded every available wall space. A gathering of curtains framed the windows and doors. The faces at dark wood tables were still turned in his direction.

'Well,' he said, startling them, as if they had thought they were invisible. They had not, he was certain, expected that he would speak to them. 'Since I seem to have your undivided attention, I wonder if there is anyone here who might be able to tell me something about Thibaud Kerjean.'

Silence.

The barman banged Enzo's whisky down on the bar top. 'You'll not find anyone here with a good word to say about Kerjean.'

Enzo poured a little water in his whisky and lifted his glass. 'Why's that?'

'Cos he's a murderous, drunken bastard, and treats his women like shit!' This came from a big man sitting with two others at a table in the far corner.

'Murderous?'

'Everyone knows he murdered the Englishman. We don't need you to come here and tell us that.'

'Well, I couldn't do that even if I wanted to,' Enzo said. 'Because I don't know who murdered Adam Killian.' He took a sip of his whisky and enjoyed the aromatic flavour that filled his mouth and the warmth slipping down his throat. Then he added, 'Yet.' He gazed around the eyes all turned in his direction. 'How do you know he treats his women like shit?'

A thin man with a cloth cap pulled at an angle over his forehead said, 'Everyone knows he beats up his women.'

'Does he? They tell you that, these women, do they?'

'It's common knowledge,' another man said.

Enzo nodded. 'I notice you say *women*, plural. So there have obviously been more than one of them. Why do you think that is, if he beats them up?'

The barman leaned forward on his elbows. 'Because they can't resist him, monsieur. God knows what it is he's got, but he's never without one. Even after the murder. In a strange way that seemed to make him even more exotic. But he's a violent man, make no mistake about that. Feral, I would call him. And unpredictable with a drink in him.'

'And why would he want to murder Killian?' He knew the answer to that. Raffin had dealt with the arrest and trial of Kerjean in the book. But he wanted to hear what the islanders thought.

'Because he ratted on him.' This from the big man in the corner again.

And someone else piped up. 'And over a woman, too. You might have known it would be. The man's little head rules his big one every time.' Which raised a laugh around the bar.

'The thing is, monsieur . . .' The barman straightened up and placed his palms flat on the bar in front of him. 'Most people here depend on tourism for their living these days. Either directly, or indirectly.' He adjusted his glasses, as if refocusing on Enzo. 'There was a fifteen per cent fall in visitors to the island the year after the murder. People who want to come and lie on the beach, or walk the tourist trails around the island don't want to think that there's a murderer on the loose. But over time, it was all forgotten.'

'Until Raffin's book came out, and suddenly it was in all

the papers again.' The man with the cloth cap was casting an unpleasant look in Enzo's direction.

The barman said, 'We took another hit then, too.'

'And now you've come to rake it all up again.' This from an older man, bearded, sitting by one of the windows, his leg up on the adjoining chair.

Enzo felt the hostility in the bar directed at him. 'If it wasn't me, it would be someone else. And there will always be a next time, and a next. Until Kerjean either leaves or dies. Or someone solves the mystery and puts an end to it once and for all.'

'And that would be you, would it, monsieur?' The big man who had first spoken glowered across the room at the Scotsman, and for the first time Enzo felt real pressure to solve this case. His very presence was raising both hostility and expectations. If he didn't meet the latter, he could only expect more of the former.

'I can't guarantee that.'

'You people never do.'

The outside door opened, and cold air flooded in with a man wearing a donkey jacket buttoned up to the neck. Oil smears stained jeans worn thin at the knee, and mud and scuff marks took the shine off thick-soled leather boots. Greasy dark hair was swept back from a broad forehead and hung limply over his upturned collar. Big hands were thrust deep in his jacket pockets, and the hubbub of conversation that had struck up once again fell away as sharply as it had on Enzo's entrance.

For a moment, Enzo wondered where he knew this man

from, before he realised with a shock that it was the same man who had confronted him as he disembarked from the ferry. It was Kerjean, blue Celtic eyes glaring darkly from a face scarred by time and fighting, but which was, nonetheless, still handsome in a brutal sort of way. Enzo had formed no clear impression of him in the rain at the jetty, except for his sense of menace. Now he felt the man's presence, which was something more than just physical. There was an aura about him, a dark charisma. And there wasn't a man in that bar who didn't feel it and perhaps fear it, maybe even envy it.

Kerjean paused momentarily, to cast an appraising glance around the room, then advanced to the bar. Enzo thought he detected a slight unsteadiness in the man's gait, and immediately smelled the alcohol on his breath as he arrived next to him, ignoring him, keeping his focus on the barman. 'Guinness,' he said.

The barman nodded, lifting a tall glass from the shelf, and slipping it beneath the tap to pour a pint of draught.

'Still here, Macleod?' Kerjean's gaze was fixed now on his pint glass, as the fine, creamy stout tumbled into it, settling to black as the glass filled.

'No, I took the first ferry back to the mainland after you warned me off.'

There was a murmur of laughter in the bar.

Kerjean's head came round sharply, and he turned dangerous eyes on Enzo. 'You think you're smart, monsieur.'

Enzo shrugged. 'Smart enough, maybe, to figure out who killed Adam Killian.'

'Oh? And who was that, then?'

'I've no idea. I thought perhaps you could tell me.'

'How could I do that?'

'It seems you knew him.'

'I came across him once. He was breathing when we met, and he was breathing when we parted.' The barman slid the islander's pint across the counter, and Kerjean took a long pull at it, before using the back of his hand to wipe away the creamy froth it deposited on his upper lip. 'You can read all about it in the transcript of the trial.'

'I will.'

Kerjean placed his pint carefully on the bar and turned to face Enzo directly. Although he was a big man, Enzo was taller. And while Enzo was churning inside, he was determined not to let it show on the outside. So he met the islander's eyes with an equally steady gaze and stood his ground. The tension in the bar was palpable, its patrons playing audience to a piece of pure theatre. 'I was tried, I was acquitted. And if you, or anyone else, wants to suggest otherwise, I'll punch his fucking lights out.'

'The only light I will be shining, Monsieur Kerjean, is on the truth. But if that's something you want to keep in the dark, then maybe you have something to hide.'

Kerjean's gaze was unwavering. 'I could take you down with a single strike, you arrogant big bastard.'

Enzo didn't doubt if for a moment. But the last thing he could afford to do was show that. 'You could try,' he said, and detected the anticipation in the bar that came with an almost collective intake of breath.

Cold air brushed the side of his face and swirled around his legs, and he heard the outside door opening once more. But whoever had opened it wasn't shutting it behind him. Enzo reluctantly tore his eyes away from Kerjean's and turned his head to see Adjudant Richard Guéguen standing in the open doorway. The *gendarme* was out of uniform, wearing a brown leather airman's jacket above jeans that concertinaed over heavy brogues, the long peak of a baseball cap pulled low over his eyes. His hands pushed themselves into his pockets for warmth. It took no more than a glance for him to appraise the situation. 'Go home, Kerjean,' he said.

Kerjean kept his eyes on Enzo. 'I just ordered a drink.'

'You've had enough already, unless you're angling to spend the night in one of our guest rooms.'

Enzo saw Kerjean's jaw tightening. Clearly a night in one of Guéguen's freezing police cells was less than appealing. Finally, reluctantly, he dragged his eyes away from Enzo to look at Guéguen. 'You can't tell me what to do. You're not even on duty.'

'A gendarme's always on duty.' Guéguen stepped aside to clear a path for Kerjean to make his exit. 'Goodnight.'

Kerjean's fury simmered silently inside him. He half turned his head towards Enzo, but this time didn't meet his eye. 'We'll talk again.'

'I'm sure we will.'

Kerjean turned and walked briskly past the gendarme and out into the dark. Guéguen closed the door behind him and approached the bar.

'He never paid for that pint,' the barman said.

Guéguen dug into his pocket and pulled out a five-euro note, dropping it on the counter.

Enzo said, 'Can I get you a drink?'

The gendarme shook his head. 'No, thank you. And I would suggest, monsieur, that you drink up and go home yourself.'

Enzo wasn't about to argue. 'Perhaps you're right.' He drained his glass and settled up with the barman. '*Bonsoir*.' He nodded at all the faces turned towards him and headed out into the night. At the foot of the steps he saw Kerjean disappearing in the direction of the harbourside bars, whose lights still reflected on the dark waters of the bay. He heard the door closing behind him and turned to see Guéguen following him out. He waited until the gendarme got down to the pavement. 'It wouldn't have hurt. One drink. Would it?'

'Monsieur, if I had accepted a drink from you, it would have been all over the island before morning.'

'So what were you doing in the bar, then? Out solo drinking or here to meet friends?'

'A gendarme has no friends. I was keeping an eye on you.'

'Oh?' Enzo raised his eyebrows in surprise. 'Following me, were you?'

'I saw your rental jeep up the road. A good thing I stopped by. Kerjean would have murdered you.'

'Like he murdered Killian?'

'I was speaking figuratively.'

Enzo grinned. 'I know. And you're right. He would have.

But I have my own personal guardian angel.' He craned to peer over Guéguen's shoulder. 'How the hell do you get your wings tucked in there?'

'I had them clipped. I don't work for the big man any more, you see. The pay was better downstairs.'

'I didn't think *gendarmes* earned that much.'

'They don't. The reward is that you get to be part of one of the most feared and hated institutions in France.' He laughed ruefully. 'That's why we have no friends, monsieur. Only colleagues.'

Enzo smiled. There was something likeable about this man. A fine, dry humour, and a sense of resolve and fair play that made you feel he was someone you could depend on in a crisis. 'The other day, you said to me you would help me in any way you could. Unofficially.'

'Yes, I did.'

'I'd like to know a bit more about Thibaud Kerjean, adjudant. The circumstances surrounding his arrest, exactly why investigating officers at the time thought he was their man. You were here. Uniquely placed to see it all first-hand. I'd appreciate your insights.'

For the first time Guéguen seemed uneasy. He glanced up the road and then down towards the harbour. 'Not here. I don't really want to be seen talking to you, Monsieur Macleod. You can bet there are eyes on us right now.'

'Where, then?'

'I'll meet you tomorrow. Two o'clock, at the Fort de Grognon. Do you know where that is?'

'I saw it signposted this afternoon when I was driving out to Pen Men.'

'You'll find it on any of the tourist maps. We're not likely to be disturbed there. And it's a place with an important bearing on the telling of the story.' His breath billowed around his head like smoke in the light of the street lamps. He flexed frozen cheeks to bare his teeth in a grin. 'It's an interesting tale.'

Lights fell out from the house across the dirt track leading along the coast to Les Grands Sables, and the gate squeaked on its hinges as Enzo pushed it open. He felt obliged to call in to say goodnight before heading across the lawn to the cold of the annex.

As he closed the gate again, he turned and looked out across the strait towards the mainland. An almost full moon hung low in a clear, black sky, reflecting in coruscating shards across the silvered surface of the ocean. The coastline between Lorient and Vannes was delineated by a line of lights like tiny glowing beads on a taut thread stretched along the horizon.

'Admiring the view?'

He turned, surprised, to see Jane Killian standing in the open doorway, light tumbling out around her and into the garden. He hadn't heard her open the door.

'It's a stunning night.'

'In the summer, on a night like this, you can light a fire on the beach and sit out with a bottle of wine, talking into the small hours. You can even go in swimming if you feel like it.

We get the full benefit of the gulf stream here. The water's always warm.'

'Not right now, I'll bet.'

She laughed. 'No.' Then her smile faded. 'I was expecting you back earlier. I prepared a meal. But I guess you've probably eaten by now.'

'Oh.' Enzo felt suddenly guilty. And at the same time annoyed. He didn't want to feel obliged to spend his evenings with her. He wasn't a house guest, after all. But perhaps he should have called to say he was eating in town. 'I'm sorry, I didn't realise.'

'It's okay. It was a casserole. It'll keep till tomorrow.'

Which trapped him into eating with her then. Enzo succumbed to a sudden sense of claustrophobia. For all that the Île de Groix was a flat stretch of rock set in an open sea, he felt cornered by its insularity, by his ability to escape it only when the ferry timetable allowed, and by the social obligations to his hostess that it seemed were impossible to avoid.

'Come in and have a drink,' she said. And he didn't see how he could politely refuse.

They went into the house, and she poured him a large whisky, and refilled a glass sitting on a small table beside her chair. Enzo wondered how many times she'd filled it already this evening. It was clear that she had been drinking. She was not drunk, or even mellow in the way that a few whiskies can sometimes affect you, but she held herself stiffly, with a kind of brittle self-control. She sat down, her legs folded up beneath her on the chair, and turned a penetrating gaze in Enzo's direction. 'You'd think,' she said, 'that after twenty years you'd get used to being lonely.'

Enzo sipped on his whisky and looked reflectively into the dying embers of the fire. 'I don't think you ever get used to it. You get to tolerate it after a while. It becomes a way of life.'

'You've had other lovers, though?'

'Oh, yes. There have been a few. Nothing that ever stuck. In a strange way, being with other women just served to remind me of what I was missing, without ever satisfying the need.' He glanced towards her, suddenly self-conscious, and wondered why he was telling her this. The whisky, perhaps. Or maybe it was simply that sharing your loneliness in some way helped to reduce it. At least for a while.

'Yes,' she said. 'Your needs never go away. Just the means of fulfilling them. Funny, isn't it, how you fill your life with other things? Work becomes a passion. Hobbies become addictions. But at the end of the day, it's still just you. And an empty glass.'

'And an obsession with keeping a promise to a dead man?'

She turned her eyes down towards her glass, as if she might find a suitable response somewhere in its gentle amber. But 'yes' was all she said. She raised it to her lips and took a small sip. 'So what did you find out today?'

'Not much. Your father-in-law's doctor is still alive. But only just, and lost in a world beyond our reach. I did see his medical records, though, but all they did was confirm what we already knew. That he was terminally ill and not long for this world.'

'Not much return for a day's work, then.'

Enzo was stung. 'Nothing comes fast in this job, Jane.

The whole point of forensic science is the examination of everything in minute detail. Conclusions are only arrived at after careful analysis of all the evidence.'

'I'm sorry, I didn't mean that as a criticism. You'd think I would have learned patience after all these years. The truth is, the more time passes the more impatient I become. It's a kind of desperation, I guess, a loss of self-control. And in the end, I suppose what it really means is that I've lost hope.' And then, as if she had somehow accessed and replayed his thoughts of the previous evening, she added, 'So relax, Enzo, you're not my last hope. That's long gone.' She smiled, but it was an unconvincing smile.

Enzo recalled the vision of her in the window the previous night, undressing to her bra and knickers, almost as if she had been putting on a show for him. She was a good-looking woman, signalling a sublimated sexuality. And he wondered why he didn't feel more attracted to her. Perhaps, he thought, the bitterness he perceived in her was muting his usually healthy appetite. He decided to change the focus of their conversation. 'I'm meeting someone tomorrow at the Ford de Grognon. Do you have a map I could take with me, so I don't get lost?'

She laughed. 'It's not easy to get lost on this island, Enzo. There are only a handful of roads.' She got up and crossed to the bureau where she found a creased and dog-eared trifold tourist plan of the island. She came and crouched by his chair and watched as he opened it up on his thighs. 'There.' She stabbed a finger at the north-west corner of the island. A small, white square marked the position of the fort. 'Just follow the main road out towards the lighthouse at Pen Men, then take the turn-off for Quelhuit and follow the road towards Beg Melen. There's a military signalling station out there. But there's a turn-off to the fort on the right before you reach it.'

'The fort belongs to the military, too?'

'Not any longer. It's nineteenth-century, I think, but abandoned now. And comes under the control of the *mairie*, I believe. You'll see there's a smaller fort right down on the coast below it. Predates it by a hundred years or so. They were built originally to protect the entry to the harbour at Lorient. Which is exactly what the Germans used them for during the occupation. They had huge guns mounted up there to provide cover for the submarine base on the mainland. Didn't do much to protect the town from the Allied bombing raids, though.'

'Is it open to the public?'

'No, it's usually kept locked up. But I think the *mairie* uses it as a base for youth activities from to time.' She paused. 'Who are you meeting there?'

'I'm afraid that's confidential, Jane.'

'Oh.' She seemed disappointed that he wasn't prepared to share with her.

'But I understand it's an important location in terms of your father-in-law's relationship with Kerjean.'

'Yes.' She looked thoughtful. 'They met there for the first time. And the last, according to Kerjean.'

'They had arranged to meet?'

'No. It was pure chance. Engineered by fate, perhaps.' And

she laughed, a laugh soured by that ever-present edge of bitterness. 'Fate again. But it was a meeting that might very well, in the end, have led to his death.'

Moonlight laid the dark shadows of trees across the lawn towards the annex. Enzo was almost at the door when a movement, caught in the corner of his eye, made him turn sharply to his right. He stood-stock still for a moment, but saw nothing, straining in the dark to give shape to whatever had passed through his peripheral vision. He scanned the imposing form of the trees standing black against the night and saw leaves that fell like snowflakes through the light of the moon, detached by the slight breeze that stirred amongst the branches overhead. Frost-brittle leaves, lying now in drifts on the grass.

He was about to turn back towards the door when this time a sound made him stop dead in his tracks. A sound like footsteps among the leaves. Soft, cautious footfalls. And then suddenly, out of the shadows, a silhouette emerged, green eyes glowing in the night, to stop and stare at him, resentment or anger burning in their gaze.

Enzo breathed more easily again. 'Damn cat!' he muttered under his breath. It was the second time the creature had startled him. He waved an arm at it. 'Shoo!' But it stood, defiant and still, watching from what it clearly felt was a safe distance. Enzo unlocked the door and went into the annex, shutting it quickly behind him again, and stood in the silence of the hall, washed by the cold, harsh light in the stairwell.

The door of the study stood ajar, as he had left it, a finger of light from the hall reaching across the floorboards to touch the books on the shelves beyond. He was almost tempted to go in, to sit with Killian in his long empty chair, and try to find a way inside his head. But he was tired, and somehow Killian seemed to have made greater inroads into Enzo's mind than the Scotsman had made into his. So he made a conscious effort to free his thoughts of both Killian and his killer, to empty his mind, and climb the stairs to a cold bed, and the oblivion of sleep.

As on the previous evening, the little bedroom was awash with moonlight, and he refrained from turning on the electric light. But as he turned to drape his jacket over the chair, he saw, once more, the light in the window opposite framed clearly by the black of the night. Jane Killian was again engaged in the process of undressing herself in full view.

She had already removed her top, and was wearing only her black bra and jeans. Reflexively, Enzo turned away. He could have stood and watched, in the certain knowledge that she could not possibly have seen him. But he was discomfited by the thought that she was undressing herself in the full glare of electric light to make him do just that. He felt manipulated, as if she were testing his male libido, sensing his lack of sexual interest in her from the start.

He stripped down to his boxers and threw back the bed covers. But, as before, he could not resist a final look. And this time saw her standing completely naked in the window, gazing out across the grass towards the annex. To his intense annoyance, he felt the first stirrings of sexual desire in his loins, and he slipped quickly between the cold sheets to douse them. He shivered and curled up on his side, pulling the blanket tight around his chin.

He closed his eyes and conjured up an image of Charlotte, with her shining, black eyes and her long, curling locks tumbling across square shoulders. Then recalled with dismay his last meeting with her at the Boneparte in Paris. *Let me know when you're in town again, and I'll apply for an audience*, she had said, as if he were the one who made it difficult for them to be together.

He flipped over on to his other side and screwed his eyes tight shut, trying to expunge the memory from his mind. As sleep descended like an angel of the night, the space it left was immediately filled by Killian's ghost. He drifted off into restless dreams of half-warmed fish.

CHAPTER TWELVE

The island was green and yellow and burnt sienna in the strong autumn sunlight that slanted across it from the south, great banks of fern turning rust-red and bleeding into the crimson leaves of the briar thicket that rose almost two metres high on every side.

Enzo eased his four-wheel drive along a bumpy mud track, ridged and pitted with holes, and turned into a metalled parking area by the gates to the fort. Earlier, he had missed the turn off, and was almost at Beg Melen when he noticed the high stone walls rising above the thicket away to his right. He had pulled up next to a sign that read, *DANGER – TROUS PROFONDS*. Deep holes on the road ahead. An abandoned white cottage, defaced by graffiti, shimmered in the sunlight beyond a stand of dark trees. Enzo managed a five-point turn on the single-track road before finding his way back to his missed turn.

There was one other vehicle in the parking area. A dark grey Renault Scenic. The morning frost had long since melted in the warm sun, and the air hummed with the sound of insects and the call of unseen birds. Ten-foot overgrown earthen banks ran off north and south, and in the distance, where the thicket fell away towards the shore, the line of the mainland was clearly visible across the shimmer of water that separated the island from the coast.

Green-painted metal gates stood open, and Enzo walked through them, following a narrow path between high walls overhung with tumbling wild growth. A low bridge spanned an outer moat to more gates, set this time into the wall of the fort. On the far side of the wall, another bridge took him across an inner moat, then through a stone tunnel in a second bank of earth. Stone watchtowers were raised at intervals all along the wall. Whoever had commissioned this fort had been taking no chances with its defences.

The tunnel opened on to a large grassy area lined with low buildings characterised by a series of arched doors and windows. Almost every available wall space was scarred and disfigured by cheap, colourful graffiti, island yobs aping their more sophisticated mainland cousins. The buildings to the right were set into mud banks and covered with grass, presumably to make them less obvious from the air. To the left stood tin-roofed barracks of more recent origin. There was no sign of anyone.

'Hello!' Enzo raised his voice and called into the silence. No response. He peered into several darkened rooms, where further archways led through stone walls to an impenetrable black beyond. Everywhere the smell of urine and damp and decay.

Stone steps cut into an earth mound at the end of the row

led up to a grassy area that concealed the roofs of the buildings beneath it.

Up here, bunkers were set into the ground and covered over with earth and grass. Concrete gun emplacements constructed along the north wall had once played host to huge German cannon that covered the strait beyond. Wide stone chimneys venting the fires that had once heated the offices and living quarters below pushed up through the ground and were covered by rusted sheets of curved metal.

Enzo heard a sound behind him and turned, alarmed, to see the uniformed Guéguen emerging from one of the bunkers. The gendarme was carrying his *kepi* in his hand and ran a hand back through his hair before pulling it firmly back on to his head. 'You startled me,' Enzo said.

Guéguen smiled. 'Pretty much as Killian must have startled Kerjean and his woman.' He turned and looked back through the arched doorway, and down the short flight of stairs he had just climbed. 'They were down there. Making love, having sex. Whatever it is Kerjean does with his women.'

And Enzo reflected that even in Guéguen he detected a hint of envy. Kerjean, it seemed, had something every man wanted. He was attractive to women. Enzo walked to the doorway and peered down into the darkness.

'Go on in. Have a look. It's not the most romantic of places to bring a woman. But, I don't think anyone would ever have accused Kerjean of being a romantic.'

Enzo walked down four steps into the former guard house. Here, he imagined, soldiers on surveillance duty had eaten and slept and taken turns on watch, ready to man the guns at a moment's notice should the alarms go off. A miserable, confined existence, a hated occupier in a land far from family and home. Scarred and crumbling plaster walls revealed patches of red brick, and a large red-lettered sign read *DEFENSE DE FUMER*. So they had not even been allowed the comfort of a cigarette.

'What on earth was Killian doing here?'

Guéguen shook his head. 'It was ridiculously innocent, really. He was out with a net sweeping for butterflies down near the shore. He must have seen the two cars parked out front and the open gates and wandered in. The fort is normally locked, so I imagine he was curious.'

And Enzo visualised how that curiosity must have led him on a route very similar to the one that Enzo had followed himself just a few minutes earlier. Peering into long-deserted darkened rooms, climbing the steps to the gun emplacements. And it occurred to him that he had just inadvertently walked in a dead man's footsteps. 'How was Kerjean able to access the place?'

'In those days he was involved with the island youth movement. And this place was used as a kind of activity centre for youngsters in the summer. He had a set of keys.'

'So Killian stumbled upon Kerjean having sex with some woman, and that was enough to motivate Kerjean to want to kill him?'

'She wasn't just "some woman", Monsieur Macleod. She was Arzhela Montin, the wife of the first *adjoint* of the mayor, a privileged and respected man in the island community. On the face of it, happily married, with two young children. Montin was a Parisian, regarded as being quite a catch for an island girl. For a woman like that to be having an affair with a man like Kerjean . . . well, it would have been the talk of the island. And it very soon was. Within a week of Killian catching the two of them together here, the story was out.'

'And Kerjean thought it was Killian who blew the whistle on him?'

'He didn't just think it. He was convinced of it. And there were dire consequences, for both Kerjean and his lover. Kerjean worked for the council at that time. A kind of *cantonnier,* involved in island maintenance. Roads, verges, hedgerows, and clearing the kilometres of pathways that criss-cross the island for walkers and *randonneurs*. It took the administration no time at all to find a reason for sacking him. He also worked as a kind of stringer for the Breton newspaper, *Ouest-France*. They couldn't get him fired from that position, but all the sources of official information that provided him with most of his copy, dried up just like that.' He snapped his fingers.

'And the woman?'

'Oh, her reward was a very messy divorce. The first thing Montin did was kick her out of the family home. And, by the time Kerjean went to trial, Montin had divorced her and won custody of the children.'

'Well, at least they still had each other. I mean, Kerjean and Arzhela.'

'Oh, no, monsieur. She refused to ever see Kerjean again. And when it came to his trial she gave some pretty damning evidence against him.'

Enzo turned his gaze towards the sun shimmering across the strait. Scraps of white sail caught the light, flashing against the petrol blue of the ocean, late-season sailors out catching the breeze. 'So what was the consensus of opinion at the time? Was Killian really responsible for letting the cat out of the bag?'

'No one knows for sure. By the time it became an issue, Killian was dead. But to be perfectly honest, monsieur, it would have seemed very out of character to me. Adam Killian was not exactly integrated into the island community. Incomers rarely are. Particularly the English. I'm sure he knew or had met Montin at some point, but I can't imagine for one moment that he went knocking on the man's door to tell him that his wife was having a relationship with the *cantonnier*.'

'So why would Kerjean think he had?'

'You'd have to ask him that. Not that I'd recommend it.' The gendarme scratched his chin thoughtfully. 'Although I imagine it was probably the timing of it all. Kerjean and Arzhela must have been pretty sure no one else knew about them. Then Killian chances upon them here at the fort, and in a matter of days it's all out in the open.'

They walked along the grassy bank in silence then, to where it rose up above the line of chimneys sunk in the earth. From here they had a panoramic view across the island, and Enzo felt the comforting warmth of the sun on his face. He tried to imagine the encounter here that day. How had Kerjean reacted? He was known for his violence and his foul mouth. Had he said or done something that had prompted the reclusive Killian to seek revenge in some way? 'What was it that first pointed investigators in Kerjean's direction?' he asked.

'Well, it was a strange situation,' the adjudant gendarme said. 'Killian was found by his cleaning lady the morning after the murder. She called the gendarmerie, quite hysterical. A radio call went out to a couple of officers who were down at the harbour in the van. By the time they got out to Killian's house, Kerjean was already there.'

Enzo turned to look at him, surprised. 'What was he doing there?'

'I told you that he was a stringer for the newspaper *Ouest-France*. He said that as a matter of habit he was always tuned into police frequencies and heard the radio call going out to our officers. Told us he'd driven straight out there. Murder on Groix! He could sell the story all over France.'

'So he got to Killian's place before the police?'

'Yes.' Guéguen pulled a face. 'Which provided a very convenient explanation for his fingerprints being found on the gate and a muddy footprint in the garden. And, as I told you, island officers in those days had no idea how to treat or secure a murder scene. So all sorts of people had trampled all over it before senior investigators arrived from the mainland.' He shook his head. 'There was hell to pay, I can tell you. And, in the end, it probably cost us the conviction.'

'What other evidence was there against Kerjean?'

'You mean other than his lack of alibi, his murder threats against Killian, and the item of personal property we recovered from the scene?' Air exploded from between his lips in remembered frustration. 'Dammit, Monsieur Macleod, if our people hadn't been so inept there's no way Kerjean would have got away with it.'

'Tell me.'

The gendarme removed his *kepi* and scratched his head. 'About two days after the murder a pen was discovered in the grass near the annex. A very expensive, hand-crafted pen – a Montblanc. Turned out to have Kerjean's prints all over it. He confessed that it was his, a gift, he said, and claimed that he must have dropped it when he went there to report on the murder. The boys from the mainland were already suspicious, and they really turned the spotlight on him then. Which is when they discovered that he couldn't account for his whereabouts the night of the murder.'

'Where did he say he was?'

'At home in bed.'

'Aren't they all?' Enzo grinned. 'So there was no one to vouch for that?'

Guéguen raised a wry eyebrow. 'For once it seems, he didn't have a woman in his bed.' He raised a finger. 'But here's the thing, monsieur. His car is always parked outside his house in Locmaria. Always. But a neighbour, coming home late that night, noticed that the car wasn't there. Even though the house was all shuttered up and in darkness.'

'So how did he account for that?'

'Said his car had broken down on the road on the drive back from Le Bourg, and he'd been forced to abandon it.'

'How did he manage to get out to Killian's place, then, the next morning?'

Guéguen smiled. 'Good question, monsieur. Of course he had an answer for it. Said he'd gone out at first light and got his car going again. Then came home and had his breakfast. Which is when he heard the police call on the radio.'

Enzo nodded. 'And no one saw him?'

The gendarme smiled. 'Not a soul.'

'You said Kerjean had threatened to murder Killian. How did that come about?'

'In a pub in Le Bourg, Monsieur Macleod. Le Triskell.'

'Oh, yes, I know it.' Enzo recalled the bar with its small deserted terrace opposite the doctor's house in the Place du Leurhé.

'One of Kerjean's favourite haunts. It wouldn't be the first time he'd got drunk there. The regulars knew him well and usually gave him a wide berth. But that night, about a week before the murder, he was in drowning his sorrows over his fractured relationship with Arzhela. He was very vocally, very loudly, telling anyone who'd listen, what a bastard that Englishman, Killian, was. How you could never trust an incomer, and a foreigner to boot. Killian had ratted on him, he said. Ruined his life. And if their paths ever crossed again he'd strike the old bastard down and dispatch him to the cemetery, where he belonged.'

They climbed down mossy and overgrown steps to the old

parade ground and headed back towards the gate at the far side.

'The thing is,' the gendarme said. 'Kerjean had motive and opportunity. He had threatened to kill the victim, was first at the scene, and had left traces everywhere. The evidence was circumstantial, sure, but the *juge d'instruction* at Vannes decided there was enough of it to proceed with a prosecution.'

'Which failed.'

'Yes.' Guéguen's mouth set in a hard line. It clearly still rankled. 'Largely because of our inept handling of the crime scene. Kerjean hired a good lawyer, who blew gaping holes through our case by exposing failures in procedure.'

They passed through the shadow of the entrance tunnel and Guéguen pulled the gates shut behind them, locking and securing them with a chain and padlock. Then they crossed the outer moat and followed the muddy track between high walls that led to the outside gates. Enzo found himself breathing more easily out here. There was something almost oppressive about the fort, open though it was. Something to do, perhaps, with its dark history. German occupation, a chance encounter leading to the destruction of lives, and perhaps even the death of Adam Killian.

Enzo had a sense of Killian almost everywhere he went on the island, as if the man was following him, haunting him. Knuckles tapping his forehead, urging him to focus, begging him to think. As if somehow it should be obvious. And there was a tiny voice nagging somewhere at the back of his head, telling him he was looking in the wrong place. *Come back*, it said. *The answer's in my study. That's where I left my message. Not here.* But Enzo was nothing if not methodical. 'What other evidence was found at the scene?' he said, and walked with Guéguen towards the cars.

'Very little. The annex, and the house itself, had been searched. Not very carefully. The killer was clearly anxious and in a hurry. The place was a mess.'

'Do you know if anything was taken?'

'No. Killian lived on his own. His daughter-in-law went through the place for us, of course, but said she wasn't aware of anything obvious that had gone.' The gendarme opened the door of his Renault. 'We found prints everywhere. Killian's. His son's, the son's wife, the *femme de ménage*. Others that didn't match anything on the database.'

'But not Kerjean's?'

'Apart from those lifted from the gate, no. We recovered three shell casings from Killian's study. No prints on those, of course. Even if there had been, they'd have been vaporised when the gun was fired. But ballistics was able to determine that the weapon used was a Walther P38. A very common semi-automatic handgun. Standard issue to German soldiers during the war. So it's quite possible that a number of those weapons found their way into circulation on the island after the occupation. You know, as trophies.'

Enzo nodded. He said, 'Adjudant, I have a couple of very big favours to ask.'

Guéguen turned inquisitive eyes on the big Scotsman. Enzo had said very little during the gendarme's exposition. Quietly listening, asking the occasional question. Whatever favours he wanted now would surely provide some kind of indication of the way his thoughts were moving. 'Go ahead.'

'I'd like, if possible, to get my hands on two items of evidence.'

'Which are?'

'The autopsy report. I take it there was an autopsy?'

'Of course. But that's a tall order, Monsieur. That report would have been submitted as evidence and would be held with everything else at the *greffe* in Vannes.'

'It's possible, isn't it, that there is a copy on file at the hospital where it was carried out?'

Guéguen exhaled deeply. 'It's possible.' And he shook his head. 'But I'm not at all sure how easy it would be to get hold of it.' He paused. 'And the other item?'

'I'd like one of those shell casings recovered from the crime scene.'

Guéguen looked at him in amazement. 'Well, even if it was possible to lay hands on one, why? I told you there were no prints on them. What could you possibly learn from a shell casing?'

'Possibly everything,' Enzo said. 'Indulge me.'

The gendarme frowned again. 'I'd love to, Monsieur Macleod, I really would. But I'm not at all sure I can. The autopsy report, maybe. But a shell casing ...' He blew air through pouting lips and gave an exaggerated Gallic shrug.

'Well, maybe you have a favour or two you can call in. I wouldn't ask if I didn't think it was important.'

Guéguen stood staring at him for a long moment before setting his jaw. 'I'll see what I can do.'

CHAPTER THIRTEEN

The Maison de la Presse was set back off the road, opposite the *boulangerie*. It was the biggest bookstore and newsagent in Le Bourg. Enzo found a parking place in the market square and wandered across the street. He wore Killian's scarf around his neck, to keep out the chill of the morning. It was another stunning autumn day, white sparkling frost still lying in the shadows where the sun had not yet fallen.

Enzo found the sharp, cold air clearing the fog from a head that was still fuzzy from too much wine the previous evening. Jane Killian had poured with a generous hand during the casseroled meal they had shared at the dining table in the main house. Gently tipsy and mellowed by the wine, she had been disappointed when he took his leave just after ten, pleading fatigue and the need of an early night.

And then he had stood in the dark of the chill bedroom above Killian's study and watched her undress beyond the unshuttered window across the lawn, knowing that she knew he would be watching. And he had found that he was very nearly aroused by the thought.

All the newspapers and sports rags were lined up in two

revolving racks opposite the counter. It took Enzo only a moment to find a copy of *Ouest-France*. He lifted it out and took it to the counter. A thin-faced, middle-aged woman with short, silvered curls cut close to her head smiled at him. 'Seventy centimes, monsieur.' He handed her a five-euro note, and she searched out his change in the till. 'You're even better-looking in the flesh.' She almost giggled. 'So to speak.' And blushed.

Enzo looked at her blankly. 'I'm sorry?'

'The photograph they had of you in the paper didn't do you justice.'

'Oh, yes.' He forced a smile. 'I've been known to crack a few lenses in my time.' It was her turn to look blank. But he pressed on. 'Can you tell me, madame, where I might be able to find back copies of *Ouest-France*?'

She frowned. 'Mmm. How far back do you want to go?'

'About twenty years.'

And her face uncreased as enlightenment dawned. 'Ah. You want to look at coverage of the Killian murder.'

'The trial, actually.'

'Oh, well, that would be about eighteen years ago now. At Vannes.'

'Yes.'

She shook her head solemnly. 'I'm not sure where you'd find editions that old. The *bibliothèque* in town here usually has the current edition for patrons of the library. But whether or not they keep back copies, I wouldn't know.' She barely paused for breath. 'I hear that man's been threatening you already.'

Enzo raised his brows in surprise. 'What man?'

'Thibaud Kerjean.' Even though there was no one else in the store, she lowered her voice and leaned confidentially towards Enzo. 'He's a bad lot. And done nothing but give this island a bad name. No one likes him, monsieur. They never have.'

'Except a whole procession of female admirers, apparently.'

She folded her arms beneath mean little breasts pressed flat by a blouse two sizes too small. 'Tramps. Every last one of them.'

'Arzhela Montin, too?'

'Hah!' The woman tossed back her head in disdain. 'Worst of the lot. Everyone knew what was going on between her and Kerjean.'

'Did they? I heard it was a pretty well-kept secret until Killian stumbled across them out at Fort de Grognon.'

'No, monsieur. It was the talk of the island.'

But Enzo was more inclined towards Guéguen's version of events, that nobody had known about it before the incident at the fort. After all, it was almost twenty years ago now, and people's memories of when they knew or didn't know about something would inevitably be suspect. He had no doubt that it had, indeed, been the talk of the island once the story was out. 'I don't suppose you know what happened to her, after the divorce.'

'Oh, she's married again now. Calls in here most mornings for the paper.'

Enzo was taken aback. 'She's still on the island?'

'Never left, monsieur. Found herself another incomer who

didn't know any better and went to live out at Quelhuit.' She
grunted. 'Almost within sight of the very place that poor Adam
Killian found her having sexual relations with the *cantonnier*.
And her married to the mayor's *adjoint*, too! She had no shame,
monsieur. Then or now.' She leaned forward again, in conspir-
atorial mode once more. 'Personally, I can't for the life of me
understand what any of these women saw in the man. He's
creepy and rude. In here every afternoon for his racing paper
and tobacco. I've always tried to be civil to him, but he's done
nothing but bite my nose off with every polite enquiry about
his health or innocent comment about the weather.'

Enzo suspected there was probably nothing either innocent
or polite that ever rolled off the tongue of the *libraire*. But as
he lifted his paper he saw that she had suddenly flushed, and
seemed flustered and self-conscious. He turned, following her
eyeline, to see Kerjean entering the store. He was wearing
the same donkey jacket as two nights previously. The same
worn and oil-soiled jeans. His hands were thrust deep in his
pockets, his head pulled down into his collar. His face betrayed
evidence of a rough evening the night before, deep shadows
beneath bloodshot eyes, a complexion that was pasty pale
and bloodless. He flicked a sullen glance in Enzo's direction,
then ignored him as he went to pick a couple of journals
from the rack.

Enzo turned back to the *libraire*. 'So where can I find the
library?' he asked.

She took a moment or two to recover her composure. 'Head
on down the street towards the port, monsieur. It's on your

left. In a converted house. It's also a *médiathèque* these days. Which just means, I think, that they have computers.'

The librarian shook her head and scratched it. A young woman, who could only have been a child when Killian was murdered. 'I'm sorry, monsieur. We don't keep back copies here. Certainly not that far back. You'll have to go to Lorient for that.'

'The library?'

'No, no. The offices of *Ouest-France* itself, in the Rue du Port. I know that they keep an archive of the Lorient edition there. And that's the edition that would carry any story relating to Groix.' She checked the time. 'If you're planning to go over there today, the next ferry doesn't leave till one-thirty.'

Time enough, Enzo thought, to browse through the paper's coverage of the trial and get the return ferry late afternoon. He thanked the young librarian and stepped out again into the morning sunshine.

A man stood directly across the road, leaning against the wall lighting a cigarette, a newspaper tucked under his arm. When he looked up from his cupped hands, Enzo saw that it was Thibaud Kerjean. Enzo stopped and the two men made eye contact. Was Kerjean following him, watching him? The *libraire* had said that he came in to the Maison de la Presse every afternoon for his paper and tobacco. Was it just a coincidence, then, he had come in earlier today while Enzo was there?

Enzo had, as he sometimes did, a foolish rush of blood to

the head, and he started across the road towards the islander. But Kerjean just pushed himself lazily off the wall and began walking away up the hill, shoving his hands in his pockets, turning his back as if to signal his contempt. Enzo stood watching him go, wondering what might have happened had Kerjean stood his ground. Enzo's intemperate behaviour in similar situations had got him into trouble in the past, and a confrontation with Kerjean in the middle of the street would not have been wise. Kerjean, a man acquitted but still suspected of murder, had probably had the same thought.

So Enzo stood for a minute, letting his heart rate subside before going in search of his jeep and a parking place near the ferry.

CHAPTER FOURTEEN

The Café de la Jetée was owned by one of the hotels that overlooked the harbour. Tables and chairs were set out on the terrace, and it was warm enough to sit in the fresh air and enjoy the late October sun. Potted plants lined one end of it, and Enzo settled himself at a table there, by the door, giving him a commanding view across the bay, and providing him with plenty of warning of the ferry's arrival.

There were some late season tourists at another table, and inside a group of regulars stood drinking at the bar. Enzo ran his eyes down the lunch menu until they came to rest on a smoked fish salad which, he thought, would go nicely with a glass of crisp white wine while he killed time before the crossing.

As a shadow fell across his table, he looked up expecting to see a waiter, and was surprised to find old Jacques Gassman standing there. The nonagenarian grinned, wrinkling a ruddy complexion. 'Monsieur Macleod. May I join you?'

'Of course.' Enzo stood to hold the old man's elbow as he eased himself into a chair.

Gassman was wrapped up warm, in a coat and scarf, a dark

blue peaked cap pulled down over his shock of white hair. He still gave the impression of a big man, undiminished by age. He had large-knuckled hands, brown-spotted by the years, and his grin revealed a row of shiny, white, even teeth that could not have been his own. 'This is my day for doing the shopping,' he said. 'And I always have my lunch here. Are you going to eat?'

'Yes.'

Gassman raised an arm and waved to someone inside, and a waitress duly appeared to take their order. 'The usual,' Gassman said.

Enzo ordered his smoked fish salad, and they agreed to share a *carafe* of white.

'How's the investigation going?'

'Slowly. I'm going to Lorient this afternoon to look at newspaper archives of the coverage of the trial.'

'Ah. Yes. Thibaud Kerjean. An unpleasant character.'

'You know him?'

'I do. Not well, of course. I don't think anyone knows him well. But well enough to know that I don't like him much.' He drew a long breath. 'So what do you think of our little island, monsieur?'

'I prefer it when the sun shines.'

Gassman guffawed. 'Ah, yes. Everywhere looks better when the sun shines. I love it. It's an unremarkable sort of place, I suppose. No dramatic features, apart from some stretches of the north-west coastline, and the beaches to the south and west, of course. But it has a perfect climate and a hidden beauty.'

'Hidden?'

'Beneath the soil. This is rare rock we are sitting on, Monsieur Macleod. Geologically quite different from the mainland. The government declared it a mineral nature reserve nearly thirty years ago. More than sixty minerals to be found. Some of them quite rare. Blue glaucophane and garnet.'

'You seem to know a lot about the place for an incomer.'

Gassman smiled ruefully. 'And how did you know I was an incomer, monsieur? The accent?'

'Well, it's not local, I can tell that.'

The old man shook his head. 'No, it's not. And even after all these years, it still marks me out as a "foreigner". But even if I had managed to shake it off, I'd always have been an outsider to the locals. You have to be born here to belong here. To be a true *Grek*.'

'*Grek*?'

He grinned. 'It's the nickname for a native of the island. Named after those big Greek coffee pots that used to sit on every fire to warm up the fishermen when they came back from the boats.' He rubbed big hands one around the other, as if he were cold or were washing them. 'But anyway, we incomers often know a lot more about the place than the folk who were born here.'

'How long since you first came to the island?'

'Ohh . . .' Old Gassman stuck out his chin and scratched it thoughtfully. 'A long time. Must be, what, nearly fifty years? I arrived in the early sixties, Monsieur Macleod, looking for a place to hide me away after the death of my wife. I didn't feel much like facing the world then, and this seemed as good a place as any to lose myself.'

'What happened to your wife?'

'Breast cancer. She was still a young woman. So much of her life ahead of her. And yet . . .' he shook his head sadly, and Enzo thought he detected a moist, glassy quality in his eyes, ' . . . it's unlikely she'd have lived this long anyway, so I'd still have lost her at some time. I just wish it had been later, rather than sooner.'

The waitress brought their wine and a jug of water, along with a basket of bread. Then the food arrived, and Enzo saw that Gassman had ordered a tuna steak with potatoes and salad. He filled both their glasses as they began to eat.

'So you never remarried?' He watched as Gassman cut awkwardly into his steak, holding his cutlery in a strange, childish grip.

'No. When I first arrived, I bought myself a cottage out on the moor near the village of Quéhello on the south side of the island. I was still hurting then, from my loss, and I kept myself pretty much to myself. I had my surgery of course, but the only people I ever really saw were my patients. I never got involved in the social scene. And never met a woman that could take the place of my wife. Not that I was looking.' He turned shining eyes on Enzo. 'Lots of things in life are disposable, Monsieur Macleod. Chuck 'em away and get another. But you can't replace people.'

'No.' Enzo looked down at his salad to charge his fork with more fish, hiding an emotional moment. He knew only too well how irreplaceable the people in your life really were. Then he glanced over and watched the old incomer's cumbersome cutting action as he attempted to dissect his tuna. 'You hold your cutlery in the most peculiar way, Monsieur Gassman, if you don't mind my saying so.'

Gassman looked up, amused. 'I do. And I don't mind. You can blame my mother for it. I'm a left-hander, monsieur, and for some reason, when I was a boy, there was some stigma attached to that. As if it were an aberration of some kind. So my mother made me hold my cutlery like a right-handed person would.'

Enzo smiled. 'Corrie-fisted we would have called it in Scotland.'

'It never felt right to me. But by the time I was grown up, it didn't feel good the other way either.' He laughed. 'So all my life, I've eaten like I have a handicap.' He breathed in and puffed himself up. 'But as you can see, it never stopped me getting the food to my mouth.'

The deep, piercing sound of a ship's horn rang out across the bay, and they looked up to see the ferry easing its way into the harbour, its wash setting all the small boats at berth rising and falling in turn.

Enzo finished his salad and drained his glass before leaving a couple of notes on the table and getting to his feet. 'I'm afraid I have to go and get my jeep into the queue,' he said. 'I've enjoyed talking to you, Monsieur Gassman.' They shook hands.

'Well, don't be a stranger, young man. Come out and see

me any time. I have only my dog for company these days, and it can get a little lonely sometimes.'

'I'll do that,' Enzo said, and he set off along the cobbled jetty to retrieve his vehicle from its parking place and get in line. It took him nearly ten minutes, and by the time he was sitting idling on the quayside, and glanced back along the jetty, the old man was gone. It wasn't until he had driven his jeep onboard and made his way up to the passenger deck, that he saw, in the distance, Jacques Gassman making his way slowly up the hill, past Coconut's and the bicycle shop. A difficult, shuffling gait. There was something oddly sad about the old man. He had lost his wife more than half a lifetime ago, and all these years later was still alone and lonely. With nothing to look forward to but the certainty of death, just a heartbeat away.

CHAPTER FIFTEEN

The Rue du Port ran along the side of the hill, parallel with the Quai des Indes, which was a deep-water channel cut into the heart of the city of Lorient from the inner harbour. There the yachts lined up side by side, touching and nudging, almost sensually, in time with the distant pulse of the sea. The street on the hill had been pedestrianised and cobbled, and young albizia trees planted all along its centre. In time they would provide dappled shade for the whole street with their frondy foliage and pink and white flowers. Now they were shedding, and the fine red and yellow leaves swirled and gathered in tiny drifts in the breeze that had sprung up.

Enzo found the offices of *Ouest-France* at number 55, and settled himself at a desk to sift through the newspaper's coverage of the trial from 1991. It was the major story of the day, achieving regular two-page spreads, with detailed reporting of evidence presented and testimony given. Enzo navigated his way through them by using subheadings as information markers, guiding him to the particular passages he was anxious to read.

Beneath the headline, A DEADLY ENCOUNTER, he found

the evidence given by Kerjean's lover, Arzhela Montin. The court reporter had wielded a colourful pen.

The pale and fragrant Madame Montin sat with hands clasped, a tremor in her voice as she told the court of her fear of the accused. Describing him as 'brutal' and 'threatening,' she nonetheless claimed that Kerjean had been a fierce and passionate lover.

'We would make love whenever and wherever we could,' she told the procureur.

Asked if she had been aware of his reputation for violence when she took up with him, she replied: 'I had heard that he was a man with a temper and prone to violence. In the early days of our relationship I saw no sign of it. But as time went on, our sexual encounters became more violent, more . . . frenzied. And he became increasingly possessive. If I couldn't see him, he demanded to know why. He insisted that I not make love to my husband, and said that he would kill any man that came between us.'

'Would you say that you were afraid of him?' the procureur *asked.*

'Yes, monsieur. In the end, I was very afraid. He was becoming totally unreasonable and quite unpredictable.'

'Then why didn't you just leave him?'

'Two reasons,' she told the court. 'I was addicted to him. He made love to me like no man had ever made love to me before.' And when the procureur *demanded to know what the second reason was, she replied: 'I was very much afraid of what he might do.'*

'To you?'

'To my husband. And perhaps to me, too.'

The accused sat cold and impassive in the dock as she went on to describe to the court the events of September 9 1990, at the abandoned Fort du Grognon on the Île de Groix. There, she and Kerjean had been engaged in a passionate bout of lovemaking when they were unexpectedly interrupted by the deceased, Adam Killian.

'Thibaud went crazy,' she said, tears brimming in her eyes from the memory. 'He was just an old man, kind of skinny and pale. But Thibaud screamed and shouted at him. Accused him of spying on us, of being a dirty voyeur. He literally chased him from the fort. It would have been comical if it wasn't so grave. I was terrified that word would get out about our affair. Thibaud was stark naked, pushing the old man across the old parade ground, slashing at his legs with a stick. When they disappeared into the tunnel I couldn't see them any longer, but I could still hear Thibaud shouting.'

'Did you hear him make any direct threats towards the deceased, Madame Montin?' the avocat de la partie civile *asked her.*

Madame Montin seemed to hesitate, and only answered after a prompting from the bench. She told the procureur: *'I heard him shout –* you breathe a word of this, you old bastard, and I'll have your ****ing hide.'

This was the lurid reporting of a tabloid journalist, and Enzo was immediately wary of putting too much store by it. The quotes were selective, feeding an unsophisticated readership's eager appetite for sex, violence and fear. But it was clear, all the same, how Arzhela Montin's testimony must have fed popular antagonism towards Kerjean and inflicted considerable damage on his defence. How quickly love had turned into something so destructive.

Michel Locqueneux, a mechanic from the garage at Port Tudy where Kerjean had his car serviced and repaired, had been called to give evidence for the prosecution. He had told the court that Kerjean had brought his car in for its annual *vidange* the morning of the day that Killian was murdered. His testimony was that the car was running perfectly when it left the garage and that there was not a single reason he could think of for it breaking down that night, as Kerjean claimed. He had also told the court that Kerjean had not subsequently brought the car back for examination. And so the fault that appeared, then disappeared so mysteriously in the course of one night, remained unexplained.

Kerjean's lawyer called several rebuttal witnesses to discredit Locqueneux, disgruntled clients who told stories of oil leaks and failing brakes and engine malfunction after servicing at the Locqueneux garage.

Several customers from Le Triskell were called to describe Kerjean's rantings in the bar the night he threatened to put Killian in the cemetery.

But as Enzo worked his way through the prosecution case, it became painfully clear that there really was no hard evidence, except for that obtained at the crime scene. The fingerprints on the gate, the footprint in the garden, the Montblanc pen.

And that was simply blown out of the water by a ruthless defence *avocat* who demonstrated beyond doubt that the handling of the crime scene and the initial investigation would have been perfect fodder for the scriptwriters of an Inspector Clouseau movie. In fact, he had made the allusion more than once, eliciting considerable laughter from the public benches. It was little wonder, Enzo reflected, that Guéguen was still embarrassed by it all, even though he had only been a trainee at the time.

The crux of the whole case, Enzo reflected as he stepped back out into the Rue du Port, revolved around the encounter at the Fort du Grognon. Only three people knew exactly what happened that day. Killian was dead. Kerjean was unlikely to provide any enlightenment. That only left the lover, Arzhela Montin. And she was still on the island, living at Quelhuit, according to the *libraire*. Enzo checked his watch. There was just time to catch the late afternoon ferry back. He would be on the island again a little after five. Time enough to drive out to Quelhuit and talk to Kerjean's ex-mistress before dinner.

CHAPTER SIXTEEN

Quelhuit was a disparate group of whitewashed cottages gathered around an old church and strung out along the north shore. Fading light washed the landscape as Enzo turned off the Pen Men road and nursed his jeep along a narrow, winding track between high hedgerows and tall oaks that shed brittle, brown leaves. Ahead, the church and the cluster of houses were silhouetted on the rise against a darkening blue sky.

It wasn't until he was almost there that Enzo realised Arzhela would no longer be Madame Montin. And he cursed himself for not stopping off at the Maison de la Presse to ask what her new married name was. But as his father had always been fond of saying, he had a good Scots tongue in his head. He would simply have to stop and ask. He pulled into a paved parking area in front of the church, drawing up next to a tractor and a digger. As he stepped out into the dusk, he felt the chill settling with the night and reached back into the jeep to retrieve Killian's scarf.

Again he was aware of the man's scent, and the sense of him there, at his shoulder, watching his progress, or lack of it.

He pushed open a gate and heard it squeak loudly in the

still of the coming night. The birds had already fallen silent, and the only sound to be heard was the sea washing gently along the shore. His footsteps seemed disproportionately loud as he crunched down the gravel path to the back door of one of a row of terraced cottages. The door was a freshly painted royal blue, and it was hard and unyielding beneath his knuckles.

The silence that followed his knock seemed profound, until a light above the door came on and startled him. The door opened to reveal an elderly lady wearing a patterned apron over a pale blue skirt. She wiped floury hands over the apron and peered at him in the light.

'Yes?'

'I'm sorry to disturb you, madame. I'm looking for the home of a lady who used to be called Arzhela Montin. I'm afraid I don't know her new *nom d'épouse*.'

The old lady seemed to lean even further out of the door, squinting up at him with beady blue eyes. 'You're that investigator,' she said. 'The one they wrote about in the paper.'

'Yes.' It seemed there was no corner of the island where he wasn't known.

'She'll not talk to you, you know.'

He was taken aback. 'What makes you think that?'

'She's never spoken about it in all the years she's been here. Keeps herself to herself, she does. Thinks she's better than us, just because she married an incomer and had her face in all the newspapers once. The centre of it all.' She snorted her derision. 'Hah! You wouldn't think it to look at her now. That a woman like that could arouse so much . . .' she searched for the right word, ' . . .passion.'

Enzo followed her directions, past the church and down the slope to where a manicured lawn led towards the seashore and a solitary white bungalow was set among the trees. He made his way through a well-kept rock garden to a conservatory built along the front of the house. The distant lights of the mainland winked and twinkled in frosted air across water that lay still and grey, like slate.

When she came through from the house to open the door and switch on the lights of the conservatory, Enzo saw what her poisonous neighbour had meant. Arzhela Leclerc, as she now was, did not fit the image of the scarlet woman at the centre of an illicit affair that had led to scandal and murder. Enzo found himself almost disappointed. She was small, no more than five-two. What might once have been a slim and willowy figure, had turned to fat, and the impression she gave was of a ball, almost completely round. Her face, though unlined, had sagged, its jawline lost in jowls, her mouth down-turned and quite unattractive.

She stood looking at him, wearing a mantle of weary resignation. 'I've been expecting you.' She stood aside, a silent invitation to enter. The conservatory was tiled and filled with fleshy-leafed potted plants. Cane furniture was arranged to take advantage of the view across the water, and she waved him into an armchair. 'My husband will be home in about twenty minutes. I'd like you gone by then. What do you want to know?'

So the neighbour had been wrong about one thing. Arzhela Leclerc seemed almost anxious to talk. 'Everything.'

She perched herself awkwardly on the edge of the settee and folded her hands in her lap, gently wringing them as she gazed for a long time at the floor, before looking up to meet his eye. 'There are things, monsieur, that I have kept to myself for nearly twenty years. When I read about you in the paper, I thought . . . it's time to tell. If he comes, if he asks me, I'll tell him. Maybe then I'll be rid of it, finally.'

Enzo found himself almost frightened to breathe in case she had a change of heart. 'What happened at the Fort de Grognon?' he said.

'Oh, nothing that hasn't been told a thousand times already. Except that I finally saw Thibaud Kerjean for the man he really was. A man barely in control of himself. A man driven by powerful urges. Sex and violence, and with a temper that released some kind of inner demon that I'd not seen before. Not like that, the way he was with that poor old man.'

'What happened?'

'He was like a man demented, monsieur. You wouldn't have been surprised to see him foaming at the mouth. I'm sure he believed that being found like that was going to be the end of us. And he was right. But not in the way he thought.' She drew a deep, trembling breath. 'He was obsessed with me, you see. Beyond all reason.'

Enzo tried hard to see her as the object of any man's obsession, but found himself agreeing with her, that it was, indeed, beyond all reason. He knew, too, that no matter how painful and traumatic the experience of all that happened to her twenty years before, it was probably the high point of her life. The only moment in it when, as her neighbour had said, she was the centre of all attention.

'I'd known for some time that it couldn't go on. But I didn't know how to end it. I couldn't ever have told him. I was scared of him, you see, scared of what he might do. But when he unleashed his temper like that on poor Mister Killian, I knew the time had come. And in that moment, I saw just how it could be done.' She glanced nervously at her watch. 'I would offer you a drink, monsieur. I could do with one myself. But we don't have time.'

She could no longer remain seated and she rose to wander through the potted plants, to fold her arms and stare out through the glass at the moon rising now over the mainland across the strait. Enzo could see her reflection in the glass, like a mirror. Had she chosen to, she could have seen his reflection too, met his eye without meeting it. But instead she gazed at, or perhaps through, her own reflected image. Dragging up thoughts from the place she had buried them many years before. A place she had never wanted to revisit but had never been able to escape. There was a sense, Enzo thought, of the confessional in all this. He as father confessor, she as the repentant seeking absolution. He wondered if it was ever that easy. 'So how exactly *did* it all end?'

After a long pause she said, 'Mister Killian didn't tell my husband, Monsieur Macleod. I did.' Another silence, as she struggled to find the right words. 'I knew he would react, you see. That it would all come out in the open. And that Thibaud would think it was Mister Killian who'd done it. I just didn't realise how ferocious my husband's reaction would be. I thought, I really thought, we could have weathered the storm. We had two lovely children, too much invested in our relationship just to throw it away. But I hadn't counted on his pride. A stubborn, utterly implacable pride, monsieur. Almost worse than Thibaud's temper.'

'And Kerjean?'

He saw her mouth set in sorrow. 'I'd seen the incident at the fort as my chance to break free. Mister Killian as a convenient scapegoat. I never for one moment, monsieur, thought that Thibaud would kill him.'

'And you think he did?'

She turned at last to face him. And nodded, almost imperceptibly. 'I do. And I've spent every moment of the last twenty years feeling the guilt. Knowing it was my fault. If I could take it all back, I would. I'd have broken it off with Thibaud and faced the consequences, whatever they might have been. It could hardly have been worse than the way it turned out.'

'Do you think that might have saved your marriage?'

She shook her head sadly. 'No.' She sucked in a deep breath. 'Because there was something else, monsieur. Something I never told anyone, except my husband. Until now.'

Enzo stared at her in the silence of the conservatory and realised what that something was. 'You were pregnant.'

A momentary fire flickered in her eyes, then died again like embers at the end of a long night. 'That's what he couldn't accept. My husband. His pride. I couldn't pretend to him it was his, because we hadn't slept together in months. And that, above all else, is what he didn't want people to know – that I was carrying Kerjean's child. When news of the affair broke, everyone thought he threw me out. But the truth is, we had made a deal. And I kept my end of it.'

'Which was?'

'To leave immediately. Go to the mainland and have the pregnancy terminated.'

'And his end was . . .?'

'To take me back, once it was done, and try to make a go of it.'

Enzo nodded. 'But he didn't keep to that.'

The fire flared again, fanned by the oxygen of her remembered anger. 'He used my absence to poison the minds of my children, to turn them against me. As soon as I'd had the abortion, he filed for divorce and got the courts to ask the children who they would rather be with – him or me.'

'And they chose him.'

The recollection still hurt. 'They left the island, the three of them, almost as soon as the divorce was granted, and I haven't seen my children since. Not once.'

They heard the sound of a car on the road by the church. It stopped, idling for a moment, before the engine ceased and they heard the slamming of a car door.

Her distress was immediate. 'That's my husband. Go now. Please.'

Enzo stood. 'He doesn't know any of this?'

She shook her head. 'Only what was known at the time. And, of course, I had my own slant on it for him. But I have a new life now, monsieur. And I won't ever speak of this again. Please go.'

Enzo nodded and let himself out, feeling how the temperature outside had dropped as he turned through the rock garden at the side of the house and saw the shadow of a man coming across the grass towards him. By the light at the corner of the house, Enzo saw that he was tall. A middle-aged man losing his hair. He wore a long coat and carried a briefcase. Enzo passed him without stopping, meeting his eye only fleetingly, and offering the merest nod of acknowledgment. Without looking round, he was aware that the man had stopped, and could almost feel his eyes on his back.

What would she tell him? That Enzo had come knocking at the door, trying to rake over the ashes of the past and that she had sent him packing? Or, having finally lanced the boil that had been slowly poisoning her for twenty years, would she now tell him the truth?

Enzo saw the last streaks of red in the western sky as he reached his car and knew that he would never know.

CHAPTER SEVENTEEN

He had forgotten it was Hallowe'en and only remembered when he stepped out of the cold and dark of the Place Leurhé into the noisy ambience of Le Triskell. The first partygoers in masks and costumes were already gathering. It seemed surreal, somehow, steeped as he was in real life tragedy and murder, to slip into this make-believe world of ghosts and ghouls.

Black curtains hung around walls festooned by skeletons and skulls, giant spiders, and pumpkin lanterns. Copious clouds of spider's web tumbled in wreaths from the ceiling, and windows were plastered with x-rays of body parts, backlit to project the images into the bar. A row of deathheads dangled above the counter, and a skeleton peered out from behind the smoked glass door of a chill cabinet.

On the drive back from Quelhuit, Enzo had called Jane on his mobile to say that he would be eating in town. He had heard the disappointment in her voice and was relieved that he was spared the prospect, at least for tonight, of succumbing to temptation and indulging in something he would almost certainly regret.

A figure in a witch's mask and black, pointed hat ballooned into his face. He smelled fresh alcohol on breath that issued from holes in the plastic. A woman's voice said, 'Not getting dressed up for us tonight, Monsieur Macleod? You could have come as Sherlock Holmes.'

A couple of pirates jostled him towards the bar. 'What will you have to drink, me hearty? Get the man a whisky, Devi. Or should it be a tot of rum?'

'What will it be, Monsieur Macleod?' Devi was a plump girl in her thirties, with a black moustache painted above ruby red lips, and blond, curly hair beneath a bowler hat. She wore a black suit and waistcoat, several sizes two small, and a white shirt and bow-tie. Charlie Chaplin, Enzo guessed.

'Whisky'll be fine.'

'I can offer you a Black Bush, if you don't mind a touch of the Irish.'

Enzo grinned. 'I don't mind slumming it for once,' he said. He reached into his pocket for some cash, but a hand held his arm to stop him. It was one of the pirates.

'No, no, that's all right, Monsieur Macleod, this one's on us.'

The three musketeers burst in from the terrace, ushering a blast of cold air in with them. 'All for one, and one for all!' One of them thrust his sword towards the ceiling and brought a loop of cobweb cascading down over their heads. A great roar of laughter went up.

'Hey, watch it!' Devi shouted. 'It took me hours to put that stuff up.' She pushed Enzo's Black Bush across the counter.

He leaned towards her, raising his voice above the hubbub. 'I don't suppose you would have been here at the time of the Killian murder?'

She grinned. 'I was sitting my *bac* at the time, monsieur. That was before I left for university on the mainland.' Her smile turned wry. 'A worthwhile interlude in my life.' She waved an arm vaguely around her. 'You can see where my doctorate in philosophy got me.'

Enzo grinned back. A Celt almost never missed the opportunity to indulge in self-deprecation. 'They say that the answers to some of the world's greatest philosophical questions can be found in a bottle.'

'In my experience, the only thing to be found in a bottle is oblivion.' Which was her recognition of yet another Celtic trait, that great capacity for self-destruction. The Celts, it seemed, were obsessed with the self.

Enzo nodded. 'I don't suppose you'd know if any of your regulars were around at that time. Several gave evidence at the trial.'

She shrugged. 'I couldn't tell you. But I know that old Robert Kerber has been a regular here for years. He might know.' She nodded towards the end of the bar nearest the door. A man in his sixties, wearing a cloth cap pulled low over a forehead with lines like scars, sat on a high stool nursing a glass of beer. He wore a checked jacket with leather patches at the elbow and a pair of frayed, baggy jeans. This was no fancy dress, and the man wore an expression of ill-concealed irritation, cocooned in his own world, making no attempt to participate in the celebrations. Enzo recognised the name at once. Kerber was one of those witnesses.

'Thanks.' Enzo lifted his glass and pushed his way along the bar, managing to squeeze in beside him. More revellers arrived: a very fat man dressed as Madame Defarge, clutching knitting needles and a metre of hand-knitted scarf; a thinner man with a beard in the role of Marie-Antoinette; and a zombie with an axe buried in his head. 'Can I refill your glass?' Enzo asked Kerber.

The old islander turned dead eyes on the Scotsman. 'You can,' he said. 'But it'll not get you anything.'

'I'm not after anything.' He signalled Devi to refill Kerber's glass.

'No?'

'Just a few minutes of your time.'

'At my age, monsieur, every moment is precious.'

'Life is precious at any age.'

'That's true.' He scratched his chin thoughtfully. 'What do you want?'

'You were here the night Thibaud Kerjean was telling anyone who'd listen how he was going to put Adam Killian in the cemetery.'

'I was, and he did.'

'Was he drunk?'

'I never knew the man, monsieur, when he didn't have a drink in him.' Kerber took a sip from his replenished glass. Enzo looked at the roadmap of broken veins across his nose and cheeks, and it occurred to him that the same could very probably be said of Kerber. But drunks rarely saw themselves as drunks, and Kerber appeared to see no irony in his words. He doubtless had the same capacity for self-deception as he had for alcohol. Another Celtic self.

'Kerber,' Enzo said, as if trying the name out for size. And then, 'Kerjean. There are a lot of Ker names on the island.'

Kerber turned to look at him as if he were an idiot. 'And a lot of Mac names in Scotland, monsieur. Son-of, right?'

'Right.'

'Ker means house. You people got named after the man who impregnated your mother. We got named after the house we grew up in. Kerber, house of Peter. Kerbol, house of Paul.' He paused. 'Kerjean, house of Jean.' He took another pull at his beer. 'Anything else I can tell you? The tonnage of tuna caught in 1933? The number of Germans billeted on Groix during the occupation?'

'You can tell me why you think Kerjean carried out his threat to murder Killian.'

'Because he's a drunk and a brute. A man who would put his fist in your face if you so much as looked at him sideways. He might have been the worse for wear that night, but his anger didn't come out of a bottle. It was real enough. And Kerjean is nothing if not a man of his word. There's not a soul who knows him, monsieur, who wouldn't think him capable of doing exactly what he said he would.'

Enzo stepped out into plunging temperatures. The night was clear and sharp, the sky newly painted black and spattered with silver. His breath billowed around his head like wreaths of mist. From inside the bar, the noise of the party followed him out on to the terrace, where the parasols, wrapped and tied, stood among the tables like guests awaiting an invitation that would never come. Across the square, the lights of a cash machine glowed in the wall of the Crédit Agricole. And he could see lights on in the doctor's house.

A narrow street led off darkly from the near corner of the square, and Enzo figured it might lead directly through to the church, where he had parked his jeep. He threw one end of Killian's scarf over his shoulder and pulled up the collar of his jacket, his hands plunged deep into his trouser pockets to keep them warm. The darkness seemed to swallow him as soon as he entered the alleyway, and he had not gone ten metres before he began to regret taking the shortcut. There were no street-lights here, and the moon was still low in the sky, casting the shadows of houses to darken his path. He slowed to take measured, cautious steps into a dark that seemed so profound he could touch it. His fingertips detected a wall to his right, and he followed it until almost walking into the side of a house. The street had taken a sharp left without warning, and he found himself with hands pressed up against a shuttered window. He tripped and almost fell over a doorstep, and stumbled forward into a deeper darkness. He cursed under his breath and his voice echoed back at him from hidden walls. Back the way he had come, he could just see the glow of lights from the square, and he was tempted simply to head back and take the long way round. But he couldn't be that far from the church now. Surely. Another turn in the street and he would see the lights of the church ahead of him. Of that he was certain.

He heard a cough. A single, muffled human bark, somewhere off to his left. And he froze. There was someone there. Now the scrape of a shoe. Leather on tarmac, and the crunch of gravel underfoot. The whisper of voices seemed to rise up into the night, but it might have been his imagination. He felt suddenly very vulnerable, and a tiny knot of fear tightened in his stomach. Spurred to find the safety of a street light, he increased his pace, keeping his hand on the wall, following it straight ahead, until it turned sharply to the right. He turned with it, expecting to see the lights of the church square ahead of him. But there was nothing but more black. He looked up and saw a narrow strip of sky above him, illuminated by the stars, almost bright somehow compared to this endless darkened street.

Another cough. More footsteps. Now he was certain that he heard the whisper of muffled voices. Someone was following him. There was no longer any doubt. Two people or more. Frosted grit scraping beneath approaching feet. He turned and hurried forward into the obscurity of the alleyway ahead of him until suddenly the wall opened up to his right, where tall gates stood ajar. They led into a large overgrown garden. The shapes of trees and long grass were just visible in the starlight before the shadow of a large house that loomed out of the night swallowed them up.

Enzo slipped between the gates and into the garden. He

could feel the frosted grass soaking his trousers from the knee down, and he waded through it, as through water, certain that if he could reach the shadow of the trees, he could crouch amongst them, and hide from his pursuers until they gave up the search.

'Hey!' he heard a man's voice shout and, startled, he began to run. The cold seemed to travel from his feet, though his legs, into his very soul, where fear closed icy fingers around his heart. It could only be Kerjean, and perhaps a couple of cronies, intent on dishing out a physical warning, doing him a little damage. Or worse. The man had been following him earlier in the day, and Enzo cursed his foolishness in straying away from the safety of the light.

Something caught and tore his trousers, causing him to stumble and fall to his knees. He felt thorns tearing through the skin of his calfs. But the sound of Kerjean and friends wading through the tall grass in his wake got him quickly to his feet, and he sprinted for the far side of the garden where the shadow of the house mired it in darkness.

But now something cold and wet wrapped itself around him, a rope cutting into his arm, spinning him around and pitching him forward. He was helplessly entangled in unseen fabric, clinging and chillingly slimy. He could smell damp and decay, something rotting and rotten. There was a loud tearing sound, and from being semi-suspended he was dumped suddenly through the long grass to the hard frosted earth below. It knocked all the breath from his lungs. He tried to get up but couldn't, as if trapped in a giant, sticky spider's web. He could hear the swish, swish, of legs running through the grass towards him, breath rasping in the night. And suddenly he was blinded by several flashlights catching him full in their glare, and he raised an arm to shade his eyes. He heard laughter. A woman's voice. A man's. And what sounded like a child.

In his confusion, he saw, beyond the lamplight, a human skull, a green face with black spots. A full skeleton stepped into the light, a hand rising through the dark to lift away the death mask to reveal the altogether less frightening face of a teenage girl. A face wreathed in smiles. Bright, shining blue eyes. And peals of laughter rising in the night air. It was a face he knew. But it took a moment for him to realise that it was Alain Servat's daughter, Oanez. Her sister stepped into the light, the owner of the witch's green face, then Alain and Elisabeth in Laurel and Hardy outfits, bowler hats above whitened faces. Alain was padded out to make him fatter, a small black moustache painted on his upper lip. All four were almost helpless with laughter.

Alain reached out a hand to help him up. 'What in God's name are you doing, man?'

Enzo had run straight into the rotting remains of a hammock strung between two trees. Elisabeth started to help him disentangle himself, while the girls continued to giggle. Enzo's initial relief gave way to irritation. 'I might ask you what you're doing following folk in the dark.'

Alain laughed. 'It's Hallowe'en, Monsieur Macleod. We're out guising.'

Elisabeth said, 'I'm so sorry, we didn't mean to scare you.

We always take the girls out guising at Halloween. We were on our way home when we saw you leaving Le Triskell, and thought you might like to come in for a drink.'

'But you're an elusive man, monsieur. Ducking into dark alleys and hiding in gardens.' Alain chuckled, still amused by the Scotsman's unusual behaviour.

Enzo tried to regain a little of his dignity, brushing away the slime deposited on his jacket and trousers by the decaying hammock. 'Oh, I'm always doing that,' he said. 'There's nothing I like better than rolling around in the freezing long grass to make myself cold and wet. It's my party trick. Do I get an apple and some peanuts?'

This sent the girls off into another paroxysm of giggles. But Elisabeth slipped a comforting arm through his. 'I'm sure we can do better than that, Monsieur Macleod. What about a nice bowl of hot soup, followed by a glass or two of whisky by a warm fire?

'Hmmm. Tough choice,' Enzo said. 'Roll in the wet grass. Or glass of whisky by the fire.'

'Well, you've already done one of them,' Alain laughed.

'True.' Enzo was slowly recovering his sense of humour. 'No choice at all, then. Soup and whisky it is.'

CHAPTER EIGHTEEN

Pale blue paint covered the walls of the Servat's living room, with the woodwork around the door and windows picked out in white. A shelf that ran around the room just above the level of the door groaned with traditional *greks* of all shapes and colours and sizes.

'They were my father's,' Elisabeth said, following Enzo's eye. 'It took him a lifetime to collect them, and I couldn't bear to throw them out when he died.'

Alain laughed. 'I leave the dusting of them to her.'

The girls had been packed off to bed, and the adults had consumed steaming bowls of hot winter soup in the dining room, along with thick chunks of homemade bread and salted Breton butter. Enzo was drying out now in front of the fire, his good humour and sense of well-being somewhat restored. It was hard not to mellow under the warmth of the doctor and his wife, and their obvious affection for each other.

Alain poured the whiskies from an antique drinks cabinet with glass doors that revealed a stunning line-up of Scots and Irish whiskies. 'It's something of a passion,' he said. 'And I collect the empties, too. One day Primel and the girls will inherit them and not have the heart to throw them out.'

'Just don't expect any of the children to dust them,' Elisabeth said. 'And I'm not sure that any of them will be as sentimental as us. I can see most of the contents of the house being sold off at the local *brocante*.'

'Never!' Alain chuckled. 'They've got their mother's hoarding genes. They might pack them away in the attic, but they'll never part with them.' He handed Enzo a glass well charged with pale amber. 'I don't know if you've ever tasted this one. It comes from the smallest distillery in Scotland. Edradour. I won't tell you how much it cost me, because Elisabeth is listening, but it was worth every centime.' He and Elisabeth exchanged smiles, and he handed her a glass before pouring one for himself. Elisabeth settled herself on the settee, and Alain stood warming himself in front of the fire and raised his glass. '*Slàinte mhath*,' he said.

Enzo raised an eyebrow in surprise. 'You know your Scots Gaelic.'

'You can't drink good Scotch whisky without knowing how to make a proper toast with it.'

Enzo raised his own glass. '*Slàinte*,' he said. Elisabeth echoed the toast and all three sipped at their liquid gold. Enzo felt the sweetness emerging slowly from behind the burn, the rich, aromatic flavour of malted barley from the Scottish glens. 'Mmmh. This is a good whisky.'

Alain beamed his pleasure and took another sip of his own. 'So how is your investigation going, Monsieur Macleod?'

Enzo pulled a face. 'Very slowly, doctor. In fact, the more I learn, the less I seem to know. I am still wrestling with the whole question of whether or not Thibaud Kerjean was involved.'

'Do you think he was?' Elisabeth asked.

Enzo shook his head. 'I really don't know. Judging by the evidence presented in court, the jury was right not to convict. On the other hand, if the police had done their job properly at the time, he would probably have spent the last eighteen years in prison.'

'So you do think he did it?' Alain said.

'I think there is some pretty damning evidence against him.' Enzo took thoughtful sips of his whisky. 'But also plenty of room for doubt.' He laughed. 'As I said, I am getting nowhere very fast. Do you know the man yourself?'

Alain shrugged. 'I've encountered him once or twice. Can't say he made a very good impression on me. But he was old Doctor Gassman's patient, and when Gassman retired another doctor in the practice took over the Kerjean file. I have only seen him, professionally, on very rare occasions. Socially, never.' He looked towards his wife. 'How about you darling?'

She nodded. 'Yes, I had dealings with him a couple of times when I was nursing at the clinic. An unpleasant sort of man.'

Enzo turned towards the doctor's wife. 'Oh, yes, I'd forgotten. The receptionist said you'd worked at the clinic.'

'Only for a short while, a very long time ago, when Alain and I were first married and he was the new kid on the block in the practice. I stayed on for a while after Primel was born. My mother was a big help looking after the baby. But with Alain's hours, and mine, it just wasn't practical, and in the end I gave it up.' She smiled, almost sadly. 'I always promised myself I'd go back to nursing when he got older. But then we had the girls, and I'm still in demand as a mum.'

Alain smiled fondly at his wife. 'She's more than just a nurse you know, Monsieur Macleod. She's a trained physical therapist. We could do with her back.'

She returned his smile. 'Maybe. Once the girls have gone to university. We'll see.'

Alain threw back his head and roared with laughter. '*On verra, on verra.*' He turned towards Enzo. 'It's been the same refrain all our married life. We'll see, we'll see. And when Elisabeth says "we'll see", it means you can bet your shirt on it. I remember once, many moons ago, we sat talking in this very room about the possibility of having more children. Primel was proving quite a handful at the time. And all Elisabeth said was, "we'll see". As you've seen for yourself, one became three. Without any further discussion, I might add.'

Elisabeth grinned. 'It's a woman's prerogative to prevaricate in the beginning and decide for herself in the end.' She sipped at her whisky. 'Without any further discussion. And, anyway, you don't make babies by discussing it.' She and Alain exchanged another smile, then she laid down her glass. 'I'd better go and see to old Émile.'

When she had gone, Alain took Enzo's glass and refilled it, along with his own. He sat down in the space she had vacated, as if needing somehow to feel close to her when she wasn't there, drawing on the warmth she had left behind. 'We were in the same class at school, you know, and I fancied her from the first time I set eyes on her.' He chuckled at the memory. 'I managed to get myself a place at the desk beside her, and used to walk her home after school. Until she got glasses, that is. Ugly, blue-rimmed things. And braces on her teeth. I went right off her then.' He laughed. 'Poor Elisabeth. She went from beautiful swan to ugly duckling in the space of a month, and couldn't understand why I wouldn't talk to her anymore.' He shook his head. 'Children can be so cruel.'

Enzo's smile was tinged with sadness. These were two people who so obviously adored each other, even after more than twenty years of marriage. He thought how different his own life might have been had Pascale lived. How many more children they might have had together. A tiny worm of envy worked its way into his thoughts, and he had to shake himself free of it. He said, 'Evidently she dispensed with the glasses and the braces, and you got back together when she turned into a swan again.'

'Oh, it was an off and on thing right through primary school, college, the *lycée*. It wasn't until I was leaving for medical school, and we faced the prospect of permanent separation, that we came to our senses and realised we didn't really want to be apart. So she came with me. We shared student accommodation in Paris. A cosy *concubinage*. She trained as a nurse while I graduated in medicine. But we didn't actually get married until I came back to the island to fill a vacancy at the clinic.'

'And was that all that brought you back? To work at the clinic?'

'There were elderly parents, Monsieur Macleod. My mother had died a few years earlier, and I knew that my father was going to need someone to look after him. Elisabeth's father was ill . . .' He paused, sipping thoughtfully on his whisky. 'But I think, in the end, I would have come back anyway. This was a wonderful place to grow up, monsieur. Paris had its attractions, of course. But I could never have seen myself raising children there. This is the only place I would ever have wanted to bring up a family.' He smiled sadly. 'The irony, of course, being that as soon as they are old enough, they leave. Can't wait to get away.'

It was some time and another couple of whiskies later that Elisabeth returned. She picked up the bottle, shocked at how little of it remained, and raised an eyebrow. 'There is no way you can drive home, Monsieur Macleod. You'd better stay over.'

'Oh.' Enzo tried to count up the drinks he had consumed in the last couple of hours. The whisky in Le Triskell, and three, maybe four, here at the doctor's house. 'That's very kind. But I was really hoping to get back. Madame Killian is expecting me.'

Alain leaned forward to look at him. 'Elisabeth's right, Monsieur Macleod. You're in no state to drive. And neither am I, I'm afraid.'

'I'll drive you back,' Elisabeth said. 'I've only had half a glass. I'm sure Madame Killian can drive you into town to pick up your car in the morning.'

As they followed the one-way system out of Le Bourg the moon was high, washing its bright, silvery light across the island. So bright, Enzo thought, that it might have been possible to drive without headlights. Elisabeth's large green SUV seemed huge in the narrow streets, but she handled it with an easy confidence, and Enzo felt comfortable in her presence, leaning back against the headrest in the passenger seat, enjoying the sense of giving himself over completely to the control of someone else, an abdication of all responsibility.

They passed a signpost pointing back the way to Port Lay. 'One day,' she said, 'if you have time, I'll take you down there and show you where I used to live. For me it is the most beautiful corner of the island.'

'Take me now.' He glanced across at her. 'It's not too much out of our way, is it?'

She smiled. 'No. A five-minute detour.' She hesitated for only a moment, before swinging the SUV around and taking another route out of town.

As they left the tiny conurbation behind them, she turned into a narrow road that wound steeply down the hillside. Enzo caught only occasional glimpses of the ocean, before suddenly it opened up ahead of them, moonlight reflecting silver across its unbroken surface. And there, the tiny harbour of Port Lay nestled among the rocks of a natural inlet that cut deep into the side of the hill.

A stone-built harbour wall cut across its entrance, leaving only the narrowest of channels for boats to come and go. In the sheltered waters of the inlet, half a dozen small boats were tethered to the quayside, overlooked by a large white house that glowed in the wash of the moon.

Elisabeth drew in at the top of the hill where a bridge spanned the beach below. 'It's hard to imagine now those tuna fleets coming in and out of that tiny little harbour. But they did, and the place was alive with activity. I used to sit on the quayside as a little girl, watching them land the catch, waiting for my dad. I knew all those faces. Island faces. Red and weathered. Such a hard life, Monsieur Macleod. We don't realise how lucky we are.' She was lost in momentary reflection. 'But we'll come back another day, and I'll show you my house, if you're interested. And the old fish processing factory.' She nodded up the hill to the right, where a large building stood dark and empty, the legacy of a way of life gone forever.

'I'd like that.'

'It looks better in the sunshine.' She revved the engine, swung across the bridge, turning sharply to the left at the far side, and accelerated up an impossibly narrow street between whitewashed cottages.

They cut back through Le Bourg and were soon heading east, along the north coast, to where the road dipped down to the beach at Port Mélite. Enzo closed his eyes, breathing in the scent of the woman at the wheel, allowing the whisky its freedom to take him where it would. It wasn't until the car drew to a halt, that he opened his eyes again, realising that he had drifted off to sleep.

A phosphorescent sea washed up on the half moon of sand in the bay below the Killian cottage. Elisabeth had drawn in beneath the trees that overlooked the beach and was smiling at him indulgently. 'You can wake up now, monsieur. Your limousine has reached its destination.'

'Oh, my God!' Enzo sat up. 'I hope I wasn't snoring.'

'Only a little. I just turned the radio up louder.' She laughed when she saw the horror on his face. 'Only joking, Monsieur Macleod.'

He grinned sheepishly. 'Enzo.'

'Well, Enzo, I am happy to report that snoring is not one of your vices. But you do talk in your sleep.'

'Do I?'

'We were having a very interesting conversation. It wasn't until we got to Kervaillet that I realised you were talking to yourself.' She laughed. 'And so was I.'

Enzo looked at her, unsure whether or not to take her seriously, till he saw the twinkle in her eye. Then he grinned. 'Thank you for the lift, Elisabeth. And I'll look forward to seeing Port Lay in the sunshine.' He paused as he opened the passenger door. 'I didn't dream that, did I?'

She laughed out loud. 'No, Enzo. You didn't dream it. Goodnight.'

He stood watching as she turned the SUV and gunned the engine, accelerating fast up the hill, back to the waiting arms of the man who loved her. And for the second time that night, he had to extinguish the little flame of envy that sprang up inside him.

He crossed the sandy parking area to the track that led to the house, and as he opened the gate, the front door swung open to flood the front garden with yellow light. Jane Killian came out on to the doorstep. 'What happened? Did your car break down?' Her voice sounded shrill, oddly strained.

'No. Too much to drink. Doctor Servat's wife drove me home.'

'Elisabeth Servat?'

He heard a tone in her voice that suggested more than surprise. 'I was at their house. The doctor had too much to drink as well.' Why did he feel the need to explain this to her? He climbed the steps to the door.

'She's an attractive woman.'

'She is.' For a moment they stood very close to one another.

Jane held the door open for him, and he transitioned gratefully from the freezing cold of the night to the smoky warmth of the cottage. He crouched by the fire, rubbing his hands together in front of its glowing embers, and noticed the empty glass at Jane's chair. He was aware of her crossing the room behind him, and looked up as she handed him a glass of whisky.

'I think maybe I've had enough already tonight.'

'One more won't hurt. I hate drinking on my own. And, in any case, I could do with another.' She refilled her own glass and sank into her chair, lifting it to her lips and watching him as he perched on the edge of the armchair opposite. 'We had a visitor tonight.'

Enzo frowned. 'Who?'

'I don't know. Someone who parked a little further up the road and walked the rest of the way so I wouldn't hear the car.'

The whisky fog in Enzo's head seemed suddenly to clear, and he found himself focusing. 'Tell me.'

'It's so quiet here at nights, Enzo. I heard the squeak of the gate. At first I thought it was you, and couldn't understand why you hadn't driven right down to the shore. I went to the window, but there was nobody there. At least, no one I could see.' She took a mouthful of whisky, and he noticed for the first time how pale she looked. 'Then I went through to the kitchen, but left the light off. And out of the window I saw someone crossing the lawn. Just a shadow among the trees, heading for the annex. So I thought then it must be you, and I opened the door and called your name.'

'It wasn't me, Jane.'

'I know that now.'

'Did you see who it was?'

Her hand was trembling slightly as she took another drink. 'I couldn't see anyone. And whoever it was wasn't responding to my call. So I turned on the outside light. It floods the whole of the back garden with light.'

'And did you see someone?'

'A figure darting through the trees, running away from the annex, and then climbing over the bamboo fence at the back.'

'Someone trying to break in, do you think?'

'I don't know. But I closed the shutters and locked up at

the back, and sat here with all the lights on waiting for you to get back. I didn't think you'd be so late.'

He drained his glass and stood up. 'I don't suppose you went over to check if there was any sign of a break-in?'

She laughed, a shrill laugh without humour. 'No, I didn't.'

'I'd better take a look then.'

She stood up. 'I'll come with you.' And she went to lift a coat from the stand in the hall and followed him into the kitchen. She turned on the outside light before unlocking the door and lifting a flashlight from the kitchen worktop.

The garden lay still and quiet, frost settling white on the grass. Enzo took the flashlight from Jane and shone it across the lawn. A trail of footprints in the frost led from the side of the house across to the door of the annex, and then away again towards the back fence, the second set spaced further apart, indicating flight and haste. Enzo crouched to examine them, but they were scuffed and indistinct, rapidly disappearing now as the frost hardened.

He shone the flashlight on the handle and lock of the door to the annex. But there was no sign of any attempt at forced entry. He heard Jane's erratic breathing at his side and wasn't sure whether it was fear or cold. He unlocked the door and pushed it open. Immediately his eye was drawn to a folded slip of paper on the hall floor. Evidently slipped beneath the door by their visitor. He turned on the light and stooped to pick it up as Jane closed the door behind them. 'What is it?' She peered over his shoulder to read it with him as he opened it up. The note was brief and cryptic.

YOU KNOW WHO I AM. WE SAW KERJEAN TOGETHER THIS MORNING. I HAVE HELD MY TONGUE FOR LONG ENOUGH, MONSIEUR. I WILL TELL YOU WHAT I KNOW AS LONG AS YOU PROMISE TO KEEP MY NAME OUT OF IT. I WON'T BE SEEN WITH YOU. MEET ME TOMORROW EVENING, 19.30, AT THE TROU DE L'ENFER. THERE IS A BUNKER BENEATH THE OLD GERMAN GUN EMPLACEMENT. I'LL WAIT FOR YOU THERE.

'Who were you with this morning when you saw Kerjean?' Jane looked up at him, eyes filled with curiosity now.

'The woman who serves at the Maison de la Presse. A skinny woman with short, curly white hair.'

'Madame Blanc? Was it her who pushed the note under the door?'

Enzo raised a skeptical eyebrow. 'Well, someone wants me to think so. What's the *Trou de l'enfer*?'

'Just about the most dangerous place on the island. Bad enough in the daylight. But you certainly don't want to be going out there in the dark.'

'Why is it dangerous?'

'Well, obviously you understand the meaning of *Trou de l'enfer*.'

He nodded. 'Literally, "hole of hell". Or "hellhole".'

'It's an enormous crack in the cliffs on the south side of the island, Enzo. Whether it was broken open by the sea, or by some geological upheaval, I don't know. But it's maybe seventy or eighty feet deep, and crumbling all along the edges. At high tide, during stormy weather, the sea rushes into it, throwing spray hundreds of feet into the air. And they say you can hear the roar of it for miles around. The devil himself calling out from hell.'

He saw that she was shivering now, in spite of her coat. The temperature in the annex had plunged, even more than the previous night. 'You're freezing,' he said, and he put his arms around her as much for comfort as for warmth. She responded, slipping her arms beneath his jacket, and around his waist to hold him tight. He felt her body trembling.

'Don't go out there,' she said. 'I'd feel terrible if anything happened to you.'

'Why would anything happen to me?'

'A lot of people have died at the *trou* in recent years, Enzo. Strayed too close to the edge and had the ground give way beneath them. They've roped it all off now.'

'So if I stay outside the ropes I'll be fine. And I'm sure you'll lend me your flashlight.'

She looked up at him, and her face seemed very close to his. He felt her breath on his neck, and smelled the whisky on it. 'Of course. But I'd still rather you didn't go.'

'Nothing ventured, Jane. That's why I'm here. You do still want to find out who killed your father-in-law?'

'Not at the expense of another life. No risks, Enzo, please. I don't like the sound of it at all.'

And in truth, neither did Enzo. Everything about the scribbled message in his hand struck discordant notes. He knew perfectly well that it was not Madame Blanc who had put pen to paper to write these words. If she'd had something to say to him she could have said it anywhere, anytime. But someone clearly wanted to get him alone in an isolated and dangerous place, and although it seemed like an obvious trap, he knew that the only way he was likely to find out who had set it was to take the bait.

CHAPTER NINETEEN

'I put a heater in your room this afternoon,' Jane said. 'I'm sorry, I should have done it before. But I didn't realise it was going to be so cold. I'd better show you how to work it.' And she disengaged from his arms and started up the stairs to the bedroom.

Enzo followed her with a strange sense of apprehension in the pit of his stomach. He was perfectly certain that he didn't need Jane Killian to show him how to turn a heater off and on. But he saw the sway of her hips on the stairs ahead of him. Smelled the faint, lingering scent of perfume that she left in her wake. And, bizarrely, he was reminded of the *Ouest-France* journalist's description of the former Arzhela Montin as *fragrant*. It was a long time since he had been with a woman, and his track record for choosing badly was only likely to be enhanced by a whisky-lowered resistance to temptation.

As he climbed the stairs, he tried to persuade himself that he was misreading the signals. But no, the three previous evenings she had undressed in the fully lit bedroom beyond the unshuttered window opposite. His apprehension began to give way to the first stirrings of desire.

The room was already warm when he entered it. Jane said, 'Close the door behind you and keep the warmth in. The heater's been on for a few hours now.'

He saw that the curtains had been drawn on the window. To keep the heat in? Or because she knew that there would be no show tonight. She took her coat off and dropped it on the bed.

'I put it here, under the slope of the ceiling, so that it would help circulate the heat around the room. You should have told me before that it was so cold in here. I'd have done it sooner.' She crouched in front of the heater. 'The controls are at the side here. Two switches, and a thermostat. I've set it to full, with the thermostat at seventy. You can adjust it as you like.' She stood up again and turned to face him. Her face was flushed now, her amber brown eyes wide. They seemed to shine, and Enzo saw a hunger in them, an intent that made his stomach flip over.

She was wearing a tight, v-necked sweater with a neckline that plunged to her cleavage. The light from the lamp on the bedside table seemed to pick out the highlights on her short, brown curls. Enzo found his eyes involuntarily drawn to the contour of her breasts, then back to fine, full lips that bore just a hint of red. His mouth was dry.

'You were watching, weren't you?' she said.

It seemed like a long time before he found a voice to reply. 'Yes.' It was barely a whisper in the still of the room.

'I want you.' Her eyes never left his, as she approached him, slowly, carefully. She stopped in front of him and ran her hands up beneath his jacket to slip it from his shoulders. 'I've wanted you from the moment I set eyes on you.'

Her hands came down again over his chest, unbuttoning his shirt, and then he felt her skin on his. Her palms brushing across his nipples. And he knew he was lost.

Only the light of the digital clock on the beside table lit the room, a faint red glow deepening shadows as they moved in slow unison beneath the sheets. Her skin felt soft and warm against his, and she seemed small and delicate beneath his hands. Her passion had an urgency about it that he calmed with gentle kisses on her neck and shoulders, feeling her rise beneath him, hips pushing hard up against him. Her fingers dug into his back, legs wrapping themselves around him, surprisingly strong. A hand slid past his waist to find him, and hold him, and guide him towards her. His mouth found her nipples, and he felt his own control slipping away.

Then the telephone rang.

'Ignore it.' Her voice whispered breathlessly in the dark.

But it was hard to maintain focus as one long, single ring followed another, penetrating, insistent. He slid his mouth across her breasts, feeling her fingers tighten around him, as the answering machine kicked in, and the voice of a man long dead filled the room.

'This is Adam Killian. Please leave a message after the tone.'

'Shit!' he heard her say, as the long tone sounded. 'I never did change the message.'

A woman's voice followed Killian's. A voice bizarrely familiar to Enzo. But it was a moment before he recognised it.

'Hello, Enzo? I hope this is the right number. Roger gave me it. He said he had no idea when you'd be back. And I can't wait any longer. So if Mohammed won't come to the mountain. . . . '

Jane had stopped moving beneath him, her grip on him slackening. 'Who is it?'

'I'll be arriving on the lunchtime ferry tomorrow. It would be nice if you could pick me up. I take it you've got somewhere I can stay. If not, you can book me a hotel room. I'll see you then.' And she hung up.

Jane and Enzo lay perfectly still in the bed, as if someone had pressed a pause button. The silence between them seemed to last an eternity. Finally, Enzo said, 'That was Charlotte.'

She slid out from under him and rolled away to lie next to him, staring blindly at the ceiling. 'And Charlotte is?'

'A friend.'

'A lover?'

He wasn't sure quite how to respond, and thought about how to frame his reply.

'Too long. Your hesitation tells all.'

'I haven't slept with her for a long time.'

'She seems very keen to see you.'

'We met in Paris before I left. She wanted to talk. But I didn't have time.'

'And she can't wait.'

'Apparently not.'

He heard her slow, steady breathing in the dark. 'I suppose you'll be wanting her to stay here.'

'I don't know. I hadn't thought about it.'

'Well, you wouldn't put her in a hotel, would you?'

'I guess not.'

'And the guest bedroom in the house is filled with boxes. So it'll have to be here.'

'I suppose it will.'

He heard the sound of the covers being thrown back, and she stood up, the silhouette of her naked body just visible in the faint glow of the clock. 'We'd better not soil the bed then. Because I really don't feel like changing the sheets.' She turned on a beside lamp and crossed the floor, picking up her clothes from where she had dropped them.

'Jane . . .'

She started to dress. 'Yes?'

'You don't have to go.'

'I think I do.'

He laid his head on the pillow and closed his eyes, listening to the sound of her pulling on her clothes, then her coat being lifted from the bed. She said nothing as she opened the door, and he heard her footsteps on the stairs, then the front door shutting behind her as she slipped out into the night.

'Damn!' His frustration echoed around the room. It seemed that even though Charlotte was unprepared to commit herself to him, she was still intent, even from a distance, on making sure that no one else could either.

CHAPTER TWENTY

Enzo sat on the terrace of the Café de la Jetée, feeling the sun warm on his face. It had finally burned the chill out of the morning air. The port was quiet today. It was *Toussaint*, All Saints' Day, and most of the shops were shut. Only the bars and restaurants and cemetery remained open.

As usual, however, a line of cars waited for the arrival of the ferry. Enzo had seen it emerging from the haze across the strait some fifteen minutes earlier, watching with an odd sense of dread as it slowly grew larger, cutting its way through water like glass. Triangles of white flashed around it, small sailboats out in the sunshine, circling like scavenging seagulls as it approached the harbour. He could see the faces of passengers on the upper deck, Port Tudy filling their eyes, that sense of excitement and adventure that always accompanied the arrival on an island. A place set apart, different, exotic somehow.

It wasn't until they were disembarking and passengers were coming up the ramp to the jetty, that he finally saw Charlotte amongst them. In spite of himself, he felt his heart skip a beat. She was taller than most of the other passengers, her long, black curls flowing out behind her. Her black coat was open, billowing around her legs as she walked. Beneath it she wore a thick, knitted grey jumper above tight, flared jeans and white trainers. A long red scarf was wrapped around her neck, one end of it over her shoulder and hanging down her back. She carried a small overnight bag. So she didn't, Enzo thought, intend to stay long. And he wondered why she had come.

He left some coins on the table beside his empty Perrier glass, and crossed the cobbles towards the end of the jetty. His head had been a little delicate this morning as a silent Jane drove him into Le Bourg to collect his jeep. She had made no reference to the night before, but the warmth she had shown him previously was gone, like frost replacing sunshine at the end of the day. A coffee and several glasses of carbonated water had banished his headache, and a mild hangover had given way to hunger.

Charlotte kissed him chastely on both cheeks and handed him her overnight bag. Then stood back and ran appraising eyes over him. 'You look tired.'

'Thank you. You look good, too.'

'You obviously got my message, then.'

'Obviously.'

'It was late when I called. I suppose you were out somewhere.'

He didn't want to describe to her the scene in his bedroom when she left her message. But he didn't want to lie either. 'I was at the house of a local doctor and his wife last night. He had some very good whisky.' He smiled. 'Too good. His wife had to run me home.'

She cocked an eyebrow and looked at him with a weary amusement that lacked affection. 'Nothing changes, then.' And he felt reprimanded, like a naughty schoolboy caught smoking behind the bike shed. 'I'm hungry. Can we eat somewhere?'

He knew, as soon as they entered the restaurant, that it had been a mistake to bring her to the Auberge du Pêcheur. The waitress beamed at him. 'It's Monsieur Macleod, isn't it? You were in the other night with Madame Killian.' As if he hadn't noticed.

When she had shown them to their table and taken Charlotte's coat, Charlotte looked at him across the flowers that sat on the table between them. 'Madame Killian?'

'It's her father-in-law's death that I'm investigating. She inherited the house where he was murdered. That's where I'm staying.'

'With her and her husband?'

'She's a widow.'

'Ah. That would explain why you dined alone with her the other night.'

'He died almost twenty years ago.'

Charlotte nodded. 'Okay. A well-practised widow, then. Do you want to tell me about the case?'

'Are you really interested?'

'Yes, I am.'

So he told her. About Killian's call to Jane the night of his murder. The study preserved intact since his death. The notes he had left for his son that made no sense. And about the man whom everyone believed was guilty, but who had been tried and acquitted. She listened intently. Dark eyes wide with genuine interest, intelligent eyes absorbing detail that he knew she would be silently processing, analysing. He had never known anyone with a more analytical mind. And she went straight to the question which had troubled Enzo from the start. 'Why would anyone bother to kill a dying man?'

'It depends on whether or not he knew Killian was dying.'

'But as you describe the situation, he was a man with only a few weeks to live. And must have looked like it. Even his killer would have seen that.'

Enzo nodded. 'It has always bothered me. The only reason I can think of for anyone wanting to kill him . . .'

'Would be to shut him up.' Charlotte finished for him. 'So when he called his daughter-in-law, he wasn't afraid of dying. He was scared of what would die with him.'

'Which is why he left the coded notes for his son.'

'Which nobody can decipher. Will you let me see them?'

'Of course.'

'And this man, Kerjean. What might Killian have known about him that he would have wanted kept secret?'

'Nothing, as far as I can see. The only thing that anyone knows for sure he knew about Kerjean was that he was having an affair with the wife of a town hall official. But by the time Killian was murdered, everyone on the island knew about that. The motive that the police attributed to Kerjean was revenge.'

'For which he would only have needed to wait a few weeks.'

'Death by natural causes is hardly revenge. Besides which,

he might have been drunk, or simply out of control. He is reputed to have a fearsome temper.'

'You seem particularly anxious to follow the Kerjean line. Do you think he did it?'

'Actually . . .' Enzo thought about it. It was good to have someone question him like this, force him to crystallise his thoughts. 'I don't think I do. But there is something about him, and his story, that doesn't ring true. It didn't then, it doesn't now.

For the first time, Charlotte smiled. And a little of the tension she had brought with her seemed to slip away. 'It's an interesting case. Maybe you'll be forced to apply reason this time, rather than science.'

'Or both.'

She tilted her head in smiling acquiescence. 'Or both.'

The waitress brought the slate menu to the table and placed it on a chair. 'The special today is roasted monkfish,' she said, and drifted off, leaving them to make their choice.

Charlotte ran her eye over the long list of choices. 'Where am I staying?'

'Killian's study is in an annex to the house. I have a room above it.'

'Just the one bed?'

He looked at her. 'Is that a problem?'

'I suppose not. I won't be staying long.'

He nodded towards her overnight bag on the floor next to the table. 'I gathered that.' He hesitated. 'Do you want to tell me why you're here?'

She shook her head. 'No. There'll be time for that.' The tension had returned. 'I think I'll go for the special.'

The afternoon sunlight was mellow as it slanted across the ocean from the south-west, losing its strength now, admitting defeat finally to the flow of cold air being dragged by an anticyclone straight down from the arctic. Charlotte gazed from the window of Enzo's jeep across flat, fallow fields and trees shedding their leaves. 'How do people pass their time in a place like this?'

'Like people pass their time anywhere. At home or at work. As you do. You might live in Paris, but you hardly ever set foot over the door.'

She turned a cold look towards him. 'Meaning?'

'Meaning you hardly ever set foot over your door. You live, work, eat, sleep, all in the same place. You might as well live on the moon for all the difference it would make.'

'Except that moon people are notoriously well-balanced and hardly ever need a therapist.'

Enzo grinned. This was more like the old Charlotte. 'That's true. I suppose you need to live in a place like Paris to keep your practice supplied with paranoids and psychotics.'

'Oh, I'm sure there are quite a few in a place like this as well.'

'Yes, but probably not enough to keep you in business.'

At the end of a long, straight stretch, the road dipped down towards the beach at Port Mélite, and Enzo drew his jeep in under the trees. Charlotte got out and walked past the stone benches to look down over the crescent of sand. The breeze from the sea blew her hair back from her face, and Enzo saw her fine, sculpted cheekbones, the line of her jaw, the slightly quizzical upturn of her lips. And he remembered why he had first found her so attractive. 'It's a beautiful spot.' She turned and looked towards the white Killian cottage with its blue shutters. 'Is that it?'

He nodded. 'Yes.'

'Then I suppose it would be only polite to introduce me to Madame Killian before you go dragging me off to your bedroom.'

Jane opened the front door and held it open for them to enter. There was a stiff, oddly formal quality in her demeanour, her smile a little too fixed, slightly strained. 'Come in. Have a seat. Can I get you tea? Coffee?'

'No, thank you.' Charlotte sat in the armchair that Jane had waved her to, crossed her legs and leaned back as if she were visiting an old friend.

Enzo could see Charlotte's look of assessment as she ran her eyes over the Englishwoman. Jane's look of appraisal in the gaze that met it was very similar. Two females of the species, each sizing up the competition the other might offer for the only available male. 'Charlotte's a psychologist in Paris,' he said, hoping to deflect them from the ritual. 'She has her own practice. And actually trained as a forensic psychologist in the States. So the Paris police sometimes ask for her help.'

'Only as a last resort,' Charlotte said. 'God forbid the

chauvinist French police establishment should have to come to a woman for assistance.'

Jane's smile immediately warmed a little, as if she and Charlotte had somehow connected, found a common cause against a mutual enemy. Men. Enzo shifted uncomfortably. He stood up. 'Anyway, I promised to show Charlotte Adam's study. If that's alright. She has a good eye.'

'Of course.' Jane stood up and held her hand out to shake Charlotte's. 'It was nice to meet you. If you need anything over there, just let me know.'

'Thank you, I will.' And as Charlotte and Enzo walked across the lawn through lengthening shadows she said, 'She's an attractive woman.'

'Yes.'

'I suppose you have dinner together every evening.'

'Actually only twice.'

As they reached the door of the annex, the black cat appeared from the side of the building, strutting past Enzo, tail raised, to rub itself against Charlotte's legs. It meowed softly, and a deep rumbling purr started up in its throat. 'Awwww.' Charlotte stooped to stroke it, and it arched its back, pressing up against her hand as she ran it back to the tail. 'What's his name?'

'I have no idea.' Enzo glared at it, and remembered the sensation of needles in his scalp as the cat landed on his head from the top of the study door. And then, again, the scare it had given him, watching from the shadow of the trees as he returned home two nights before.

'Is it Jane's?'

'I don't know whose it is.'

Charlotte looked up, detecting his tone. 'I didn't know you had anything against cats. You like Zeke well enough, don't you?'

'Zeke's not like other cats,' he said, and meant it. Charlotte's cat was more like an alien, with cropped cream fur on a skinny body, and saucer eyes in an overlarge head. 'This one's been haunting me. Prowling around the place at all hours. Even managed to get inside once, I don't know how.'

She laughed and stood up. 'Maybe it's the ghost of Adam Killian.'

But he didn't return her laugh. Almost exactly the same thought had passed through his own mind during those darkly unreal small hours of the morning. Not a serious thought, of course. But the same one to which Charlotte had just given voice. He felt a slight shiver run through him, and wondered if it were just the cold.

He was careful not to let the cat slip in unnoticed this time, holding it at bay with his foot until he had closed the door. He turned on the lights and pushed open the door to Killian's study. Charlotte walked in and stood in the centre of the floor. Her eyes were everywhere, running along the shelves of books, casting their gaze across his desk, the blood stain on the floor. 'Oh my,' she said. 'You can feel him.'

Enzo nodded. 'You can.'

'Such a sense of the man in this room.' She turned towards Enzo. 'Undisturbed for nearly twenty years?'

'Yes.'

'It's like he's still alive. Every facet of him is here. The room is like the embodiment of his spirit. A place where it still resides, still lives.' She turned, bright-eyed, towards him. 'Oh, Enzo, he's talking to us. Telling us about himself. All we have to do is know how to listen. Show me the notes.'

So he took her on a tour of the cryptic messages left by Killian for his son. The message list and Post-it on the fridge. The entry in the desk diary, the Post-it stuck to the desk lamp. The upside down poem on the wall. She shook her head, mystified. 'All in English,' she said. 'If you can't make sense of it, I don't know how I can.' She returned to the bookshelves, and wandered along them, scanning myriad titles. 'What was his profession?'

'He worked at the University of London. An expert in genetics in the field of tropical medicine.'

She raised her head and let her eyes wander along a colourful array of books on the subject. 'Hmmm. Yes. He wasn't English, though, was he?'

Enzo raised his eyebrows in surprise. 'How do you know that?'

She turned and ran her fingertips along a line of books on a middle shelf. 'What native English speaker would have so many books on English grammar and vocabulary? Unless he taught it, of course.'

Enzo smiled. 'Can you tell me what nationality he was?'

'Polish, I'd say.'

This time he raised his eyebrows in astonishment. 'How do you know that?'

She pointed to another line of books on an upper shelf. 'It seems his interest in history extended to only two countries. England and Poland. One his adopted home, the other the land of his birth. That would be my guess anyway.'

'Congratulations, Mademoiselle Roux, you've just won a set of steak knives and a holiday for two in sunny Warsaw.'

This made her smile. But it was a fleeting smile, lost as her focus returned to the room. She crossed to Killian's work bench, touching nothing, but staring at it for a long time. Then she opened the filing cabinet and let her eyes wander along the rows of tabs on the suspension files. A, B, C . . . She slid the top drawer shut and opened the one below it, fingering the files, as if something might communicate itself by touch. Then she crossed to his desk and went through the drawers one by one, touching nothing this time. Just looking. After which she stood for a long time, arms folded, her scarf hanging down almost to her knees, eyes drifting around the room, taking in the pictures and display cases so neatly lined up on the opposite wall, one above the other.

Enzo watched her. He had been attracted to her physically from the first moment he met her. But it was her mind that had seduced him. When they were good together it was wonderful, but that was only too rare. The distance she kept between them frustrated him to distraction. While he would have given himself to her completely, she prized her independence above all else, and had made it only too apparent that she would not give it up for him. He dragged his eyes away from her to look around the room again. 'Killian had a very ordered mind,' he said.

Charlotte looked thoughtful. 'More than ordered, Enzo. Obsessive. This was a man fixated. Everything had to be in its place. A place he created for it.' She pointed. 'And those display cases on the wall. Look at them. He must have measured from the ceiling. And between the frames. I bet there's not a centimetre's difference between them. I can visualise him as a man consumed by the need for routine, of doing the same things in the same way every day. Bringing order to the chaos of life.' She wandered over to look more closely at the display cases. The rows of insects neatly pinned to pristine backboards. 'A man drawn to insects. Creatures that live short, unfettered lives, but lives which also revolve around rite and routine. Think of the bee, the ritual dances, the order of the hive. The organisational qualities of the ant. The apparent randomness of the butterfly. Such a short life, but compelled to spend it flying from one flower to the next – one of nature's pollinators. The lives of insects must have seemed extraordinary to him. Compelling, but contradictory. Free but ordered. Short but intense.'

'So what does all this tell you about him?'

She turned pensive eyes in his direction. 'It would be my guess that this man spent time in prison.'

Of all the conclusions she might have reached, this was not one that Enzo could ever have foreseen. 'Why?'

'People who lose their freedom cling to things that give their lives meaning, Enzo, a reason to exist. Order, routine, ritual, something that marks the passing of time, gives it shape and form.' She raised an eyebrow. 'Am I right?'

'I have no idea. If he was in prison in Britain, or in Poland, Jane either doesn't know or hasn't told me.'

'Better ask her, then. Over one of your dinners together.' And with a dismissive wave of her hand, she banished Adam Killian back to the grave, as if he were of no importance. She was done with him. 'And now you can show me where I'm going to be spending the night.'

He lifted her overnight bag from where he had laid it on a chair, and led her into the hall and up the stairs to the tiny attic bedroom. She looked from the window across a lawn where the last light of the day lay in long, autumn yellow strips, divided and subdivided by the trees along the west side of the garden. The dew was already settling on the grass and would soon turn white as it froze in the tumbling temperatures. She turned her back to the light and cast curious eyes around the room, settling finally on the unmade bed.

Enzo missed the cold that clouded them suddenly. He was distracted. It was almost seven, and he knew it would take him nearly thirty minutes to drive south to the *Trou de l'enfer*, and his rendezvous with the writer of the note. 'I'm going to have to leave you for a while,' he said. 'I have a meeting in half an hour.'

'How long have you been sleeping with her?'

The question came straight out of left field and caught him completely off-guard. 'What?'

'You've only been here four nights. So either you're a very fast worker, or you knew her already.'

Enzo felt his face flush and wondered why he should feel any guilt. She had no right to make him feel guilty. 'What are you talking about, Charlotte?'

She nodded towards the bed. 'Two people slept here last night. A quite separate imprint left by heads on each pillow.'

Enzo glanced towards the rumpled sheets, and saw where Jane's head had left a deep depression on the left-hand pillow. He had spent the night curled up alone on the right side of the bed. He was damned if he was going to defend himself, but he did. 'We've never been mutually exclusive you and I, Charlotte. You were the one who made that the rule, right from the start.'

'Men find love so easily,' she said. 'Or, at least, sex. They always seem to confuse the two. I don't think I want to sleep in a bed where you made love to another woman the night before.'

He sighed his exasperation. 'I didn't. I might have. But your call put a stop to that. You want to hear it?' He crossed to the answering machine on the bedside table. 'Your message will still be on the tape. A real passion killer. What was it Jane said as she left . . .? Oh, yes. "We'd better not soil the bed. Because I really don't feel like changing the sheets."' His finger hovered over the replay button.

'Don't!'

He swung around to face her. 'What do you want, Charlotte? Jane Killian doesn't mean a damned thing to me. But I'm not made of stone. And you're never there.' His voice stopped abruptly, cut off by the shock of seeing the silent tears that ran down Charlotte's cheeks. Her fine, brown eyes were blurred and lost behind them. 'What's wrong?' His question sounded feeble, hopelessly inadequate in the face of her obvious distress. He stepped towards her to lay a hand of concern on her cheek.

But she brushed him aside, crossing to the bed to sit on the very edge of it, her hands folded together in her lap. She seemed oddly crushed, and fragile in a way that belied the strength he knew she possessed. 'I'm pregnant.'

Two simple words, almost whispered, that would change his life forever. The shock of them left him bereft of something to say, and holding his breath. He stood in the silence of the room, hearing the blood pulse through his head. Finally he found his voice. 'How?' And no sooner had he uttered the question than he realised how absurd it was. A thought not lost on Charlotte.

'Law of nature, Enzo. You fuck a woman without protection, there's a good chance your sperm will find her eggs.'

He felt a stab of anger that wasn't entirely without justification. 'I thought you took precautions.' It's what she had always told him.

'Accidents happen.' She wiped away the tears with the back of her hand, and ran a fingertip beneath each eye to remove the smudged mascara. She was regaining control of herself. But it was clear she was hanging on to it by the merest thread.

'When?'

'Oh, about three months ago. Remember, you were up in Paris for that conference? We had dinner. You bought that bottle of Saint Julien. What was it . . .?'

'Château Lalande-Borie, 2004.'

'Yes. And then we went back to my place. Drank armagnac and made love.'

Enzo remembered it well. It had been a long and passionate night. Charlotte had been warm and affectionate during that visit, anxious to spend time with him, almost frenetic in her lovemaking. 'You're sure it's mine?'

Her head came round sharply. A look that might have turned him to stone. 'I'm not like you, Enzo.'

He felt both reprimanded and angry, and fought back. 'I haven't seen you in three months, Charlotte. You haven't returned a single one of my calls. And suddenly you show up out of the blue and tell me you're pregnant – with *my* child.'

Her voice was tight with tension. 'There is no other man in my life.'

'There would be no other woman in mine if you had been prepared to commit to me.' His anger subsided as quickly as it had spiked, and whatever else might have flooded his mind, he believed she was telling him the truth. She was carrying his child.

'I've had a sonogram,' she said. 'It's a boy.'

Enzo closed his eyes. He had two beautiful daughters. And could never have wanted for anything more. And yet somehow, in some way that he had never allowed himself even to think about, a son would have made his life complete.

'I wanted to tell you in Paris. But not in a café, when you were rushing for a train.'

Even as she spoke he remembered his rendezvous, and cursed inside. 'Charlotte . . . can we talk about this later?'

She looked up, eyes wide in disbelief. 'What's wrong with now?'

'I told you I have to go. I have a rendezvous in about twenty minutes. I'm late already.'

'Then cancel it.'

'I can't.' He recalled the words of the note that had been pushed under the door. *I have held my tongue for long enough, monsieur. I will tell you what I know as long as you promise to keep my name out of it. Meet me tomorrow evening at the Trou de l'enfer. I'll wait for you there.*

'What can possibly be more important than this?' The accusation in her eyes was almost more than he could bear. He looked away.

'Nothing, Charlotte. Believe me. But if I miss this chance, there might never be another to learn about Killian's murder.' He drew a deep breath. 'We have the rest of our lives to talk about our child.'

She fixed him with an unblinking focus that was very nearly painful. 'Well. No mistaking where your priorities lie, then. You'd better go.' He returned her gaze, filled with conflicting emotions, before finally turning towards the door. 'But take this thought with you.' He turned back. 'This is *my* child, Enzo. Not *ours*. And any decision about his future will be mine, not yours.'

CHAPTER TWENTY-ONE

Enzo drove through the tiny settlements of Créhal and Kerigant, heading directly south into the deepening gloom, descending at last into a copse of tall Scots pines where a parking area had been hacked out of the mud and stone. When he turned out his lights, everything around him seemed plunged into darkness. He decided to wait for a moment until his eyes had grown accustomed to it. So he sat clutching the wheel in front of him, his thoughts still dominated by Charlotte's news and her parting remark. If she had meant it to haunt him, it had.

Now, for the first time, his focus shifted, and he began to feel apprehensive. He reached into the glove compartment to take out Jane's flashlight and flick it on as he stepped from the jeep. The bitter cold caused the skin on his face to tighten as it made contact. The stink of damp, rotting vegetation assailed his olfactory senses, and in the far distance he heard the roar of the sea, driven against the cliffs by the tide. Killian's scarf was tied around his neck, his jacket buttoned over it, and he wore a thick pair of woollen gloves.

Even so, the cold was already penetrating his outer layers, and he could feel his body temperature dipping. He aimed his flashlight around the car park to pick out a track leading up through a tangle of gorse and bramble to the coastal footpath that led towards the clifftops.

There was no other vehicle visible, and he knew with unerring certainty now that he was allowing himself to be lured into a trap with eyes wide open. If he were to be sensible about it he would get into his car and drive back to resume his conversation with Charlotte. But he knew that to date he had made no progress at all towards dscovering who had murdered Killian, and that this might provide the only fingerhold he had on the case.

He pulled up his collar and headed quickly up the footpath, following it around to his right until the trees opened out into a wide area of rock and grass. It joined a gravel road leading to a wooden gate which was closed but not locked. A sign warned that no vehicles were allowed beyond this point.

There was more light here, the last of it dying in the west as the moon began its steady ascent into the November sky, and he found he could see without his flashlight. He passed through the gate and strode purposefully along the mud track towards the top of the cliffs. He could see light shimmering on the ruffled surface of the ocean beyond, and he heard the growl of it as it beat itself against the rocks a hundred feet below. The southern elevation of the island opened out all around him, and he could see, off to his right, a black slash where the ground fell sharply away into a deep cleft.

Now he heard a sound like wind blowing through trees, and a deep sigh, as of phlegm crackling in a constricted throat. Strangely human, and yet oddly unnatural out here on the clifftops. He saw a sign and turned his flashlight on it. A warning to take extreme care. Here, a father and two children had recently lost their lives, it said. Incongruously, there were three holes in the metal *panneau*, made by what looked like pellets from a shotgun. It wasn't only the cliffs that posed a danger, then.

Rope was pegged along the line of the *trou*, about six inches off the ground, creating a safe passage towards the distant gun emplacement out on the point. But it looked more to Enzo like a tripwire than a safety measure. Signs everywhere warned not to step beyond it.

Enzo edged closer to the innermost edge of the *trou*, and saw that the fissure in the cliffs ran a good hundred yards back from the sea. In the dark, it was impossible to see how deep it went, but the roar of inrushing water was almost deafening, amplified by the widening of the chasm towards its topmost edge, which created a megaphone effect.

He turned then, criss-crossing the ground ahead of him with the beam from his flashlight, and steered a safe course between the ropes out towards the distant point.

As he approached the one-time German gun emplacement, he saw that it was little more than a concrete platform surrounded by a low, broken-down wall. Beyond it lay a slab of concrete at ground level, the roof of the bunker where soldiers on duty must have spent their days and nights sheltering from the elements. The ground around it was strewn with rock and smashed-up pieces of the gun mounting. He picked his way carefully through them until he reached the steps leading down to the door of the bunker. They, too, were broken, and overgrown. He trained his flashlight into the dark below, picking out empty beer cans and the detritus of tourist picnics and teenage misadventures. The acrid smell of stale urine rose to greet him.

He stopped to listen, but could only hear the wind and the sea. 'Hello!' he called, and his voice was immediately whipped away in the breeze and lost in the ether. His earlier apprehension was hardening into fear. He should never have come.

He looked back in the direction of the car park. He had a clear view in the moonlight now towards the distant trees. There was no one to be seen. Nothing to be heard. He could simply head back to his car and drive off. Back to Port Mélite and Charlotte. To ask her what she had meant about the child being hers and not theirs. To hell with Adam Killian and his damned secret messages! What did any of it matter anyway?

But he didn't move, the beam of his flashlight still directed into the darkness below. He cursed his own stubborn stupidity as he touched his fingertips to the wall and began making his way down to the opening where once a steel door had shut out the wind and rain. The door was long gone, as was the glass and even the frame in the window opening beside it. His foot struck an empty beer can that clattered away into the dark, and he stood still again, listening once more, before swinging his flashlight through the doorway and directing its beam into the bunker. A shadow passed through it. He heard a rush of air, and something flew into his face. Something soft, flapping

in panic. He thought he heard a distant scream, before realising it was in his head, and he called out involuntarily. The
flashlight almost fell from his hand as he raised his arms to
protect himself – and then it was gone, whatever it was. Into
the night. And all that he could feel was the pumping of his
heart, and all he could hear was the rasping of his breath. A
bat? A bird? He had no idea. But his legs were like jelly. He
saw now that the bunker was empty. Graffitied walls, a floor
strewn with litter. The stink of human waste.

He turned and ran quickly back up the steps. And as he
emerged on to the open sweep of the clifftops, he felt how
the wind had got up. Stronger than before, and softer in his
face. A change of weather. Milder air from the south-west, and
with it, large swathes of dark cloud scudding overhead. For
a moment, the moon was obscured. Just as if someone had
flicked a switch, the landscape around him was plunged into
darkness. And then light washed again across the cliffs, racing
in from the sea and off across the rise of the land towards the
north-east.

Enzo stepped up onto the broken cement plinth of the gun
emplacement and looked around. There was no one to be seen
anywhere. This had all been a wild goose chase. Someone's
idea of a joke, perhaps. Damn them, whoever they were!

The moon vanished again behind a bank of cloud. He felt,
more than heard, the movement behind him. Some sixth
sense caused him to turn, just in time to see a shadow rise up
above him. Then his head was filled with light and pain, and
he felt his legs buckle beneath him. The concrete beneath his

feet was hard and unforgiving as he hit it with the full force of his body weight, his flashlight clattering away. He heard the air escape his lungs in a rush, and he panicked as, for a moment, he couldn't seem to draw another breath. Then he heard his own voice in his throat, a long, painful gasp, as he finally refilled his lungs.

Half-turning at the scrape of leather soles, Enzo rolled himself over to look up and see a figure looming over him, arms raised to strike again.

From somewhere he found the strength to scramble to his feet, and stagger towards the perimeter wall of the platform, fuelled by pure adrenalin. He tumbled over it, and on to the frost-hardened ground below. He gasped involuntarily as the force of it emptied his lungs once more. But one single, sharp intake of breath, and he was on his feet again. Shaky legs somehow carried him forward, half running, half staggering. He glanced back to see his attacker coming after him, silhouetted against the horizon, moving quickly and easily in his wake.

The moon emerged from behind the clouds, their shadows chasing him back the way he had come, towards the dark line of the trees at the car park. He didn't look back. Just ran. His breath tearing at his lungs now, his body crying out for oxygen to power this sudden, unexpected, and painful burning of energy.

He could hear the footsteps behind him. Closer now. Also running. He felt panic rise inside him. And then the sky carpeted the land below it with darkness again. He was running blind now, back towards the gate and the warning sign peppered with buckshot. He could no longer see it, or anything else.

Something cut into his leg, just above the ankle, and he found himself flying headlong into space. The damned rope pegged around the *trou* to keep people away. And he remembered thinking how it had seemed more like a tripwire than a deterrent. Again he hit the ground, spreadeagled across grass and rock. And as he tried to get to his feet, felt a jarring pain in his right knee. It almost buckled beneath him as he hobbled forwards, uncertain now of his direction.

He could hear the roar of the sea deep in the folds of the *Trou de l'enfer*, a hundred feet below. But the noise seemed to be all around him. He was stunned, confused, but scared to stop. With no idea now where his pursuer was, he turned towards where he thought the gate might be. Light cascaded over the cliffs once more as the wind tugged at his jacket, and he saw the deep, dark slash of the *trou* immediately ahead. Almost at the same moment, the ground beneath his feet slipped away. Frozen mud and rock crumbling and tumbling into darkness, and Enzo felt himself falling through space, down into this crack in the earth that led straight to hell. The call of the devil below filled his ears. And in that moment he knew that his life was over, that whatever Charlotte might have meant by her parting words, it no longer made any difference. His unborn son would never know his father.

For the third time, a hammer blow knocked all the wind from his lungs, and pain filled his world. Arms, legs, head, chest, back. But he was no longer falling. He was lying prostrate, in an odd, twisted position, the wind whipping around him, his ears filled with the sound of the sea venting its anger on unyielding gneiss. By the light of the moon he could see it far below, frothing, phosphorescent, furious that it had failed to claim him.

He lay perfectly still, breathing hard, screwing up his eyes against the pain, frightened to move in case he couldn't. Finally he removed a glove and lifted a hand to his head. He felt warm blood on his temple, then raised himself on to one elbow and bent each leg at the knee. Miraculously, it seemed that there was nothing broken. He tilted his head to look up towards the sky. The lip of the gorge hung ten to fifteen feet above, a wedge of black that cut hard across the sky. He couldn't see any way of getting back up there, and knew that none of the ground around him could be trusted to take his weight.

He seemed to be on a narrow ledge of some sort that ran across the sheer wall of the rock. He let his head fall back, and lay breathing in short, stertorous bursts. If he lay here for long enough he would die of exposure. If he tried to climb back up, the chances were that he would fall to his death.

The line of black above him was broken, suddenly, by a shadow leaning over to peer down into the chasm. Enzo must have been plainly visible, lying twisted on this shelf of rock, and he wondered why his attacker would risk coming so close to the edge. Perhaps to be certain that Enzo was dead and to finish him off if he wasn't. He lay perfectly still, looking up at the silhouette looking down, and both remained like that for some minutes, until finally Enzo could stand it no longer. 'Help!' he shouted. 'Help me!' Though he had no expectation whatsoever that any help would be forthcoming.

Almost immediately, the figure above withdrew from sight, and Enzo was left staring at an unbroken sky, the moon flitting in and out of the clouds, its light switching off and on, like the flickering filament of a dying light bulb. He closed his eyes and listened to the roar of the sea, aware of the light and dark that washed over him, breathing slower now, and feeling his bruised and bleeding body stiffen with the cold.

Finally, he decided that he would risk the exposure rather than the fall, hoping to survive till daybreak and the chance of someone coming by, someone who might hear him calling for help. But even as he thought it, he realised how unlikely it was that anyone would be out along the cliffs in the early morning light. In the season, there was every chance he would be discovered by the dozens of *randonneurs* who trekked around the coastal footpaths. But they were into November now, and tourists to the island were few and far between. He felt the mantle of despair settle on him, like the darkness that fell as the moon vanished yet again.

He was not sure how long he lay, shivering, half-unconscious, before becoming aware of a sound like someone hammering. The repeated smack of metal on metal. Regular strikes, sharp enough to be heard above the constant commotion of the sea. It came from above, and did not sound that far away.

'Hello!' he shouted into the night. 'Is there anyone there?'

And the hammering stopped.

He held his breath. Nothing. No response. The hammering did not restart, as if he had chased it away with his calls. He felt despair settle on him like dust. Maybe he had simply imagined it. He lay listening intently for several minutes, but there was no further sound.

Then suddenly something fell on him, tumbling over him, heavy and rough, and he yelled out in fear and surprise. He sat up, supporting himself on one arm, trying to make sense of it. His fingers closed around something coarse and thick, and he realised it was a rope. Someone had thrown a rope over the edge of the cliff. Long enough that it had coiled around him on the ledge, the end of it falling away from his grasp now and dropping into the darkness below.

He held on to it with both his hands and pulled hard. There was no give whatsoever. It seemed firmly anchored to something up on the clifftops. And yet, he realised, if he was to use it to haul himself up to safety, he would have to trust it completely. With his full weight. The very thought sent shivers of apprehension through him. He could picture himself only too clearly, almost at the top when it gave way, sending him tumbling backward through fresh air to his death.

Who had thrown him this lifeline, and why? Why didn't he show himself and call out to see if Enzo was all right?

'Hello!' Enzo shouted again into the night. 'Goddamnit! Who are you?'

But only the wind replied, moaning through the fissures in the rock and wrapping itself around him, cold fingers robbing him of strength. Even if he decided to trust his life to the rope, he was not certain he had the power left to pull himself out.

Slowly he managed to get to his feet, balancing precariously, forced now to trust the rope. He yanked hard, several times, and still it remained rock solid. He stood for several moments, teeth clenched, eyes closed, summoning the courage and the strength to give it a try.

He pulled up the end of the rope, and wrapped it several times around his waist before knotting it securely. If he fell, and the rope held, he would survive. If the rope failed to hold, he was dead. He reached up as far as he could, grasping the rope with gloved hands, and braced his legs against the face of the rock, pushing himself out. Fully committed now, he knew that his life was in the hands of whoever had secured the other end. It was not so much a question of trust, as of blind faith.

Inch by painful inch, Enzo worked himself up the cliff face, feet searching for footholds to brace him as he moved his hands up the rope, one over the other. His arms began to ache, his legs trembling, his strength ebbing away, slowly but surely. Desperation clutched his heart with icy fingers. He gritted his teeth against the pain and kept going, never once looking up until the very last, when he felt his hand crushed between the rope and the rock, and realised he was almost there. Rock and earth was crumbling all around him, sending showers of debris down into the black. He threw an arm over the top and grasped the rope, pulling with all his might, kicking a leg over the lip of it to give himself extra purchase.

And then he was up on the high crest of the cliffs, fully in the open, shadow and light racing to greet him as he rolled himself over and over until he was sufficiently clear of the edge to feel safe.

He lay on his back looking up at the moon, arms and legs spread wide. And with relief, came an urge to weep. So he closed his eyes and took deep, steady breaths to calm himself, before finally getting stiffly, painfully, to his feet and untying the rope from his waist. He looked around and saw that the rope was tethered to a stout metal crowbar driven at an angle deep into a crack in the rock. It could hardly have been more secure.

He stood shakily, the wind whipping around him, and looked all along the line of the cliffs and back towards the woods. There was no sign of either his attacker or his rescuer. And he wondered if they were one and same person, and if so, why? All he knew was that by some miracle he was still alive, and he was grateful for that.

He stepped over the rope that delineated the supposedly safe walking area and started stiffly back towards the car park.

It was with an enormous sense of relief that he slipped into the driver's seat and pulled the door shut. He started the engine, turned the heater up full, and laid his head back against the headrest and closed his eyes. Every muscle in his body ached. He waited until the engine had warmed up and he felt the heat coming through, before slipping the jeep into reverse gear and accelerating backward to turn. The whole vehicle shuddered and he almost stalled it. He braked, slipped into first, and tried to go forward. The same thing.

Enzo opened the door and jumped out to see what was wrong. The offside front tyre was flat. He cursed out loud and raised his eyes to the heavens. To have to change a wheel now, after all he had been through, would be the final straw. With anger fuelling determination, he stalked around to where the spare wheel was bolted to the back of the vehicle. Which is when he noticed that the rear offside tyre was flat as well. And the rear nearside tyre. Despair gave way to anger as he walked briskly to the other side of the jeep and saw that the front nearside tyre was also flat. He crouched down to run the tips of his fingers over the deep slash cut into the tyre wall, and closed his eyes, breathing out through clenched teeth.

Not content with almost killing him, his tormentor was determined that he would now have to walk across the island in the dark to get back to Le Bourg. Enzo stood up slowly and leaned both hands against the roof of the jeep, his anger simmering dangerously inside him.

There would be a reckoning.

CHAPTER TWENTY-TWO

Lights burned in several windows of the doctor's house as Enzo pushed open the gate and followed the path through the jungle that was the front garden up to the door. He heard the weary hammering of his knock echo along the hallway behind it. And after a moment, footsteps approaching. The door opened, and the Servats' elder daughter, Oanez, peered out at him.

For a moment her face was frozen in something like shock, or disbelief, before she let out a shriek that almost burst Enzo's eardrums. He recoiled, startled, as Elisabeth, followed by Alain, appeared hurriedly in the hall behind her and looked at him in astonishment.

The doctor said, 'For God's sake, man! What's happened to you?'

It wasn't until he saw his reflection in the hall mirror that Enzo realised why Oanez had screamed as she had. His face was streaked with dried blood. Most of his hair had pulled itself free of the band that held it in a ponytail, and, where it wasn't matted with blood, hung wild and unkempt over his shoulders. His jacket and trousers were bloodstained and filthy, the lower half of his right-hand trouser leg almost hanging off where it was torn open at the knee. He was pale with the cold, and shivering.

'Come in, come in, for Heaven's sake.' Elisabeth took his arm and led him through the dining room to the kitchen and sat him in a chair at the kitchen table. The whole family gathered round to stare at him as he described how he had been attacked at the Point de l'Enfer and fallen into the *trou.*

Alain boiled up some water and poured in disinfectant, and began methodically cleaning the wounds and scrapes around his head as he talked, holding him steady as he winced from the pain of the antiseptic. He didn't tell them who he had been expecting to meet, or why. Only that it was connected in some way with his investigation into the Killian murder.

'Did you get a look at who did it?' Elisabeth said.

Enzo shook his head. 'It was too dark.'

Alain tipped his head to one side and dabbed carefully at a gash on his right temple. 'But you have your thoughts?'

'I do.'

'And?'

'It could only have been Kerjean.'

Elisabeth said, 'Are you sure?'

'No. But if it wasn't him and he didn't murder Killian, then it must have been the real killer who attacked me out there.'

Alain secured a dressing over the wound. 'And do you have any idea who that might be?'

Enzo breathed out his frustration. 'No, I don't.'

Alain stood back and looked at him. 'You're going to be

black and blue by tomorrow, Monsieur Macleod.' He smiled wryly. 'You'll make a pretty sight.' Then he crouched down to examine Enzo's knee and drew a sharp breath. 'Going to have to get these trousers off you, I'm afraid. That's a terrible gash in your knee. I might have to put stitches in it.'

The girls were sent out of the kitchen as Enzo removed his trousers with difficulty. Then he sat with eyes closed while Alain cleaned the wound and injected anaesthetic into the knee, before taking needle and thread and closing it up with four neat stitches. The doctor smeared his handiwork with disinfectant cream before placing a dressing over it.

When Enzo opened his eyes again, he found Elisabeth there holding out a glass. He smelled the whisky immediately.

She smiled. 'Something for the pain.'

He took the glass with still trembling fingers and sipped a mouthful of amber heaven, letting it trickle slowly back over his tongue, burning down his throat and into his chest. 'I don't know how to thank you both,' he said. 'During the walk back across the island, the only thing that kept me going was the thought of getting here. I'd never have made it back to Port Mélite.'

'Well, I'm glad it was us you came to. Here.' Elisabeth passed him his trousers. 'I've sewn up the knee.' She grinned at her husband. 'A little more neatly than Alain did yours.'

'I made a wonderful job of it,' Alain said. He smiled at Enzo. 'Don't listen to her. You'll be left with barely a scar. But you'll probably need a new pair of trousers.'

They each supported an arm as Enzo stood up to pull his

trousers back on, and then slump into his chair again to finish his whisky.

'Now,' Alain said, 'we'd better call the police.'

'No,' Enzo said quickly.

Elisabeth looked at him, perplexed. 'But, Enzo, someone just tried to kill you.'

Enzo shook his head. 'I don't think so. If he'd meant to kill me, I'd be dead by now, or still lying on that ledge. The irony of it is, he actually saved my life. Whatever his intentions, killing me wasn't one of them.'

Alain said, 'But he attacked you, assaulted you, slashed your tyres. These things are all matters for the police.'

But again, Enzo simply shook his head. 'No. They're between him and me.' He looked up to see their shared disapproval. 'But I'd very much appreciate it if one of you could run me home.'

Alain took the SUV right up to the gate of the Killian cottage and came around to the passenger side to help Enzo out. All of Enzo's muscles had stiffened up, and he was finding it hard to move. The anaesthetic had also worn off, and his knee was hurting like hell.

'Do you need a hand into the house?'

'No I'll be alright from here, thanks.' Enzo shook his hand. 'I owe you, doctor.'

'You owe me nothing. Just take care that none of those wounds becomes infected. Come and see me if things aren't healing properly.'

'I will.'

By the time Enzo had reached the door of the cottage, Alain had reversed back to the parking area and turned the SUV. Enzo watched as the headlights dwindled into the distance, and turned as the door opened.

Jane's initially cold expression dissolved immediately to shock, and then concern. 'Oh, my God! What's happened?'

'It's a long story.'

She took Enzo's arm as he hobbled into the warmth of the living room to find Charlotte curled up in one of the armchairs. Discarded dinner plates lay on the floor, and glasses of red wine stood on the tables beside each chair. 'We were hungry and couldn't wait for you,' she said. And then saw the state that he was in. She stood up, immediately anxious. 'My God, Enzo! Are you alright?'

'Not really. Turned out it wasn't so much a rendezvous as a trap.'

Charlotte said, 'What happened?'

He slumped into the settee and let his head fall back. 'If you put a drink in my hand I might think about telling you.'

'I'd better open another bottle, then,' Jane said. 'And I'll heat up something for you to eat.'

It was almost an hour before Charlotte helped Enzo across the lawn in the dark to the annex. They heard the cat before they saw it. It emerged meowing, and running from the shadows, to press itself up against Charlotte's legs as it had done earlier. Enzo hissed at it and it ran, startled, back into the darkness.

'Poor thing,' Charlotte said.

He unlocked the door, and they immediately felt the chill as they stepped inside. When they got to the bedroom, Enzo turned on the heater and glanced out of the window. The shutters on Jane Killian's windows were firmly closed tonight and would, he imagined, remain so for the rest of his stay. Which, in many ways, was a relief. He turned to find Charlotte watching him. She was slightly flushed from too much wine, her eyes almost glassy.

'You shouldn't be drinking,' he said.

'Why not?'

'You're pregnant.'

'I'm not sure what gives you the right to care. It's me who's carrying him, not you. Though maybe not for much longer.'

He stood completely still, staring at her. 'What do you mean?'

'I haven't decided yet whether to go ahead with it or not.'

The shock of her words stung him, like a slap in the face. 'You wouldn't . . .'

'The child deserves better than us, Enzo. And what kind of father would you make? Think about it. Are you someone your son could look up to? Twice married, old enough to be his grandfather. Climbing into bed with every other woman he meets, drinking too much.' She paused for emphasis. 'Putting your work ahead of family and friends.'

'That's not fair!'

'Isn't it? Take a good look at yourself, Enzo.'

And the words of the Scots bard, Robert Burns, came back

to him. *O wad some power the giftie gie us, to see oursels as ithers see us.* He closed his eyes. After all the years of estrangement from Kirsty, they had in the end reached a kind of rapprochement. Sophie, he knew, adored him. His career in forensic science had been replaced by a new one teaching biology and forensics at a top university. He hadn't done so badly. But after Pascale's death he had searched, and failed, to find love. Her life – and death – had shaped his.

'And then, what kind of mother would I make? A singular woman. Idiosyncratic, eccentric, way too independent. I'm just as brutal in my own self-analysis, Enzo. Would I be prepared to give up my work, my independence, my life? I've never done it for any man. If I were to do it for a child, my life as I know it would be over. By the time I got it back, you'd be seventy. And what would I have to look forward to then? Caring for you into old age?'

'If that's how you feel . . . I mean, if you're really serious about terminating the pregnancy, why did you even tell me about it? What did you come here for?'

She turned dark eyes on him, and he felt their intensity. 'I was hoping you might give me a reason not to.' There was a long silence. Then, 'And what do I find? The night before I get here you've been drinking too much and end up in bed with another woman. You'd have slept with her if I hadn't phoned when I did. And now you're out getting into fights in the dark and falling off cliffs. It would be laughable if it wasn't so serious.'

He held her gaze. His voice was low and steady. 'I'll give

you one perfectly good reason why you shouldn't have an abortion.'

'Yes?'

'We created a life together, Charlotte. But we have no right to end it.'

She gasped in frustration and turned away. 'I didn't know you'd found religion in your old age.'

'I haven't. But I've spent a lifetime catching people who take lives. I'm not about to sanction the taking of one myself, just because it might not be convenient to you.'

She turned back. Eyes blazing. 'He's not growing inside of you, Enzo. You don't have to give birth to him. And where are you going to be when he's growing up?'

'Right there. Sharing the responsibility.'

'Oh? Just like you were with Kirsty?'

Of all the wounds inflicted on him on this dark November night, that was the deepest, and hurt the most. Not least because it was so unfair. 'I never turned my back on Kirsty,' he said. 'Never. It was her mother who closed that door on me. Used her own daughter as a stick to beat me with.' But no matter how many times he told himself this simple truth, he still couldn't shake off his sense of guilt.

They lay in bed, not touching, both of them awake in the dark for a very long time. Enzo lay on his back, staring blindly at the ceiling. Everything that had happened to him tonight was somehow overshadowed by Charlotte's situation. For the first time in his life he wished he were twenty years younger, and regretted the wasted years and the passage of time. Time that was against him. Charlotte's bald statement of fact that by the time their son had reached adulthood Enzo would be seventy had stunned him. He still saw himself as the young man he had been thirty years before. The idea that he would be seventy in the not too distant future was shocking. Seventy! How was it possible? Where had his life gone? And yet to think like that, he knew, was to throw away all the good years to come, to accept the mantle of old age and discard his youth as spent, like the greater part of a dwindling fortune.

He was not quite sure when it was that he finally drifted off into an uneasy slumber, but when he awoke with a start from some disturbing dream, the digital read-out on the bedside clock showed 2.43. He lay for several minutes, listening to his own breathing, before becoming aware that Charlotte was no longer in the bed beside him. He turned his head and saw the light from the stairwell in cracks around the door, and reluctantly he slipped from the warmth of the sheets to find his dressing gown and slippers.

Charlotte was sitting in the captain's chair behind Killian's desk, the black cat curled up on her lap. She ran gentle fingers back through its long fur, and Enzo could hear it purring from the door.

'I heard him meowing outside and let him in. I hope you don't mind.'

'Would it matter if I did?'

She smiled. 'No.' Then, 'I couldn't sleep.'

He nodded.

'I spent some time looking at Killian's notes.'

'And?'

She shrugged. 'Perhaps if they were in French. But I can make no sense of them.'

He moved into the study, closing the door behind him, and sat in the chair facing her. 'So what did you talk about tonight, you and Jane?'

'Oh, all sorts of things. She's a sad creature, Enzo.'

'How so?'

'Her parents split up at an early age, and she never really bonded with either of them. It was one of the reasons she was so drawn to Peter. His relationship with his father. The first time, she said, she'd known a real family. Like being a part of something special. I think she was as much in love with Adam as with Peter.'

Enzo shook his head. 'My God, you never stop playing the psychologist, do you?'

'I don't play at it, Enzo. It's what I do. People find it easy to talk to me. You did once, too.'

'Don't project your faults on to me. You're the one who never talks, never telling me what's in your head. I'm a damned open book.'

She scratched the cat under its chin, ignoring Enzo's jibe. Whatever thoughts they had provoked, she wasn't about to divulge them. The cat stretched its head back, eyes closed. 'Killian himself would have made an interesting subject. The immigrant who sees his heritage as a stain on his new nationality. A Pole who wanted to be more English than the English and, when he couldn't quite achieve it for himself, invested all the time and effort in his son. He turned Peter into the archetypal Englishman, baptised in the Church of England, sent to public school.'

Enzo chuckled. 'And educated at a Scottish university.'

'I don't think Adam Killian saw any difference. Only the Scots see themselves as different from the English. To the rest of the world British, English, Scottish, it's all same thing.' She cocked an eyebrow and tilted her head, expecting a challenge. When none came, she just shrugged. 'Anyway, Adam made sure that no one would ever know that Peter's roots couldn't be traced all the way back to the Norman conquest. They played word games together when Peter was still a boy. All designed to expand his vocabulary, provide him with an unassailable grasp of the language, mould him into the Englishman Adam had always aspired to be.' She gazed thoughtfully off into the middle distance. 'Jane's tragedy was that she lost them both within a few weeks of each other. No sooner had she found her family than she lost it.' She looked up. 'A little like you, I suppose, with Pascale.'

Enzo nodded. The thought had not escaped him.

The cat stretched and stood up, before stepping gingerly onto the desk top and looking cautiously at Enzo from a safe distance.

'And what did any of it matter? That search for an identity, a nationality. With both of them dead, the family line ended there.' She paused. 'Just as mine will end with me, unless I have a child. I guess that's the thing about being the daughter of adoptive parents. With no surviving blood relatives that I know of, I feel a certain responsibility. A certain reluctance to let my passing be the end of a whole thread of human history. But that is a decision I have yet to make.' She examined Enzo in the cold, harsh light of Adam Killian's study. 'Not a problem for you, of course. With two daughters that we know of, and God knows how many other progeny that we don't.'

Air exploded from Enzo's lips in exasperation. 'That's completely unfair, Charlotte. I've made mistakes in my life, sure. Who hasn't? But I'm not the one who's kept our relationship at arm's length. And I'm certainly not going to walk away from the responsibility of our child.'

Charlotte ran the flat of her hand back over the cat's head, following the curve of the spine to its tail. 'Maybe. But I'll tell you this. Whether or not I have the baby is a decision I will be making on my own.'

And Enzo felt a chilling sense of finality in this.

CHAPTER TWENTY-THREE

The landscape through which he had trudged in the dark looked very different in the sunshine of the following morning. Picture postcard clouds, like tufts of cotton wool, tumbled across a watercolour wash of pale blue, and the insipid yellow November sunshine brought the warmth of the south with it on the edge of a brisk wind.

The mechanic from Coconut's said little as he navigated his Land Rover among clusters of cottages, winding through rolling countryside towards the flat, open clifftops of the southern elevation. Before leaving the garage he had listened to Enzo's tale of tyre-slashing vandalism with an ill-concealed scepticism, passing thoughtful eyes back and forth over the Scotsman's bruised and battered face. Whatever he believed, he merely muttered oaths and imprecations. Then he threw four spare wheels in the back of the Land Rover.

They would, he said, have to report this to the *gendarmes*, and Enzo's insurance would be picking up the tab.

In the parking area at the *Trou de l'enfer*, the mechanic examined each of the tyres and shook his head in disbelief. 'Never saw anything like it,' he said. 'Not here, not on the island. It could only have been an incomer that did this, monsieur.'

'You've been here a long time, then?'

'All my life.'

'Always worked at Coconut's?'

His laugh was sour. 'No, monsieur. I used to have my own garage in Port Tudy. Service and repair. It was a good going business until that damned trial.' He opened his tool box and prepared to start jacking up the jeep.

Enzo frowned. 'The Kerjean trial?'

'Damn defence lawyer destroyed my reputation, monsieur. And those customers that gave evidence, claiming my work was substandard? Lying bastards! All with axes to grind. But it's hard to keep a business going in a place this size when folk spread those kind of stories about you. It was in all the newspapers, and on the telly.'

And Enzo realised that this was Michel Locqueneux, the mechanic who had serviced Kerjean's car the day before the murder. 'So what did you really think, then, of Kerjean's story about his car breaking down?'

Locqueneux shifted his focus away from the wheel nuts he was loosening to cast a withering look in Enzo's direction. 'He was a damn liar! There was nothing wrong with that car. If he'd really had a problem, why didn't he call me? Kerjean's not the sort to let something like that go.'

'He claimed to have fixed it himself.'

'Hah! Kerjean couldn't change a wheel on a toy motor, monsieur, and I doubt if he's ever lifted the bonnet of a car in his life. Except maybe to top up the wash-wipe. He might be good with words, but he doesn't know the first thing about cars.' He pulled off the front nearside wheel, and it rolled away a couple of metres before toppling over.

'You didn't say anything about that in court.'

'No one asked me, monsieur. The *procureur* was an idiot, and the defence lawyer was too busy trying to make me look like one.'

Enzo watched, then, in thoughtful silence as Michel Locqueneux changed all four wheels, stewing in his own bitter memories. When, at last, he was finished, Enzo said, 'Kerjean still lives in Locmaria, doesn't he?'

'More's the pity. There's not a soul on this island who wouldn't have liked to see the back of him eighteen years ago.'

'Except for a certain number of ladies, I gather.'

Locqueneux curled his lips in distaste. 'God knows why. Must be some kind of animal attraction he has. Because that's what he is, monsieur. An animal.'

Locmaria was built around a sandy bay on the south-east corner of the island, a jumble of fishermen's cottages tumbling down the hill to the beach and a handful of houses that looked out over the water towards the harbour wall and a rocky promontory beyond.

Enzo parked opposite Le Bateau Ivre, which translated literally as *the drunken boat*, a pub whose darkened windows were filled with strange *papier mâché* pantomime characters. Captain Hook. Puss 'n Boots. He peered through the glazed panels of the door and saw a young man moving around inside behind the bar. He pushed at the door and it scraped and rattled as it juddered open. A bell rang.

'Sorry, monsieur. We're closed.' The young man was sweeping out.

'I'm looking for Thibaud Kerjean's house.'

The man paused mid-sweep and peered at Enzo. If he recognised him, he made no sign of it. 'And what would you be wanting with a man like that?'

'A little chat.'

'Pfff.' The young man exhaled through lips pressed against his front teeth. 'You're more likely to get a mouthful.'

'I take it this is his local watering hole?'

'It would be, monsieur. Except that he's barred. He does his drinking in Le Bourg.'

'So where will I find his house?'

'Take the road around the east side of the bay, monsieur. There's a row of cottages facing the water. Kerjean's is the stone-faced house with the well in the front garden.'

Numerous small sailing vessels and fishing boats were moored out in the still waters of the bay, whitewashed cottages on the rise above the rocks along the west side, the sea beyond glinting like cut crystal in the low-angled sunlight. Enzo walked past several cottages facing west across the bay, stopping finally at the dry stone wall that bounded the garden of a neat, stone-faced cottage with a cobbled courtyard and a circular stone well sunk in its centre. A battered green Citröen van sat out in the courtyard. White shutters were opened on the windows and two sets of *portes-fenêtres*. The three dormers in the roof were all shuttered over.

Enzo walked to the front door where a black anchor hung on the wall. He breathed deeply, summoning resolve and determination, and pulled the rope on an old ship's bell bolted to the stonework. The peal of it rang sharply out across the bay, startling a line of seagulls on the quayside. There was no sound or sign of life from within. He rang the bell again. More vigourously this time. It was more than possible that Kerjean was still sleeping off whatever excesses he might have indulged in the night before.

Finally, he saw a movement behind the glass, and the door swung open. Kerjean looked bad in the cold light of day which revealed a sickly pallor and deep shadows beneath his eyes. Silvered stubble covered his face, and his hair was a bird's nest of tangled, greasy curls. He wore a flannel robe, and his bare feet drew the cold from a stone-flagged floor. He squinted at Enzo from behind puffy eyes.

'What the fuck do you want?'

'A word.' Enzo heard the tightness in his own voice.

Kerjean stared at Enzo for a long time, conducting some internal debate. At length he said, 'You look like shit.'

'So do you.'

And for the first time, Enzo saw a smile light Kerjean's face. The man whom everyone believed had murdered Killian let the door swing open and he turned away into the interior without a word. Enzo followed him into a large, square kitchen. Next to the door was a window that would flood the room with pink light at sunset. Opposite, a panelled glass door led out to an east-facing terrace. A long table sat in the centre of the room. A wood-burning Rayburn stove was set against the north wall, while cupboards and cabinets lined the others, shelves cluttered with jars and glasses and crockery. A little residual warmth emanated from the stove, and the table was littered with half a dozen empty beer bottles and the congealed debris of the previous night's meal.

Enzo closed the door behind him. Kerjean found a pack of cigarettes on the table and lit one. He turned towards the Scotsman. 'So what word do you want, exactly?'

Enzo glared at him, barely able to hide his anger. 'You bastard!'

Kerjean stood his ground and smirked. 'That's two words. And I've heard them before.'

'You nearly killed me last night.'

'I saved your bloody life, for what it's worth.'

'You don't deny it, then?'

'Why should I? It's just you and me here and now. Your word against mine.'

'Why did you do it?'

'Why did I do what?'

'Save my life.'

'Contrary to popular opinion, monsieur, I am not a killer. But in spite of all my warnings, you'd been nosing around asking about me, poking your nose into the past. So I decided it was time to rough you up a bit, provide a little incentive to send you on your way.' He chuckled. 'But I didn't expect you to go throwing yourself into the *Trou de l'enfer*.'

Enzo's anger rose up through him as if from his feet. A sudden, unstoppable surge of it, fuelled by a furious rush of adrenalin. Kerjean never saw the big fist that swung at him out of the gloom until it hit him square on the side of the head, sending him crashing across the kitchen table. His legs buckled and he toppled on to a chair, and then to the floor.

Enzo heard the sound of Kerjean's head striking hard, unyielding stone, but in that moment he was more concerned with the pain in his hand. Sharp, stabbing, all-consuming. He called out involuntarily and clasped and unclasped his fist, waving it around, as if it might be possible to shake away the pain. For a moment, he feared he had broken bones, and was relieved to find that all his fingers could still move. He rubbed the palm of his left hand soothingly over knuckles that were already beginning to swell.

Kerjean was stunned, pulling himself first to his knees, then steadying himself with a hand on the table as he swayed from side to side, blood trickling from a split cheek and a gash on the opposite temple. He shook his head and growled. A deep, feral growl that rose up from his diaphragm, and Enzo was reminded of Michel Locqueneux's description of him as an animal. Kerjean dragged himself to his feet and turned murderous eyes on Enzo.

Enzo faced him down, breathing hard, heart pounding, fist aching, but clenched once more, ready to strike again in spite of the pain. Perhaps it was something he saw in Enzo's eyes, a determination to stand his ground no matter the consequences, that extinguished the fire in Kerjean. He was ten years younger than Enzo, and still fit despite his drinking. Had he chosen to make a brawl of it, he would almost certainly have come out on top. Instead, he went almost limp, all the tension draining from him, and he stooped to pick up his cigarette from where it had fallen on the floor.

'I suppose maybe I deserved that,' he said, and he drew a deep lungful of smoke, touching his fingertips to his cheek, feeling the blood and then looking at it on them.

Enzo saw the change of body language and relaxed a little. But he was still tense, and still hurting. 'For God's sake, man, why don't you just tell me where you were the night of the murder?'

Kerjean flicked him a surly glance. 'You must know the story by now.'

'Only the one you told at the trial. But your car was running perfectly, Kerjean, and you're no mechanic. So why wasn't it sitting out there the night that Killian was murdered.' He tipped his head towards the door, and the courtyard beyond.

Kerjean stared at the stone flags, taking several long drags at his cigarette, before crossing to a cupboard and lifting out a bottle of Islay malt and two glasses. He banged the glasses on the table and filled them both. Then he lifted one and held it out to Enzo.

Enzo hesitated. Much as he enjoyed a glass of good Islay whisky, it was only just after ten in the morning, and this much whisky could ruin the rest of the day. But he felt that he was on the point of a breakthrough here, and he didn't want to let it slip through his fingers. He lifted the glass. '*Slàinte*.'

'*Yec'hed mat*.'

Both men sipped at the pale liquid in silence.

Kerjean ran his tongue over dried lips, savouring the taste of it. 'I love that smoky, peaty taste of the island whiskies. It's like drinking the earth itself. It connects you to the ground that feeds you.'

Enzo nodded, saying nothing, waiting for Kerjean to speak. And even as he looked at him he saw, for the first time, beyond the image that the world had of him. There was a strangely attractive quality about his eyes, and the line of the jaw. Even the way he held himself. A kind of dignity, not yet entirely excoriated by the drink.

'I was with someone who shouldn't have been with me.' His voice sounded slightly hoarse, as if reluctant to give up the secret it had held for so long.

'A woman?'

Kerjean pursed his lips and cast Enzo a look. 'What do you think?'

'But you'd only just broken up with Arzhela Montin.'

Kerjean took another mouthful of whisky, and swilled it around his gums. 'I can't help it, monsieur, that women find me attractive. Or, at least, used to. When I was younger. And sober.' He paused. 'Arzhela was gone.'

'Why didn't you tell that to the police?'

Kerjean sucked in more whisky, followed by more smoke,

and turned dead eyes on his visitor. 'I might be many things, monsieur, but I would never betray a woman's trust.'

'Even if it meant going to prison?'

'Even if it had meant that.' He held Enzo steady in his gaze, almost as if challenging the Scotsman to contradict him.

'Then it's a pity the women in your life didn't show the same loyalty to you.'

Kerjean frowned. 'What do you mean?'

'You always believed that it was Killian who told Montin about you and his wife. It wasn't.'

In the nearly sixty seconds of silence that followed, Enzo became aware for the first time of the slow tick, tock of an old grandfather clock in the corner of the room. 'How can you possibly know that?'

'Because I know who told him.'

'Who?'

Enzo took another sip of his whisky. 'Tell you what, Monsieur Kerjean. You tell me who you were with that night, and I'll tell you who told Montin about you and Arzhela.'

Kerjean drained his glass and put it on the table to refill it. He waved the bottle towards Enzo. 'Another?'

Enzo had barely drunk half of his. He shook his head.

Kerjean raised his own to his lips and took another large mouthful. Then he turned his gaze back towards Enzo. 'No,' he said. It was a simple, and very final, statement.

Enzo placed his glass carefully on the table. 'In that case, as far as I'm concerned you stay right in the frame for Killian's murder, Kerjean. Until, or unless, I find out different.'

CHAPTER TWENTY-FOUR

Doctor Jacques Gassman's cottage stood at the end of a long, narrow, pot-holed road that cut through the banks of gorse and broom that smothered the moor between Quéhello and the sea. Its freshly whitewashed walls contrasted sharply against the crisp, clean blue of the ocean beyond. The shadows of clouds passed across the moor like riderless horses, and Enzo saw smoke whipped away from Gassman's chimney top by the stiff sea breeze.

As he parked at the side of the house and stepped out into the freshening sou'westerly, he smelled the wood smoke. The bittersweet smell of oak, not dissimilar to the smell of the peat they burned in the Scottish north-west.

He went around to the front garden, pushing open a rickety green gate, and knocked on the door. There was no response. He knocked again, and saw the doctor's Range Rover parked in the shelter of a lean-to on the far side of the house. So the old boy was at home. He tried the door handle and found that the door was not locked. He pushed it open, and leaned in to a gloomy living room with a staircase at the far side. Several doors led off from it. The only one that was open revealed a tiny kitchen, sunlight streaming into it from a south-facing window.

'Hello?' His voice sounded dully in the silence of the house. He heard the tick of a clock, saw oak embers glowing in the *cheminée*, smelled wet dog hair, and from the kitchen something simmering on the cooker. Soup or a stew. 'Hello?' Still nothing.

He pulled the door closed and walked back up the path to the gate. The tiny patch of lawn was bald in places, over-grown in others, flowerbeds choked with weeds. He supposed that when you were in your nineties, caring for your garden slipped down the list of priorities.

Then, in the distance, his eye was caught by a flash of red scarf, and the sound of a dog barking carried on the wind. He saw the familiar blue peaked hat of the old doctor just above the line of the thicket and realised he must be out walking his dog. Enzo set off along the still frozen mud track to greet him. They met a few hundred metres from the house.

'How are you, Monsieur Macleod?' Gassman grinned to show off his too white, too even dentures and grasped Enzo's hand firmly in his. His golden Labrador was old, too, and walked stiffly like his master. He looked up at Enzo with sad, world-weary eyes and sat down to wait patiently until the two men would finish talking. 'What on earth have you done to your face?'

Enzo's hand went instinctively to the bruising below his eye. 'A nasty fall.'

Gassman regarded him thoughtfully for some moments. 'It's a fine morning.'

'It is.'

'Old Oscar likes nothing better than to take me out for a walk on a morning like this.' He ruffled the dog's head. 'That right, boy?' He grinned. 'It's thanks to Oscar I'm still alive.'

'Oh? How's that?'

'The walking, Monsieur Macleod. Out every day in all weathers. Four, five kilometres sometimes. I would prescribe it to anyone with a dodgy heart or ambitions for longevity.' He grinned. 'That and the odd glass of whisky.'

They turned and started walking, by unspoken consensus, back towards the house. The two men and the dog.

'You've not been out this way before?'

'No.'

'Then you'll not have seen the monument to your fellow countrymen.'

Enzo looked around, surprised, seeing nothing but empty moorland. 'Monument?'

Old Gassman smiled. 'Well . . . a commemoration. But a well-kept one. They're not forgotten, those men that died here.'

The monument turned out to be two dark blue plaques bolted to a rock in a tiny clearing in the thicket. A short path led to it from the main track. There was a representation of a twin-engined airplane painted with the markings of the RAF. Inscribed in white beneath it was the legend, *They saw Groix for the last time – 12 August 1945*. And the names of four British airmen who had died when their plane crashed on the island. Their ages ranged from twenty-two to twenty-six.

'Such a waste of young lives,' Gassman said. 'Even though it was the British who bombed Lorient to oblivion, the locals preferred them to the Germans. It takes a long time for a nation to live down the humiliation of occupation. The Germans were still hated here when I arrived in the sixties.' He chuckled. 'I should know. I was mistaken for one by a few folk when I came at first.'

Enzo turned curious eyes on the old man. 'Why?'

'My accent, monsieur. And, I suppose, my name. It's a little Germanic.'

'So where are you from, originally?'

'Alsace.' He chuckled. 'Over the years, it has been German as much as it has been French. So it's probably not surprising that my accent made me sound a bit like one of the *Boche*. And it was just over fifteen years since the Germans had left, so the hatred was still fresh in the memory.'

'Was it hard, then, to be accepted here, as an incomer?'

'No, no. A doctor is very quickly at the heart of any community, Monsieur Macleod. Folk forget all about where you're from when you're prescribing something to take away their pain.' He laughed. 'Or draining a carbuncle.'

They retraced their steps towards the track that led back to the house.

'So what is it that brings you away out here then?' the old man said. 'Not the pleasure of my company, I'm quite sure.'

Enzo smiled. 'Just a couple of questions, doctor, that I thought you might be able to answer for me. Regarding one of your former patients.'

The old doctor flicked sharp eyes towards the younger man. 'I'm still bound by the Hippocratic oath, you know.'

'I understand that. And I wouldn't dream of asking you to breach it.'

'Good. Because I wouldn't. What patient are we talking about?'

'Thibaud Kerjean.'

'Ahhhh. I should have seen that coming.' He shook his head sadly. 'As a doctor there's not much I can tell you about him. It's plain for everyone to see that the man has a problem with the drink. And the most I ever treated him for were the cuts and bruises he got from brawling in bars.' He pointedly scrutinised Enzo's bruised and cut face.

'I guess, as a doctor in the practice, you must have known that Adam Killian was terminally ill?'

'Yes, I did. But I don't see what that has to do with Kerjean.'

'I just wondered, if there was any way that Kerjean might have known about it, too.'

'Pah!' The old man waved a hand in the air, and his exclamation drew a slightly startled look from the Labrador. 'He certainly wouldn't have heard it from me. And to be honest, I never exchanged more than a few words with the man. So I wouldn't have known what he knew or didn't know about anything.'

'Oh, okay.' Enzo was hardly surprised. It had always been a long shot. Sometimes doctors knew more about their patients than others. But it seemed that no one had ever got close to Kerjean, except for a handful of women.

'You might ask Elisabeth, though. She spent more time with him than any of us.'

Enzo turned to look at the doctor. 'Elisabeth Servat?'

'She was a nurse in the practice when Alain first joined.'

'Yes, she told me.'

'Specialised in physical therapy and re-education. As I recall, Kerjean had a fall on his boat and broke a leg in two places. Elisabeth went out to his place at Locmaria twice a week for a couple of months to get him walking properly again.' He chuckled once more. 'Two to three hours a week in the man's company. He wasn't the most forthcoming I've ever met, but they must have talked about something.'

Enzo stopped for a bite to eat in Le Bourg, and it was early afternoon by the time he got back to Port Mélite. Charlotte and the baby had been on his mind all morning, a constant distraction gnawing away at his concentration, like back pain or a toothache that never lets you forget it's there. He was determined to confront her.

Jane Killian's car was parked, as usual, beneath the trees above the beach. When he got out of his jeep he heard the tick, tick of cooling metal coming from beneath its hood. So she had recently come back from somewhere.

He was halfway across the lawn towards the annex when he heard her voice calling to him from the house. 'If you're looking for Charlotte, she's not there.'

Enzo stopped and turned. 'Oh. Is she with you?'

Jane shook her head. 'No, Enzo. She's gone.'

He stood staring at her for a moment. 'Gone where?'

'Left. The island, I mean. I took her to the ferry late this morning.'

Enzo felt the colour rising on his cheeks, his skin stinging, as if he had been slapped. And he wondered if Jane was taking pleasure in this. 'Okay. Thanks,' was all he said.

He went up to his room and was struck by its emptiness, a reflection of the way he felt inside. The rumpled bedsheets where they had lain together in chaste self-consciousness seemed to mock him. A reminder of just how great the gulf between them had become. That they should have spent a night together without holding, or kissing, locked in silent conflict, words expressed earlier in the evening endlessly repeating in the mind, like ticker-tape headlines crossing the screen of a twenty-four hour news station.

Choked by a sudden claustrophobia, he hurried back down the stairs and out into the garden, breathing deeply. The black cat that had taken a shine to Charlotte was stretched out on the lower limbs of the nearest tree, watching him with affected disinterest. He turned away and walked briskly around the side of the house to the gate. He couldn't face Jane right now.

On the far side of the parking area, three houses and a smaller cottage sat up on the bank in an elevated position, looking over the beach, and he wondered how it must feel to live this close to the sea. To feel its moods, suffer its tempers, hear its constant breathing. Like living with an unpredictable lover.

He thrust his hands in his pockets and wandered down the track to the sand. The tiny bay was protected by low cliffs rising at either end, and fingers of black, shining rock that extended into the brine. A flock of seagulls floated and frolicked in the water at the far side of it. The sand was firm, compacted. The tide had withdrawn to reveal the full crescent of silver, marred only by the arc of seaweed deposited below the high tide mark.

Enzo followed the line of the water, just beyond its reach, feeling the wind in his face, smelling the seaweed and the salt air. But it couldn't blow away his depression. At his time of life, he should have been looking forward to grandchildren. Not to being a father again. And yet there was still an ache in him, somewhere deep inside, an urge to try again. To get it right this time. To be the father he had always wanted and meant to be.

The child that he and Charlotte had made, their son, was another chance. Certainly his last. Surely there was some course of action he could take, some power of persuasion he could exert to prevent Charlotte from doing the unthinkable.

PART THREE

CHAPTER TWENTY-FIVE

Unable to face an evening alone with Jane, Enzo had spent the afternoon driving round the island, walking the sands of the long inlet at Port St. Nicolas and leaving his tracks in the deserted sandbank at *Les Grands Sables*, before washing down fresh seafood with a chilled chardonnay in Le Bourg.

It was dark when he got back to the house. There were still lights on, but he went around the side and headed straight for the annex. For once, Jane did not come to the door. Perhaps she was as anxious as he was now to wrap this whole thing up and leave the island. He had been here for days and made no progress whatsoever, except perhaps for discounting in his mind the thought that it was Kerjean who had murdered Killian.

A drunk, an intemperate brawler, a lover who attracted women like flies to shit, he had about him, nonetheless, a certain integrity, a sense of honour that Enzo had divined from their brief, brutal encounters. It was time to refocus.

He went up to the bedroom to drop his bag on the bed and

check his e-mail on the laptop. There was a message from Sophie. A simple, six-word message that touched his heart. 'Missing you, Papa. I love you.'

He sat for some time, staring at it, before looking up through the window, across the lawn towards the house. Jane's bedroom window was firmly shuttered. He stood up wearily and went back downstairs to the study. As he switched on the light and walked in, he recalled Charlotte's words. *Enzo, he's talking to us. Telling us about himself. All we have to do is know how to listen.* Enzo stood listening, running his eyes over everything that had become so familiar to him. The ordered rows of books on the shelves, the tidy workbench. The desktop with the open diary. The fridge door with its magnets and message list, and single, discordant Post-it. The bloodstained floorboards, the bullet holes in the wall.

He remembered asking Guéguen for a copy of the autopsy report and for one of the shell casings. But since he had heard nothing from the gendarme, he assumed that neither of these things was likely to find its way into his hands. Which was disappointing. None of this was going well. He looked around again. If Killian was speaking, why couldn't Enzo hear him? He closed his eyes, and the silence seemed deafening.

He shivered now, as he pushed his hands into his pockets and wandered over to the workbench to look at the upside-down poem by Ronald Ross on the wall. Canting his head to one side, he tried to read it again but gave up and lifted it down on to the desktop, propping it the right way up against the wall.

This day relenting God
Hath placed within my hand
A wondrous thing; and God
Be praised. At his command,
Seeking his secret deeds
With tears and toiling breath,
I find thy cunning seeds,
O million-murdering Death.
I know this little thing
A myriad men will save,
O Death, where is thy sting?
Thy victory, O Grave?

What on earth was it all about? And who was Ronald Ross? Enzo walked over to the bookshelves. Surely Killian had kept an encyclopedia. He scoured the lines of books until he found a row of twelve dark green volumes. *Everyman's Encyclopedia*, A to Z. The books looked old. He lifted one down at random and checked the publication date. 1957. So they were well out of date. Still . . . He ran his eyes along them searching for the volume RAG to SPI, so that he could look up Ronald Ross.

It wasn't in its place. He frowned. In its stead was the first of the twelve volumes, A to BAL. It seemed almost inconceivable to him that Killian would have filed them out of order. He checked to see if something else had replaced the first volume, and found that the missing RAG to SPI was now there. The two had been transposed. Who by? Killian? If he had done it, then it could have been no accident. For the first time, Enzo felt a sense of excitement, saw the very first chink of light, and heard perhaps the very first distant echo of Killian's voice.

He placed the two books on the desk, and sat down in Killian's chair to look at them, struck by the chilling sense of occupying a dead man's space, of following in his invisible footsteps.

The first volume he opened was RAG to SPI, and he flicked through the pages to see if there was an entry for Ronald Ross. To his surprise, the search was facilitated by the presence of a blank yellow Post-it stuck on the page with the entry. And Ross's name itself had been highlighted with a yellow marker pen. The entry was headed, *Ross, Sir Ronald (1857–1932) Brit. Physician and poet.*

Enzo read that Ross had been born in India, the son of a British general. He had trained as a doctor, and in collaboration with a scientist, Patrick Manson, had explored the theory that malaria was transmitted to man via the mosquito. Following years of perfecting a technique for dissecting the stomach of the mosquito, he had finally made the breakthrough which won him his Nobel Prize – on a day that he thereafter named Mosquito Day. The date was August 20 1897, and it was the day he discovered, in the stomach wall of a dissected mosquito, the *plasmodium* long identified in the blood of malaria sufferers as the cause of the disease. In celebration, Ross had written his poem, supposing that his discovery would lead to a cure for malaria.

Enzo was puzzled. He read and reread the entry. But there was nothing in it that seemed in any way connected with what had happened here on this tiny Breton island off the north-west coast of France. Of course, Killian was interested in insects, which might explain his admiration of Ross and his poem. But how was it relevant, if at all?

He sat thinking for some time before absently picking up the volume A to BAL, and riffling through its pages, almost without thinking. Something caught his eye and made him stop. A flash of yellow. Another Post-it. He flipped back through the pages until he found it. It was stuck to the left-hand page, and written on it, in a bold, tidy hand, in capital letters, were the words, HE DID NOT DIE. The blue ink of the pen was as crisp and clear as the day it had been applied to the paper, never having been exposed to light until now.

Enzo stared at it wondering who Killian was referring to, before his eye was drawn to a yellow highlighted entry on the opposite page. *Agadir*. He found himself frowning again. Agadir, he knew, was the southernmost port on the Atlantic coastline of Morocco, at one time regarded as the sardine capital of the world. He read through the entry, most of which involved itself with a dispute between France and Germany over territorial claims on the North African country.

Again he was mystified. What possible relevance could this have to Killian's murder? And yet the words, HE DID NOT DIE, lingered in his consciousness, as if lasered into it.

He closed both volumes again and sat looking at them. There had to be, he felt, some connection between Agadir and the poem by Ronald Ross. And yet, if there was some correlation there, he could not for the life of him imagine what it might be. He touched the books with tactile fingers, as if hoping something might transmit itself to him simply through contact. And then it occurred to him that a more up-to-date entry for Agadir might prove more illuminating. He searched the shelves once more, looking for a more modern encyclopedia but found nothing, and almost gave up before remembering that he could do an Internet search from his laptop.

Enzo brought the computer down to the study and set it up on Killian's desk. He moved the diary to one side and placed his laptop in front of him, plugging in his USB stick and dialing into his mobile provider's high-speed Internet connection. Up came his Google homepage, and he typed in AGADIR. It produced more than six million results, the first of which was the Wikipedia entry on the Moroccan seaport.

Reading through it, nothing immediately struck him as significant. Located near the foot of the Atlas mountains, where the Souss River flows into the Atlantic ocean, Agadir was, he read, one of the world's most important sardine ports. It was also an important commercial port and tourist town, with its long strip of sandy beach. It wasn't until he reached the section on the city's history that he found his interest suddenly piqued. The entry read:

At 15 minutes to midnight on February 29 1960, Agadir was almost totally destroyed by an earthquake that lasted 15 seconds, burying the city and killing thousands. The death toll is estimated at 15,000. The earthquake destroyed the ancient Kasbah.

Of course, Enzo realised, the entry in the *Everyman Encyclopedia* had predated the earthquake by three years. If Killian had possessed a more recent edition, might he have marked out the section on the earthquake? Fifteen thousand had been killed by it. And Killian had written on the Post-it, HE DID NOT DIE. Had someone thought to have died in the quake actually survived it?

He spent some time browsing through accounts of the earthquake. Some gave the death toll at over 16,000, others gave the time of the quake at anything between fifteen and twenty minutes before midnight. What was clear was that most people had been indoors, and that buildings with structures hopelessly inadequate to withstand even a minor earthquake had simply collapsed, killing almost everyone inside. In fact, a third of the population of the city had perished in that brief fifteen seconds.

There were entire sites dedicated to photographs of the dis- aster. Graphic images of a city reduced to rubble. Twisted and mangled buildings whose roofs hung in suspended animation just inches from the ground. An aerial shot of the original walled kasbah, utterly devastated, only a handful of buildings in the old, medieval hilltop city left standing. Bodies buried beneath tons of masonry had never been recovered, and the kasbah had never been rebuilt. It was almost inconceivable to Enzo that so much damage could have been done in such a short space of time, so many lives taken without warning.

In the end, he was overtaken by fatigue. He closed down his computer and trudged wearily upstairs to the bedroom.

And as he lay between the icy sheets, aware as never before of the emptiness of his bed, he knew that somehow, in some way, he had just made a breakthrough. But Killian's voice was still too far away. Enzo was simply unable to hear the words with sufficient clarity to make any sense of them.

It was sometime after four in the morning that he woke, sitting bolt upright, feeling cold air on hot skin. He was sweating, wide awake and staring into the darkness. Five hours of shallow sleep seemed like no more than five seconds. And yet his mind had never stopped, taking him on a restless journey through the shattered remains of Agadir, the elusive shadow of Adam Killian always just out of reach, his voice a distant call, words lost in the crashing of falling masonry and the death cries of fifteen thousand other voices.

And Enzo had only one thought in his mind. He had not checked the row of encyclopedias to see if any of the other volumes were out of place. He cursed himself out loud, and heard the dying echo of his voice swallowed by the night. He had been too tired, insufficiently focused. But, still, it should have occurred to him before now.

He swung his legs out of the bed, slid his feet into his slippers, and slipped on his silk robe. He turned on the bedside light, screwing his eyes up against its sudden brightness, and started back downstairs to the study.

The room seemed to be waiting for him. Its stillness, in this darkest hour of the night, was so dense Enzo felt he could almost touch it. He had the strangest sense of premonition, of something just beyond his grasp that would soon be his. He was uncertain whether it was that, or the cold, that made all the hairs stand up on the back of his neck. The bloodstain on the floor seemed darker, somehow, the bullet holes in the wall freshly made, the dust of shattered plaster hanging in the air, along with the smell of cordite.

He was, he knew, letting his imagination run away with itself, and yet he could have sworn that he was not alone in the room. Killian himself was there, somewhere in the stillness, willing him to listen, to hear his voice.

Enzo rounded the desk and ran his index finger along the line of dark green *Everyman* encyclopedias.

'Damn!' His voice shattered the stillness of the night. Two further volumes had been transposed. NYA to RAG and SPI to ZYM. If he had only taken the trouble to look last night, he would have seen them immediately. He lifted them down, and placed them on the desk in front of him as he sat in Killian's chair.

From somewhere out in the garden he heard the deep-throated yowling of a cat. It came chillingly out of the night, penetrating the dark and the quiet. Enzo stood up and crossed to the window, opening it and pushing out the shutters. Light from the room washed across the lawn. In the shadow of the trees at the far side, he saw the black cat pacing restlessly in silhouette, howling at the night. For a moment it stood still, to turn luminous green eyes in his direction.

For several seconds it seemed to Enzo as if he were trapped, a rabbit caught in the headlights of a car, before he closed the window. Ruffled, he remembered Charlotte's playful allusion to the cat as being perhaps Killian's ghost. Absurd, of course, but still he could not shake off the sense of another presence in the room, of eyes watching his every move, of a voice whispering silent encouragement that he couldn't hear.

He went back and stood at the desk to open the volume NYA to RAG with trembling fingers. He drew his thumb across the open pages of the book and let them flick past it, until his eye caught the flash of yellow he had been hoping for. He flipped back until he found it. Once more, the Post-it was blank. But on the opposite page, the entry for *Paris* had been marked with the same yellow pen. The entry was five pages long, and Enzo flipped slowly through them all looking for a highlighted passage, something that would guide him to more specific information. But there was nothing. All that had been singled out was the word *Paris* right at the head of the entry. So perhaps, he thought, Paris itself was the clue. The city. The place. But why?

He set the open book on the desk and lifted the volume SPI to ZYM. This time he found the Post-it among the W entries, and highlighted on the opposite page was the name Simon Wiesenthal. Enzo stood staring at it, his skin prickling all over his skull. He looked up and saw his reflection in the window. The black robe with the red dragons, the tangle of dark hair tumbling wildly over his shoulders, the silver streak running back from his forehead. A sudden movement startled him. He refocused, and saw the black cat on the outside window ledge, staring in at him.

He turned his eyes down again to the page. Wiesenthal, he knew, was the most famous of the post-war Nazi hunters, responsible for tracking down dozens of fugitives so that they could be brought to justice for crimes against humanity. Although this 1957 entry was long out of date, Enzo read it anyway.

Wiesenthal was an Austrian-Jewish architectural engineer and holocaust victim who had survived four and a half years in the German concentration camps of Janowska, Plaszow, and Mauthausen. After the war he began working for the US army, gathering documentation for the Nazi war crimes trials at Nuremburg. Then, in 1947, he and thirty other volunteers had founded the Jewish Historical Documentation Centre in Linz, Austria, to gather information for future trials.

In the same way that Enzo had made the assumption that the entries on Ronald Ross and Agadir were somehow linked, he felt there had to be some connection between Wiesenthal and Paris. But what? There was nothing in this old entry that gave any clue as to what it might be.

And so, as before, he turned to the computer, rebooting it and connecting again to the Internet. For a moment he paused to take in Killian's desktop. His laptop sitting on it at an angle, four open volumes of the *Everyman Encyclopedia*, the desk diary pushed to one side. Killian's sense of order would have been grossly offended. Google popped up on his screen, and he turned his concentration back to the search, typing in Simon Wiesenthal and hitting the return key. There were more than half a million entries. Again, he went to Wikipedia and began reading.

The man had written three books on his experiences and opened numerous centres around the world before dying in 2005 at the age of ninety-six. Still, Enzo could not find any logical connection to Paris. He clicked on a link to the entry on the Simon Wiesenthal Centre in Los Angeles and read its mission statement describing it as 'an international Jewish human rights organisation dedicated to repairing the world one step at a time.' Quite a task, Enzo thought.

He scrolled down the entry until he came to the section on Office Locations. There were five other centres around the world. New York, Miami, Toronto, Jerusalem, Buenos Aires. And Paris. Enzo held his breath. Perhaps this was the link he had been looking for.

He went back to Google and tapped in *Simon Wiesenthal Centre Paris*. More than thirty-two thousand links appeared. But the third from the top took him directly to the website of the Wiesenthal organisation's European operation. The office was in the seventeenth *arrondissement*, in the rue Laugier, and had been established there in 1988. Before Killian's death. Had he been in contact with them for some reason? If so, surely they would have a record.

Enzo scrolled down the home page until he reached the contact details at the foot of it. There was an email address and a link that opened up his emailer. He tapped in a subject line, KILLIAN CONTACT, and composed a short mail.

Sirs,

I am conducting an investigation into the death of a British citizen in France in 1990. I have reason to believe that he may have been in contact with you around this time. His name was Adam Killian. I would be most grateful if you could tell me if you have any record of such contact. My bona fides can be checked by following the link (below) to my page on the website of the University of Paul Sabatier, Toulouse, where I head up the faculty on forensic science.

With best wishes,

Professor Enzo Macleod.

He hit the send button and off it went, carrying with it more hope than expectation.

For a long time he sat just staring at the screen, until it almost burned out on his retinas. He leaned his elbows on the desk and rubbed his eyes with the heel of his hands, and then blinked them, bloodshot, in the direction of the window. The cat was still there, pressing itself against the glass, still staring in at him.

For the second time Enzo was startled awake. This time, it was sunlight streaming through the unshuttered windows of Killian's study that woke him. At some point in his deliberations, he had cleared a space on the desk in front of him and folded his arms on the desktop to create a pillow for his head. He had closed his eyes, intending simply to rest them while he thought. And now, three hours later, he had woken almost rigid with the cold.

Pale yellow light slanted in at a low angle, falling across the chaos that was now Killian's desktop. He straightened himself stiffly, painfully, and stretched his arms above his head as he yawned. The cat was gone, along with the still of the night. Enzo shivered. He stood up and stamped several times to try to get the blood back into his feet.

He replayed everything he had learned, everything he now knew. About Ronald Ross and his mosquito poem. About the earthquake in Agadir, the man who had not died, and the Simon Wiesenthal Centre in Paris. More than ever, he was convinced that none of this connected to Thibaud Kerjean. The man had been a blinding red herring, both then and now. He had stolen the focus of every investigation into this case, when all the time the clues had been in the books.

Enzo stood stock-still.

Even as the words formed in his mind, realisation dawned. He tipped his head back and yelled at the ceiling. 'Jesus Christ!' His voice reverberated around the room. Why on earth had he not seen it immediately? It was so childishly simple. And yet, how often was it that the most obvious was overlooked? That the most cunning place to hide anything was always in plain sight?

CHAPTER TWENTY-SIX

Strands of mist washed up all along the shore, lingering among the trees where splintered sunlight seemed suspended in long, slanting fingers. The dew on the grass, almost white, sparkled like frost in the early morning light.

Enzo felt it soak through his slippers as he crossed the lawn, leaving dark tracks in his wake. He pulled his robe tightly around himself as he banged hard on the back door of the house. He knew that Jane was up, because he had seen the smoke drifting lazily into the sunlight from the chimney on the east gable. But like Enzo, she had not yet dressed, and peered at him, dishevelled and a little bleary, through the crack in the door that opened up.

'Oh!' She seemed startled to see him. 'I'm still a mess.'

'So am I.'

'I can see that.'

He could barely contain his impatience. 'Look, it doesn't matter what either of us looks like, I've made a breakthrough.'

She opened the door a little wider, forgetting her appearance. She looked older in the cold light of day, without make-up to paper over the early morning cracks. 'In Papa's murder?'

'Yes.' He scratched his head. 'Listen, you told Charlotte that when Peter was a boy, his father used to play word games with him to increase his vocabulary.'

'That's right.'

'What games?'

She shrugged. 'Peter never said. I have no idea.'

Enzo reached out his hand to take hers. 'Well, I do. Come on.'

'Hey! It's freezing out there!'

'Tell me about it.' Enzo almost dragged her across the lawn behind him. She ran to keep up. They both left wet footprints on the floor as Enzo led her into Killian's study. She looked at the mess of open books on the desktop, and then at Enzo. 'What have you found?'

'Messages. Left in the encyclopedias. Pages marked with Post-its, entries highlighted with a marker pen.'

'What messages?'

'Nothing that makes much sense to me yet. Although that'll come, I'm sure. But the point is this. Just ask yourself. Where were the clues?'

She looked at him blankly.

'Where did I find these clues?' He waved his hand at the open volumes on the desk.

She shrugged, not fully understanding. 'In the books, I guess.'

'Exactly.' He took her hand again and dragged her across the room to the tiny kitchen leading off it. He ripped the Post-it off the fridge door and handed it to her. 'What does it say?'

Her face was a mask of incomprehension. 'You know what it says.'

'Read it out loud.'

She sighed in exasperation. 'The cooks have the blues.'

He looked at her expectantly, waiting for the penny to drop. But it didn't. 'Haven't you ever heard of Doctor Spooner?' She frowned. 'Reverend William Archibald Spooner. A lecturer at New College, Oxford, in the nineteenth century. He was an albino, and had occasional problems with the spoken word, a nervous tendency sometimes to transpose initial letters. It used to amuse his students so much they started inventing their own transpositions, and called them Spoonerisms.' He paused, eyes shining, and she looked again at the Post-it in her hand.

'The books have the clues,' she read. And she looked up, her face suddenly flushed. 'Oh, my God!' Her eyes turned towards the magnetic message board and she prised it free of its grip on the fridge. This time she read, 'A fit of the blood will foil the beast.' Her eyes darted towards Enzo, infected now by his excitement. 'What does that mean?'

'I have no idea. But we're going to find out, Jane. I know we are.' He took her hand again. 'Come and look at the others.' And they crossed the study to Killian's desk.

Jane unstuck the Post-it from the desk lamp and read it out. 'P, one day you will have to oil my bicycles. Don't forget.' She turned puzzled eyes on Enzo. 'Boil my icicles?'

He made a face that conveyed his own lack of comprehension and pulled the desk diary towards him. This time he read out the transposed message himself. 'P, I was fighting a liar, but now there's no more time, and all I'm left with is a half-formed wish in the roaring pain.'

Concentration furrowed Jane's brow. 'Fighting a liar?' She paused. 'Kerjean?'

Enzo shook his head. 'I don't think so.'

'Well, if not him, who?'

'I don't know. Yet.'

'And what is a half-formed wish?'

'I guess it was something he was in the process of doing, but unable to finish. Something that would help him to defeat, or unmask, the liar he was fighting.'

'And the roaring pain must have been the suffering of his illness.' The tide of emotion that had risen in Jane was visible in eyes that brimmed with tears. 'Oh, God . . . Poor Papa.'

Enzo cast his own eyes over the open volumes on the desktop. The Post-its and highlighted entries. And he wondered what any of it had to do with Wiesenthal and Agadir and Ronald Ross. Killian had not made it easy. But, then, he must have been paranoid his killer would find and destroy the evidence after he was dead. He had been relying on his son to see the wordplay at once, and then be inside his mind to unravel the puzzle. Somehow, Enzo had to get himself inside Killian's head, too.

CHAPTER TWENTY-SEVEN

Dressed now and warmed by the full English breakfast that Jane had prepared for him, Enzo retraced his footsteps of yesterday along the beach at Port Mélite: footsteps erased by the tide. But the tracks Killian had laid down were not lost. Just obscured. And, one by one, Enzo was uncovering them, like an archaeologist brushing away the dust of time. He still had no idea where they would lead.

How to get inside Killian's head. That was the problem. He was missing something, he knew, and that one key would probably unlock the secret. He ran through all the clues again. Ronald Ross and his mosquitoes, Agadir and the man who had not died, the Simon Wiesenthal Centre in Paris. And the notes. What could he have meant by boiling the icicles? Who was the liar he had been fighting? Was it the same man who had not died in Agadir? He thought back to the phone call Killian had made to Jane the night of the murder. Might there have been something he said that night that Enzo had missed?

He turned and looked back along the beach. Tall chestnut trees were shedding the last of their leaves around the stone benches that overlooked it. The houses sharing the rise sat square and solid, cheek by jowl, facing the sunrise like old friends greeting the day. Across the shining waters, the Breton coast smudged the horizon. It was a magical spot. Sheltered and private. There was an intimacy about it, spoiled only by the stain of a man's murder. The thought jarred, like a discordant note in a dreamy symphony. Enzo turned and walked briskly back to the house.

When he got to the annex, he sat once again behind Killian's desk and surveyed the clues laid out before him. He had brought through the Post-it and message pad from the fridge and laid them out alongside the diary and the Post-it from the desk lamp. The encyclopedias were all open at the relevant pages. And against the desk lamp itself he had propped Ronald Ross' framed poem about mosquitoes. His eyes were drawn to a line of it which made sense now in the context of Ross' discovery. But somewhere, far away in the back of his brain, sparking neurons were making almost subliminal connections. *I find thy cunning seeds, O million-murdering death.* The plasmodium found in the mosquito's stomach, of course. But with Killian's fondness for wordplay, might there be some hidden meaning here? *O death, where is thy sting? Thy victory, O Grave?*

Whatever connections he was making deep in his subconscious, they were, for the moment, eluding his conscious mind. As a distraction, he went online to check his email and saw that there was one waiting for him. It was from someone called Gérard Cohen. He opened it up.

Professor Macleod,
Your email was forwarded to me by the Wiesenthal Centre first thing this morning. Although retired now, I worked there as an investigator in the late eighties and most of the nineties. I can confirm that I did, indeed, have correspondence with a certain Adam Killian in the spring of 1990. I am very sorry to hear that he was murdered. This must have occurred not long after I met him in Paris in July of that year. I am intrigued to know more.
    Gérard Cohen

Enzo felt his excitement mounting. He immediately composed his response.

Dear Monsieur Cohen,
Thank you for your prompt response. I will, of course, be only to happy to share with you everything I know about Monsieur Killian's murder. However, I would be most grateful if first you could tell me what it was that you and Monsieur Killian were discussing?
    Thanking you in advance,
    Enzo Macleod

Within a matter of minutes his laptop alerted him to Gérard Cohen's response. He must have been sitting at his computer waiting for a reply.

Professor Macleod,
The subject of my correspondence with Monsieur Killian, and our subsequent meeting is, as far as I am concerned, confidential. I do

not feel at liberty to discuss the details by email with an unseen,
unverified correspondent. If, however, you are prepared to come
to Paris to meet me face to face, I will make a judgment then on
the question of how much, if anything, to reveal.

With best wishes,

Gérard Cohen.

Enzo sat thoughtfully tapping his right index finger on the edge of the desk before reaching a decision. He hit the reply key again, suggesting a meeting the following afternoon. Cohen's response was, again, almost immediate. He would meet Enzo, he said, at the door of the Wiesenthal Centre at four.

Enzo immediately pulled up the SNCF website to book a rail ticket from Lorient to Paris the following morning, then sat staring at the screen. Vague thoughts were beginning to take form and coagulate in his stream of consciousness. Any correspondence between Killian and Cohen would have been by conventional mail in 1990. So where was Killian's end of that correspondence? Jane had made no mention of any such letters being found among his belongings. And surely they would have been significant enough to mention.

His thoughts were interrupted by the ringing of his mobile. He fished in his pocket to find it.

'Hello?'

'Enzo, hi. It's Elisabeth Servat. How are you recovering from your ordeal the other night?'

In truth, Enzo had almost forgotten about it. He laughed. 'Fine. Thanks to you and Alain.'

'Good.' She paused. 'I got up this morning and saw the sun shining and thought this would be a good day to take Enzo to Port Lay. You said you wanted to see it in the sunshine.'

Enzo hesitated for only a moment. 'I would like that very much.'

'Great. I've just packed the girls off to school, and Alain has a surgery this morning, so I'm free any time you are. Shall I come and pick you up at Port Mélite?'

'Sure.'

'And afterwards we can go into Port Tudy and hook up with Alain. We quite often meet for lunch at the Café de la Jetée when the girls are lunching at school. Would that be okay?'

'Sounds perfect, Elisabeth.'

He could hear the pleasure in her voice. '*Géniale*. I'll see you in about half an hour, then.'

For a long time after he had hung up, Enzo sat thinking before finally getting up and crossing the lawn to the house. The black cat was sitting at the base of one of the trees washing its face. It paused mid-wipe, one paw poised behind its right ear, to watch as Enzo knocked on the back door. When Jane opened it, dressed now, her face softened by freshly applied make-up, he said, 'Whose cat is that over there?'

She peered across the garden and shrugged. 'No idea. I've never seen it before.' She held the door open, and he stepped up into the kitchen. 'Any developments?'

'I'm going to Paris tomorrow to meet a man from the Simon Wiesenthal Centre. Apparently he and your father-in-law exchanged letters in the spring of 1990, and met in Paris in July of that year.'

Jane raised her eyebrows in surprise. 'Really? He never mentioned anything about that to us.'

'There were no letters among his belongings?'

'No, there weren't. I'd have noticed if there were. Coffee?'

'Sure.' He sat down at the kitchen table as she poured them each a cup. 'Jane, I want you to think back to the telephone conversation you had with him the night he was murdered.'

'What about it?'

'Tell me again how it went.'

She placed their cups on the table and sat down. For several moments she was lost in a distant memory. 'It's very clear to me. Still. Even after all these years. I can almost hear him.'

'What did he say?'

'He didn't want me to speak, just listen. Said he knew that Peter wouldn't be back from Africa till October, and that if anything were to happen to him in the meantime, Peter was to come straight here.'

'And he explained why.'

'Yes. He said he had left a message for Peter in his study, and that if he died before Peter got back I was to make sure nobody disturbed anything in the room. He was so insistent on that.'

'Did you ask him what kind of message?'

'I did. But he just said that no one other than Peter would understand it. And that it was ironic that he was the one who would finish it.'

'Peter?'

'Yes.'

'Finish what, exactly?'

'He didn't say. He said . . .' And she thought hard, trying to recall his exact words. 'It's just ironic that it's the son who will finish the job.' She sighed. 'I wanted to know why he couldn't tell me. And he said it was too great a responsibility. Peter would know what to do.'

But Enzo wasn't listening anymore. Those connections his brain had been making deep down in his subconscious were fizzing upwards now, like bubbles breaking the surface of his consciousness. And he knew it wasn't science that had made the connections. It was intuition. But it would be up to science to provide the proof and, in the end, just maybe lead to the truth.

CHAPTER TWENTY-EIGHT

After the cold of the last few days, the warmth in the sun was extraordinary, like a return to late summer or early autumn. It laid its clear yellow light across the ocean like reflective glass and cut deep shadows into the sheltered waters of the tiny harbour at Port Lay. Boats tethered to the quayside strained and bumped and groaned on the gentle swell. An old man sat on the harbour wall with rod and line, dozing in the late morning sunshine. Anything taking his bait would have disturbed his peace. There was not another soul around.

Enzo and Elisabeth stood high on the east bank looking down on the harbour below. They had driven up past the deserted fish processing plant and parked in an overgrown patch of ground that had once been the car park. Whitewashed cottages with slate roofs and blue and pink shutters climbed the hillside among trees that clung stubbornly to thin soil. The sea breathed through the throat of a harbour that sucked water in and out with the ebb and flow of the tide, and the plaintive cries of seagulls overhead were a lament for way of life long gone.

'That's my house just up there.' Elisabeth pointed to a

bungalow with a steeply pitched roof overlooking the harbour on the far side. She laughed. 'Well, not *my* house. The house where I grew up. My mother still lives there.'

Enzo tried to picture the scene that Elisabeth had described the other day, of tuna boats in full sail plying in and out of this tiny harbour, the quayside crowded with fishermen landing their catch, seabirds clustered around the crates of fish as they lined up along the quay. But it was an image almost impossible to conjure out of this tranquil little inlet. It existed now only in photographs and in the memories of those for whom it had been a reality. If he could have seen it through Elisabeth's eyes, then he might have pictured something quite different.

He glanced at her and saw the fondness in her gaze as she peered back through the haze of years towards her childhood. 'Must have been a special place to grow up,' he said.

She smiled. 'It was. Of course, like all island girls, I hoped to marry a man from the mainland and escape. When you are a child, the island is your whole world, filled with endless possibilities. But when you get older the water that surrounds you makes it feel like a prison. It shrinks, becomes confining, and you start to feel trapped by it. In the end, I had to leave.'

'But you came back.'

She laughed. 'Only because I was daft enough to marry a fellow islander. Of course, Alain is still only first generation. His father's family came from Paris. But his mother was an island girl just like me, so he has genuine island blood in him.' Her smile faded. 'But all our children will leave in the end, and there'll be no one to look after us like we looked after our parents.'

They gazed in silence for a while, enjoying the sunshine and the peace, and the comforting sound of the ocean. Enzo silently rehearsed his change of subject, before he turned his eyes towards her and said, 'I wanted to ask you, Elisabeth . . . about your home visits to Thibaud Kerjean in the late summer of 1990, after he broke his leg.'

She didn't move, and there was not the slightest change of expression on her face. But it drained of colour, and a glaze like cataracts crossed her eyes. It felt like a very long time before she spoke. 'You know, then.' It wasn't a question. Her voice seemed very tiny, lost in the blink of an eye on the edge of the offshore breeze that caressed their faces. Enzo said nothing, almost holding his breath. His question had been innocent enough, but Elisabeth had read more into it than he could ever have anticipated. 'I've been dreading this for twenty years. Did Thibaud tell you?' She turned searching eyes on him, something like fear in them now. And consternation. She shook her head. 'Why would he do that now, after all these years? He was prepared to go to prison back then to protect me.'

Enzo's mind was racing. But his voice was calm, and gave no indication of the turmoil behind it. 'What on earth did you see in him, Elisabeth?'

Now she looked away, her expression pained, her eyes lighting on the house where she had grown up, wishing perhaps she could be transported back there, to the innocence of childhood. 'Alain and I were going through a difficult time. I'd just given birth to Primel and, after the initial joy of it, I sank into the most terrible post-natal depression. I was almost suicidal, Enzo. The baby was keeping us awake most nights. Endless, endless crying. My nerves were shot to pieces. And so was our relationship. Alain coped with it all much better than I did, but even so, things had never been worse between us.

'My mother was looking after Primel during the day, and I was still working part-time at the clinic. Alain thought it would be good for me to be out of the house, getting a break from the baby.' She drew a deep, tremulous breath. 'Which is when I got to know Thibaud. After he broke his leg and Doctor Gassman assigned me to his physical re-education.'

She ventured a look towards Enzo that pleaded for under-standing.

'I can't even begin to explain to you what the attraction was. I hardly know myself. People knew he was a womaniser. He had a terrible reputation. The first time I went to his house I was really quite nervous.' She breathed in deeply, eyes closed, reliving some distant memory. 'But there was something about him. I . . . I never saw the side of him that other people talked about. I never saw the temper that woman described in court. He was gentle and sensitive. And unexpectedly intelligent. And . . .' She searched for the words. 'He gave me something I needed then, Enzo. Something I wasn't getting from Alain. I can't even tell you what that was. Understanding, reassurance maybe.'

She was wringing her hands in nervous distress, watching

herself doing it, unable to bring herself to look at him again.

'It didn't last long. But it was very intense. Very passionate.'

'And the night of the murder?'

'He was with me. My mother was looking after the baby here at Port Lay, and I telephoned Alain to say I would stay over, too. As far as he ever knew, that's where I was. But I was with Thibaud. A holiday cottage that he looked after for some Parisians. It's where we always met. Right out on the point, near Kervedan. No neighbours.' She sighed deeply, shaking her head. 'Then over the next few days, when suspicion began to fall on Thibaud for the Killian murder, I was in a panic. You have no idea. I was his only alibi.'

Silent tears rolled down her cheeks.

'I knew that to speak up would mean the end of my marriage. I was prepared to do it, Enzo, I really was. But Thibaud wouldn't let me. Point-blank refused. And in the end he was cleared, thank God. It restores a little of your faith in our system of justice.'

'And if he'd been convicted?'

She turned to face him now, brushing the tears from her face. 'I wouldn't have let him go to prison, Enzo. Even though he was prepared to do that. I couldn't have lived with myself. I would have had to come forward then.'

Enzo thought about everything he had read and heard about Thibaud Kerjean. He was a drunk, a brawler, a woman-iser who beat up his women. He had the temper of a madman. Not one person had a good word to say about him. It was hard to reconcile that with the picture Elisabeth painted. A man of honour and integrity, who had been prepared to sacrifice his own freedom to protect her reputation and her marriage. And yet, hadn't Enzo himself experienced that other side of him, too? The human face behind the gorilla mask. Kerjean had attacked and assaulted him. But he had also saved his life. He was no more a murderer than Enzo or Elisabeth. Just a deeply flawed, deeply troubled man.

Almost as if reading his thoughts, Elisabeth said, 'I see him sometimes in the street now, and it is shocking to see how drink has reduced him. He's the merest shadow of the man he was. He doesn't acknowledge me. Won't even meet my eye. I think, in a way, he knows what he has become and is ashamed of it.'

'And now?' Enzo said. 'How are things between you and Alain?'

She turned sad eyes on him, filled with regret. 'They couldn't be better, Enzo. I love him. I always have. What happened between Thibaud and me was . . . it was an aberration. I lost my way for a time, but I found my way back in the end. I never really wanted to be with anyone but Alain.' The regret in her eyes dissolved into apprehension. 'Are you going to tell him?'

Enzo shook his head. 'No. Your secret is in safe hands, Elisabeth. You have my word on that. I never really believed that Kerjean had done it.' He turned a thoughtful gaze out across the water. 'But there have been developments now. And I'm looking in another direction altogether.'

CHAPTER TWENTY-NINE

Elisabeth dropped him off at Port Mélite to pick up his jeep. She had said little on the drive back from Port Lay, and Enzo guessed that she was now dreading the lunch with Alain at the Café de la Jetée. How could either of them behave naturally with her husband after the revelations that had passed between them? Enzo almost suggested calling it off, but it might have seemed unnatural to cancel.

'I'll see you in about fifteen minutes then,' she said, and he stood and watched as she accelerated her SUV up the hill, back towards Le Bourg. He was about to get into his Suzuki when he heard Jane calling him from the house. He turned to see her coming down the path to the gate.

'You just missed Adjudant Guéguen,' she said. And she waved a large manila envelope at him. 'He left this for you and asked you to call him.'

Enzo went to meet her at the gate and took the envelope.

'You seem very close with the doctor's wife these days.' She watched him carefully.

'She's a nice lady,' Enzo said. 'And very happily married.'

Jane nodded, and he saw what looked like regret in her

eyes. 'When you get back from Paris, I'll probably be gone. But keep your key. Feel free to use the place.' She paused. 'Any further developments?'

Enzo hesitated for a long moment before he said, 'I can tell you one thing with absolute certainty. It wasn't Thibaud Kerjean.'

Jane searched his face with inquisitive eyes. 'And do you have someone else in mind?'

He nodded slowly. 'Actually, I do. But I'm not quite sure yet just why.'

He didn't open the envelope until he was sitting behind the wheel of his jeep. He waited until Jane had gone back into the house, watching for the door to shut, before he tore it open. Inside was a stapled document about nine pages long. He turned it over to look at the front page. It was a copy of the autopsy report on Adam Killian. There was a handwritten note paperclipped to it.

Here's the autopsy report you asked for. Please don't show it to anyone else. I hope to have a shell casing to give you by tomorrow.
   RG

Enzo smiled. He wanted to punch the air, but restrained himself. Guéguen must have gone out on quite a limb to obtain these for him. But he knew that the shell casing, in particular, could prove crucial. He checked the time. He could take five minutes to look through the autopsy report, and only be a little late for his lunch with the doctor and his wife.

He flipped first to the pathologist's conclusion. Nothing unexpected there. Killian had died from three bullet wounds to the chest, one of which had ruptured his heart before passing straight through him. Another had lodged in his spine, severing the spinal cord. Either one would have killed him. The third had punctured his right lung and exited through a wound in his back.

Enzo skimmed through the initial examination, and leapfrogged through the opening of the chest cavity to the dissection of the organs. When he finished, he sat frowning for almost a full minute, thinking hard, before searching back through the paragraphs he had just read, looking for something that wasn't there. Finally, he closed the report and sat staring out at the empty beach in front of him. He was filled with confusion, and consternation, and dread building in the pit of his stomach.

Enzo was full of apologies for being late when he arrived at the Cafe de la Jetée. Alain and Elisabeth were sitting on the *terrasse* with old Jacques Gassman. 'I got held up at the house,' Enzo said. 'There were messages for me.'

Alain shook his hand vigorously. 'That was very inconsiderate of you, Monsieur Macleod. Dammit, man, we've had to sit here drinking while we waited for you.'

Enzo grinned and shook hands with the old doctor. 'Good to see you again, Doctor Gassman.' He noticed that Elisabeth's smile was a little frozen. Then cast his eyes over the empty glasses on the table. 'Let me get you all another before we eat.'

But Doctor Gassman got stiffly to his feet. 'Not for me, thank you, Monsieur Macleod. I must be on my way. Don't want to spoil lunch for you young folk.'

'Oh, don't be silly,' Elisabeth chided him.

But the old doctor just raised a hand and smiled. '*Bon appétit*,' he said, and he shuffled off across the cobbles towards where his Range Rover was parked at the quayside.

Enzo lifted the glasses from the table. 'Same again?'

'Please,' Elisabeth said. 'We're both on red.'

When Enzo got to the bar inside he cast a quick glance back towards the door. Both Alain and Elisabeth were facing towards the harbour, and he could see old Gassman behind the wheel of his Range Rover, starting the motor. He turned back to the counter. The barmaid was busy serving someone else, and he carefully set out the three glasses in front of him. For a moment, she had her back turned as she poured a measure of *pastis*, and he lifted one of the glasses by its stalk and slipped it quickly into his shoulder bag.

When he looked up again, he saw a vacant-eyed regular at the far end of the bar watching him. The man was unshaven, and wore a Breton peaked cap pushed back on his head. The glass in front of him was empty. There was no way he had not seen Enzo slipping the wine glass into his bag. Enzo almost blushed. It was the first time he had ever been caught stealing a glass from a pub. He recovered a little of his composure, winked at the man and put a finger to his lips.

The barmaid turned towards him, and he gave her his best smile. 'Three glasses of red please, for the table on the terrace, and whatever my friend at the end of the bar there is having.'

'Cognac' she said, and turned immediately to lift his glass and fill it from the optic. A slight smile passed across the lips of the man with the peak cap as he lifted his glass towards Enzo, winked, and took a sip.

'I'll bring them out,' the barmaid said.

Enzo felt the warmth of the sunshine on the back of his neck as he took his seat at the Servats' table. 'Suddenly we have an Indian summer,' he said.

Alain nodded. 'Sometimes it happens that way. Just to lull us into a false sense of security before winter comes to force us back indoors.'

'Pity I won't be staying to enjoy it.'

Elisabeth raised an eyebrow in surprise. 'You're leaving us?'

'I'm going to Paris tomorrow. Not quite sure when I'll be back.'

'To do with your investigation?' Alain asked.

'Yes.' He could see that he had piqued their interest, but was not going to volunteer any further information. Instead he changed tack completely. 'Tell me, doctor, do you have any idea when it was that Doctor Gassman first came to the island?'

Alain shrugged. 'I would just have been a kid. Sometime in the early sixties I would guess.'

'You couldn't tell me any more specifically than that?'

'I'm afraid not.' Alain tilted his head a little, a slight frown of puzzlement about his eyes.

Elisabeth said, 'You can find out, of course, from the *mairie*. They are bound to have a record of when he first arrived in the commune.'

'Yes, of course. I'll do that.'

Their drinks arrived, and they chinked glasses and wished each other good health before sipping on soft red wine, rich with fruit and tannins.

'So . . .' the doctor said. 'What about Kerjean? Is he still in your sights?'

Enzo shook his head. 'No. Not at all. If there's one person on this island who I know for sure didn't murder Killian, it's Thibaud Kerjean.' He took another sip of his wine.

'You have another suspect, then?' The doctor was looking at him, wide-eyed with curiosity.

'Perhaps. I'm not sure yet. I'm still looking for a motive. But I'm hoping that's what I'm going to find in Paris.'

CHAPTER THIRTY

The *mairie* stood in the corner of the Place Joseph Yvon, in an old two-storey house opposite the church. On Groix, the town hall had been given the more elevated status of *Hotel de Ville*, which was emblazoned black on white, above a small, semi-circular balcony from which the tricolour furled and unfurled in the afternoon breeze.

Enzo climbed a short flight of steps to an arched doorway and pushed dark blue doors into a tiled foyer. Through frosted glass he saw a staircase wind its way up to the second floor. The *accueil* was through an opening to his left.

A young woman behind the counter raised her eyes and smiled. There was clear recognition in her smile, giving way almost immediately to a quizzical curiosity. 'Can I help you, monsieur?'

'Yes.' Enzo beamed at her and thought what an attractive woman she was. Something of that assessment must have transmitted itself to her, for she beamed back. Flattered, and not uninterested. Enzo leaned on the counter, lowering his head confidentially. He saw her eyes widen, sensing that he was about to admit her to some inner circle where secrets might be shared. 'I was wondering if you might be able to tell me when certain individuals first came to the island.'

She nodded slowly, realising that to answer in the positive would lead to the sharing of a confidence that would indeed make her a part of that inner circle. 'I'm sure I can.'

Enzo's smile faded suddenly, and he lowered his voice. 'But I need to be certain that I can rely on your absolute discretion.'

She lowered her voice to match his. 'Of that, Monsieur Macleod, you can be quite certain. Any information that passes between us will do so in the strictest confidence.'

Enzo smiled.

The breeze had stiffened again during the afternoon, but was still soft on the skin. Enzo looked south, out across the sparkling waters of the Bay of Biscay, and saw smoke being whipped away on the edge of the wind as soon as it rose from Jacques Gassman's chimney. The whitewashed stone cottage was probably somewhere between a hundred and fifty and two hundred years old, and had survived every assault the winter sou' westerlies had thrown at it over nearly two centuries. It seemed to stand braced, once more, for the winter to come. Weary but resolute. It was nothing new.

Enzo abandoned his jeep and walked around to the front of the house, clutching the manila envelope that Guéguen had left for him at Port Mélite. To his disappointment, he saw that the old doctor's Range Rover was not parked in the lean-to. Either he had not yet returned from town, or he had come and gone again. Enzo decided to wait.

He tried the door, and found that, as before, it was not locked. Gassman's old labrador was stretched out in front of the dying embers of the fire, and raised a lazy head to cast a glance in Enzo's direction as he came in. A few sniffs in the air was enough to satisfy him that Enzo was someone he knew, a scent matched as accurately as a fingerprint to the catalogue of smells filed away in some compartment of his memory dedicated to that purpose.

Enzo crossed the room and crouched down in front of the fire to ruffle the dog's head and ears, further reassurance if any were needed. But Oscar had already closed his eyes again, and issued only the merest whimper of acknowledgement. Enzo stood and looked around the room, checking his watch impatiently.

The place smelled of old age. Of stale cooking and body odour. And the ever-present perfume of dog hair. Enzo perched for some minutes on the edge of the armchair nearest the fire, watching as glowing logs slowly crumbled to ash. But he couldn't contain his impatience for long. Or his curiosity, and he stood and began to wander around the room, touching things. Ornaments, books, a discarded pair of reading glasses, a framed photograph of an attractive young woman. Black and white, dated to early or mid-twentieth century by hairstyle and make-up. It was strange, he thought, how photographs from an era when the world was at war and millions had died seemed somehow innocent. It was, he imagined, Doctor Gassman's dead wife, taken when she was still barely more than a girl.

The kitchen door stood ajar. The door next to it was closed.

Enzo paused, listening, certain he would hear the Range Rover from a distance if it approached. He opened the door next to the kitchen and found himself in a tiny room cluttered with filing cabinets and bookcases, an antique writing bureau, and a small worktable strewn with books and magazines. Gassman's study. On the wall hung another framed picture of the woman out in the living room. A little older, but still attractive, with bright, smiling eyes, blond hair catching the light that slanted at an angle across her face.

Enzo wandered around the cramped little *bureau*, running eyes over everything, and felt uncomfortable, prying as he was into another man's private world. The top of the writing bureau was rolled back, revealing shelves and dockets stuffed with papers and stationery, paperclips and pens. And Enzo found his eye drawn to an open compartment on the upper left side of the desk where a stack of what at first sight appeared to be thin maroon notebooks was held together by a thick elastic band. But they weren't notebooks. He saw the gold crest of the *République française,* and the word *Passeport* embossed beneath it.

Why would Gassman have so many passports? He reached for the pile and removed the elastic band. And as he riffled through them, realised that Gassman had kept all his old passports dating right back to the nineteen-fifties. A glance through the photographs in each took him on a journey back into the old man's youth. Like rewinding time. But it was the passport that covered the period of the early sixties that interested him most. He stopped and flicked through its pages, looking at the visas and immigration stamps of a man who had done quite a bit of travelling in his younger years. And what he saw confirmed both the records at the *mairie*, and his worst fears.

He heard the sound of a vehicle, and glancing up saw Gassman's Range Rover bumping along the narrow track towards the house. He quickly reassembled the passports into their stack and snapped the elastic around them, replacing them exactly as he had found them. Then he hurried through to the living room and opened the front door. He would be in the front garden by the time the vehicle rounded the house.

His face was flushed, and he breathed deeply to try to slow his heart rate. He was certain he knew now who had murdered Killian. All he needed was the proof, and an understanding of why.

When he got back to the annex, Enzo sat in the dead man's seat and booted up his laptop. He made a search for the website of the University of Leicester in the English midlands, and from there to the page dedicated to his old friend Doctor John Bond. He clicked on a contact link that opened up a fresh email and tapped in a title. *Shell casing*. Then he moved his cursor into the text box.

Hi John,
  It's been a long time, but I've seen you a lot in the news this last year. I was wondering if I could trouble you to do a big favour for an old friend . . .

CHAPTER THIRTY-ONE

As on the day he arrived, the weather had closed in again. Low, bruising cloud scraping the hilltops, blown in on a wind from the south-west that was mild but wet. The rain fell in a fine, wetting mist that was sucked in under the umbrella that Jane had lent him. Enzo lowered his head, squinting through the rain searching for the name of the boat that the gendarme had given him on the phone.

The pontoon that ran between the boats in the tiny marina rose and fell with the swell of the water in the harbour, making him feel a little drunk. He glanced up and saw that the line of houses and hotels that lined the Port Tudy quayside had almost vanished in the smirr. The rattle of cables and the cries of seagulls filled his ears.

And then there it was. White, painted on a blue plaque. *La Bohème*. Metal hawsers running up the mast fibrillated in the wind, whining, metal vibrating against metal. Enzo stepped onto the shiny wooden boards at the stern of the little yacht, clutching a cable to steady himself, then pushed open the door that led down to the shelter of the cabin. A few steps took him out of the rain to where Adjudant Richard Guéguen sat on an upholstered bench seat along the starboard side. There was a table between facing benches, and a small galley at the far end. Curtains were drawn on the side windows. Enzo slipped into the bench opposite Guéguen, propping his folded umbrella against the wall, rivulets of rainwater streaming from the point of it across the floor.

The air was stale and damp in here, and it was almost dark, cracks of grey light around the curtains providing the only illumination. The two men sat in silence for some minutes. Then Guéguen said, 'Anyone see you get on board?'

Enzo shrugged. 'There aren't many people around in this weather. And it's early yet.'

The gendarme nodded. 'Was the autopsy report any good to you?'

'It was.'

Guéguen raised an eyebrow. 'What did you find?'

'It's what I didn't find that made it interesting.'

Guéguen frowned, dark eyes laden with curiosity. But Enzo did not elucidate. 'Did you manage to get the shell casing?'

'I did.' The younger man pushed a hand into the pocket of his dark blue waterproof jacket and pulled out a clear plastic ziplock evidence bag. He dropped it on the table, and Enzo heard the clunk of the brass shell casing on its wooden surface. He picked it up and held it towards the light creeping in around the window. The casing of the 9mm Parabellum bullet felt surprisingly heavy.

'You know how it gets its name?' he said. 'Parabellum?'

Guéguen shook his head.

'It's from a Latin phrase, *si vis pacem, para bellum.*'

'Meaning?'

'If you seek peace, prepare for war.'

'There will be a war break out if anyone upstairs finds out I gave you this.'

'They won't hear it from me.'

'I still don't understand what you want with it. There were no fingerprints found on it.'

'I know.' Enzo laid the shell casing in its bag on the table and pushed it back towards Guéguen. 'I need you to do me another favour.'

Guéguen leaned back and shoved out his jaw. 'You're pushing your luck, monsieur.'

Enzo delved into his shoulder bag, and brought out a green Tupperware food box. He prised off the lid to reveal a dirty wine glass with polystyrene granules packed around it. 'There are probably two or three sets of prints on this glass. I think one of them may belong to our murderer. I need you to pack it up securely and send it along with the shell casing to a colleague of mine in England. If there's a match, then we've got our man.' He pushed a slip of paper with a name and address on it across the table. And then a sealed white envelope. 'And put this in with it.'

Guéguen leaned forward and peered at the glass, then looked up at Enzo, eyes wide, intrigued. 'Who do you suspect?'

'I don't want to say anything until I am sure. I'd send it myself, but I don't have time. I have to catch the train to Paris from Lorient in just under two hours. So I need to be on the next ferry.'

The gendarme frowned and shook his head again. 'I still don't understand. If there's no fingerprint on the shell casing, how can it match with anything on the glass?'

'Because,' Enzo said, 'there's a chance that there *is* a fingerprint on the casing. Just not one that's visible with conventional techniques. You see, . . .' he leaned forward, miming to illustrate his words as he spoke, ' . . .the killer would have had to load the magazine with bullets, pushing each one in with his thumb against the pressure of the spring. And if he did that, then he will have left an invisible print.'

The skin around Guéguen's eyes crinkled with consternation. 'How?'

'Because the natural sweat present on the fingers reacts with the metal of the casing, in effect engraving the fingerprint invisibly into it. Sweat is a complex mix of water, inorganic salts like sodium chloride, and other oily compounds. These have a corrosive effect on the brass. And, in fact, while the heat generated by the process of firing the bullet will have obliterated any normal prints, it will actually have burned the sweat print more deeply into the metal. My colleague, Doctor Bond, has invented a technique for making those engraved prints visible.' Enzo smiled. 'Deceptively simple, really. He applies a 2,500 volt electrostatic charge, then dusts the casing with a fine carbon powder which clings to the areas of metal corroded by the sweat. And, bingo! You have a fingerprint. Unfortunately the technique has not yet been granted a patent, so the only person in the world who can carry out this test is Doctor Bond himself. Which is why we have to send everything to him.'

The gendarme stared at him, almost open-mouthed. 'That's amazing, monsieur. The number of cold cases that could solve . . .'

Enzo nodded. 'It's a technique that can also be used for recovering fingerprints from exploded terrorist bombs. A conclusive way of catching the bomb makers. It's going to revolutionise crime detection.' He stood up. 'But for the moment, let's just hope that it nets us Killian's murderer.' He reached out a hand to shake Guéguen's, then lifted his umbrella.

As he stepped from the boat to the pontoon he saw, through the mist of rain, the lights of the ferry approaching the harbour. The wind whipped at his umbrella, making it difficult to hold. He tipped it in the direction from which the wind blew, and teetered unsteadily back towards the quayside. He was climbing the steps to the quay just as the ferry slipped through the narrow harbour entrance, a blast of its horn ringing around the little enclosed bay.

Fifteen minutes later, as he gazed from the rain-smeared window on the passenger deck, he saw Adjudant Guéguen emerging from *La Bohème* to make his way back to shore, Enzo's Tupperware box tucked beneath his jacket.

It was, Enzo supposed, a long shot. The killer might have worn gloves when he loaded the gun. Or the magazine could have been preloaded. In either of those circumstances, any print recovered from the shell casing would not belong to the man who murdered Adam Killian.

He turned away from the window and found a seat, and when finally the boat had completed its turn in the relatively calm waters of the harbour and headed out again into the strait, he set his sights for the moment not on who murdered Killian, but why. The answer to that, he hoped, was waiting for him in Paris.

PART FOUR

CHAPTER THIRTY-TWO

Paris, France, November 2009

The Simon Wiesenthal Centre in the Rue Laugier was located in a four-storey brick building opposite the narrow Rue Galvani. A stone-faced ground floor was accessed through an arched doorway. An equally stone-faced Gérard Cohen met Enzo in the entrance as arranged. He was a small man, clutching a large leather briefcase, and was completely bald. He had a lined, almost wizened face and small, black, suspicious eyes. He wore a dark blue suit that had seen better days. Enzo noticed how, under the jacket, the cuffs of his white shirt were frayed. His collar was crumpled, and his tie too tightly tied. He had a small, neatly trimmed silver moustache above too-full lips that were purple and shiny wet. Enzo thought that he must be at least seventy-five.

He shook Enzo's hand with a firm but brief grip. Enzo reached for the door to hold it open for him. But he shook his head. 'I no longer have an office here, monsieur.' He nodded along the street towards the Café Liberté on the far corner of the Rue Guillaume Tell. 'But you can buy me a drink.'

He walked with quick, shuffling steps along the street, almost running, and Enzo had to work to keep up with him. It was still dry in Paris, and mild. But a leaden sky presaged the coming rain that Enzo's train had earlier outrun. They passed the Shri Ganesh Indian restaurant with its maroon canopies and crossed the street diagonally to the opposite corner, provoking a flurry of car horns.

Cohen took a seat by the window and Enzo slipped into a chair opposite. The café was also a *tabac* and sold lottery tickets, and so there was a constant stream of clients. It was noisy, customers barracking at the bar, the rumble of diesel engines out in the street, and the tinny, wasp-like buzz of motor scooters whizzing past. Ideal for an exchange of confidential information. The place smelled of stale alcohol and fried onions, but the smokers stood out on the pavements these days, so they were spared the fugg.

Enzo could see from the nicotine stains on his fingers that Cohen was also a smoker. He could smell the stale smoke that clung to his clothes but wasn't certain if it was the enforced abstinence from cigarettes or some deeper insecurity that made him so nervous. The one-time Wiesenthal investigator kept glancing from the window towards the *quincaillerie-droguerie* opposite, as if there might be someone watching them from across the street. He constantly interlinked and unlinked his fingers on the table in front of him.

Enzo felt unsettled by his apparent edginess. 'Is there any reason for us to be concerned about meeting like this?' he asked.

'Not that I know of, monsieur. But there are usually eyes on us.'

Enzo frowned. 'Whose eyes?'

'The Nazis'.' The word rolled off his tongue almost casually.

Enzo nearly laughed. 'Surely those days are long gone? The people you went after following the war are dead or too old to be a threat.'

'Yes. But there is a new generation, monsieur. And they regard the people we hunted as heroes. And those who hunted them as vermin to be exterminated.'

The barman came to their table and they ordered beers.

Cohen fixed him with a penetrating stare. 'So. How can I help you?'

'You know how you can help me. I want to know what you and Adam Killian wrote about in your exchange of letters. Why he came to see you.'

Cohen scratched his chin, and an alien-like tongue darted out to pass quickly over his already wet lips before withdrawing again behind yellowed teeth. He looked at Enzo pensively. 'I checked you out, monsieur. You have quite a presence on the Net.'

'Yes,' Enzo agreed ruefully. 'Unfortunately I do.'

'It's where I live these days.'

Enzo frowned.

Cohen explained. 'On the Internet. I spend most of my waking hours online. It's incredible, you know, just how much Nazi propaganda there is out there masquerading as fact, how many sites there are where the neos meet to exchange ideas and intelligence. They are stitching themselves back into the fabric of our society, without our even being aware of it.'

Enzo looked at him speculatively, wondering if he was just another paranoid conspiracy theorist, or whether there was any truth in his assertions. 'Are you going to tell me about Adam Killian or not?'

Their beers arrived, and Cohen took a long pull at his, holding his glass in a hand that shook a little as he raised it to his mouth. 'Did you ever hear of a man called Erik Fleischer?'

Enzo shook his head.

'He was a young Bavarian doctor, newly qualified when war broke out. He was taken under the wing of a certain Aribert Heim, an SS doctor assigned initially to the concentration camp at Mauthausen in Austria. You probably know Heim better by his nickname. Doctor Death.'

Enzo raised an eyebrow in surprise. He had been vaguely aware of newspaper articles about Nazi hunters closing in on the last surviving Nazi on the most-wanted list from World War Two. The press had called him Doctor Death, and he was rumoured to be still alive and hiding somewhere in Patagonia.

'Anyway, Fleischer was Heim's assistant, and for several months in 1941 they carried out the most horrific experiments on Jewish prisoners at Mauthausen. They injected numerous substances directly into their hearts just to see what physical reactions they might cause. Things like petrol, water, various poisons. The eyewitness account of a Mauthausen survivor told of a young eighteen-year-old boy being taken to their clinic with inflammation of the foot. Fascinated by his level of fitness, they discovered that he played football. But instead of treating the foot inflammation, they anaesthetised him, opened him up, dissected one kidney, removed the other, then castrated him. Finally he was decapitated, and Heim boiled the flesh off the skull so that it could be put on display.'

Enzo felt the hairs stand up all over his body, raised by a mix of anger and revulsion, and he washed the bad taste quickly from his mouth with another gulp of beer.

'Heim went on to another camp at Ebensee, near Linz, and ended up in Finland. Fleischer went to Majdanek concentration camp near Lublin, in Poland, where he earned the nickname of "The Butcher". He continued his experiments on prisoners with various forms of poison and surgery, before being assigned to a field hospital on the eastern front. After the war he went back to Bavaria and set up a very successful gynaecology practice in Munich.'

Cohen glanced nervously from the window and took several more mouthfuls of beer.

'The war crimes people finally caught up with him in 1951. But the Nazis still had a well-oiled early warning system and escape network in those days. He was tipped off and got away, leaving behind a wife and two children.'

'He just disappeared?'

'At first, yes. It took investigators nearly ten years to find him again. But we're pretty sure they did. Our operatives tracked him down finally to the Moroccan seaport of Agadir. He had given up his medical status and was working under the name of Yves Vaurs as the manager of the city's fishmarket.

They had been watching him for several weeks, photographing him, making comparisons with photographic evidence already possessed, before deciding to move in.'

And suddenly everything started falling into place for Enzo. He said, 'On the night of February 29 1960, right?'

Cohen blinked beady, suspicious eyes at him. 'How do you know that?'

'I'll tell you in a moment, Monsieur Cohen. What happened that night?'

'Well, I'm assuming you're aware that an earthquake destroyed most of the town.'

'Yes.'

'All three operatives died in the quake. Missing, presumed dead.'

'And Fleischer?'

'As far as we knew, he was also killed. His apartment block in the old kasbah was completely destroyed. There were no survivors from that building.'

'So you stopped looking for him?'

'We would have pursued him all the way to hell and back, Monsieur Macleod. But death robbed us of that option. Case closed.'

'Until Adam Killian contacted you.'

'Well, he didn't come to us with any fresh information, if that's what you mean. But he did arouse our interest, yes.'

'What did he say?'

'When he first wrote he was just looking for information about Fleischer. He didn't say why. I sent him the standard background that we put out to the press when we believed he was still alive. We had several exchanges, then, before he telephoned me at the centre one day, asking if he could meet me here in Paris.'

'Why did he want to meet you?

'Because, as with you, monsieur, there was a limit to how much I was prepared to give out by mail or by telephone.' He drained his glass. 'I could do with another of these.'

Enzo caught the attention of the barman and ordered another two glasses of beer.

Cohen waited until he had a fresh glass in his hand before he continued. 'He was interested to see any photographs we had of Fleischer.'

'And you were able to show him some?'

'I let him see some of those we had in the file. Fleischer was still a young man then, of course. Killian spent a long time looking at them, and then asked if he could keep them.'

'You gave him copies?'

'No, monsieur, I did not. He was very disappointed. But we were not prepared to let them pass into general circulation.'

'Did he say why he was so interested in Fleischer?'

'No, he wouldn't tell me.'

'Did you arrive at any conclusions about that yourself?'

'It seemed to me pretty clear that he thought he had found Fleischer and was looking for some way to confirm his identity.'

'But you didn't take that too seriously?'

'No, monsieur. We used to be inundated with claimed

sightings. Most of them, of course, were either fanciful or malicious. Besides . . . Fleischer was dead.' He paused, swirling his beer around in his glass, staring into the bubbles that foamed to the surface. 'He wanted to know if we had any other means of confirming Fleischer's identity. Other than photographic comparison, that is.'

'And did you?'

Cohen raised his eyes to scrutinise the Scotsman's face, hesitating for a moment, as if pondering whether or not to respond with the truth. Finally he said, 'Yes, we did.' He paused. 'And still do.'

'How?'

'At Mauthausen, monsieur, there was a young prisoner who had trained as a hairdresser. He was assigned to cut the hair of the SS officers who ran the camp. And because he made such a good job of it, they kept him alive. An older prisoner, a lecturer in science at the University of Vienna before the war, persuaded him to smuggle out a lock of hair from each of the officers. These were preserved, noted, dated and hidden. The old professor believed they would provide an ideal way of proving the identity of these criminals after the war.'

Enzo nodded. For decades, examination of hair under a comparison microscope had provided forensic scientists with a good, although not foolproof, basis for identifying both victims and criminals.

'And he was right. Although the old professor did not survive the camps himself, the young barber and his hair clippings did. And they were used, along with photographic evidence and eyewitness accounts, to convict several war criminals in the years that followed.'

'And you still have a sample of Fleischer's hair?'

'We do. Monsieur Killian and I went on to exchange several letters on the subject. He was anxious to ascertain that the hair would be available for scientific testing, if requested.'

Enzo sat back in his chair and raised his eyes towards the ceiling. Suddenly the note Killian had scribbled on the shopping list on the fridge door made absolute sense. *A bit of the flood will boil the feast.* Which, with the Spoonerism reversed, translated as, *a fit of the blood will foil the beast.* Somehow Killian had obtained a DNA sample from the man he suspected to be Erik Fleischer. Although still in its infancy in 1990, DNA comparison was already being employed by forensic investigators to identify criminals. Killian had worked in the field of tropical medical genetics, so he would have been familiar with the technology. A simple comparison of mitochondrial DNA between the hair and the suspect would have provided definitive proof of identity.

His mind was flitting with butterfly randomness among myriad thoughts flooding his brain. Killian would have needed a sizeable sample to make the comparison. Somehow he must have got that. But how? And where had he hidden it? He opened his eyes again to find Cohen watching him.

'You think Fleischer didn't die in Agadir?' the old man said.

'Adam Killian was certain he didn't.'

'So you believe he found someone that he thought to be Fleischer?'

'Yes.'

'But how would he know? How would he ever have suspected?'

Enzo shook his head. 'I have no idea. But your hair sample gave him the means by which he thought he could prove it. Do you have a photograph you can show me?'

'Yes, of course.' Cohen lifted his briefcase on to the table and took out a fat manila folder. Enzo watched as he thumbed through yellowing documents with official stamps, extracts from registers of birth and marriage, reports, correspondence, photographs. Dozens of photographs, including several old, blurred prints from his youth. A smiling young man giving no clue as to the monster within. Finally Cohen separated out an eight by ten black and white print and pushed it across the table towards Enzo. 'That's probably about the best, taken around 1945 we think.'

'What about the ones taken in Morocco?'

'Unfortunately the photographs taken in Agadir were lost with our operatives in the earthquake.'

Enzo took out his half-moon reading glasses and perched them on the end of his nose to peer at the print Cohen had given him. Fleischer stood grinning self-consciously for the camera. He was in uniform, but holding his cap in his hands. It had clearly been blown up from a smaller print and was grainy, but quite sharp. His face was thin and pale. He had a thick head of black hair and cautious eyes. Enzo stared at it for a very long time. There was something familiar about the face, although it was difficult to say what. Something, perhaps, in the set of the jaw or the line of the mouth. But this had been taken more than sixty years ago. If the man in the photograph were still alive, he would be in his nineties now. Virtually unrecognisable.

'And you, monsieur?'

Enzo looked up, eyebrows raised, to meet Cohen's naked curiosity.

'Do you believe he found Erik Fleischer?'

'Yes, I do,' Enzo said. 'And I also believe he is still alive.'

CHAPTER THIRTY-THREE

From the gallery beyond the living and working area, Enzo stood in the semi-darkness looking down into the well of the building, where Charlotte conducted her patient consultations in the indoor garden. The rain, finally, had caught up with him, and he heard it battering now on the glass roof overhead, almost drowning out the musical tinkle of the artificial stream in the garden below.

From here he could also see into her bedroom, glass walls opening onto a view of the garden beneath it. A bedside lamp cast a warm glow around it, and he saw the rumpled sheets of her unmade bed. A bed he had shared with her many times, always aware of how exposed they were to the view of anyone standing where he stood now. It had always been an inhibiting factor.

But not for Charlotte. She had laughed at the idea of feeling watched and told him the story of the two Italian soldiers billeted during the war with the former owners of this one-time coal merchant's in the thirteenth *arrondissement*. On the day of liberation, the elderly couple had murdered the soldiers and buried them under the floor of the former coal store, an area now cemented over and providing the foundation for Charlotte's indoor garden. They had told her this when selling her the property, and she had been amused by the idea that her home might be haunted by their ghosts. If anyone was watching them, she had once told Enzo, it would be her Italians. And who could deny them a little entertainment after their lives had been cut so brutally short?

'Will you stay for something to eat?'

He turned and saw her standing at the top of the short flight of steps leading up to her office. He had not heard her hang up the phone. 'No, I won't. I have to get out to Charles de Gaulle tonight. I'm booked into one of the airport hotels.'

'You could have stayed here,' she said. And when he didn't respond, added, 'You know I have a guest bedroom.'

He felt unaccountably disappointed. He might be the father of her child, but it seemed he was no longer welcome to share her bed. 'The flight to Morocco leaves early. It made more sense to be at a hotel out there.'

'Then why are you here?' The light was behind her, and he couldn't see her face. But her body was outlined in silhouette. Tall and willowy, dark curls falling abundantly over her shoulders. He felt the pain of their estrangement acutely.

'We have unfinished business.'

'I don't think so.'

'You left Groix before we had the chance to talk.'

'There was nothing left to say.'

He drew a deep breath to calm himself. This meeting with her had been on his mind all throughout the long rail journey from Brittany. He had rehearsed so many things in his mind. What he would say, how he would say it. And now the spotlight was on him, he seemed paralysed by stage fright. But perhaps it was only the outcome he feared.

'Was there some other reason for your visit?'

He hesitated. 'You said, at Port Mélite, that you thought Killian might have spent time in prison.'

'Ahh.' She came down the steps. 'The ulterior motive. There's always an ulterior motive with you, Enzo, isn't there?'

He closed his eyes and exhaled slowly, cursing himself for his stupidity. He had given her the perfect opportunity to deflect his questions, to change the focus of their exchange. Now anything he might say would be construed as opportunistic and lacking sincerity. He decided to let the Killian question drop. 'No. Our child is both my primary and my ulterior motive. Nothing else matters.'

'Oh, good. So I have your undivided attention, then.'

'Yes, you do.'

She turned away, sauntering along the gallery, trailing her fingers along the handrail, before turning back to face him. 'Well, I suppose it's only fair to tell you that I have made a decision.'

He felt the blood turn cold in his veins. If she had opted for termination, there was, in truth, almost nothing he could do about it. 'And?'

'I've decided to go ahead and have the baby.'

His sense of relief was almost overwhelming. 'Oh, Charlotte, I'm so glad.'

'But there's a condition attached to it, Enzo.' She stared at him for a long time. 'The child will be mine, not yours. You may be his biological father, but I really don't believe that you are suitable to raise him. For all sorts of reasons, most of which we've already discussed.'

He opened his mouth to argue the point, but she cut him off. 'For heaven's sake, Enzo, for once in your life think about someone else for a change.'

Enzo bit back a retort.

'I'll raise him on my own. And at my own expense. I'll not take a centime from you. I don't want you having any claim on him of any kind. He will be entirely my responsibility, and he will never know that you are his father.'

He stared back at her in disbelief. The cold lack of emotion in her words was unnerving.

'That's the price of your son's life, Enzo. Your choice. But if you can't accept it, then I'll go ahead with the termination.'

CHAPTER THIRTY-FOUR

Agadir, Morocco, November 2009

The taxi bumped and rattled its way along the highway from the airport. Dust rose in the hot air all around, almost obscuring a desolate landscape of sand and scrub. After the cool autumn temperatures in France, it seemed incongruous to be back in shirtsleeves and sandals. Enzo felt the sweat prickling across his forehead. There was no air-conditioning in the car, and the air blowing in the driver's open window did little to cool him. It was close to thirty degrees centigrade, the African sun bright in the southern sky, and Enzo had been forced to dig out his sunglasses from their winter hibernation in the bottom of his bag.

During the three-hour flight, he had stared blindly out into the endless blue, lost in a turmoil of thoughts about Charlotte and his unborn son. Thoughts that had kept him awake most of the night, listening to the flights coming and going, trying to reach some decision about a course of action. In the end, he had realised that he was powerless to do anything. At least until the child was born. Then, with the fear of termination no longer an issue, he could surely make some legal claim on the child. But he had been haunted, during all those waking hours, by the words that Charlotte had used to cut him open and lay him bare. *For heaven's sake, Enzo, for once in your life think about someone else for a change.*

He gazed from the window as the outskirts of Agadir grew up around the arterial route that led unwaveringly towards the town centre. Almost fifty years after the quake, it still looked like a town in ruins. Unfinished apartment blocks sprang up like weeds from the dust and rubble. Roads had been laid out around gap sites, and satellite dishes grew like fungus on unrendered cement. Here and there was the odd splash of colour, red, green, blue, amongst all the grey. Shops and stalls selling clothes and groceries. Enzo was reminded of video footage he had seen on television of a bombed-out Beirut.

As they neared the coast and the centre, they passed walled villas slumbering in the shade of tall trees, rows of shop fronts open for business. The traffic thickened, like cholesterol constricting the bloodflow, until they reached the boulevard that followed the shoreline along the tourist strip. Luxury hotels, palm trees, manicured lawns.

Enzo saw the curve of the beach, a deep crescent of golden sand washed by warm north Atlantic waters. It stretched away into a hazy distance, where the land rose above the docks at the north end and the remains of the old kasbah stood on the hill above.

Enzo tapped the driver on the shoulder. 'Could you take me to the kasbah?'

The driver shrugged, without turning. 'Nothing to see there, monsieur.'

'All the same . . .'

He shrugged again. 'Sure.'

Major new motorways converged on an enormous circular junction at the foot of the hill where the original city had once stood, and the driver turned off, circumventing road works and bumping over broken tarmac before heading up towards the walls of the kasbah. The road wound steeply around the hillside before spilling them out into a large paved parking area.

'You walk from here,' the driver said. 'I'll wait for you.'

Enzo stood looking out over the wall that bound the car park down on to the docks below, the marina, and the port where all the fishing boats were tied up in rows. Then he turned to brave the touts and stallholders who lined the climb towards the old gate. He brushed aside offers of carpets and jewelry, pottery and camel rides, bottles of soda and food proffered by filthy fingers. Faces that were hopeful on his approach spat imprecations at his back, and he passed through the old gateway, climbing up broken steps into the kasbah itself.

He had not known quite what to expect, but when finally he arrived, there was nothing to see. The old broken-down city walls contained only rubble, sand, and dusty desert shrubs clinging obstinately to cracks in the parched earth. An old man in a timeworn *djellaba*, his head wrapped in grey cloth, followed him around, holding out a black kid goat.

It was almost impossible to imagine this as a thriving town of streets and apartments, restaurants and souks, a place thronging with people and life. Those who had died here remained here, beneath the buildings that had fallen on them. Like one enormous cemetery where the bodies of many thousands were entombed for eternity, a reminder, if any were needed, of the forces that nature wielded over man.

And here, too, was where the three operatives of the Wiesenthal organisation had died as they were closing in on the war criminal, Erik Fleischer. The same place that Fleischer himself had supposedly perished. But all Enzo could see now in his mind's eye was the yellow Post-it stuck between the pages of the *Everyman Encyclopedia* in Killian's study. *He did not die.*

In the shadow of the hill, the road ran around the perimeter of the docks. Huge rusting sheds shimmered in the heat, and the hulking carcasses of half-built boats stood, ribs exposed, like the skeletons of strange beasts long extinct. The decaying remains of ancient fishing boats sat up in the dry docks like the rotting remains of beached whales, and hundreds of small, blue-painted fishing craft were tied up to lines of wooden posts stretching across the inner harbour.

The fish market and the *Office National des Pêches* had been rebuilt since Fleischer's day, a big square cream-coloured concrete building with pale blue stripes. A long gallery high up in the apex of the roof ran from one end of the building to the other, and windows all along its length looked down on to the trading floor below. Fish were beautifully laid out in colourful patterns in rectangular wooden boxes contained within numbered lots. Silver sea bream, red mullet, yellow snapper, sardines, white-coated buyers clustered around them in bidding frenzies. Raised voices echoed around the chamber as Enzo walked along the shiny wet concrete of the gallery with the latest in a long line of Fleischer's successors.

Ahmed el-Ghoumari was a personable young man with dark smiling eyes and unblemished olive skin. He wore an expensive suit, with a white shirt and red tie. His black shoes were polished to an impossible shine. He did not look like a man who managed a fish market.

'Your *father's* uncle?' he said.

'No, he was on my mother's side of the family. She was Italian, but her mother was French. Uncle Yves is the missing piece of the family jigsaw.'

'Of course, so many people died in the earthquake, their bodies never recovered. But I'm afraid Yves Vaurs was long before my time. I wasn't even born then.' Ahmed el-Ghoumari laughed, an infectious laugh full of unselfconscious good humour. 'The only one I can think of who might have been around in those days was old Khalid.' There was an affection in his smile as he spoke the old man's name. 'Long past retirement, but no one has ever had the heart to ask him to go. He works in the accounts department now as a runner.' He chuckled. 'I use the word "works" advisedly. And it is probably about thirty years since he ran anywhere. He sits in the office and smokes cigarettes, passes comment on the world, and has long lunches in the fish restaurant down the road. He will be only too happy to talk to you, monsieur.'

Khalid was even happier when Enzo offered to buy him lunch. He wore a grey and cream *djellaba* over faded jeans and open sandals, and he pulled the hood of it up over his baseball cap as they ventured out into the midday sun. He was an old man with a sun-dried face the colour and texture of a walnut. He walked with a limp and a stick, and had a hand-rolled cigarette permanently glued between his lips at the right-hand corner of his mouth.

Fish restaurants lined the road that led to the harbour, little more than prefab huts with open frontages and lines of plastic tables and chairs shaded by huge white parasols. Old Khalid ordered mixed seafood platters for them both and a jug of Pepsi-Cola. Enzo could have done with a beer or a chilled white wine. But neither was an option. Prodigious amounts of fried fish, prawns, and squid arrived on two enormous platters, and Khalid began gorging himself as if he hadn't eaten for a week. For a man half Enzo's size, it seemed as if he might be capable of eating twice as much.

'I was really just a *gamin* when Monsieur Vaurs was the manager here. Eighteen or nineteen. I started out on the fishing boats when I was twelve, but crushed my foot in a stupid accident when I was seventeen. I wasn't fit for the fishing after that. It was Monsieur Vaurs who took me on here. Gave me a job when no one else would. He was a good man.'

Enzo remembered Cohen's tale about the young prisoner in

Mauthausen with the inflamed foot and wondered if Fleischer and Vaurs could really be the same person.

'Poor guy. Died in the earthquake. But just one of thousands, so maybe no one really grieved for him but me. I was lucky, lost no family. But everyone else was too busy grieving for parents, wives, husbands, children. It was a terrible time, monsieur. You have no idea.' He spat out some fishbones on to the plastic table cover and wiped his mouth with the back of his hand before slurping several mouthfuls of Pepsi.

'Yves lived alone then?'

'As far as any of us knew.' Khalid grinned suddenly, revealing a mouthful of gaps and yellow stumps. 'Though there was a rumour about an affair with the wife of some politician.'

'Who?'

'Oh, I wouldn't know, monsieur. No one did. Maybe it was just a story. But he had a certain ... *mystique* ... about him. You know? A sort of swagger. Self-confident. Like a man who was screwing the wife of someone important.' He laughed. 'He had the style of the French. You could have believed anything about him.'

'Everyone thought he was French then?'

Khalid looked at him blankly. 'Why wouldn't they, monsieur, since that is what he was?' He opened a tin that he produced from some hidden pocket, and took out a badly rolled cigarette. He lit it and sucked in a lungful of smoke. 'Come to think of it, I might just have a photograph of him somewhere at home. There was a party to celebrate someone's retirement, and all the staff were there. There were a lot of pictures taken that night. I have a few of them. Or, at least, I did at one time.'

The taxi took them deep into the rebuilt heart of the new Agadir. Apartment blocks lined narrow streets with shops and stalls and spindly trees with dusty green leaves shading donkeys and bicycles. Khalid talked non-stop with their driver in Arabic, sitting next to him in the front seat of the battered Volkswagen, smoking profusely. Enzo sat on his own in the back, staring from the window at the blur of colour and people that smeared his vision. He wasn't really looking, lost still in the despond into which Charlotte had plunged him.

The entrance to Khalid's apartment block was in a shaded alleyway that climbed steeply off the main drag. Enzo paid the driver and followed the old man through an archway and up a tiny staircase to the third floor. The heat was stifling and increased as they climbed. Arab music was blasting out somewhere from a badly tuned radio, and the sound of raised voices rose with the heat from the street below. They squeezed past several bicycles padlocked together on the landing and stepped over boxes and bric-á-brac cluttering the hallway just inside Khalid's tiny apartment. A single room served as a living, dining, kitchen area, with a curtain closing off a recess with a bed. The floor and every available space was littered with the detritus of this man's life. Newspapers, books, empty food cartons, bottles, dirty plates. All the windows were open wide, and the fetid air of the apartment vibrated to the hum of countless flies.

'Have a seat,' Khalid said over his shoulder, as he searched the drawers of an old dresser.

Enzo looked around. But he could not have sat without moving things off chairs. 'That's all right,' he said.

Finally, the old man turned towards him, clutching an envelope of old photographic prints, grinning widely, his eyes screwed up against the smoke that rose into them from his cigarette. 'Got them.' He started leafing through the faded prints, colours that had long since lost their lustre, chuckling and muttering to himself as he recognised forgotten faces, and dredged up long lost memories. Eventually he let out a deep sigh of satisfaction. 'Ahhhh.' And he held out a dog-eared print for Enzo to take. 'Yves Vaurs is the one in the middle.'

Here was a group, standing awkwardly together, smiling self-consciously for the camera. Women with covered heads, a couple of men in *djellabas*, the rest in suits. The faces of people long dead. Enzo wondered how many of them had died in the earthquake.

The man in the middle stood taller than the rest. He had a fine head of thick, black hair and smiled more easily than the others. Although older, it was, unmistakably, the same man in the photograph Gérard Cohen had shown him. Proof, if any were needed now, that Erik Fleischer and Yves Vaurs were one and the same man. A man who had not died, as everyone believed, in the terrible earthquake of 1960. A man who was still alive and living on a tiny island off the coast of Brittany in France.

CHAPTER THIRTY-FIVE

There was something a little unreal about being back on the island after the heat and the bright sunlight of North Africa. Here the air was the colour of sulphur, the sky low and bruised. He'd had some hours to acclimatise himself again to the late French autumn during the long train ride from Paris and a blowy crossing on the ferry. But the wind whipping rain into his face as he disembarked at Port Tudy still came as a shock, stinging his skin red and soaking his jacket and trousers as he struggled with his umbrella to cross the street to Coconut's car rental.

The rain had eased by the time he drove down the hill into Port Mélite, and a dark cloud of depression descended on him as he prepared to unravel the last of Adam Killian's long-obscured message to his son. It would, he knew, lead him to a place he had no real desire to go.

Jane Killian was surprised to see him. 'I didn't expect you back so soon. Actually, you're lucky you caught me. I'm just packing.' She headed back upstairs, and he followed her up and into the master bedroom. A suitcase lay open on the bed, clothes folded neatly around it. 'I'm getting the ferry late afternoon. How was Paris?' She continued to lay items of clothing carefully into the suitcase.

'Wet. But I've been a little further afield than that.'

She turned to look at him. 'Oh? Where?'

'Agadir.'

She seemed surprised at first, then nodded slowly. 'The entry Papa marked in the encyclopedia. What did you find there?'

'A man called Yves Vaurs who was supposed to have died in 1960, but didn't.'

She raised her eyebrows in surprise. 'You actually met him?'

'No. But I talked to someone who knew him. And saw his photograph, a photograph of the same man whose picture I also saw in Paris. A man called Erik Fleischer.'

She stared at him, consternation drawing together frown lines between her brows. 'None of this is making very much sense to me, Enzo.'

He hesitated, turning for a moment to gaze from the window across a dripping wet garden towards the annex. Then he turned back to her. 'Why didn't you tell me that Adam Killian spent time in a concentration camp during the war?'

She turned almost instantly pale, before a blush of pink appeared high on her cheeks, just below the eyes. 'How do you know that?'

'I'm guessing. Am I right?'

She drew her lips into a tight line and nodded. 'Yes. But no one in the world knew about that. Except Adam himself, and Peter. And, of course, me. Although Papa never knew that Peter had told me.'

'Majdanek concentration camp near Lublin, in Poland, right?'

Her eyes opened wider. 'How can you possibly know all this?'

He ignored her questions. 'Why was it such a secret?'

'Oh . . . I don't know.' She waved her hand vaguely through the air. 'All part of Papa's denial of his past, I guess. Of his Polish origins. Although Peter knew about it, he said Papa would never speak of it. Never. And he made Peter promise not to tell anyone.'

'But he told you.'

'We were husband and wife.' There was a defensive tone in her voice. 'We had no secrets between us. But I kept my promise of silence to Peter. That's why you'll find no reference to it or record of it anywhere.' Her eyes were troubled, confused. 'But I don't understand . . . If you found out about it, does that mean it has something to do with his murder?'

Enzo nodded. 'It has everything to do with his murder, Jane.'

The same chill as always permeated the annex. Enzo's depression deepened as he pushed open the door and stood under the naked electric light bulb that hung in the stairwell. He dropped his overnight bag on the floor, not sure how much longer he would be here, but reluctant to take it upstairs, as if to do so was committing him to another cold, lonely night in the attic bedroom.

With the tips of his fingers spread wide, he pushed the door to Killian's study, and it swung slowly inwards. The shutters were still open, and the gloomy light that filtered through the trees in the garden fell through the window and cast dark shadows in every corner. Until he flicked the light switch and flooded the room with cold, harsh light.

Somewhere in here was the final piece of the Killian jigsaw. And he was determined to find it. He walked to the window and stared out into the garden, the trees black with rain, the lawn sodden and patchy. He caught a movement out of the corner of his eye and turned to see the cat that had been haunting him since his arrival. It was sauntering across the grass, tail high, the end of it curled round at the highest point and quivering. Almost as if sensing his eyes on it, the cat stopped and stared at the window. Enzo could see its black coat glistening in the wet. What a miserable life, he thought. Always shut out in the cold and rain. And he wondered whose it was and why it had chosen the Killian garden as its home turf.

On an impulse he went back into the hall and opened the outside door. The cat was no more than eight or ten feet away. He left the door wide, and stood back, an invitation made by body language alone. The animal stood completely still, staring at him, but made no move. Enzo waited for several minutes before the cat finally sat down and continued to stare, clearly unprepared to accept his offer of truce.

'Okay, stay out in the rain then,' he said, and immediately felt foolish for talking to it.

He left the door open and went back into the study. For a moment he stood gazing at the bookcase, then rounded the desk to look at the Post-its he had left lying on it, the message pad, the open diary, the poem propped against the lamp.

What was missing?

He answered his own question immediately.

The letters sent to Killian by Gérard Cohen. His killer must have found and taken them. But Killian would have wanted Peter to see them, surely? For without them his clues would have been almost impossible to decipher.

Enzo had got there without the letters, but there was something else missing. The sample of Fleischer's DNA that Enzo was certain Killian had somehow obtained. He lifted up the Post-it from the fridge. *A fit of the blood will foil the beast.* What else could he have meant? A fit of the blood, a matching of the DNA. But where was it?

He slumped into Killian's captain's seat and let his eyes wander over the desk in front of him. They came to rest on Ronald Ross's framed poem. What in God's name did the poem have to do with anything? And even as he posed the question in his head, the answer came thundering back to him, loud and clear. Mosquitoes! He pulled open the top right-hand drawer and saw there what Jane had called a *pooter*, a home-made contraption of plastic tubing inserted into each end of a clear plastic film container. Made for capturing and transferring insects. There, too, were the insect repellent and the bottle of lactic acid which he knew, in combination with carbon dioxide, was a recognised mosquito attractant.

Damn! Like the tumblers of the combination lock on a safe, everything was suddenly dropping into place.

He stood up and began running his eyes along the shelves of books behind him. There was a whole section on entomology, subdivided into various primary insect species. There were long runs of old journals published by various British entomological societies, *The Entomologist's Record*, *The Entomologist*. There was a small subsection dedicated to the mosquito. Enzo pulled out the first in the row, a slim volume of only eight pages. *Collecting Mosquitoes*, by Eric Classey. It was subtitled *AES Leaflet 11* and had been published in 1945 by the British Amateur Entomologists' Society. Next to it was a series of slender green paperbacks on the life of the mosquito. Five volumes. With trembling fingers he lifted them one by one from the shelf and riffled through their pages, certain that his eye would be caught by a yellow Post-it. But there was nothing, and he rapidly felt his excitement subside into disappointment.

It was only as he lay the last of them on the desk that he noticed its full title, *The Life of the Mosquito, Part 6*. But there were only five books. He checked each volume in turn. Part four was missing. He lifted his eyes and ran them quickly around the room as if he somehow expected to see the missing volume there in front of him where he had never noticed it before. Stupid! He turned back to the bookshelves. Was it filed somewhere else, out of sequence? It would take some time to check.

A noise made him turn his head, and he saw the black cat sitting in the doorway watching him. It held his eye for nearly a minute, before lifting its right paw to drag across its head from behind the ear, lick, and drag again, cleaning itself, wiping the raindrops from its fur. Even as he looked at it, Enzo found himself jumping focus, his gaze settling on the Post-it that had been stuck to the desk lamp. *P, one day you will have to oil my bicycles. Don't forget.*

'Boil my icicles.' Enzo's voice was barely more than a whisper, but it seemed to reverberate around the room. The cat paused mid-lick and looked at him. And suddenly Enzo's face split into a grin. 'You clever old bastard!' he shouted, and the cat turned and fled.

Jane heard him calling from the kitchen and came to the top of the stairs. 'I'm still up here.'

After a moment he appeared in the downstairs hall. His eyes were wide and shining with excitement. 'Jane, I need a hair-drier, do you have one?'

She looked at his hair, neatly tied back in its ponytail and frowned. He had told her he was going to the annex to unravel the final pieces of Killian's message for Peter. She frowned and said, 'You're going to wash your hair now?'

He almost laughed. 'No. It's not for my hair. Do you have one?'

'Of course. But what's it for?'

'Just bring it over to the annex. You'll see.'

By the time she got there, clutching her travel hair-drier, Enzo was in the tiny kitchen. The door of the refrigerator was open wide. He took the drier from her and plugged it into the wall socket above the worktop. He had already unplugged the fridge. 'You said you'd never defrosted this in all the years since your father-in-law's death.'

'It was never very high on my list of priorities. The thing must be thirty years old. And I never kept anything in it.'

Enzo pulled open the door of the tiny icebox at the top of the fridge. It was choked, almost to bursting, with ice and frost, folds of frozen condensation formed over the years sealing it completely closed. He switched on the hair-drier and directed its blast of hot air directly on to the ice.

She looked at him as if he were mad. 'What on earth are you doing?'

'Just what Adam asked Peter to do. I'm boiling his icicles.' He smiled at her consternation. '*P, one day you will have to oil my bicycles. Don't forget.* My guess is that this icebox was probably already pretty furred up, even then. But not entirely. I reckon there was maybe just enough of an opening for your father-in-law to push something past the ice, so that it would be hidden from casual view. And who would think to defrost it to see if there was anything there?'

The ice was already starting to melt and drip down through the fridge.

'You'd better get a basin or something to catch the water, and a chisel or a big screwdriver.'

When she returned with a bucket, and a large, flat-headed screwdriver, water was now pouring from the freezer. Jane placed the bucket beneath it and took the hair-drier from Enzo, allowing him to start prising the melting ice from the roof of the icebox. But it was nearly fifteen minutes before a large slab of it finally released its twenty-year grip and allowed him to start easing it free with burning cold fingers.

He dropped it into the sink and unplugged the hair-drier, and stooped to peer into the darkness of the icebox. It was still partially obscured by ice. There was something there, but he couldn't see what it was. Carefully, he slid his right hand beyond the remaining ice until his fingers made contact with cold, wet plastic. It crinkled at his touch. After several attempts, he managed to catch a corner of it between his index and middle fingers, and slowly eased it out.

Jane peered over his shoulder at the opaque plastic bag in his hands. 'What is it?'

'Looks like one of those ziplock food bags.' He grabbed a dish towel and wiped it dry, then pinched the plastic tab and unzipped it before reaching in to lift out the missing *Life of the Mosquito, Part 4*. It was icy-cold to the touch, but perfectly dry. Taking great care not to damage it in any way, Enzo laid it on the worktop and let it fall open where it would. Between pages 56 and 57 lay the perfectly preserved squashed corpse of a mosquito, its last blood meal rust-brown now, staining the page in a small irregular patch the size of the nail on his little finger.

Jane looked at it, utterly mystified. 'I don't understand.'

But Enzo was smiling. 'A clever man, your father-in-law,' he said. 'Ingenious. He must have wondered how on earth to get a DNA sample from him.'

'From who?'

'Erik Fleischer. A Nazi war criminal hiding here on the Île

de Groix. Killian must have recognised him from his time in Majdanek concentration camp. Or at least, thought he did. He hadn't seen the man for forty-seven, forty-eight years. He needed to be sure. A DNA sample would do it, something to match with the lock of Fleischer's hair that the German authorities still possessed.'

'How would a mosquito help him do that?'

'Because the last thing it must have done on this earth was feed on the blood of Erik Fleischer. Not a big enough sample in 1990 to extract sufficient DNA. But Killian would have known that the PCR process of amplification was just months away. And that if he kept it cool for long enough, it would provide the damning evidence to prove Fleischer's identity. Even if Killian died in the meantime, the evidence would still be there. Dammit, it's still here twenty years later.' He closed the book and slipped it back into its ziplock bag. 'We need to continue to keep it cool. It's now evidence in a murder case.'

He plugged the fridge back into its wall socket, closed up the freezer compartment and took away the bucket of water. Then he placed the plastic bag containing the book on the middle shelf and closed the door.

He turned to find himself trapped in Jane Killian's penetrating gaze. She said, 'Do you know who he is? This Erik Fleischer. Or, at least, who he's been pretending to be all this time?'

Enzo's face clouded, and the lights dimmed in his eyes. 'Yes, Jane. I'm pretty sure I do.'

CHAPTER THIRTY-SIX

Guéguen's blue Citröen van with its red and white flashes on the hood and blue light on the roof rocked in the strength of the unrestrained wind that lashed the south coast. It was the only vehicle in the gravel parking area at the foot of the hill as Enzo drove down, peering through his rain-streaked windscreen to see the breakers smashing over the rocky outcrops at the point.

The rendezvous at the Pointe des Chats had been the gendarme's idea. Since acquiring the autopsy report and the shell casing, he had been paranoid about being seen with Enzo. Hence his choice of meeting place. No one was likely to stumble upon them by accident on a stormy November afternoon by the unmanned lighthouse on this exposed southwest point of the island.

White spume rose high into the air, whipped away on the edge of a wind approaching gale force, obscuring for a moment the orange cowling of the lighthouse that poked up above bowed trees. Enzo drew his jeep in beside the police van and transferred quickly through the rain from one vehicle to the other. Even in the time it took him to cover the few feet between them, he got soaked, and he sat breathing hard in the passenger seat, rain streaming down his face. He turned to see the gendarme watching him carefully. He wore his dark blue peaked *kepi* and a waterproof jacket with a single white horizontal stripe over his gendarme-issue blue pullover and trousers. There was a large white envelope laid across his knees. The windows of the Citröen were already steamed up to opacity. He said, 'Your friend in England responded very quickly.'

Enzo glanced at the envelope. 'What did he find?'

Guéguen shook his head in pensive admiration. 'You're an amazing man, Monsieur Macleod.' He passed the envelope to Enzo and, as the big Scotsman opened it up to remove several printed sheets, added, 'He emailed me a PDF of his findings.'

Enzo scrutinised the printouts of the PDF. Photographic images of digital fingerprints, brief comparison text, and a short note for Enzo.

'As you can see, he did indeed find a print on the shell casing. And, as you suspected, there were several sets of prints on the wine glass you asked me to send him. But one of them was a perfect match.'

Enzo nodded. The very final piece of this long lost puzzle finally snapped into place. But it gave him no satisfaction. His heart weighed like lead in his chest.

Guéguen could not contain his curiosity any longer. 'Whose are they?'

But before Enzo could respond, a burst of white noise issued from the gendarme's police radio. The voice of the duty officer back at Port Tudy crackled across the airwaves.

'We've got a suspicious death, Adjudant. Out at Quéhello. Dubois and Bonnet are already on their way. And Doctor Servat has been notified.'

'Who's dead?'

'Old Doctor Gassman. The postman found him earlier this afternoon. Looks like suicide.'

'Damn! I'm on my way.' Guéguen turned sad eyes towards Enzo. 'I have to go. We'll need to continue this another time.'

'Would you mind if I came with you, Adjudant Guéguen?' Enzo's voice was hushed, and barely audible above the roar of the wind and the sea outside. He had a sick feeling in his stomach.

The gendarme frowned. 'Why?'

'Because I think there is a good chance that Jacques Gassman's death is related to the murder of Adam Killian.'

By the time they got to Gassman's cottage out on the moor beyond Quéhello, several vehicles had already pulled up on the patch of gravel next to the west gable: a van from the gendarmerie, Alain Servat's dark green SUV, an ambulance from Le Bourg, and the *facteur*'s yellow *La Poste* van, the postman himself slumped in the driver's seat, his pale face visible through the rain-distorted side window.

Enzo ducked his head into the rain and followed Guéguen inside. He recognised the smell of the place instantly. Old age and dogs and stale cooking. But there was something new that hung in the air now. A distant whiff of gunshot and the sharp rust-like smell of dried blood. The living room seemed smaller, crowded as it was with people. Two *gendarmes*, Alain Servat, two ambulance men, and now Enzo and Guéguen. The air in the room was cold, the fire long gone out. From upstairs came the pitiful, hoarse yelping of old Gassman's dog, howling for the dead.

Guéguen raised his eyes towards the ceiling. 'What in God's name is that?'

'His dog,' one of the *gendarmes* said.

'Oscar,' Enzo said, and everyone turned to look at him. There was a momentary hiatus during which it became clear that everyone else was wondering why he was there.

'Yes. Oscar.' The gendarme acknowledged the name. 'It was Oscar's barking that alerted the postman to something being wrong. He came in and, well . . .' He moved to one side. The others followed his lead, clearing a space to reveal the body of the old man slumped over the table at the far side of the room, the table where he had taken his solitary meals and where he had ended up, it seemed, taking his own life. It did not take the presence of a doctor to tell that he was dead.

His head lay in a large, sticky pool of blood that had already lost its lustre. It was rapidly browning as it oxidised and would leave a permanent stain in the wood. A Walther P38 semi-automatic pistol was clutched in the retired doctor's right hand. Enzo's eyes dipped to the floor, where he saw a single, discarded brass shell casing.

'Jesus,' Guéguen whispered. He had gone quite pale. Enzo knew he must have seen many dead bodies during his years in the service, but death was something you never got used to. And if you did, it was only because something had died inside of you.

'Looks like a pretty classic suicide,' the other gendarme said. He hesitated. 'Except . . .'

Guéguen looked at him sharply. 'Except what?'

'Well, you know, people usually leave a note. A message, a last thought. So when we got here, I looked around to see if I could find one. I found this in his bureau.' He held up an old, worn, leather identity wallet. Enzo noticed that he had taken the precaution of wearing latex gloves before handling anything, a measure of the improved procedures that Guéguen himself had introduced.

'What is it?'

'Identity papers, Adjudant.'

Guéguen frowned. 'Well, his identity's not in doubt is it?'

'It could be now.' The gendarme opened up the wallet. 'These are wartime identity papers, sir, issued by the German Reich to an SS Officer named Erik Fleischer.'

There was a long silence, broken only by the howling of the wind outside and the rain driving against the windows on the south side of the house, until Enzo's voice resonated softly around the room. 'Could you show me where exactly you found that, officer?'

All heads turned in his direction, and the gendarme flicked a look in the direction of his adjudant, seeking some indication of how to respond. Guéguen gave an almost imperceptible nod of his head.

'It was in here, monsieur.' And the gendarme turned through

the open door behind him. Enzo, followed by Guéguen and the second gendarme, went into Gassman's study after him. 'Just here, in this little open compartment at the top right-hand side of his writing bureau.' He placed the wallet inside it, then lifted it out again. It was where Enzo had found the pile of Gassman's old passports held together by an elastic band. His eyes flitted over the rest of the bureau, but there was no sign of them now.

There was a polite cough in the doorway behind them, and they turned to see Doctor Servat standing there. Enzo hadn't paid him much attention until now. He looked wan, tired. His coat hung loose and damp on his shoulders. 'Shall I tell the ambulance men to take the body away now?'

'No.' Enzo spoke quickly, and was again aware of everyone's eyes on him. 'Nothing should be moved, or touched. This is a crime scene.'

'How can you know that?' Guéguen said.

Enzo pushed back through to the living room and approached the body. Guéguen followed him and turned to the two ambulance men. 'Wait outside please.' And the two men cast sullen eyes at the adjudant, feeling cheated by their exclusion from this moment of high drama.

Enzo waited until the door closed behind them. 'For a start,' he said, 'Jacques Gassman was left-handed.' He looked round to see all their eyes focused on the gun in the old man's right hand. 'If you were going to kill yourself, particularly by shooting yourself in the head, you would want to be sure you didn't botch it. If you were left-handed you would take the gun in your left hand, I think.' He turned to Guéguen. 'And if your ballistics people at Vannes run a check on the gun he is holding, I'm pretty sure they'll find it was the same weapon used to murder Adam Killian.'

It was Alain Servat who broke the silence this time. 'Are you saying that Doctor Gassman murdered Killian?'

'No, I'm saying that someone would like us to think he did.'

Guéguen said, 'You've lost me, Monsieur Macleod. I think you'd better explain.'

'Well,' Enzo said reluctantly, 'at the risk of incriminating myself, I will have to confess to poking about among Doctor Gassman's private papers myself just a few days ago.'

'You broke in?' This from one of the *gendarmes*.

'No. I was here to see him about something else. He was out, so I let myself in. The door wasn't locked. And I suppose I let my curiosity get the better of me. I had just come from the *mairie*, where I had established the date of the doctor's first arrival on the Île de Groix.'

'Which was when?' Alain Servat asked.

'May 1960. About two months after an earthquake that killed around sixteen thousand people in the Moroccan seaport of Agadir. I didn't really believe there was any link between Gassman and events there, but as it happened, I was able to satisfy myself that I was right.' He looked around the faces watching him. Faces that were a study in fascinated incomprehension. Nobody knew quite what to ask next. So he pressed on.

'In that same compartment, officer, where you found

Fleischer's identity papers, there was a bundle of Gassman's old passports dating back to the 1950s. If Gassman had been in Morocco in 1960, there would have been immigration stamps in his passport to show that. Entry and exit.' He paused. 'There weren't.' He waved a hand towards the identity wallet still clutched by the gendarme who found it. 'There was no identity wallet in that compartment. Just the passports. But I'm willing to bet that if you look for those passports now, you'll not find them.'

'Meaning?' Guéguen's concentration was completely focused on Enzo's face.

'Meaning that someone took them and replaced them with Fleischer's identity papers, so we would think that Gassman was really Fleischer. The same person who killed him. The same person who murdered Killian. The same person whose fingerprint we recovered from the shell casing in Killian's study.' He stooped to the floor and took out a pencil from an inside jacket pocket. Carefully, he slipped the pointed end of it inside the spent shell casing and stood up again, holding it up for them all to see. 'The same person whose fingerprint, I am sure, we will also find on this one.'

The wind outside was gusting now to gale force and beyond. They heard it whining in the rafters and rattling the window frames and blowing cold air around their feet. Upstairs, poor Oscar still barked and yelped, his voice almost completely gone now.

'I think you'd better tell us a little more about this Fleischer,' Guéguen said.

Enzo drew a deep breath. 'Erik Fleischer is a Nazi war

criminal. Investigators on his trail thought he had been killed in the 1960 earthquake in Agadir. But Fleischer didn't die in the quake. He escaped and ended up here under an assumed identity on the Île de Groix, a place he thought he would be safe, where no one would ever recognise him in a million years. Except that someone did. A former inmate of the Majdanek concentration camp in Poland, where Fleischer had experimented on prisoners with poisons and surgery.'

'Adam Killian was that inmate?' Guéguen's eyes were wide now in amazement.

Enzo nodded. 'Killian was a Polish national who spent nearly two-and-a-half years at Majdanek. By some miracle he survived both the camp and the war, to end up in England taking British citizenship and retiring finally to this quiet Breton island to pursue his hobby of studying insects. I guess the last thing he expected was to come face-to-face with the man he knew as "The Butcher."' He laid the shell casing carefully on the table top. 'But he wasn't sure. So, somehow, he obtained a sample of Fleischer's DNA for comparison with some of the man's hair still held by investigators in Germany.'

'So,' Guéguen said, 'Fleischer realised that Killian knew who he was and murdered him.'

The gendarme with the identity wallet was getting excited. 'And if Doctor Gassman was killed to make us think he was Fleischer, that must mean that the real Fleischer is still alive.'

'Oh, yes,' Enzo said. 'Erik Fleischer is still very much alive.'

'Who is he?' Guéguen said.

Enzo turned towards him and gave him a long, hard look.

Finally he said, 'We won't know that for sure until we match up the DNA sample that Killian obtained.'

'You mean you have it?'

'I mean that Killian hid it somewhere in his study, preserved somehow until such times as a comparison could be made. Positive proof of Fleischer's identity.'

'Where in his study?'

'Well, that'll be a job for your forensics people when they arrive from the mainland tomorrow to start the investigation into poor Doctor Gassman's murder. They are going to have to take Killian's room apart brick by brick, until they find it. And find it they will, of that I am absolutely certain.' He drew a deep breath. 'In the meantime, you had better seal off the crime scene here. And I'll make sure that nobody tampers with anything at Killian's place until the *police scientifique* arrive.'

Guéguen stared at him for a long time, and Enzo could almost see the thought processes passing before his eyes. Eventually, the adjudant said, 'You told us you came here to see Gassman about something else, the day you found his passports.'

'That's right.'

'Related to the Killian case?'

'Yes.'

'Do you mind telling us what that was?'

Enzo shrugged, and gave a little half smile. 'It's almost irrelevant now. I wanted to ask him about Killian's autopsy report. About something that wasn't in it that should have been.' And it was clear from the finality of his tone, that he was not, for the moment, going to tell them what that was.

CHAPTER THIRTY-SEVEN

Somewhere a shutter was banging in the wind. Several times Enzo had thought about getting up to find and secure it. But he knew that would be a mistake.

The sound of the rain pounding against the window was almost deafening, and the wind whistled and whined through every space in this old building. Even as he lay in bed, the covers pulled up tightly around his neck, Enzo could feel the draught on his face.

Sleep had never been an option. But as the hours passed, he had found his eyes growing heavy, and he blinked fiercely now to keep himself from slipping away. And then, suddenly, there was no need. He was wide awake, sitting bolt upright in the bed, fully dressed beneath the sheets. The bedside clock told him that it was a little after two. He listened intently. There was no doubt about it. Even above the din of the elements, and the banging of the shutter, he had heard the sound of breaking glass, a sound that cut through the night, slicing its way into his consciousness. His mouth was dry, and his heart beat faster than was good for him.

He swivelled in the bed and slipped his feet into his trainers at the bedside, bending quickly to tie them before reaching for Killian's old walking stick with the owl's head handle. The same stick that Killian had taken with him the night he left this room and went downstairs to his death.

Enzo gripped it tightly not as an aid to walking, but once more as a weapon, hoping that he would not have occasion to use it as such. He stood up and crossed to the door, wincing at the squeal of the hinges as he pulled it slowly open. The stairwell was in darkness. The door to Killian's study, he knew, was closed at the foot of the stairs. With one hand on the wall, he felt his way down the steps one at a time. He tensed each time the wood creaked beneath his weight, hoping that the sound of the storm would drown it out.

He had no idea how much the element of surprise might work in his favour. But it was preferable to being heard coming. Or seen. Which is why he did not switch on the light. In the tiny hall at the foot of the stairs he stopped, listening, and felt the cold air circling around his legs as it blew in from under the outside door. Or was it coming from Killian's study? Strangely, the sound of the wind and rain seemed louder from the other side of the study door.

Enzo closed trembling fingers around the door handle and pushed it open. He felt the rush of air in his face, and was startled by the pool of light on Killian's desk. The old man's Post-its, his long hidden messages to his son, blew around the floor. Enzo turned his head towards the window. Splintered glass was strewn across the floorboards beneath it where the stain of Killian's blood was a constant reminder of his murder.

The wind and rain blew through the broken window, and the outside shutter swung back and forth, beating out an erratic tattoo against the sill.

Enzo stepped into the room and felt spots of rain on his right cheek. A movement in his peripheral vision brought his head sharply around to the left as Alain Servat stepped out of the shadows. His brown eyes burned with a dark intensity. Gone was the wry amusement that normally crinkled them. His sallow skin looked bleached and stretched taut. His sandy hair seemed to have turned grey almost overnight.

He held a small pistol in a hand raised and pointed at Enzo's chest. Enzo had a moment of paralysing fear. It would be easy for the man simply to pull the trigger, and Enzo would be gone in a heartbeat. He caught his breath and tried to stay calm.

'I was expecting you before now,' he said.

Alain blinked several times, clearly struggling to contain some inner turmoil. 'Monsieur Killian wasn't surprised to see me either. Put the stick on the desk.'

Slowly, so as not to spook him, Enzo laid Killian's walking stick on the desktop. 'Why did you kill him?'

'Because he was going to expose my father as a monster. The Butcher of Majdanek. One of the most notorious Nazis never to be brought to justice.' He paused, as if somehow that was explanation enough. But Enzo's silence drew him on. 'No one, and I mean no one, was more shocked than I was to discover my father's true identity. When Killian first came to me, it seemed so monstrous, incredible. I just couldn't bring myself to believe it.'

'What made Killian come to you at all?'

A shadow crossed Alain's face. Of pain, or misery, or hatred. A shadow like death. 'Because my father was poisoning him.' He almost spat out the words. 'During a consultation he caught a glimpse of a tattoo inside Killian's left armpit. The identity number given him at Majdanek concentration camp. And he realised that Killian must have been an inmate there. That was when it dawned on him why Killian was seeking so many consultations when there was, apparently, little or nothing wrong with him. He had recognised my father from his time in the camp.'

'So your father invented an illness for him?'

'Yes.' Alain ran a tongue over dried lips and moved towards the centre of the room, keeping his weapon trained on Enzo. His hand was trembling slightly. 'He sent him for x-ray at Lorient, then falsely diagnosed lung cancer.'

Enzo stepped slowly away from the window and the wind and rain at his back. He said, 'I realised that when the pathologist made no reference in the autopsy report to a tumour in either lung. It's why I went out to see Doctor Gassman that day. Just to confirm that if there was one, it would have been mentioned.'

Alain nodded. 'It's what I feared most at the time. Had there been a proper investigation the *enquêteurs* would surely have noticed its absence. My father had been poisoning him with thallium, you see, claiming it as a treatment, but in fact inducing all the symptoms of a man in the final stages of terminal cancer. Of course, the pathologist had no reason to test for thallium in his blood or tissue. The cause of death was clear. Three bullets in his chest.'

He took a deep breath and allowed his eyes to close momentarily, before they snapped open again, quickly, resuming their intensity and their focus on Enzo.

'Somehow, belatedly, Killian realised that my father was killing him, not treating him. That was when he came to me and told me the whole story.' He shook his head. 'You cannot for a moment imagine how I felt, Monsieur Macleod. The depths of horror and despair that revelation brought me to. Of course, I immediately confronted my father. He was already entering the early stages of senility, and he confessed to everything. Just like that. As if these were normal memories that a father might recall for his son. I can remember going to the toilet afterwards and vomiting. I was, literally, sick to my stomach.'

And now there was something else in Alain's eyes. Something like self-pity, an appeal for understanding that he knew was unlikely ever to to be forthcoming.

'I couldn't let Killian tell the world that I was the son of a monster. It would have ruined my life, monsieur. Elisabeth's life. The life of my son. A whole family forever more seen in the eyes of the world only as the progeny of Fleischer, the Butcher of Majdanek.'

Enzo felt a taste like bile rising into his mouth. 'So you took your father's old service pistol and turned into a monster yourself.'

'I was protecting my family!' Alain's voice rose in pitch, as if by protesting more loudly he might drown out the accusation in Enzo's tone. 'My father's life was virtually over anyway. No purpose would have been served by exposing him after all these years. No lives would have been saved.'

'Just one taken.'

Alain's eyes flickered away from Enzo's, unable to face the reflection of his own guilt. 'Killian knew it,' he said. 'Saw it in my eyes, I guess. That I would never expose my father, or my family. He knew it had been a mistake to tell me.'

Sudden anger overwhelmed guilt, and he turned burning eyes back on Enzo. 'It was all history, dead and buried with Killian. And then, twenty years on, you arrive. Raking over long-cold ashes, rekindling the fire. And getting far too close to the truth for comfort.'

'So you murdered old Gassman, trying to make it look like suicide, attempting to pass him him off as Fleischer.' Enzo was almost overwhelmed by the anger and guilt that washed over him in almost equal measure. 'The worst of it is, I probably put the idea in your head that day when I asked you if you knew when Gassman had first arrived on the island. And I thought I was simply deflecting you from the fact that I already suspected you.'

Alain stared resolutely back at him, making no attempt to deny it, and for a moment Enzo was almost tempted to charge him and knock him down, squeezing the life out of him with his own hands. But he knew that he would be dead before he took two paces, and that nothing could extinguish his own sense of regret.

He found control from somewhere and spoke in a calm, even voice that belied his inner torment. 'What you didn't realise, of course, was that Killian had taken DNA from your father. And that the Wiesenthal Centre had a sample of his hair. Poor old Jacques Gassman would never have been identified as Erik Fleischer. You killed him for nothing.'

'He was an old man.' The sudden callous quality in his voice provoked a spike of anger that overpowered Enzo's guilt.

'After ninety-four years, he didn't deserve to die like that.'

Alain said nothing for a very long time, and Enzo found his eye drawn to his finger on the trigger. It almost seemed to be caressing it, and fear returned. Then finally Alain said, 'How did you know it was me that murdered Killian?'

'You left fingerprints on the shell casings. Fingerprints that couldn't have been recovered twenty years ago. But time and technology caught up with you, Alain. I took your glass from lunch the other day so we had prints to compare them to.'

Alain frowned. 'But you must have suspected me even then.'

Enzo nodded. 'Something Killian said in that last phone call to his daughter-in-law and that was confirmed by the date of your father's arrival on the island. I found that out at the *mairie* when I went to check on Gassman. Gassman came in May, more than two months after the earthquake in Agadir. But your father was here within three weeks.' He saw the doctor's jaw clench and unclench.

'What was the something that Killian said to his daughter-in-law?'

'He told her it was ironic that it was the son who would

finish the job. I had taken that to mean that he didn't expect to live, and that it would be up to his son, Peter, to finish his work for him, whatever that was. But it was the word *ironic* that troubled me. Why was it ironic?' He answered his own question. 'Because he also expected Fleischer's son to finish what *his* father had started. As you said, he must have seen it in your eyes. Knew that you would never let him expose your father. That you would finish the job your father had started and kill him yourself.' Enzo shook his head. 'I didn't want to believe it, Alain. I really didn't. But Killian did, which is why he set the clues for his son in such a way that you would never find them, or understand them even if you did. And why he hid the sample of DNA in a place you would never think to look.'

Alain breathed his frustration through clenched teeth. 'I searched everywhere for anything that might implicate my father. All I found was correspondence between Killian and someone at the Wiesenthal Centre in Paris.' His eyes were a reflection of the confusion of thoughts that must have been tumbling through his head. 'How on earth did he get a sample of my father's DNA?'

'I'll show you if you like. It's in the kitchen.' He opened an outstretched palm towards the kitchen door. 'May I?'

Alain nodded mutely and stepped aside to let Enzo past. Enzo moved cautiously into the kitchen and switched on the light. He opened the fridge door and lifted out the ziplock bag, removing the book from inside. Alain approached the door, his gun still trained on the Scotsman. But his eyes were filled now with puzzled curiosity as Enzo opened up *The Life of the Mosquito Part 4* to reveal the squashed and preserved insect with its last blood meal between pages fifty-six and fifty-seven.

'Your father provided this little creature's last supper. Enough blood there, with PCR amplification, to provide a perfectly acceptable sample for comparison.' He looked up to see a weary resignation pass across Alain's face. 'He knew it had to be kept cool, of course. So where better to hide it, than in the choked-up icebox in the fridge?' He slipped the book into its bag and placed it back in the fridge, turning now to face the doctor with the cold realisation that the time for talking was nearly over. There really was nothing much left to say.

Enzo saw that the hand which held the gun was trembling now, almost uncontrollably. His mouth was so dry he could barely separate his tongue from the roof of his mouth.

'So. What now? Are you going to kill again, rather than face the shame?'

Alain stared at him, his face a passive mask, hiding the kaleidoscope of emotions that must have been revolving behind it. 'Yes,' he said. And although he had spoken very quietly, his voice filled the tiny kitchen. He raised the gun, and Enzo saw the barrel from which the bullet would come. The bullet that would kill him. And it was like looking into the tunnel of his life, a tunnel where all his years were behind him and only darkness lay ahead.

Then suddenly Alain crooked his arm and pressed the barrel to his forehead.

Enzo heard his own voice shouting, 'No!', almost as if it

had come from somewhere else. But out of the darkness came hands, emerging from shadows. He heard a scuffle and raised voices as Alain was pulled backwards into the room, and the sound of a gunshot brought momentary deafness.

White plaster dust showered down over Guéguen and the two *gendarmes* who accompanied him, before Alain Servat was pushed up against the wall and handcuffed.

Enzo realised how rapidly he was breathing, and it took him a moment to find his voice as Guéguen turned towards him. 'Jesus,' he said. 'You left that late. What if he'd pulled the trigger while the gun was pointing at me?'

Guéguen managed a pale smile. He, too, was shaken. 'Then I guess, monsieur, that Doctor Servat would have been charged with three murders instead of two.'

Enzo looked beyond him, catching a glimpse of Alain's white face as he was led away, and he wondered if there could possibly be something in the genetic code that predisposed a man to kill so easily. Or was it simply, as the bible had said, that the sins of the father shall be visited upon the son a thousand times?

A movement at the broken window caught his attention, and he saw the luminous green eyes of a cat glowing in the dark as it sat on the sill watching Killian's murderer being taken away.

CHAPTER THIRTY-EIGHT

It was hardly any time after the ferry had slipped out from the comparative shelter of the harbour and into the grey swell of the strait that separated the island from the mainland when Port Tudy was swallowed by the rain. Vanished, like some imaginary place from celtic mythology, lost in the mists of time.

Enzo dragged himself away from the window and retook his seat in the salon. Pale winter faces huddled into the shoulders of coats beneath hats, dripping umbrellas laid below seats to send tiny rivers of water back and forth across the floor with the rolling of the boat. Celtic faces, hacked out of the gneiss by the wind and the rain and the sea.

He thought about old Fleischer sitting drooling in his wheelchair, lost in some world beyond reach. A man who had taken the lives of others without conscience, who had delivered pain and misery and death in equal measure. A man who would never face the justice he so richly deserved.

And he thought about his son. A man prepared to kill rather than face the shame visited upon him by his father. A man who, unlike his father, *would* face the judgment of his peers but leave behind him a wife and children who deserved better.

And Adam Killian, a man who had survived the Nazi death camps, only to die at the hands of the next generation. And his son, Peter, who had never had the chance to unravel his father's final message.

Fathers and sons, he reflected. A sad end. And he wondered how things might end up for *this* father and *his* son in the years that lay ahead.

Read on for an exclusive preview of
Book Five of The Enzo Files

BLOW
BACK

CHAPTER ONE

Cahors, south-west France, October 2010

He had bearded and washed the scallops, wonderful fat, succulent *noix St. Jacques* that the fishmonger in the covered market across the street had reserved for him. They purveyed the delicious aroma of the sea without a hint of fish. He had sliced them in half, along the round, with a razor sharp knife to make medallions, then left them to drain on kitchen paper, their milky sweet juices absorbed by the softness.

Now he plated up the salad. A few fresh green leaves. Lettuce, baby spinach, rocket, and a drizzle of thick, sweet dressing made with a syrupy balsamic, carefully gathered in a corner of the plate. He turned back to the stove. His Calphalon nonstick sauté pan was smoking hot. Tiny pools of bubbling melted butter and shimmering olive oil ran across its surface as he tipped it one way, then the other, before dropping in the *St. Jacques*. The sizzling sound of searing scallops filled the room along with their sweet smell. Sixty seconds, and then he flipped them over, pleased with the caramelised crust on the cooked side. Another sixty seconds, and he slipped a thin metal skewer through the side of the fattest of them, deep into its centre, before extracting it quickly and raising it to his lips. The merest touch told him that the scallops were warmed to the middle, and therefore cooked. But only just.

Quickly he arranged five medallions in an elegant heap next to the salad on each plate and swivelled towards the table, one in each hand, to deliver them to the two facing place settings. He had already poured tall glasses of chilled, crisp Gaillac *blanc sec* from Domaine Sarrabelle. Hélène looked wide-eyed at the plate in front of her and breathed in deeply. 'My God, Enzo, they smell fabulous. You'd have any woman eating out of your hand if you served up food like this every evening.'

Enzo grinned. 'Maybe that's the idea.'

Hélène raised a sceptical eyebrow. 'Hmmm. If only.'

'But in any case, I'd rather you ate them off the plate than out of my hand, *commissaire*. And quickly. They won't keep their heat for long in these temperatures.' No matter how high he turned up the central heating, the pervasive cold of this early onset winter weather seemed to fill the apartment. Only the heat of the oven and the gas rings seemed to hold it at bay. As he sat down to slice through a scallop and spear a forkful of salad, he glanced from the French windows across the square towards the floodlit twin domes of Cahors' gothic Saint-Etienne cathedral. The rain slashed diagonally across his line of sight, and he almost imagined he saw an edge of sleet in it. Which would be unprecedented for late October in this ancient Roman city.

'Delicious.'

He turned his head to find Hélène beaming at him, as his *St. Jacques* melted in her mouth. She washed it over with a sip of *blanc sec*, then dabbed fine, full lips with her napkin.

She was still a handsome woman for all her forty-odd years. Hair normally piled up beneath the hat of her uniform, tumbled in luxuriant elegance across square shoulders. Only the sixth woman in the history of the *République* to be appointed Director of Public Security to one of the country's one hundred *départements*, she had never quite seen the joke in Enzo's refusal to call her by her name. He referred to her always as *commissaire*, as if it were somehow amusing. She had reflected, more than once, that it might also be a subtle way of his telling her that their on-off relationship was doomed never to progress to intimacy. She popped another scallop in her mouth. 'I'm afraid there are still no developments in our attempt to identify who's been trying to kill you.'

Enzo studied her thoughtfully, distracted by the delicate caramel flavour of the scallops mixing with the sweet, vinegary flavour of the balsamic, and the crisp, slightly bitter tang of the greens. He prepared his palate for the next mouthful with a generous sip of wine and shrugged dismissively. 'Well, it's over a year since the last attempt. So maybe whoever it was is already dead, or behind bars.' But he knew that was unlikely. With four of Roger Raffin's celebrated cold cases already solved, and only three remaining, someone out there would be increasingly anxious to stop him.

Hélène, too, looked less than convinced. But she decided

on a change of subject and slipped the last morsel into her mouth before taking a piece of bread to mop up the juices that lingered tantalisingly on her plate. 'Where's Sophie these days?' She glanced around the apartment as if expecting to see her suddenly appear.

'Ah,' Enzo said. 'I'm glad to say I finally persuaded my daughter to resume her education. I was very disappointed when she dropped out of university to go and work at Bertrand's gym.'

'Oh?' Hélène feigned interest. 'What's she studying?' And she was surprised to detect a hint of evasion in Enzo's response.

He leaned across the table to take her empty plate and carried the two of them back to the breakfast bar. 'Oh, she's away on a *stage*. Just a few weeks' work placement.' He paused. 'I'll be with you in a moment.'

And he turned his attention to the main course. A *filet mignon de porc* which he had marinated in hoisin, five-spice, and honey, and then roasted in a hot oven. He removed it now from the tinfoil he had wrapped it in before cooking the *St. Jacques*, and cut it into moist, tender discs which he arranged on a warmed plate. Over the meat he drizzled a reduction of the marinade, then served the cubed, honeyed roast potatoes which had been crisping in the oven on a bed of rosemary.

'*Voila!*' He delivered his plates to the table like a magician presenting the denouement of a complex trick. He grabbed a bottle of red and expertly removed the cork. 'Some oak-aged syrah to go with it. Enough strength and fruit in it, I think, to stand up to the sweetness of the pork.' He poured them each a glass.

'*Mon dieu*, Enzo!' Hélène surveyed the plate in front of her, breathing in its aromas. '*Are* you trying to seduce me?'

He grinned. 'It's not exactly three-star Michelin quality, *commissaire*. But anything that can persuade you to slip out of your uniform for the night can't be bad.'

She smiled demurely, knowing that his flirtation was empty of intent, but enjoying it all the same. Her knife cut through the meat as if it were butter. A little sauce, a cube of honeyed roast potato. She closed her eyes to savour the taste. 'You missed your vocation in life.'

Enzo laughed heartily. 'It's just a hobby, *commissaire*. I'm not at all sure I would have wanted to spend my life slaving seven days a week in a hot kitchen like Marc Fraysse.'

She regarded his smiling face, his dark hair drawn back in its habitual ponytail, greying now, but not enough to hide the silver streak in it. His eyes sparkled with life and amusement, one brown, one blue, and she thought how handsome he was for a man in his fifties. 'Is Fraysse the next on your list?'

His smile clouded a little, and he nodded. 'Actually I'm leaving for Puy de Dôme in the morning.' He paused. 'An early start.'

Which she took as a hint that he did not anticipate her staying the night. She raised the wine glass to her lips to mask her disappointment.

ACKNOWLEDGEMENTS

I would like to offer my grateful thanks to those who gave so generously of their time and expertise during my researches for *Freeze Frame*. In particular, I'd like to express my gratitude to pathologist Steven C. Campman, M.D, Medical Examiner, San Diego, California; Grant Fry, Lead Forensic Specialist, Orange County Sheriff-Coroner Department, California; Doctor John Bond, head of forensics, Northamptonshire Police, England; Professor Joe Cummins, Professor Emeritus in Genetics at the University of Western Ontario, Canada; Hubert Piguet and Yves Gomy of the *Société Entomologique de France*; my namesake, Peter May (no relation), of the British Amateur Entomologists' Society; Adjudant-Chef Didier Le Gac, Gendarmerie, Île de Groix; Claude Guiader, Maire-adjoint, Île de Groix; Brigitte Adam, journalist, *Ouest-France*, Île de Groix.

READ THE RED-HOT COLD CASE SERIES

PETER MAY

THE ENZO FILES

Enzo Macleod – ex-pat Scot, one-time forensic expert, and stubborn to the last – is investigating France's most confounding murders, which until now have been consigned to the unsolvable list.

He won't give up until the last drop of spilled blood has been avenged. The only trouble is – the killers have been warned. And now they are watching . . .

The Love of
Her Life

KATE McCABE

HACHETTE
BOOKS
IRELAND

First published in Ireland in 2016 by Hachette Books Ireland
First published in paperback in 2016

1

Cataloguing in Publication Data is available from the British Library.

ISBN 978 1 47360 972 3

Typeset in Cambria by Bookends Publishing Services.
Printed and bound in Great Britain by Clays Ltd, St Ives plc.

Hachette Books Ireland policy is to use papers that are natural,
renewable and recyclable products and made from wood grown
in sustainable forests. The logging and manufacturing processes
are expected to conform to the environmental regulations of the
country of origin.

Hachette Books Ireland
8 Castlecourt Centre, Castleknock, Dublin 15, Ireland

A division of Hachette UK Ltd
Carmelite House, 50 Victoria Embankment, London EC4Y 0DZ

www.hachettebooksireland.ie